The Fulfillment

LAVYRLE
SPENCER

The Fulfillment

AVON BOOKS NEW YORK

AVON BOOKS, INC.
1350 Avenue of the Americas
New York, New York 10019

Copyright © 1979 by LaVyrle Spencer
Interior design by Kellan Peck
Library of Congress Catalog Card Number: 99-95371
ISBN: 0-380-97851-2

First Avon Books Hardcover Printing: November 1999
First Avon Books Mass Market Printing: October 1979

AVON TRADEMARK REG. U.S. PAT. OFF. AND IN OTHER COUNTRIES,
MARCA REGISTRADA, HECHO EN U.S.A.

Printed in the U.S.A.

FIRST EDITION

QPM   10 9 8 7 6 5 4 3 2 1

www.avonromance.com

With love
to my grandma, Bessie Adamek,
whose recollections made it possible.

My perpetual thanks to Judie Coscio,
Darlene Schaeffer, and Denise Brusseau,
who were my impetus, my conscience,
and my critics whenever I needed them . . .
and to Kathleen Woodiwiss, for writing
The Flame and the Flower in the first place . . .
among other things.

Chapter 1

The truth had long been settling on Jonathan Gray, sneaking into his resisting corners, but it had finally resounded in the deepest part of him. He'd prayed it wasn't so, hoped that if he willed it untrue it would be. But it was true. He knew it. At last it had to be faced . . . and dealt with. After denying it all these years, it had come to Jonathan Gray that he was infertile.

Jonathan and Aaron had suffered together in that winter when it had happened, as they'd suffered most of their childhood illnesses together. As only brothers they'd shared everything from the tin cup on top of the water pump to the bed they'd slept in all their growing years, so it was only natural that what one got, the other one got, from the croup of babyhood to the head colds of childhood and, finally, the mumps of adolescence. It was the mumps that had done it.

Who's to say why they'd stayed up on Aaron and moved down on Jonathan. Their ma had tried everything from packs of icy, burning-cold snow to poultices of boiled beans, but Jonathan's swelling genitals had stubbornly refused to subside.

It was one of the few times he ever remembered Doc Haymes coming out to their house, and maybe that had something to do with his mistrust of the man now.

"There's nothing I can do that you haven't already done, Mrs. Gray," the doc had said, and those words rang now in Jonathan's memory. He blamed the doc because Haymes had found no way to take away the pain.

When it was over and done with, they'd all said not to worry because it wasn't a sure thing he'd been damaged. Probably he'd end up with more babies than he needed, they'd ventured.

But he'd been married seven years and there were no babies yet. He and Mary had been trying all that time, and now it seemed almost certain there wouldn't ever be any babies.

And that old fool Haymes hadn't helped matters recently, either. For the life of him, Jonathan couldn't figure out why Mary listened to Haymes's farfetched notions. Now he had her counting the days on the calendar with some nonsense about some days it can happen and some days it can't. That riled Jonathan. Somebody ought to shake some sense into that old fool's head, but Jonathan was a peaceful man and it wouldn't be him that did it. Besides, the old fool seemed to keep Mary hopeful. So Jonathan stifled his tongue and went along with it when she announced it was the right day to try again. But he cursed Haymes half of the time for giving her false hopes.

But the pretending got harder and harder and the bed seemed smaller and smaller as their lovemaking brought no babies. The strain was rife between Jonathan and Mary, and nothing would ease it except the baby they both wanted and couldn't have.

It wasn't clear in Jonathan's head just when the notion had come to him, but it was somewhere back during the past winter. He'd had time to mull it over in his mind, holding it, weighing it, measuring it, rolling it back and forth as he might work a lump of spring soil, wondering just when it'd be ready for its mating with the seeds.

When it first came to him he was sitting where he was now, right here in the family pew after Sunday services, soaking up the good closeness of himself and the Lord after all the others had left the two of them alone for a while. It was a time he enjoyed best. Let the others yammer away, exchanging gossip in the churchyard like they always did on a Sunday. He'd rather spend his last few minutes here.

He'd been reading his Bible, easing his eyes over some words there, when he came to a verse that held his mind from wandering on: "Take unto thee Aaron thy brother and his sons with him." At first it was Aaron's name that held him, made him go over it one more time. It was hard to say who had taken whom unto whom, for Aaron and Jonathan still shared their childhood home, and had since their parents had died. But as for who was doing the "taking unto"—now that was hard to say. For they shared the home place equally, although, strange as it was, the land had been left to Jonathan while the house and outbuildings had been willed to Aaron.

Their pa knew what he was doing when he left things that way. It was a sure bet that Jonathan would never leave the land. He loved it too much. Aaron, on the other hand, was held more loosely to the land. Hadn't he already left it once and taken a fling in the city? But he'd come back after a year of that wildness. He'd come back to the home place, and you might say Jonathan had taken Aaron unto his land while Aaron had taken Jonathan unto his house. Seven years ago when Mary married Jonathan, she was taken into the lives of both brothers, as wife to the one, as true friend to the other. And that suited them all just fine.

Jonathan was pondering all this after he'd read that Bible verse the first time, and he wasn't quite ready, in his peaceful, unsuspecting state of mind, for the downright disturbingly sinful idea that entered his soul after he reread the verse a third time. "Take unto thee Aaron thy brother and his sons with him."

It was the part about Aaron's sons that started the notion rolling around in Jonathan's brain. For Aaron had no sons. Aaron wasn't married—yet!

But before he was married . . . suppose Aaron sired a son for Jonathan!

From the moment the thought entered Jonathan's head it wouldn't leave. It just lodged there like a fishbone sticks in your throat and no amount of hard swallowing or eating dry bread is going to make it move. You keep thinking you can forget it's there, but you can't.

And that surely was the way of it with the notion he'd taken about how he and Mary could get a son.

The sinfulness of it filled Jonathan with shame. But that didn't make the idea disappear. Instead, it made him conjure up reasons why it might be less than sinful after all—and now he'd gotten himself to the point where the idea seemed almost sound.

Oh, he'd done plenty of praying over it, and time and again he'd asked the Lord's forgiveness for it. But then, hadn't he been reading the Bible when he'd first gotten the idea, and right here in the Lord's house, under His very eyes?

Through the end of the winter and early spring Jonathan had watched Mary and Aaron together. They had an easy way with one another, almost easier than between Mary and himself. But they were strictly friends, observing the proprieties between brother-in-law and sister-in-law no differently from the way Jonathan thought they should.

"Thou shalt not covet . . ." gave Jonathan hours of troubled thoughts. It ran itself through his mind a thousand times, but after the thousandth time he still told himself that there was no coveting between his wife and his brother. Might they not therefore be sinless if they did this thing at his bidding? If there were sin involved, Jonathan would willingly accept it.

He'd thought about it long enough now, and it had even come to him that the perfect time was in the offing. Soon he'd be off to Minneapolis to buy the Black Angus bull. And so, on a sparkling May morning in 1910, Jonathan Gray decided the time had come to put it to them.

Once the decision was made, Jonathan apologized to the Lord one last time, left the quiet church, and stepped into the brilliant late-morning sun.

Mary was standing amid a gaggle of Garner children, their mother—her Aunt Mabel—at its core, Uncle Garner at its fringes. Mabel Garner's voice, as always, could be heard above most in the churchyard. As Jonathan approached, she was saying, "It don't hardly seem like my Catherine here could be old enough to be a bride yet, but I reckon she grew up since you left us, huh, Mary?"

"Catherine, I'm so happy for you," Mary said, kissing her young cousin on the cheek.

"Well, here you are, Jonathan!" Mabel Garner's voice boomed again. "You're either powerful good or powerful wicked, needin' that much time in church!" Her boisterous laugh followed. She was almost as big as Jonathan, wattle-chinned, red-faced, bespectacled, good-natured, and well-loved. Jonathan was used to her outspokenness by now, and it didn't bother him anymore. With her whole brood around her, she resembled a mother turkey, her head higher than theirs, gobbling away while herding the young ones.

"Come over here, boy!" Every man was a boy to Aunt Mabel.

When Jonathan neared the group, Mary said, "Aunt Mabel's just told me that Catherine and Mike are to be married in June." Jonathan had inherited this bunch of cousins when he married Mary, so it was more or less family news that the oldest of them was to marry.

Preoccupied as he was with other thoughts, Jonathan found himself hard-pressed to join in the felicitations. But the women were giddy at the news and couldn't be hurried away from each other, so Jonathan waited on the fringe of the group. Uncle Garner and he talked man-talk.

Jonathan's attention was now and then diverted to Aaron, who was across the dusty stretch of yard where the rigs were tied, leaning against a wheel next to Priscilla. From the way she cocked her head and blinked up at him from under her bonnet, it was apparent that Jonathan didn't have a day to waste. Pris meant to have a wedding ring on Aaron's finger, and then it would be too late. Sunday was the perfect day for doing the asking, the one day a week that they slowed their pace and let the farm do the same. The chores, milking and feeding the stock, were about all they did. It was the Lord's Day, and they used it as such. Plenty of time to approach Mary and Aaron and put it to them, time for whatever would follow after he'd asked it.

"Jonathan, you'd better listen up a bit better, 'cause by the looks of it you'll be going through the same thing soon with that brother of yours over there," called Aunt Mabel. "If ever I saw a lovesick calf, it's Priscilla Volence. You know weddings always come in threes, and Catherine's will be only the first one of the summer!"

"Well, it's what we're hoping for, isn't it, Jonathan?" Mary asked, glancing at Aaron and Pris while taking Jonathan's arm.

"That's Aaron's lookout and none of ours," Jonathan said, "but yes, we're hopin'."

They all moved toward the rigs, and Mabel Garner's voice preceded them. "You gonna shine that wheel all day, boy, or you gonna drive that pretty li'l gal home?"

The head capped with a wealth of russet curls came up, and a hand waved at Mabel Garner. Aaron was a slightly younger version of Jonathan, slim-bodied, straight-nosed, wide-mouthed, although his lips were more crisply etched. Aaron had an eternally amused look about him. Crinkling his brown eyes in a smile, he called back, "I see a morning in church didn't put much benevolence in you, Aunt Mabel. Your tongue is just as disrespectful as always."

"Never mind my tongue, boy, just watch your own!" she hollered. Then, more quietly, she added, "That boy's got the same spunk his pa had." She watched Aaron and Priscilla mount their buggy and leave the churchyard, followed by Jonathan and Mary.

Moran Township was still reaching for its prime. The grass along the roadside was a pale shadow, like the beard of a youth not yet shaved for the first time. The willows along Turtle Creek wore fat, adolescent buds, promising soon to burst into the fullness of maturity.

So it seemed with Mary. She was something to behold, Jonathan thought, looking like a schoolgirl, eagerly leaning forward, hands on knees, nostrils to the wind, sniffing it, tasting it. Sitting as she was, she might be mistaken for a child. Her form was so slight that it seemed the knot of honey-brown hair at the nape of her neck must weigh her down. The only hints of maturity about her were small breasts, evident only when she drew in her breath beneath her woolen coat, sucking in the spring as if some of its fecundity might remain with her if only she could capture it long enough. She was a woman waiting for the same awakening that Moran Township awaited, awaiting the fullness of her season.

Jonathan knew this. From the corner of his eye he studied her, her eyes the blue of a summer cornflower, always wide, excited. Her little face, so childishly round of cheek, told of her Slavic ancestry. When she smiled, her eyes became larger, rather than narrower. It was this that gave her the look of expectation and gaiety. Too, Jonathan had never seen her pout or sulk or feel sorry for herself, and perhaps it was this everlasting zest that made him hopeful now.

"There's just nothing in this world as good as April!" Mary claimed now, nose still windward. "Except maybe May!" Then in her typical, ebullient fashion, she raised her arms skyward and recited:

> *"April away!*
> *Bring on the May!*
> *But never too soon*
> *For then it is June."*

Then her hands slapped back down upon her knees, shoulders hunched as before.

How in tarnation was a man supposed to reply to a thing like that? Most of the time, like now, Jonathan didn't answer, for there was no answer in him, not in words anyway.

"Just imagine waking up one year and finding that April and May had skipped by without stopping . . . I don't think I could stand it!" she bubbled.

Jonathan thought she talked like a child sometimes, and he wondered if it was because she had no child to do its own talking.

She was going on, ". . . but I guess April and May can't pass fast enough for Catherine and Mike. Just imagine, Jonathan, a June wedding, and Catherine's at that! Oh, it'll be lovely; Aunt Mabel will see to that.

And we'll dance . . ." Here she raised her arms again, a bit of her skirt caught up in her fingertips, swaying to the imaginary music. Jonathan enjoyed her merriment but found himself unable to respond to it, which was often the case with Jonathan.

So, with the Minnesota breeze ushering them home, they rode, the quiet man and the childlike woman, following the rig that skimmed the gravel ahead.

When Aaron Gray left Moran Township a couple of years before, Priscilla Volence had been just another of the gawky kids up the road. By the time he returned, the gawkiness had become female allure. Everyone in Moran Township knew she'd set her sights on him the first time she'd seen him back at the Bohemian Hall. When his head snapped around for a second look, he found her meeting his stare boldly before the expression on her face softened. The gossips of Moran had hashed over every move the couple had made since then. And now they were sure Aaron and Pris weren't long for the altar.

If Priscilla had her way, they'd be dead right. She'd been ready for marriage since that first time she saw him after his return from the city, and he knew it perfectly well. But Aaron was put off by the idea. She'd worked her simple wiles on him in the plainest country ways possible: being available whenever he called, making no firm demands, letting him see how well prepared she was to handle a family and a home. Their farms were so close together that he'd had countless occasions to see her handle her younger brother and sisters, helping her mother with the never-ending house chores, her father with the field chores. Oh, she was prepared for marriage, all right. All she needed was the asking. But there was no pushing Aaron Gray. He seemed satisfied to woo her until they both started losing their hair, and nothing could get a proposal out of him.

And what did Aaron think? Riding through that April morning, taking Priscilla home in her father's rig, he recognized how deeply he'd settled himself into her family. He was so comfortable with them all that it seemed as if he were already a part of them. Maybe that was why his hackles rose when he thought of marriage. It seemed he and Pris had never had the chance to think about marrying before everybody in the township had the knot tied for them.

He admitted that he'd given Pris more than enough reason to expect his proposal. They'd been constant companions for the last year, and once, but only once, they'd been more. Granted she'd given in to him only once. But that was enough to build her assumptions on. The memory of that encounter didn't set lightly on Aaron. He knew she wasn't the type to dally with every young buck in the county. Indeed, he'd been her first. And just because that was true, Aaron felt a responsibility toward Pris. But it made him feel he was being forced toward marriage. And he simply wasn't ready for marriage.

Still, habits are hard to break, and spending time with Pris wasn't exactly a hardship. She was pretty, she lived close by, and they had fun together. So here he was again, headed down to her place to while away a Sunday, driving her pa's rig like he'd already married into it!

None of the others in Pris's family had gone to

church that day. Agnes, her mother, was due with her fifth baby. Coming up the rise now where his own driveway angled off to the left, Aaron asked, "You want to go straight home today, or should we have breakfast with Jonathan and Mary?"

"It's best I get straight back," Pris answered. "Ma will need help with the meal and all."

From behind them Jonathan saw Aaron's hand wave a farewell. The lead rig continued over the crest of the hill toward the Volence place, which lay a quarter mile beyond, at the bottom of the hill.

"Looks like they're not stopping for breakfast," Jonathan observed.

Mary watched the dust settle ahead of them, saw the rig disappear over the crest of the hill, and felt a wisp of loneliness dim the bright day. She would miss their usual Sunday breakfast together. The house would seem empty. Mary thought about the bustling Volence household with all those kids and didn't blame Aaron for preferring it to their own silent house, which always seemed a little bigger and a little quieter on Sundays. Well, at least she could escape to the garden today, Mary thought, shaking off the bothersome emptiness, but what she said was, "Agnes will be needing help. It's best they didn't stop, anyway."

Newt Volence came charging down the driveway on his stubby six-year-old legs, a-hollering all the way, "Ma's havin' the baby! Ma's havin' the baby!"

"You git down to the barn and stay there!" Pris yelled as the rig passed Newt in the dusty gravel. She was down and running to the house before Aaron could bring the rig to a full halt. When he stepped down,

Newt was right on his feet, pulling at his hands and hollering, "Do I gotta go to the barn, Aaron, do I? Pris can't make me!" And little drops of spit came flying out where his tongue peeked between his teeth.

"Better do like she says, Newt, so you won't be in the way," Aaron said.

"She just doesn't want me to hear if Ma does some yellin'."

Aaron laughed and reached down to grab Newt under the arms and hoist him up, astraddle his own waist.

"How do you know that?"

"Jimmy Martin said his ma did plenty o' hollerin' last time," Newt confided, "and so did Clara when her calf was born."

There was no arguing with that, Aaron decided, and offered to keep Newt company down in the barn with his sister Gracie—for a while, anyway. Cora was sixteen, so it seemed she'd be allowed to remain in the house.

As it turned out, the baby was nowhere near to being born yet. The day lengthened and Aaron stayed, entertaining the young ones, getting news now and then from the house. Clem Volence wandered in and out of the house, and Aaron wondered what a man said to his wife at a time like this. Pris fixed sandwiches when the sun was well past midday and brought them to the barn for Aaron and the kids. She said Aaron needn't stay, but he did. The afternoon dragged on. Finally, near suppertime, she sent Aaron to town to fetch Doc Haymes. Riding past his own place, he saw Mary coming from the hen house clutching an apron full of eggs. He waved and she waved back, stopping to watch him disappear toward town.

On his return trip it was dark outside, but the lights were on at home. The house looked good and he wished he could pull in and stay, but he thought it best to hang around the Volences' until he was sure he wasn't needed any longer.

Doc Haymes wasn't far behind him. Priscilla was relieved when she saw both rigs pull in.

"Nothing yet," was all she said before she and the doc went inside, leaving Aaron in the damp chill, uncomfortable and restless.

The barn was warmer, drier, and Aaron found the kids bedded down there, so he joined them, alternately dozing and waking, finding his thoughts hazily reconstructing the memory of Pris and himself, that one time in the hay in the chill of a February night.

Later she came without a lantern, and Aaron awoke at the sound of her entering below. He came down the ladder from the mow. Turning, he nearly bumped into her in the darkness.

"Mama had a boy," she whispered.

"How are they faring?"

"They're both fine."

"Is the doc still here?"

"No. He offered to give you a lift home, but I fibbed and told him you'd most likely be sleeping the night in the barn. I wanted to talk before you got away. Let's go outside in the air."

He took her hand and led her out into the crisp, glittering night. As he carefully closed the barn door,

holding the latch from making its customary click, Pris
sighed, a confession of how long the day had been.

Aaron turned and drew her into his arms, pushing
her head down until it nestled beneath his chin.

"Tired?" he asked.

She moved her head, and it bumped his chin.
"But happy."

"Yes, I reckon everyone is, now that it's over.
Won't Newt be happy he's got a brother?"

She pulled away from him momentarily. "Oh, I
should have checked on the kids. Are they all right
up there?"

"Yes, yes, don't worry over them. They're tuck-
ered, too, and sound asleep."

"You know, you didn't have to stay in the barn. Ma
just meant for Newt and Gracie to stay out from
underfoot."

"I was more comfortable out here, too," he admitted. "How did Cora take it?"

"Oh, you know Cora . . . never misses anything.
Sixteen and snoopy." Pris laughed, remembering Cora's
grown-up attempts to be helpful and her undisguised
chagrin at the sounds going on in the house.

"And you, Pris, what do you think of it all?" Aaron
asked, brushing a hand across her cheek, the memories
from the hayloft still fresh in his mind.

"I guess it's more beautiful every time it happens.
I remember when Newt was born, and it was something to treasure. But now that I'm older—of age, you
might say—well, it's just about the most beautiful thing
there could be. You should have seen Mama and Papa
together afterward. I guess there's no time two human
beings feel closer than after a birthing." She paused, as

if expecting a reply, but when he made none she went on, "Thank you for staying, Aaron. I appreciate your taking to the little ones the way you do and keeping them from underfoot."

"I couldn't very well run off without knowing whether it was a boy or a girl, could I?" He leaned back and smiled down at her.

"Which would you rather have, Aaron, a boy or a girl?" she asked, and there was a catch in her heart, a moment of uncertainty during which she knew it was a mistake to press Aaron. She sensed his withdrawal. His hand dropped down from her face, where it had been, and the night cooled the skin he'd been touching.

"What difference does it make?" There was an edge of annoyance in his words.

"Things like that matter to a woman," Pris replied. "She'd like to think they do to her man."

Her words formed a cinch around his gut, and he felt it tightening in a way that needed escape, like he imagined strangling must feel.

"Am I your man?" he asked. There was no warmth to the question.

"I don't know. Are you, Aaron?"

He knew damn well what she was trying to lead him to, and the worst part of it was she had every right. But he wasn't ready to be confronted.

"Don't push me, Pris," he said.

"Have I ever pushed you?"

"Maybe push is the wrong word. Maybe it's pull."

She said nothing, and he turned to walk toward the drive. In spite of his reluctance to speak of marriage, he felt he owed her something. He could feel the hope springing in her, and in himself there was something akin to pity because he hadn't the same nesting urge she had.

They walked together, but apart, near the corncrib and toward the road. The moon highlighted things: her hair—mussed now—an old, misshapen sweater she'd thrown on against the chill, her downturned face.

He took her hand in apology and drew her against his side. They walked very slowly, their hips bumping in a familiar way with each step, until by some unspoken agreement they stopped. He knew it had to be brought out into the open, and she'd done her part, more than a woman should have to. His silence belittled her, and she deserved better.

He eased his hold on her hand and very lightly stroked his thumb up and down her own, feeling her shiver as he did.

"Pris, I know what you want," Aaron said, and his voice was so quiet that her breathing seemed a roar in her ears.

He stood beside her, unmoving, except for the warm thumb that kept stroking across hers. She waited for him to go on, but he just stood there, the thoughts so quietly loud around them that perhaps they were already spoken.

"What is it I want, Aaron?"

He swung to face her then, and gripped both her hands so hard they hurt. As if unable to look at her, he put his face up toward the sky instead. "Oh God, girl . . . you want me to marry you, and I should be askin' right now." Something told her his eyes were closed, and she heard him swallow.

"But you're not?"

He looked down at her then, but she was looking

at the ground. She wondered if Aaron could feel the heat of her face through the night chill.

"No, Pris, I'm not. I'm just not ready for it yet. And that makes me feel guilty."

"Is it something I did?" she asked, meaning the time she gave herself to him, blaming herself for it.

He held her right hand in his, and with his free hand ran the length of her forearm, up and down again and again from wrist to elbow.

"It's nothing, Pris, nothing you did. Please believe me. It's got to do with me, not you. People had us marching down the aisle before we even got used to the changes we saw in each other. We sort of fell together like, living so close like we do. And it's for sure I enjoy being here—I mean I like your folks . . . the kids . . . and you."

He put a hand under her chin and made her look up at him as he asked, "Do you know what I'm saying?"

"No." The word was choked out.

"I'm saying I've been unfair to you. I've come around here for a year now, and I can feel all the threads tightening me to you . . . and some days I feel like they're strangling me because I'm not ready to be tied down yet. That's the part that's unfair to you. Folks in these parts see me coming to call, and right away they say she's Aaron's property. Nobody asks me, and nobody asks you. Meanwhile, the others who might take a fancy to you keep away, thinking it's all set between you and me. It seems I can't have the pleasure of you without us taking vows."

"I never said that, Aaron."

"No, *you* never did, but it's the truth, nevertheless.

Do you know what I was doing up there in the loft tonight while I was waiting for you? I was remembering the time we made love up there, and wishing it would happen again. Even though I don't want to marry yet, and even though I know what . . . well, how guilty you felt after the first time. And if I keep hangin' around here, I'm going to keep after you until it does happen again. So I think it's best I leave and make way for somebody who'll think of marriage first and haylofts second. With me aside, other fellows might feel more welcome around here."

"But they aren't welcome, Aaron. You're the only one I want."

He reached a hand behind her neck and pulled her face against his neck. "I know that, Pris, and I want you, too. But wanting and marrying are two different things to a man. To a woman they're the same."

She felt the heat of her face centered now in her eyes, and tears spilled.

"Don't cry for me, Pris, don't."

"I know why you're saying all this," she cried, her voice muffled. "It's because of what I let you do last winter. If I hadn't held myself so cheap, you wouldn't, either."

"That's not true," he argued. He had to make her see it wasn't true. "I'm the one at fault for that. I knew you couldn't . . . knew I shouldn't . . ."

Finally she said, "If I hadn't given in then, you'd be asking me to marry you now."

"That's got nothing to do with it."

"Wasn't I good enough?"

He pulled her roughly against him, put his arms clear around her shoulders, which were jerking quietly.

"Jesus, Pris, don't do this to yourself."

And then, to comfort her, he lowered his mouth to hers. As she always could, she made his body surge with desire. She opened her mouth without thinking, and in that slackening movement he lost himself. Her arms clung to his neck, fear of losing him a threat that hurt more than the slats of the corncrib digging into her back.

With his fingers between the wooden slats behind her head, he pulled the length of his body against hers, and she could feel what the kiss had started. One of Aaron's hands left the slats and found her breast inside the old woolen sweater, and he made a groaning sound, while his body betrayed him.

She pushed in denial against the hand on her breast, but he held her pinioned against the corncrib wall, her head firmly against the slats and his mouth holding her still. She struggled until she could twist free and gasp, "No, Aaron, not again! If you set out to prove you can make me want you, you did! But I can't."

His angry words cut her off.

"I didn't set out to prove anything by you, and you know it! I'm just not made of a goddamn lump of stone, Priscilla. I can't turn my body on and off like you can!"

"Just what are you aiming to do here, Aaron? Threaten to leave me so I'll give in to you again?" Her anger matched his, making her accuse him when she might not otherwise have done so.

"That's a cheap accusation and you know it. It's hardly worthy of you."

"Do you think just because I want to marry you, you have the right to act as if we're already married?"

"I don't stop to make lists of rights—or wrongs—and maybe if you didn't, you'd quit trying to push me into marriage and give your body what it's panting for!"

She slapped him then, and it cracked through the April night, stunning them both into silence.

He broke it first.

"I'm sorry, Pris. But a man has physical needs, and I'd say I've done quite well, pressing mine as little as I have."

"Well, go press them somewhere else. Go try one of the chippies at the Bohemian Hall Saturday night. After all, their price is cheaper than mine. All they want is money. I demand marriage in return for my favors."

Meaning to hurt her, he backed a step away, bowed slightly, and said with quiet sarcasm, "Ah, yes, if favors they could be called."

He had hit his mark, and he heard her sharp, sucking breath of surprise and shame, and he wanted suddenly to grab back the words. But she was running up the drive toward the house, and it was too late.

She heard him call her. There was apology in his voice, but she was too humiliated to hear it. She heard only the words that cheapened what they'd once done together. They hurt more than the absent proposal ever had.

Mary was lying awake when she heard Aaron's steps on the gravel. A glance at the alarm clock in the moonlight showed it was well past midnight. Jonathan was snoring lightly, and she lay listening to his snores and waiting to hear Aaron come into the house downstairs. Glancing at the clock again, she wondered if she

LaVyrle Spencer

had really heard footsteps. Ten minutes had passed, and Aaron hadn't come in. Climbing over the foot of the bed, she jostled Jonathan, who rolled over. He made a snuffling sound but continued sleeping. Grabbing her chenille robe from the back of the bedroom door, she made her way into the dark upper hall, where no moonlight touched the floor. The familiar railing guided her down the squeaky stair more surely than any moonlight could have done.

Aaron was home, all right, sitting on the back porch step, looking all worn out. His elbows rested on his knees, and one hand hung limply down while the other massaged the back of his neck. If it hadn't been for the moving hand, she'd have thought he was asleep.

"Aaron? You okay?" she whispered.

"What're you doing up?" he asked.

"I couldn't sleep for wondering about Agnes. Is everything all right down there?"

"Yeah, it's just fine. The baby's a boy."

"A boy . . ." she repeated, her voice like the trailing-away note of a mourning dove, wistful and uncertain.

"Did you see him, Aaron?"

"No, not yet," he said, and he knew she wanted to hear far more of it than he was able to tell her. He patted the step beside him and hitched himself over a bit. "Come on out," he invited in an indulgent tone. "There's room for two, and I can tell you're not going to let up till I tell you all I know."

She eased the door shut behind her and squatted on the wide step above him, hugging her long robe around her ankles and knees against the damp.

"It took a long time, did it?" she asked as she settled.

But he didn't reply, as if he'd forgotten he'd invited her out there.

"Aaron?"

At the sound of his name he seemed to waken.

"Oh, longer for Clem and Pris than for Agnes, probably."

She laughed. "Honestly, Aaron, the things you say. No sympathy for poor Agnes?" But her tone was not accusing. "Now tell me about it."

"I would if I knew more, but I spent most of the day with the kids in the barn, then riding into town to fetch Doc Haymes."

"Aah," she said, a little disappointed.

"Best let Agnes and Pris do the telling, Mary. They know more of it than I."

She was disappointed for sure. She longed to hear of the birth. She wondered about all Aaron couldn't tell her, about all the mystery involved in a birth that no one but a mother could know. She huddled there while he puzzled in silence over thoughts of his own.

As if he'd come to a decision, Aaron straightened, then leaned his elbows back onto the step behind him with a weighted sigh.

"Ah, I think I've been a damn fool," he mumbled, more to himself than to Mary.

"You trying to convince me or you?"

"Not me, for sure. I don't need any convincing."

She said nothing, waiting for him to go on when he chose. It was cold. She curled her bare toes away from the concrete.

He half turned on the step below her, so she could see his face profiled with the moonlight behind it, and he saw her bare feet on the same cold concrete step.

He moved and took them onto his warm thigh and covered them with the hem of his Sunday suit jacket, which he still wore. Over the hem he placed his hand, and between Aaron and Mary there was a natural warmth that had nothing to do with his taking her feet upon his thigh to warm them. He did it without conscious thought, for they'd always had that careless way between them. They'd always counted themselves lucky at the friendship they enjoyed, knowing Jonathan was not the reason. They'd have been friends even if Jonathan were neither Mary's husband nor Aaron's brother.

"I hurt Pris tonight, on purpose, something I never thought to do. We argued and I ruined her day for her—after the birthing and all. I shouldn't have done that."

"Is all the blame yours? It takes two to anger, doesn't it?"

"It takes two to do a lot of things." Then he grew quiet, the silence more telling than the words.

"So it's finally come to that?"

"Yes, finally. She'll have it no other way. And damn my hide! I'm just not ready. But she can't see it my way, and I can't see it hers."

"You've given her reason to look at you with marriage on her mind, Aaron, you can't deny that. You've seen no one but her for a good year now. Could be she's a right to expect more than walks in the moonlight."

"Maybe I've a right to expect more, too."

Once he'd said it he felt coarse and guilty, and he supposed he must seem so to Mary.

"That's what you fought over, then?"

"Aha," he confessed, "I told you I'd been a damn fool."

"Well, I reckon many other men have been equally as foolish as you, then."

"It ought to be Jonathan I talk to about this," Aaron said.

"Jonathan isn't a man for talking, though, is he?"

It was true. Aaron had always been able to talk with Mary far easier than with Jonathan.

"A man's needs can sometimes be bigger than his common sense, you know? And women have a hard time understanding that. But a woman's needs are so different."

"A woman's needs aren't different at all, and don't you think they are. We all want pretty much the same—marriage and love and children."

"In that order?"

"Most of the time."

"It doesn't always happen so for a man."

"That's nature, Aaron."

"Yeah, well, nature's been giving me a hell of a time lately, then."

"Maybe it hasn't been easy on Pris, either."

"Whose side are you on?"

"I can't take sides, Aaron. You know I can't. I care enough about both you and Pris to want to see you happy. Both of you."

She paused.

"But you see, Aaron, there's something you should understand, and it's what happens to a woman when another woman has a baby. It's like nature plays a trick on her, makes her think of it as her own. Hearing the news the first time, she'll hold fast to her own belly, just as if it were growing there. And no matter who the father is, for a time he seems special—as if she herself had been touched by him. Why is it she asks so many questions of an expecting woman? Well, it's because the more she hears, the more she shares—the discomforts and the joys. She hears about the quickening, and for a time *it's hers,* too. She hears of a heartbeat, and it might as well be beating inside herself. And the birth—she takes a share in that, too. And to see a newborn child is to want one of her own, whether she already has two—or twelve. It doesn't matter. Because that's the trick nature plays on her. It makes all women think of babies in terms of themselves."

Under his hand Aaron could feel her toes, curled tightly now, as some might clench a fist in intensity.

"You plead Priscilla's case too convincingly for it to be only her case," Aaron said, smoothing his hand over her feet, looking down at them. He looked up at her, huddled shivering above him. "I'm sorry, Mary, for being selfish and going on about myself."

She drew her robe tighter about her.

"No, Aaron, that's not true. If you're selfish, then so am I, but I don't see us that way. I see us as two people who have to talk about what needs saying."

"Don't excuse me so lightly. I should have had more sense than to go on—"

"More sense than to what?" She cut him off. "To air a few feelings that needed airing? That's all we're doing, you and I."

And it was all they were doing. But it occurred to Aaron how unseemly it would be if anyone knew how freely they'd talked. Here in Moran Township the straitlaced matrons would not understand that a talk so personal could take place innocently. He was amused at the thought of some pucker-faced old harridan pursing her mouth in sour shock. Gossip was the thing they thrived on, and Aaron disliked it.

"Oh, but if the town gossips could hear what we've been talking about, they'd choke in their sleep."

It hadn't occurred to her before, but the thought of it brought a bubble of mirth to her lips. "Oh, Aaron, I expect they would," she laughed.

And the night, sealing them against self-consciousness, carried their laughter on its uncensoring ear.

Chapter 2

Out in the fields was the place where Jonathan did his best thinking. There he found expressions and feelings that seemed to avoid him everywhere else. Between him and the land, it seemed, he could work out most anything. All of his twenty-eight years he'd lived on this land, and it had never failed him. At times he felt he might have sprouted right out of it, breast-fed by its nectars, nurtured by its grains, and made secure by its perennial richness. When in doubt, the land was there. It gave back all he put into it. So he gave it his best. He worked it in love, and it returned his faith.

Walking on his soil that spring afternoon, he thought how easy it was to drop a seed into it, how effortlessly the land returned it. Far easier to ask a return of that kind than to ask what he was setting out to ask of Aaron and Mary.

"Consider, Aaron, if you were to father Mary and me a child."

He said it aloud, and it was good on his ears. Yes, that'd do just fine as a beginning. What would come to follow he couldn't guess, but Jonathan was fey to do the asking, no matter what. He would keep his arguments all stored and ready to voice—somehow—and would divine just how to voice them when the time came.

But the time never came that day, while Jonathan's words were fresh on his mind. He returned from his walk in the late afternoon, and Aaron wasn't home yet. At chore time, he still hadn't returned. Then when the milking was done and Jonathan returned to the house, Mary said she'd seen Aaron heading for town and figured he'd gone after Doc Haymes for Agnes.

So Jonathan went to sleep that night with the question unasked, but through the following day it remained in his mind just as he'd rehearsed it, and by the end of the day, when they were all three in the kitchen around the big old claw-foot table, he was tense from the weight of it.

One thing worked in his favor. Agnes Volence had had her baby last night, and Mary had that queer urge to talk about it, like she always did after news of a birthing.

"We'll have to all go down there to visit, as soon as it's respectable. Maybe the end of the week or so." She was mending something she held on her lap, and she didn't look up.

Aaron was drawing a handful of cookies from an old molasses pail in the middle of the table. He glanced at Mary, reading her intention immediately.

"You wouldn't be planning to do a bit of matchmaking while you pay your little social call, would you?" he asked.

"Why, Aaron, no such thing. It's just common politeness to visit the new parents. You know that."

"It's not common politeness to go calling within a week of the birth. Agnes will more'n likely still be in bed."

"And what better time to take a cake down there than when they're likely to appreciate it?"

She looked across at Aaron and put the thread in her teeth to bite it off. When she bit something off she was prepared to chew it, and he figured the sooner he made his peace with Pris the sooner Mary'd let up on him. He shrugged his shoulders and said, "We'll see. What do you think, Jonathan?"

And then Jonathan did the strangest thing. He jumped. Or flinched, rather.

"Jonathan?"

Mary couldn't see Jonathan's hands, for the oilcloth cover hanging over the edge of the table hid them from sight. But she could tell he was wiping his palms on his thighs.

"Is something wrong, Jonathan?"

"Wrong?" But Jonathan had a frog in his throat, and he had to clear it before he could continue. "Just that everybody is having babies but us."

He didn't look at Mary, so he missed seeing her eyes drop quickly back to the work on her lap.

"Excuse me . . ." Aaron rose from his chair as if to leave.

"No. I want you to listen," Jonathan said, staying

his brother with a hand on his arm. "I got something to say, and it's for both of you."

Aaron glanced at Mary, but she kept her eyes on her needlework. He sat back down slowly.

"We've been married seven years now. That's a long time. And there are no babies."

"I think this is between you two, and I've got no place in it." Aaron started to rise again, but a word from Jonathan stopped him.

"Stay."

And though Aaron stayed, he did so reluctantly while Jonathan went on.

"We all here know what happened when we were boys—how we both got the mumps, Aaron, you and me. They left me"—here Jonathan swallowed—"I mean, we all know I can't father babies."

"We don't know that for sure, Jonathan," Mary said. "I haven't given up hope."

"Well, I gave up hope, Mary, and you're just fooling yourself anymore," Jonathan said.

"There's no call to hurt her," Aaron said quietly, remembering what they'd talked about the night before.

"Well, this place needs children, and they won't spring from me."

Jonathan's palms were cold and damp on his thighs. His tongue, like a thick, swollen cork, threatened to stop up his mouth.

"But you, Aaron, they could spring from you." It came out half question, half something else. But it was out. Before he dissolved in his own sweat, Jonathan hurried on. "You're the natural one, Aaron. You're my brother. You see how there ought to be a child, don't you? It's not a thing I ask lightly." He looked at Mary, and her hands were still, her face expressionless.

Aaron's impatience erupted.

"I'm getting pretty damn sick of everybody in five counties pushing me to get married. First it's the townspeople, then it's Pris, then Mary, and now you, Jonathan. It isn't bad enough that the others push only for a wedding. Here you are, pushing for an heir! If people would leave us alone, maybe I'd be more in favor of the idea, but I'm not even ready to marry Pris yet, let alone have babies!"

"I'm not talkin' about you and Pris."

"Well, what the hell are you talkin' about?"

Jonathan's Adam's apple rose and slid back into place. This whole thing had gone wrong from the start. Mary had a puzzled look on her face. He wanted to ask this for her sake, too. He wanted to give her this, but how could he get her to understand? The sweat rolled down his temple. Dampness made dark stains on his blue cambric shirt.

"I said, what are you talkin' about?" Aaron repeated.

It was now or never.

"I'm talkin' about you and Mary."

The silence in the room was broken only by the tick of the pendulum clock on the kitchen wall.

"Me and Mary?" Aaron asked it in a quizzical way, as if he weren't sure he'd heard the question right. He didn't look at her, but he sensed her awful stillness, and it cracked the outer layer of his disbelief.

"Before either of you say anything, I got to ex-plain—"

"Christ almighty! Explain! If I understand what you're asking, you got more than explaining to do. You got some apologizing!" Aaron was on his feet now and leaning toward Jonathan across the table. "There's nothing between Mary and me. Nothing! Do you hear me, brother?"

"I know . . ." was all Jonathan could get out before Aaron raged on.

"Mary's your wife, man! Your wife! You'd best look at her and see what you've done in the last minute here." Aaron pointed a shaking finger at Mary. She sat staring at Jonathan with enormous eyes, her mouth working.

And Jonathan knew he need not plumb too deeply to see how he'd hurt her.

"Why, Jonathan?" she asked at last, and her voice was a quiet croak.

"I want us to have a son, and I give up hoping I could father one. It came to me that you and me had those mumps together, Aaron, but you being those four years younger than me, well, they didn't go down on you like they did on me, and I figured—"

But Aaron cut him off again. "Oh, no, you don't! You don't lay the guilt on me, Jonathan. Yes, we suffered side by side and you came out of it worse off than me, but that doesn't mean I owe you this that you're asking."

"I didn't mean you owe me. You know I'm not handy with words. But I thought about this plenty over the whole winter, and it appeared to me you and Priscilla were getting mighty close, so before you up and married I thought—"

Once again he was cut off, this time by Mary.

"Oh, Jonathan, you thought of it all winter? You planned on asking us all that time?" There was such hurt and bewilderment in her eyes that both men looked away rather than see it.

"Aaron's your brother. I'm your wife. The asking aside, did you think of the sinfulness of it? Did you think of that?"

"I did. And I've done some praying over it, and I'll gladly take the sin onto myself if there is sin. But there's nothing between you and Aaron. You said so, Aaron, and I could see that. Maybe the sin lays in the *coveting*, like the commandment says."

"You can't just bend and twist the words to suit your needs! You took those words and you chiseled off all the corners till they fit some hole in your scheming head where you wanted them to fit, and that makes it right?"

"I said I'd accept the blame, Aaron."

"Accept, hell! You'll accept nothing because there'll be nothing to accept! No blame! No sin! No baby! It makes me laugh to think you even believed we could get by with it. Just how do you think the fine women of Moran Township would take to one of their own showing up at church with a bastard son in her arms? Have you thought of what they'd do to Mary?"

"They'd never know it wasn't mine, Aaron. Look at us. You know how much we look alike? The child would have the looks we both got from Ma and Pa. Nobody could look at it and say it's yours, 'cause if he looked like you, he'd look like me, too. And I'd call it mine. It wouldn't be no bastard."

Aaron still stood leaning on the table, glaring across at his brother.

"I think the only bastard here is you!" he shouted.

Mary leaned toward him and touched his arm,

firmly but quietly demanding, "Sit down, Aaron. There's been enough hurt done here already. We'll not add more by saying things we'll all regret later."

Aaron sat down, but the black look of rage stayed on his face.

"Jonathan," Mary said, "I never complained about there being no babies, and if I acted like I held you responsible, I'm sorry. But what you're asking is wrong. It's wrong for Aaron and me, and it's wrong for you. How could you ask such a thing?"

Jonathan swallowed a great lump of love for her that welled up in his throat. He needed to make her see that he'd asked it out of love, but his wooden tongue was not easily commanded.

"Mary," he began, but the words were so hard to place between them, "Mary . . . I . . . it was a thing I wanted to give you, like I couldn't give you a baby."

"To give me, Jonathan?"

"Every woman should have the chance . . . I couldn't see no other way to give it to you."

Tears welled up in Mary's eyes, and a confusion of feelings tightened her chest.

"There's nobody else I'd ask except Aaron," Jonathan went on, "I thought maybe he'd see it my way, like maybe some deed of goodness he could do you . . . and me, too."

"But Jonathan, there's got to be love before . . ." Here Mary looked at Aaron, and for the first time she became embarrassed. His anger was partly under control, and with its going she had no defense against self-consciousness.

"It's not as if there's no love at all," Jonathan said. "And I can see the need in you, Mary. I can see you need what nature intended. Would it be unkind if Aaron could give you that?"

She could see that Aaron's jaw was tightly clamped shut, the muscles quivering as he kept his silence. Suddenly the things they'd said last night, those confidences exchanged so innocently, became laden with meanings neither Aaron nor Mary had intended, and her eyes flashed quickly away from his when she sensed that he was thinking the same thing.

"And for myself," Jonathan was going on, "well, there'd seem more purpose to working the land with a son to take it on one day. He could even tie this place together again—the whole place might be his—not split apart like Pa left it to us two."

Aaron leaned his elbows on the table and folded his knuckles together, pressing them against his chin while he scowled at Jonathan.

"You weren't kidding when you said you'd thought about this all winter, were you? You damn near planned the whole future for us, didn't you, Jonathan? Only you never said how we're all supposed to live with this when it's over and done. That's it! It'd never be over and done. It'd be a guilt we'd carry forever, can't you see?"

"I can see it could be that if we let it be. But it could be a blessing in many ways."

"Jonathan, you're being a self-righteous hypocrite, and you've never been before. I can't believe what you're saying." And Aaron shook his head, as if doing so would negate all that Jonathan had said. He covered his face with his hands and listened to his brother.

"I'd just ask you both to think about it, and consider if . . ." But his words faltered at last.

With his face still in his hands Aaron said, "Jonathan, you realize that you're sitting in my house and what I'm considering right now is asking you to get out of it?" Then he rubbed his hands downward, as if to wipe away his weariness and clear his eyes. When he did, he saw Mary with her eyes on her lap, hands idle, and the look on her face made him instantly sorry for what he'd threatened.

"Aw, hell, I didn't mean it. For better or for worse, we're here sharing the place, and I'm not throwing you out, neither of you. Pa sure picked a hell of a way to split up this property, though."

"I'm sorry," Mary said then, and Aaron realized she was frightened.

"Mary, I didn't mean that like it sounded. You belong here as much as Ma ever did, and you've got every right to be here. It's your home whether it belongs to Jonathan or me—that part doesn't matter. When I marry is time enough for us to change it." Then, in an effort to dispel the overwhelming oppression around them all, he added, "Right?"

No one answered. Just the ticking clock imposed itself on the quiet.

"It doesn't bear thinking about, Jonathan, and it never could," Aaron said, "whether I marry Pris or not. Suppose I do marry her? Then she's part of this, too. There's such a thing as faithfulness, and I feel it, whether I'm married yet or not."

"I figured when you went to the city there were other women."

"What I did in the city is no business of yours! Any women I knew there have nothing to do with this or with Pris."

"Oh, Jonathan, don't!" Mary cried, and there were tears on her face at last. "Don't say any more. We are not *things,* not animals you can pen up together at mating time!"

"I said it all wrong, I know."

"And you've said enough!" Aaron charged, pushing his chair back and rising in one angry movement. "Just don't say another word. Not one more word." And he slammed out the door, leaving Mary and Jonathan in its reverberations. But before the air had quite stilled he came back and stood just inside the kitchen door, looking across the room at Mary.

"I'm sorry, Mary," he said. "I had no part in this." And she knew he'd felt it necessary to clarify that point after all he'd told her the night before. But he'd slammed back out before she could say, "I know."

She could not face Jonathan any longer, so she picked a jacket from the hook behind the kitchen door and went out, too, closing the door more quietly than Aaron had. But the click of the latch censored Jonathan as firmly as when Aaron had slammed the door.

Aaron took his anger to the barn. He stormed down the yard, flung the barn door open, and charged inside. It was clean and quiet, no work to be done. And nobody to listen to his arguments. In frustration he slammed his open palm against a wooden beam.

One would not guess it just then, but he was a man of easy temperament, usually slow to anger. His way was the way of light response, a word of jest. He was uncomfortable with anger and tried to avoid it.

How, then, had the last two days spawned such belligerence in him? Like mushrooms during long summer rains, the events of the last two days had sprouted out of nowhere, growing so fast they seemed to close around Aaron. He was angered because they'd grown out of his control.

It didn't help when Aaron recalled all the remarks he'd made last night to Mary, remarks that echoed now with implication he'd absolutely not intended.

"Nature's been giving me a hell of a time lately. It takes two to do a lot of things. A man's needs can sometimes be greater than his common sense." Did I really say all those things to Mary, he thought. The memory of how he'd let his foolish tongue run wild blistered his conscience now, creating bubbles of fear, fear that Mary might somehow mistake his intentions, especially after all that was just said in the house.

He knew both Jonathan and Mary understood the reason he'd left the farm for the city two years before. He'd gone to give them privacy, hoping they'd accomplish in his absence what hadn't happened while he lived with them. Feeling like the outsider in his own house, he'd left it to them, gone to that miserable city to work in sweatshops among strangers, giving Jonathan and Mary time alone. But nothing had come of it, and after a year Jonathan had written, asking him to come back home. It was a two-man farm. They'd made it so after their pa died. In his absence, Mary had worked in his place. But she was a small woman, city-bred, and much as she loved the country, she never did take to field work. They all knew it was hard on her. And Jonathan wanted Aaron to come back, and so did Mary, he wrote. Aaron had come, and gladly—leaving behind the hated city and carrying with him the memory he now ruefully referred to as "the time I went to town."

Now the memory came back to Aaron, and with it the threat that he might have to leave the farm again. Surely there'd be no living together as they had before. Why, he couldn't sleep in the house tonight! Not on the other side of their bedroom wall!

So Aaron climbed to the haymow, still simmering. But the hay was nearly all gone from the loft, and what was left lent small comfort, compacted as it was from months of winter storage. He was exhausted after the long day yesterday at the Volences', the turmoils of tonight, and last night's arguments. When the heat of his anger cooled somewhat, he was left in the comfortless barn, tired and cold, and he finally gave in and returned to the house and his room, sleeping like a drugged man, worn beyond caring who was on the other side of the wall.

When Mary came back to the house, it was dim and still. Jonathan had left a lantern in the niche at the bottom of the stairs. There was nowhere for her to go except to bed, but she wouldn't take the lantern up. She couldn't face Jonathan yet, even in the dimmest lantern light.

She blew out the flame and made her way up the dark stairwell, hoping he would be asleep. But the house was old and dry, and it creaked, signaling to Jonathan she was coming.

He lay very still, with his arms folded under his head, watching her come in and change into her nightgown in the moonlight. She brushed out her hair and braided it, taking an endlessly long time. His heart beat out the minutes until she finally climbed over the foot of the bed to her place between him and the wall.

It had always been a spot where she'd felt such security, with Jonathan there on the outside, but tonight she felt trapped in it, held there by Jonathan's elbows, which loomed just above her pillow. She knew he wasn't asleep, but hoped he'd say nothing. When he spoke quietly in the dark, she jumped, realizing how tense she'd been.

"Mary?"

She didn't answer.

"Where'd you go?"

"Just walking."

"You gave me a scare, being gone so long."

"I didn't think you'd miss me if I didn't come back."

She couldn't help saying it, even though she knew it wasn't so. She wanted him to know how he'd hurt her.

"You know that's not so, Mary. This is where you belong."

"Yes. In your bed, not Aaron's."

"You've been seven years in my bed, with no babies."

"And you need one that bad, you'd send me to Aaron?"

"It was a way that come to me, Mary."

"Well, it's no way at all."

Jonathan inhaled deeply. "I said it all wrong, I know. I meant to say it better, so you'd understand."

"Oh, Jonathan, it doesn't matter how you said it, it only matters you did. There's no good way to ask a thing like that."

"But don't you see? It's something I wanted for you, too. I see you going year after year and still lookin' like a child yourself . . . and everybody else has got more kids than they need. I can see the need in you."

"But you had no right to ask it of Aaron and me." In an impatient voice she continued, "It's not a seed you just borrow like a punkin seed, Jonathan. You might want a punkin like the one in your neighbor's punkin patch, but planting a punkin seed is different than a man's."

He was quiet then, still lying with his head on his arms, looking at the ceiling. After a space he said, "I had such plans for the place, you know, always thought of working it into something even better to pass on to a son."

She lay, like him, staring at the ceiling.

"I was proud of all those plans, too, Jonathan. That summer I came from Chicago to Aunt Mabel's—why, I had no intention of staying. I was only coming to help her out for the summer. When you came along in Uncle Garner's threshing crew and started talking about this place, I could nearly see it before you ever brought me here. You made me proud of all the plans you had, and I was willing to share them with you. But this plan now—there's no sharing it."

"Are you sorry you came to this place with me, Mary?"

"I'm not sorry I came, Jonathan, only sorry about this . . . this obsession you have, about the baby."

"Obsession?"

"You've got it in your head that without a son you're working for nothing. But that's not true. You've got . . . we've got . . . a lot. And yes, I'd like a child, too, but I'm not willing to sell my soul to get it. I'm not going to let the need of it change me like it has you."

"Change me?" He turned his head to look at her beside him.

"Didn't it change you, Jonathan?"

He didn't answer.

"Well, then, how did you come to where you could ask what you did tonight?"

He knew she was crying then because she turned her face toward the wall.

"I did wrong, Mary," he said, and reached out to touch her, not knowing much about comforting her, for he'd never had much cause to do so.

"Oh, Jonathan, how can we face Aaron in the morning?"

"We'll weather it, Mary." It sounded hopelessly inadequate even to Jonathan, but he didn't know what else to say.

"How?" Her crying was audible now.

He patted her arm, leaning above her on an elbow. "We'll weather it somehow," he repeated. Her arm under the nightgown was warm, folded across her chest, and he could feel it rise and fall with her breathing. She never cried, and Jonathan realized what a feeling of concern those tears had evoked in him. She was such a child—and he hadn't thought to hurt her this way. How could he take away that hurt?

"We could try again," he said, moving his hand onto her breast, feeling her stiffen at his touch.

"This way? And then you think this will wash away all the sourness of today like you wash away the clabbered milk from a pail? Well, it takes a while in the sunshine to air that sourness out, Jonathan. I might need a while of sun, too, before I sweeten."

She made a shrugging push with her shoulder, nudging his hand off her breast until he retreated it to her arm. It was the first time she had ever denied Jonathan.

"What does that mean, 'sweeten'?"

She was exasperated that he could fail to understand the depth of her hurt, and her reluctance to quickly accept him again.

"Sweeten means sweeten! I mean I can't just so quickly forget what you would have me do with Aaron if you had your way. Now, here you are, wanting your way with me again. Well, which is it you want, Jonathan? I can't follow your change of mind fast enough."

"You're talking nonsense. I only meant to comfort you."

"Well, it was no comfort. The kind of comfort I need is the kind that starts with 'I'm sorry' and builds from there."

"I didn't mean to hurt you by it."

"But you aren't sorry. Are you, Jonathan?"

His hand squeezed her arm lightly as he answered, "For the hurtin', yes. For the askin', no." Then he lay back down with his hands folded beneath his head, as before.

"If you're not sorry, then we're in bad shape."

"We been in bad shape, as far as a baby is concerned, for years. And you're getting where you're grabbing at even those ideas Doc Haymes has been putting in your head. But I've gone along with that, and it didn't work, either. It's just more proof I can't be no father, that's all."

"But I believe what he says is reasonable, that a woman is . . . well . . . that a woman is prime on special days each month. We just haven't given it enough time."

"Well, if it's so reasonable, then maybe it'd work in your favor with Aaron. It'd prove to me that Haymes was right."

"Is that how you figured it? And then what about afterward? Did you figure I'd be your wife again and we could pretend nothing ever happened between Aaron and me?"

"I don't know. I thought if he was to marry Priscilla, it might all work out."

"You and I have to work things out and leave Aaron out of it."

She seemed to be suggesting that maybe she was sweetening a bit, but her next words belied that.

"I never turned you away before, Jonathan, and I know it's not right, either, but I got to have some time to mend my mind a bit. Let's just both drop off and work on that mending for now."

She turned on her side, facing the wall, shutting herself away from him, and even though his caress had been meant only as a consolation to her, he found now that her cold, curled back raised a yearning he hadn't known was there. For, as she said, she'd never turned him away before.

Chapter 3

$\mathcal{A}$aron awoke to the sound of the lifter and lids ringing through the house as Jonathan made a fire in the kitchen range. It had become Jonathan's job, by tacit agreement, just as filling the woodbox in the evenings had become Aaron's. Making the fire had been something their pa did when he was alive. It was a task for the man of the house, and no matter that Aaron's ownership ought to give him that status, the four years' difference in their ages made it fitting for Jonathan to assume the role.

Aaron was only sixteen and Jonathan twenty when that load of potatoes had overturned, burying their ma and pa as they delivered the wagonload to the potato warehouses in Browerville. It had been natural for Jonathan to take over as the head of the house.

They worked the land together, but it was Jonathan who signaled their first spring seedings, gauged the need for cultivating, judged the grain's maturity, called for its reaping and threshing, decided how much of the harvest would be sold and how much kept for seed, which fields would lay fallow and which used for grazing, which section of woods needed thinning at woodcutting time, which sow would be slaughtered, which cow would be bred, which heifers would be kept and which sold.

His decisions were not so much edicts as effects, for they were born of his oneness with the land, his simple knowing of its every need. Aaron sensed this and accepted it without rancor, even when Jonathan wrote, "Come home, Aaron, the farm needs you." He came back from the city then, and things were pretty much as they'd been before.

But now, hearing the iron ring of the stove lids, it seemed Jonathan called him, ringing the lids like a schoolmarm might ring the bell for a tardy pupil, and Aaron resented it for the first time.

When he came into the kitchen it was empty but the fire was snapping. Jonathan had already gone to the barn and Mary wasn't up yet. Standing by the range, savoring its heat on the chilly morning, he made an effort to shake off his resentment, blaming it on the argument they'd had last night. But it stayed with him while he took his jacket from the hook behind the door and shrugged it on, heading outside.

The April morning was lost on Aaron, spring's specialness remote from his mind. The yard, still half-locked by winter, waited for spring to release it. The transient robins hadn't returned yet, but the ever-present sparrows twittered around the chicken coop and granary, looking for kernels the chickens had missed. Pale patches of green showed across the yard where the first brave grass had poked its way into the new season, hesitating as if reserving the right to duck back under if it didn't like what it found. Inside the barn the cows, grown heavy and lazy over the winter, turned inquiring eyes on him as he entered. A couple of barn cats came out of somewhere to sit on the step of the big, open, east door, nosing the air and waiting to cadge their cream. Everything was the same as always. Everything except Jonathan and Aaron.

They worked silently together, their routines meshing from long practice: filling the troughs with fodder, squatting on their milk stools, making the empty pails ring, setting the froth-topped pails aside, filling the tins for the cats, moving to the next cow. But neither spoke. The words of the night before were still between them. Aaron had too many more he'd like to add, while Jonathan had too few. Knowing they'd only make the situation worse if they hashed it over again, both remained silent.

Mary saw them coming up the yard with the milk pails and was determined to keep things sensible. If she knew anything about these two, she knew they'd brood and stew until there'd be no living with either one of them. They came into the kitchen, mouths drawn. She was bound to set them right. Doubtful herself, fearing her own misgivings, she nonetheless resolved to do her best to restore peace among them.

"Mornin', Jonathan. Mornin', Aaron," she said as they set the pails down.

They answered together, but then the room was quiet again and Mary's heart fluttered again with doubt. She went to the breakfront and got a clean dish towel, as always, and went to wet it at the sink. Aaron turned toward the cistern at the same moment she did. Any other day he'd have pumped the handle while she wet the towel and squeezed it, but today he hesitated, backed off, and left her to do it herself. She took the pails into the cool, concrete buttery under the stairs and covered them with the wet towel as she always did. Before going back into the kitchen, she placed her hands to her cheeks, then dropped them to smooth her apron and chastise herself for being so vulnerable in Aaron's presence. She could see it was up to her to settle him down. Aaron was as twitchy as a cow's tail at fly time.

"Hurry with your washing, then," she called, coming up out of the buttery into the kitchen again. "Breakfast is all ready."

The men never washed until after chores, and they did it at the kitchen sink, stripping off their shirts while they did. The kitchen range and the sink were side by side on the north wall. Usually, while Mary took up the food, Aaron was beside her, washing. But today he left his shirt on, opened up the front, and washed himself inside it, suddenly self-conscious with her moving about right there beside him. When he came to the table his shirt had damp, uncomfortable spots where he'd gotten it wet.

"Are you spreading today, Jonathan?" she asked, passing him a bowl of fried potatoes.

And Jonathan was forced at last to talk.

"It's thawed. It's ready to spread."

"Have some side pork, Aaron." She thrust the platter toward him. "Which field are you starting with?"

She looked directly at him, forcing him to answer in an everyday way.

"I suppose the south ten." They always fertilized the south ten first, but Aaron knew what she was up to, and to make it easier on her, he added, "Right, Jonathan?"

Jonathan looked briefly at his brother, nodded his assent, and answered, "Yup, the south ten."

It was a start, anyway.

"Before you go out there, will one of you fetch me the big crock from the shed? I need it for the pork today," Mary said.

They answered at once:

"Sure, Mary."

"Yup."

She quelled the irritation that rose in her stomach as they glanced at each other hesitantly across the table.

"Thank you, Jonathan." She settled that.

They went out after breakfast, putting on boots at the back porch step and heading off across the yard. Jonathan returned with the crock she needed, then left again. During the day she'd catch sight of them at times out in the barnyard where the frozen pile of manure was thawed enough to use. They need time to thaw, too, she thought, watching them pitch together, filling the spreader before it disappeared out to the field again. She wondered what they had to say to each other, but when they were out of sight she returned to her pork. It took her mind off them for a while, anyway.

Pork was their mainstay. It was butchered in the fall, after the freezing weather had settled in for good.

The frozen pieces were stored in a wooden barrel on the north side of the house until the weather warmed enough that it might spoil. Then, what remained was fried down slowly until its fat rendered and could be poured around the meat again, preserving it for the warm months ahead.

Mary worked with the pork all during the day, packing the crock until it was full to the top. The house reeked, and in the afternoon she opened the windows and the back door to let the spring breeze freshen it.

She could hear Jonathan whistling somewhere outside and knew his spirits must be lighter than they had been that morning. The first field work usually did that to him, made him more alive than at any other time of year. She and Aaron sometimes teased Jonathan about his whistling, telling him the robins wouldn't return until they heard him. It was just a thing Jonathan did. The feelings he couldn't put into words, he warbled in his tunes.

All day, Mary felt herself caught in the middle between Jonathan and Aaron. When they came in for supper, the crock was sitting on the floor, all packed with fried-down pork and fat. When she tried to lift it, they both offered to help. Aaron ended up doing it. Why had such small favors suddenly taken on the hint of chivalry? It had never mattered before who helped her do small things.

At supper, Aaron flinched when he reached for the sugar bowl at the same time she did. She pretended not to notice.

"Tomorrow I aim to get this grease smell aired out of here," she said. "I think we can get along without the heater stove in the front room. If you two would move it out, I'd do it all properly and give the front room a good spring cleaning tomorrow."

"Spring getting to you, Mary?" Aaron asked, reaching again for the sugar bowl.

"I guess it has. Me and Jonathan both, I guess. Did I hear you whistling today, Jonathan?"

But her effort fell flat, for Aaron made none of his usual jokes about his brother's whistling. There followed an uncomfortable silence.

Finally Aaron said, "We can take the wood stove out after supper, so it'll be out of your way come morning."

"Yes, do that."

When they were done eating, she cleaned up the kitchen while they dismantled the black stovepipe and carried it in pieces out to the back porch, followed by the stove itself and the silver asbestos pad from the floor under it. It was dirty work, and they needed washing to get rid of the soot they'd gathered while doing it. Mary had finished putting the kitchen back in order and left it to them. Aaron's unaccustomed modesty had made her uncomfortable once already today while he was washing up. But he'd better snap out of it, and quick, she thought, because she wasn't catering to such foolishness after today!

Jonathan finished washing first and turned the sink over to Aaron. Aaron was dipping warm water from the reservoir when Jonathan said, "You know that Black Angus we talked about this winter?"

"Yeah."

"You still in favor of me buying it, like you said?"

"You know more about it than I do. If it sounds like sound business, then go ahead."

"Mary said the same thing."

"Then do it. You don't need our okays, but you got 'em just the same. So what's holding you up?"

"Nothin'. Nothin' at all," Jonathan replied.

Aaron was bent over the washbasin lathering his face and neck when Jonathan continued.

"Except, I'll have to make a trip to Minneapolis to do it."

"Mary'd enjoy a trip like that."

"She agreed to stay behind and help you with the sowing. I figure we won't have it done yet when it's time for me to go."

"You know she can't take the field work," Aaron argued, not able to say that Jonathan must not leave her behind, no matter what.

"It'll only be for a few days, is all."

"When you going?"

"Cattle Exposition is the last week in May. I'd want to go then to get my pick of the bulls. And so I can talk to the sellers and learn a little more about the breed."

"There must be someplace around here you can buy one and save yourself the trip."

"Like I said before, nobody in these parts ever tried breeding Angus. All they think of is pork. I mean to get the jump on the beef business around here. The magazines say beef is the way the whole country'll be eating before long, and they claim it's Angus they'll prefer."

They'd talked this over during the winter, and Jonathan, as usual, made good sense.

"So go ahead if you've decided. Maybe we'll have all the crops in by then. It's hard to tell."

"You sure you don't mind?"

"Naw," Aaron mumbled into the towel.

"Good."

Jonathan left the kitchen and headed upstairs to bed. Left behind in the kitchen, Aaron leaned both hands on the edge of the sink, gripping it, staring down at the floor. He felt drained. Only one day since Jonathan had brought this unspeakable idea up among them, and his nerves were already strung out like fence wire. Now his brother had taken it one step further, providing a time when he and Mary would be left alone. Hah! If it weren't so absurd, it would almost be laughable. But there was nothing funny about the situation at all. Today he'd acted like a schoolboy, flinching every time Mary came within touching distance, but he saw that this must end and knew he'd best treat her like he always had before. It seemed best now, too, if he patched up things with Pris. The sooner the better.

In the morning Aaron seemed more like his old self. "Leave some walls standing," he teased, "don't scrub the plaster off."

"No chance, the way this place is built," she threw back at him as he left the yard with Jonathan, "but I can guarantee it won't smell like fried-down pork tonight." It was a relief having him treat her again as he had in the past. It worked on her like a tonic, and she tore into her work feeling lighter than she had since this whole thing had started.

She spent the morning scrubbing the walls with borax to combat the summer insects that might creep indoors. She boiled the lace curtains in turpentine water until they were bleached, rinsed them in gum arabic, and stretched them on the wood-and-nail frame to dry. She took the stovepipe pieces from the porch into the yard and brushed the insides of them, making them ready for summer storage. She was just finishing when Aaron came up the board path at dinnertime.

He laughed as she stood up to go into the house with him.

"You look like you're the rag that's been drug through the stovepipe," he teased, touching some soot on her nose. But she instinctively shied away from his touch, just as he'd done from hers the day before. She brushed distractedly at her nose, annoyed by her skittishness. Then she turned toward the house.

"Dinner's hot," she said as Jonathan came up the walk. They all went inside together.

In the afternoon she scrubbed the horsehair sofa with naphtha, took cold tea to the varnished woodwork, beat the rugs that had hung on the line all day, washed the windows with vinegar water, and ironed the antimacassars. She loved this old house and had felt comfortable with it from the very first. She had a feeling for it much the same as Jonathan had for his land. It was her domain, and she took pride in it. The house reflected her love just as the fields reflected Jonathan's. It had been built by his grandfather, the first Gray to homestead the land in the mid 1800s. Jonathan and Aaron both told the story of how their grandfather had earned it by doing stumping for others here in Todd County. Using nothing but a grub hoe, he'd removed stumps, clearing the land for a mere ten dollars per acre until he'd earned enough to buy his own farm. His first crops of corn and potatoes had been planted among the tree stumps he'd not had time to clear from his own acreage that first season. Thus, his first harvest had been taken from among the stubbled remains of the trees he'd felled and timbered for the building of his own homestead. Aaron was the one who was fondest of telling that story, maybe because the house was his now. But Mary often remembered it herself, and the spirit of that first homesteader burned in her with pride. True, the house was Aaron's, but she'd been its caretaker for seven years and there was no use denying it would be hard to leave it when Aaron got married.

It was late afternoon when the room was put back in order. The curtains hung in crisp peaks, scratching against the wall; antimacassars lay crisply on the arms and backs of chairs. Spirits of lavender on a lump of salt ammonia sweetened the air like summer, and the old decorative plate covered the chimney hole high up on the wall. Mary studied it, sitting in the kitchen rocker, which took the place of the heater stove for the summer. The plate pictured an old mill beside a brook, surrounded by velvety grass and heavy trees. She'd studied it often and knew it as well as the rest of the house. Most times the peaceful scene filled her with a homey contentment.

It lent no such satisfaction today. She was weary. While her hands were busy, she'd held her worries and doubts at bay, but now, when she relaxed her guard, they assaulted her anew. As if Grandfather Gray had come walking across the velvety grass by the mill up above her, wondering why she sat so forlornly in his old front room, she answered his unasked question.

"Seems like your grandsons need me between them to settle down this hornets' nest here, but I feel like I've already been stung by both of them. Jonathan first with this whole fool thing—he's the one who stirred it up. And then Aaron, acting so skittish. And both of them carrying on like fools. I wish you were here to talk some sense into them both. I could use a steadying hand, too, maybe."

Then, realizing she'd been talking out loud, Mary thought what a goose she must seem. She stamped a foot and got up from the rocker to make supper, muttering, "Great big fools . . ."

It was a busy week that left little time or energy for paying social calls, so they didn't make it down to Clem and Agnes Volence's to see the new baby. The field work started in full force for the men, and spring housecleaning filled Mary's days.

They were up early, worked too long, and ended the days weary. It really would be best to wait until Agnes was up and about again, Mary thought, and put off the visit to the following week.

Aaron hadn't had time to go down to settle things between himself and Pris, either. But they always went to the Bohemian Hall Saturday nights, and he figured they'd have time together then to straighten things out.

On Saturday night he cleaned up, hitched up the buggy, and headed down the hill to the west. As he turned into the Volence driveway, the corncrib seemed to accost him, and he recalled Pris's anger in its full force. She was going to take some gentling tonight, he knew, but he could handle almost anything after the week he'd just been through.

He left the horse and rig under the box elder and walked up on the back porch. It was bright inside, and someone was playing the organ in the front room.

When he knocked, he heard footsteps running; then the door flew open and Newt and Gracie stood there grinning.

"How come Pris ain't goin' to the dance with you?" Newt questioned without preliminary. Cora nudged Newt's ribs.

Aaron chucked him under the chin and said, "Well, I hope she is. I came to get her just like always, didn't I?"

"But her'n Cora already went with the Kveteks." The Kvetek family lived across the road.

"I told her she best wait and see first if you was comin' to get her," Gracie told him, "but she was in a huff and said she wasn't waitin' around no longer."

Aaron ruffled her hair and said, "That's okay, honey. I'll see her down at the dance hall, anyway. How's that new baby?"

"He looks just like me," Newt bubbled. "Ma said."

"Well, we'll come down soon and see him, okay?"

"Wanna see him now, Aaron?" Newt asked hopefully, pulling on Aaron's hand.

"I better get down to the dance before Pris finds another beau. But I'll be back soon, huh?"

"Okay, Aaron."

He left them waving him off and headed for the hall. Priscilla had never gone off to the dance like this, not since they'd been going together. He hadn't thought about her not being home—she'd always been before. Tonight, just when he'd decided to play things her way, now when he needed her there to steady him, she'd decided to stomp off to the dance and show him what-for. Well, maybe he deserved it, but why—oh, why!—did she have to choose right now?

The Fulfillment

The Bohemian Hall was heaving like the sides of a winded horse. Aaron could feel the ground shake clear outside. Settling the horse and rig, he could hear the sounds of the Shymek brothers, hard at the music. The lilt of the piano came through the windows, joined by a fiddle and concertina.

The hall served as Grange, polling place, township meeting house, and theater for school programs. Every Saturday night it was a dance hall—and the Bohemians gave it no pity. Inside, Aaron could feel the rhythmic quaking of the plank floor as the dancers beat it to a polka step.

The building was fronted by a small room that served as kitchen or taproom, depending on the occasion. The large main room was lined with tables and benches on three sides. Aaron scanned the scatter of benches, looking for Pris. He saw Cora first, for she sat facing the door at a table with Mr. and Mrs. Kvetek and their two daughters. Pris sat with her back to the dance floor, but the minute Cora saw Aaron she quickly leaned toward Pris. He detected a slight turn of her head in his direction, but she gave him only a quarter profile.

So she's still got her back up, he thought.

The dancers were dancing a waltz as he began threading his way through the crowd toward her to ask her to dance, but two single men reached Pris just as Aaron began to make his move. She walked out to the floor with one of them. Aaron had worked his way too near the Kveteks' table to change course now, and as he passed it he glimpsed Pris waltzing off to his right, while Cora called, "Hi, Aaron," with a singsong inflection he didn't like one bit and a glance toward Pris.

Smart-aleck snot-nose, he thought. He heard her and one of the Kvetek girls giggle as he moved off toward the taproom to buy a beer. He stayed back there by the wooden kegs to down the beer and consider the situation.

Pris didn't waste much time hangin' out her shingle! But he'd told her this was what he wanted, hadn't he? She was dancing with Willy Michalek again, and all Aaron could do was wait it out. But she finished the whole set with Michalek, and Aaron had another glass of beer while he waited for a new set to begin.

When the music struck up again, he crossed the floor and stepped behind Pris's chair. "Dance, Pris?"

"Sure, Aaron," she accepted.

The two punks across the table didn't smirk or giggle this time, but avoided looking at him as he took Pris onto the floor.

"What did you tell Cora about us?" he asked. "She acts like I'm a cockroach she just found in her cream."

"I didn't tell her anything about us. There's nothing to tell."

"Well, she seems to think she should defend you."

"Maybe I need defense against you."

They were dancing now, but she stayed her distance and he didn't press her, didn't pull her against him in the old way.

"I didn't come here to fight," he said.

"What, then, to make a conquest?"

"No, to make an apology." And he meant it.

"It's too late for that. I don't want it anymore."

"What do you mean 'anymore'?" he asked.

"I mean I've had time to do some thinking this week, and I've decided you're right. Why should I put all my apples in one basket? Maybe I'll pass a few around."

"Come on, Pris, let me take you home and we can at least talk this out."

"Sorry, Aaron, I already told Willy Michalek he could take me home."

He really hadn't figured she'd move that fast, and it irked him.

"Passing your apples around already?" he couldn't help taunting. "Look out, Priscilla, too many passes and you'll be applesauce."

There was a sudden stab of pain in his right foot as Pris's heel mashed it onto the floorboards. He tightened his grip around her waist with his arm and lifted her until her toes dangled above the floor. His foot hurt like hell, but it took both feet flat on the floor to hold her aloft.

"Aaron, you put me down this instant! If you don't I'll smash something else!" And her legs were thrashing against his. But he held her as she was, her hips pressed smack against his, her breasts tight against his chest, and an arm still around his shoulders. She grabbed a handful of his shirt to keep from tipping sideways.

"Anything you say, Miss Applesauce," he grinned as he let her slide down against the front of him, all the way to the floor.

"You want someone to take home?" she flung at him. "There! Try one of them?" And she pointed to the group of chippies who were near the door in their usual place. "They're more your type!"

The dance was done, and she spun off toward her table. He followed, trying to appear as though he were showing her back to her place. But it was easy to see she was practically running to escape him.

Well, he'd known she'd take some gentling, hadn't he? He'd give her a bit more time and then try again. He'd see her at church tomorrow. Maybe then he'd have better luck.

But the following morning when he approached her in the churchyard, he could tell she was as sour as she'd been the night before.

"Hello, Priscilla," he said, attempting to neutralize her with an engaging smile.

She was having none of it.

"Will you come and have breakfast with me and Jonathan and Mary today?"

"I hardly think so," she answered coldly.

"How long are you going to keep this up? I apologized, didn't I? Will you give me a chance to make it right?"

"You had your chance for a whole year."

"Well, I'll take another day if you got it." He tried to take her elbow, but she avoided his touch.

"I don't think you'll take anything more from me."

"Did you have that good a time with Michalek last night?"

"At least he's a gentleman."

He grew angry. His crime had been wanting her and having demonstrated it, that was all.

"Pris, it isn't every day I push you up against the corncrib wall. Can't you forget it?"

"Aaron Gray, you stand here making light of it right smack on the Lord's doorstep!"

"I figure the Lord's got enough to do without slappin' my hands for putting them where He intended they ought to be put, anyway."

He was teasing, but he never should have said that, for she swirled in a quick, dust-lifting turn and strode away, and Aaron realized he'd only made matters worse.

Each day that went by now with himself and Priscilla still at odds made Aaron more determined to settle their quarrel. He gave it no words, but there was a feeling that he had to get Pris to take him back before Jonathan left on his trip.

If Aaron had known last winter that his approval of the plan to purchase a bull would lead to the situation he now found himself in, he would have objected then. But arguing about whether or not Jonathan should make the trip was now impossible. What would Mary think if he raised objections? That he was afraid of what might happen if the two of them were left alone?

4

𝒯he fields of Moran lay at their blackest best, for the most part. The harrowing was nearly done, but the heavy drags had turned rocks up, seeking them out of their hiding spots and laying them bare and discovered above the ground, looking like blocks of salt on the peppery earth.

The tin bottom of the stone boat screeched along on the complaining soil, and with each "Hiyup!" the horses worked harder at their growing load. Jonathan did very little whistling during stone-picking. The only breath he could spare was for the whistle that escaped his pursed lips when he'd hoisted another stone up and dropped it onto the stone boat, the great reflex expulsion of breath seeming to lend him strength for handling the next stone.

It was Friday morning when Jonathan straightened and stretched his back, glancing sideways at Aaron.

"We're going over to Volence's tonight. You coming along?" Jonathan wondered why Priscilla hadn't come home with Aaron for breakfast last Sunday, as usual. He'd also noted that Aaron hadn't been down the hill to her house for over a week. He guessed something was amiss.

But Aaron only answered, "I reckon so," and stooped to pick up another stone. "It'll do us all good to get away for a while."

Abiding by local custom, Mary baked a cake to offer on this first visit to a family with a new baby. Also following local custom, Clem Volence went down to his cellar and brought up a quart of golden, home-made dandelion wine to treat the visitors. Between the cake and wine, the children, and the babble of excitement over the unexpected call, the coolness between Aaron and Pris went quite unnoticed. Newt monopolized Aaron's lap once they were seated around the kitchen table. The child's nonstop chatter was welcome, for it filled the chasm that gaped between Aaron and Pris whenever their eyes met. She had greeted him with a civil hello but made sure when they were all seated that her chair wasn't next to his. Mary caught Priscilla's quick retreat from Aaron's gaze and looked for some sign of reconciliation between the two of them, aware of its importance to her.

The baby was awake, and Cora brought him into the kitchen, taking him straight to Mary with great sisterly pride.

"You wanna hold him, Mary?"

Cora bent near Mary's shoulder to show off the prize.

"I'd love to if it's all right with your mama."

" 'Course it is," Agnes assured her with a laugh. "By the time you have your fifth one, you're just too glad to have someone else do the holding for a change," she added.

The warm shape felt foreign. The baby was quiet, though awake.

"What's his name?" she asked.

"James," Newt said importantly, "but we're gonna call him Jimmy while he's little."

The baby's eyelids were nearly transparent, and he had no brows at all. There were tiny white newborn dots on his nose, and his mouth with its slightly swollen upper lip sometimes sucked at nothing.

"Ain't he cute?" Newt asked, and though she wasn't too sure about it, Mary answered, "He's plumb beautiful, Newt. Anyone can see that."

She hadn't any of the knack for talking inanities to an infant and would have felt foolish trying it in front of all these people. But the longer she held Jimmy, the nicer he felt. He was a good size in her arm, and the little lumps and bumps of his tiny body kind of fit as they lay against her. He had an uncommonly good smell about him, not unlike the barn cats after they had drunk fresh milk. He moved his feet inside the blankets, and the little movement felt right against her stomach. Sometimes the tip of his tongue peeked through rosy lips, and she marveled at the smallness of it, just as she did at his tiny fingernails and earlobes.

As always, the men were talking weather, crops, and planting—always foremost in their minds at this time of year. The remainder of April and May would be spent putting the crops in, the last of May always an unspoken deadline they aimed for.

"I don't know if I'll be done by the end of May this year," Jonathan said, "but if I'm not, Mary said she'd give Aaron a hand getting in the last of the seed corn. I'm taking the train down to Minneapolis in the last part of May, to the Cattle Exposition."

Mary looked up. With a sudden shock she realized what he was talking about. The Cattle Exposition . . . the Black Angus . . . but it was long ago when they'd talked about it. She hadn't given it a thought for some time. Now she felt a tremor run through her.

He meant to leave her and Aaron alone. Why hadn't Jonathan said anything more about this to her? Why was he telling everyone here about his plans to make the trip, sealing them with finality by doing so?

Mary met Aaron's eyes briefly across the table, and he realized that Jonathan had not spoken to her about this since they'd all talked it over together last winter. His puckered brows clearly told Mary that Aaron was aware of Jonathan's plans and that they didn't rest well with him.

The baby had fallen asleep, and Pris took him off to his bed but returned from upstairs to the living room and began playing the organ. It was getting late, and Aaron knew they'd soon be leaving. If he wanted to talk to her, this was his chance. When he got up to leave the kitchen Newt would have followed him, but Agnes sent him packing upstairs to get ready for bed. Aaron was grateful.

Priscilla had her back to Aaron when he came into the living room. He came up behind her and put his hands on her shoulders, but she continued to play, pumping the foot pedals and creating a gusty sound that wafted louder than his voice, giving them a sort of privacy.

"We have to talk," he said to her back.

"Uh-uh," was all she said.

"How long are you going to keep this up?"

"I don't want to talk to you or see you anymore," she said.

"Turn around and look at me when you say that," he challenged her.

"It would be the same, looking at you or not."

He swung her by the shoulders until she spun around on the revolving organ stool to face him. Her hands had slid across the keys, and discordant notes swooned to a telling silence as the bellows lost air. The voices in the kitchen waned momentarily. Then the sound of scraping chairs told Aaron they were preparing to leave.

He lowered his voice. "Will you come outside so we can talk this over like two adults?"

"No. I have to help Mama put the kids to bed."

"Okay, have it your way," Aaron conceded. "But I'll come down and get you for the dance tomorrow night."

"I'm going with Willy," she said.

"Next Saturday then."

"Don't waste your time, Aaron," she said dryly.

"Okay, have it your way for now." Then he went to join the others at the door and say his goodnights to Clem and Agnes.

The ride home was uncomfortable. While the trap seated two comfortably, it crowded three. Aaron sat nearly atilt in his corner, stretching an arm along the back of the seat to widen the space where Mary sat wedged. Although her left shoulder found space behind Jonathan, her right nested warmly against Aaron. His leg bolstered hers, and his armpit contoured her shoulder. In days past they'd ridden this way unaware of crowded limbs. That was no longer true.

In bed later, sealed inside the dark, Mary said to Jonathan, "I didn't know you planned to go to the Cattle Exposition."

"We talked about buying the bull last winter," he reminded her.

"Yes, but that was . . . before."

"You mean you don't want me to buy one now?"

" 'Course I do, but do you have to go to Minneapolis to do it?"

"If I'm to get the purebred I want for starting the herd, then yes."

"I can see you're dead set on going."

"Aha."

"When?"

"In five weeks."

She knew how badly he wanted to buy his first bull, but she knew, too, that the trip fell in with his other thoughts. She couldn't let him go along assuming everything would go as planned while he was gone.

"I know you want that bull terribly bad, Jonathan, and what I said last winter I'll stick by. I'll help Aaron with the corn if it's not done yet—so you can go—but don't expect to come home and find me changed, because I won't be."

His voice came lightly from his pillow. "That's fine, Mary." But his tone implied, "We'll wait and see."

She felt the spinning of events whirling on in spite of her, like when she was a child trying again and again to catch the spinning box-elder seeds that spiraled down toward her outstretched hands. She'd been told it was lucky to catch the seeds before they touched the ground, but always just before they fluttered into her grasp they reeled out of reach. Events now whirled around her, leaving her unfavored and luckless. She'd thought Jonathan had accepted her and Aaron's refusal, and now he'd come up with this other ploy to nudge his notion into reality. She was convinced now that his going served his other purpose. Divining that, Mary knew she must now try to reconcile her differences with him, take a step toward a normal relationship in light of his coming trip. It was she who'd turned him away in the first place, she who must turn toward him again.

"Jonathan, I'm sorry I turned you away," she said.

She needed to say no more, for the dandelion wine had warmed him and he rolled onto his side and took her in his arms. But before kissing her, he said, "I reckon you had reason."

His lovemaking was familiar, for its pattern never changed. When he reached for her, she was there in her own familiar way, and when he rolled her onto her back and entered her, there was a comfortableness that seven years had created. But when he lay spent, they knew there were other things between them tonight.

In her there was a desperation, a clutching effort to settle this tension among the three of them.

And for Jonathan there was a kind of resurging hope.

The trip, the buying of the bull became a panacea for Jonathan. The bull symbolized all he hoped to accomplish, and he spent elated hours imagining herds of hornless Black Angus cattle roaming over the land, all because he had had the foresight to buy one small bull.

Ah, but that bull would be something.

Planting the small grains of wheat, oats, and barley during the following weeks, he contented himself with dreaming of the Angus. Aaron, pouring seed to fill the grain drill, wished that his brother would cease whistling for just one day, but Jonathan leaned to his work, whistling his way through the seeding. Aaron worked beside him while they finished the wheat planting and moved to the oats. They worked long days, staying in the fields to use even the last dusk-lit hour for sowing. But after the long hours with the sun in their eyes in one direction and the dust in their mouths in the other, evening chores waited for them. Jonathan seemed unaffected by the hours of arduous labor, but while milking at the end of the day, Aaron's hands ached, the winter-softened skin burned from the leather reins he'd pulled all day. It didn't warm him toward his brother any, either. Aaron continued to simmer at Jonathan's satisfied air.

Full spring rounded on them suddenly, bringing all her best out of hiding: bloodroots, Indian turnips, wild arbutus, and more. Dandelions with bitter leaves needed sweetening into wine, wild asparagus appeared on the dinner table, watercress made its once-a-year appearance in spring runnels, and comfrey needed gathering for next winter's medicinal brews. Even the ditches burst into an array of color as Indian tobacco, pennyroyal, and crowfoot blossomed again. The arborvitae berried, evergreens candled, oaks spoke after their long silence, elms blossomed and seeded, and birches popped their bark. Liverwort, trillium, and wake-robins appeared in the woods while the garden perennials shook their winter-flattened hair.

And everywhere the animals nested. Squirrels outspokenly hurried every which way. Gophers disappeared into the ground with bits of grass in their mouths. Swollen garter snakes and toads frequented the garden. The paired wrens returned to their house in the low-branched mountain ash. The barn cats had a litter somewhere, the female reappearing thin and slack, her underbelly swaying as she walked. Hens clucked in their nests, stubbornly refusing to lay again until they felt something alive move beneath them. The geese were laying and would continue as long as their eggs were taken. Mary collected them each day and kept them carefully until there were the fifty she wanted for a summer flock, when she would put them under the "clucks" and let them have their way, but meanwhile she turned the goose eggs over daily, sprinkling them with water as the mother goose would have done with her bill.

Nature reaffirmed itself in celebration. And the three who lived and worked so closely with it felt its urgency.

But in mid-May, Mary's monthly flow started. She returned to the house and tore clean rags, stubbornly refusing to let it bother her. At midday she tore more and washed those from morning, taking them to spread on the sumac bushes in the woods behind the outhouse. She never hung them on the clothesline between the birches in the yard, for she thought they'd be indelicate strung out there, the stains never completely bleached clean. So they lay on the sumacs, covering the scarlet buds that were promising to bear leaf soon, she still stubbornly saying to herself, "I don't care, and I hope Jonathan knows it!"

But the thought came unbidden: two weeks from now when he goes off to Minneapolis, it'll be the time of the month Doc Haymes and I believe in . . . the time he says a woman conceives . . .

She'd never been able to convince Jonathan to accept what Doc Haymes held to be true. But just like the animals, there were changes in her body then, swellings and flowings, tenderness and sensitivity that it lacked at other times. She could never say to Jonathan, "See, feel, I'm different now," for he had always refused to believe the theory. But he knew darned well that she held it as true, and she wondered if he would notice those rags out there on the sumacs and figure ahead.

The sumacs were the last to leaf, and Jonathan caught glimpses of white through the redness of the licorice-whip branches, knowing what was out there again. He'd listened to Haymes's carping and lived with Mary's hopefulness long enough to reckon the days, counting them off from now until his trip. Not really admitting to himself their significance, he muttered, "Flap-doodling old fool!"

Chapter 5

$\mathcal{T}$he following Saturday, they went to town with the double box buckboard to buy potatoes for seed. The seat was wider than that of the trap, so they rode uncrowded, Aaron handling the reins. His hands were raw, and he felt every shift of the leather in his palms.

They dropped Mary off at the Mercantile store and went off to see to the buying of seed potatoes. She shopped from a long list, for it had been a while since she'd come to town. She selected tinned foods, fresh crackers from the barrel, and visited with Sam Motz while he weighed the coffee beans and the seeds she'd selected for the garden, measuring them out by the ounce into small paper sacks. He drew vinegar from the wooden barrel in the strong-smelling back room and returned the crock jug to her, corked and filled. She treated herself to touching and admiring the bolts of materials, thinking of a dress for her cousin's up-coming wedding. Sam asked if she'd care to buy a length, but she had no eggs to trade that day, and, knowing the bill would run high as it was, she said no.

She savored her time in the store as she savored its smells—pungent, dry, sweet, and spicy all mixed in one. Acquaintances from town came in, and she visited with them.

Later, she waited under the awning on the boardwalk for the men to come back for her, but when the wagon pulled up, Aaron was alone. He said he'd be right back and went inside to pay the bill, then carried the boxes of food out, putting them on top of the potatoes that now lined the bottom of the wagon bed. When Aaron came out of the store for the last time, Mary was sitting on the high-sprung seat. He had a brown-striped candy stick in his mouth and handed one up to her before climbing up to take the reins.

She took the proffered candy, a peace offering, self-conscious again with him beside her.

"Where's Jonathan?" She knew they'd already finished at the feed and seed store.

"He stopped off at the railroad station," Aaron answered.

"The railroad station?" Her rising note questioned why.

"To check out the price of a train ticket to Minneapolis and a schedule."

"He really means to go, then?" she asked.

"Yes, it looks that way," Aaron admitted.

The strain was showing on his face. There were two deep, parallel furrows between his eyes. Maybe it was from frowning into the sun all day, but she suspected it was less from the sun than from their situation. He looked thinner and tired. She wished she could smooth his worry from him, dust it away with a light brush of fingers, but she now dare not touch him.

It was just a couple of blocks to the railroad depot, and as Aaron turned the horses toward it, he knew he had only the space of that three-minute drive to convey the thoughts it had taken him weeks to straighten out in his head.

"Mary, if Jonathan leaves, I'll have to stay. The place can't run itself. But honest, Mary, I'd never lay a hand on you . . . you know that. What Jonathan said is bound to be running through your mind, and now with him getting set to leave us like he said, I just don't want you worrying about what's going to happen. Because nothing's going to—I swear to you, Mary."

It was the first time he'd said anything about it since Jonathan had brought it all up, and, try though she might, she couldn't hold that heat from leaping to her face. Aaron was looking directly at her, holding the candy stick forgotten in his hand. She returned his gaze as steadily as possible. "Oh, dear God, Aaron, don't you think I know that? Did you suppose I don't trust you?" Seeing the color mount to his face, she knew what it had cost Aaron to say what he had.

"Well, it had to be said, Mary. We all shut up and never said a word about Jonathan's wishes, but it can't fester inside forever. Now it looks like he really means to run off to Minneapolis, and there's nothing we can do about it. I just had to tell you, to put your mind at ease." Then his attention turned again toward the team he was driving.

"Aaron," she said, also looking now at the horses

that pulled them toward the depot, "Thank you, but you know I'd trust you even if you hadn't spoken up."

"Even after what I said on the back porch that night?" The memory of his frank admission still burned him.

"I could ask the same thing after what I said on the porch, too."

"No, you're . . . well, you're Mary," he said, as if just being Mary put her above reproach, above compromise.

It was silent then, but Aaron heard what he'd said, and it suddenly sounded as if he'd said he could never consider her womanly, female, as if she hadn't the wherefore necessary to attract him. That wasn't the way of it at all, and he hoped she wouldn't think so. Jonathan had already robbed her of enough pride, but God, how the girl had stood up and refused to be cowed. Not many would have shown the spunk she had.

They were pulling up to the depot building then, and he turned her way and asked simply, "Friends?"

And she nodded, her eyes lighting with relief and warmth. "Friends."

Jonathan stepped outside just as they approached, and climbed aboard. When they were on their way home he said, breaking the silence, "The train pulls through at noon on Sundays. I'll be going a week from tomorrow."

"Time enough between now and then to get a good start on the spuds, if not finish them," Aaron said, and Jonathan noticed an old, easygoing roll to his brother's words.

"If the weather holds, we should get them all in this week," Jonathan mused.

"Quartering spuds has never been my favorite job," Mary put in. "I'll be glad when the wagon is empty."

"Maybe the day'll come you won't have to quarter spuds—if this Angus turns out to be all they say. I figure one Angus calf'd bring in the same money as ten acres of spuds."

"First you gotta buy the calf, then raise the herd, Jonathan," she reminded him, and there was the old note of teasing in her voice.

"How much do you figure the bull will cost you?" Aaron asked.

"I won't know till I get there. The only prices I've read about are on-the-hoof for slaughter."

Their ride passed in pleasant conversation that genuinely eased the tension among them for the first time in days. What Aaron had said so openly to Mary had at last relaxed the knot of wariness they'd been feeling. Jonathan too found himself drawn into the camaraderie that had been absent among them for too long.

When they arrived home, Aaron pulled up under the elms. The wagon didn't need unloading. The potatoes could wait there until they were quartered for planting.

"If you don't mind, Jonathan, I'd like to start the chores early," Aaron said. "I'm thinking I'll go down to Pris's and see if she'll go to the hall with me tonight."

"That'll be fine, Aaron," Jonathan agreed.

Mary felt that Aaron's plans put the capper on this healing day. He's going back to Priscilla at last! If she'll only take him back, everything will be fine.

Mixed in with her relief were small tuggings, whimsical longings to go to the dance herself. It had been so long since she'd been down to the hall on a Saturday night. They used to go often when they were first married. She was still young, and she felt the urge for a little socializing. It would do Jonathan good to get away from the farm for the evening, too. While he didn't care much for dancing, he enjoyed a cold beer and a bit of visiting.

Jonathan was already unhitching the horses, and she hurried to speak up before he finished.

"Jonathan, I think we could all use a little relaxation. You've been working hard, and it'd do you good to get away a bit. Why don't we go up to the hall, too?"

He was already releasing the traces from the collar. He didn't think he needed to go to the hall to relax. He could do that right here at home, just sitting on the porch looking out over the fields. But Mary hadn't been away much lately, except for Sundays at church and the visit to Volences' a couple weeks ago. She probably could do with an outing.

He didn't answer immediately, so Mary hurried on while he ducked under the horses' heads to the wagon tongue. It didn't look like he wanted to go. He was releasing the horses as if to stay home.

"I wouldn't mind going in the wagon, and Aaron could take the buggy and the mare. It doesn't matter about the potatoes. Nobody'll bother them." There was pleading in her voice.

He hadn't meant to make her beg. After all, it was a perfectly natural thing, her wanting to go out for a bit of Saturday night fun.

"That'd be fine, Mary," he said then. "I'll feed and

water the horses, though, and leave 'em off the wagon till we go."

She was already racing up to the house as fast as she could, with a small box of groceries in her arms. Jonathan thought, I'd better hurry with the chores. Looks like she'll slam supper together quicker than greased lightning. I'll eat it cold if I don't move myself. Leading the horses toward the watering trough, he felt pleased that Mary was snapping out of the mood that had kept her tight and silent these past weeks. But he'd known she'd come around. Just like lightning, too, she had too much spark to hide it long.

Mary met Aaron coming out the kitchen door after setting a heavier box of groceries inside.

"What did he say?" he asked her, but he knew from her flying skirts as she jumped both porch steps at once what Jonathan had said.

"He said you can take the mare and buggy and we'll take the wagon." She was slamming stuff around in the kitchen, hurriedly putting the supplies away, and he could hear the staccato sounds as he sat on the back step and pulled his work boots on. He knew full well it was she who'd said he could take the buggy. A man didn't go a-courting in a wagon full of potatoes, but Jonathan would never think of that.

It was just as Jonathan had thought. She had her chickens and geese tended to in record time and was calling the men to supper while they hustled the milk pails up the yard. He didn't have to worry about eating it cold, though, for she had been in too much of a tizzy to make a hot meal. The range was piping, though, and she'd found time to pump bathwater in the midst of her headlong hurry.

The meal was a hurried affair, and dishes disappeared from under their noses before the men could get around to seconds. What held the dishes in one piece was hard to say, the way she threw them into the dishpan, rattling and clacking and chinking as she rushed.

Aaron brought in the washtub from the porch. There was no need to ask who'd be first tonight. If they didn't clear out and leave the kitchen to Mary, she'd jump into the tub with her clothes on.

Aaron decided he'd take a pail of warm water upstairs for his own bath rather than wait for the kitchen to be free. It would save time. It was getting late, and he'd better be on his way. He wished now that he'd taken the time to drive over during the week and ask Priscilla in advance, but there should be enough time to get down to her place, do the asking, and make it to the hall in time to get a table. But suppose she said she was going with Michalek? He made up his mind that if it turned out that way, he'd pursue her at the dance, Michalek or no Michalek.

Up in her bedroom after her bath, Mary opened the wardrobe and took out a dress of yellow dimity. Its raised twills caught the waning light from the window. She took a chemise from the dresser drawer and put it on, looking in the mirror at her image. During the week she wore a simple homemade binding over her breasts, but her wedding chemise was still good, and fit her youthful shape just as it had seven years before. She buttoned her long petticoat around her waist before taking the celluloid hairpins out of her hair. It fell down her back, and as she combed it she had to pull it over her shoulders to stroke its full length. She began to reform the knot at the base of her neck, but a thought crossed her mind, making her drop the hair back down.

She had already gotten Jonathan to agree to go to the dance. That was a step in the right direction. Perhaps she herself could do more to bring back the old closeness. For the first time, it crossed her mind that as the seven years of their marriage had progressed she had paid increasingly less attention to her toilette. She kept herself clean and neat, and the childless state of her body had kept it firm and youthful. But maybe there was more she could do to rekindle the light that, with the passing years, had faded from Jonathan's eyes. Most farm women had plenty to keep them busy without fussing over affected hairdos and painted faces. She had been no different.

But here, tonight, in the favorable twilight that shone on her profile, she again raised her arms and combed the cascading hair high on her head. Securing it there with curved metal combs, she lit the kerosene lantern on the dresser, then dug through the bottom dresser drawer until she found what she sought, the long-unused curling iron. She heated it over the lamp chimney. Then, separating a tress of hair, clamped and rolled it up. She could smell the acrid odor of singed hair, but as she continued she got the feel of it back after all these years and gauged her heating better so the iron didn't singe her hair anymore. When she'd finished the coiffure, she found a small jar of petroleum jelly and dipped her little finger into it, running it across her lips, leaving them glistening. The last thing she did, on impulse, was to turn to the faded old wallpaper that surrounded the room with red morning glories. Wetting her fingers with her tongue, she touched a morning glory, and its dye left her fingertips pink. She smoothed the color on her cheeks. She thought how lucky she was to have two men working the fields, so that she was spared that job most of the time. The sun had not had a chance to toughen her skin. Smoothing the color onto it, she wondered if Jonathan would notice.

The yellow dimity dress fell over her petticoat, and its buttons pulled it tightly over her midriff as she worked them as far up the back as she could reach. The neck was cut square and high, but it showed the shadows of fine, small round bones below her neck. She had no cologne, but in the bureau drawer among the linens was a small sachet pillow filled with lavender. She found it and pinned it on her chemise between her breasts, reaching in easily where the unbuttoned bodice was still slack at the top.

There was only one thing more she needed, and here it was, easily found: a smile, making her face a perfection, all for her husband.

Taking a last look at herself in the mirror, Mary clasped her hands together, pressing them tightly against her throat. Please, oh please, Jonathan, she wished silently. The simple wish encompassed countless hopes. If only he would know them.

Aaron, too, had taken pains with his preparations. He'd worked to smooth his curly hair until it lay thick and clean around his smooth-shaven face. He wore his worsted Sunday suit and a white shirt with a crisp, starched collar buttoned tightly onto the neckband. A black bow tie was giving him trouble now as he stood in the kitchen by the wall mirror above the sink. But he managed it finally and hoped the effort wouldn't prove fruitless, that his appearance would speak for itself, telling Pris that he'd made a special effort for her.

He was splashing bay rum on his face when a golden reflection in the mirror stopped his hands in midair. Mary had rounded the corner from the steps and was coming into the kitchen. Her path held her in his mirror until she swerved toward the washtub on his right. She had come up near and behind him and bent down to squeeze the cloth from Jonathan's bath-water. He turned and looked down at her bending fig-ure and saw the honey-colored curls that fell on each side of her neck. The top three buttons of her dress were unbuttoned, and he saw the white cotton of a garment on her back beneath it. She seemed to be bending down a long time over the tub, and he contin-ued staring at the back of her neck.

She straightened then and turned to face him, and the bay rum and lavender all mixed in the air between them, and it was heady as warm spring wine. She saw his tanned skin redden slightly above the white collar. His russet hair glistened, and as she looked up at it, one unruly curl sprang loose onto his forehead. His brow shone. His blue eyes took in the details of her high, pink cheekbones and shiny lips. Her hair did not have the usual part down the center, but was skimmed back tightly, clearing her face before it and giving it an open look. Behind the yellow lace that ran across the top of her dress he saw without glancing down that her breathing was quick.

They had each prepared themselves for someone else. Yet, as they stood facing each other in perfection, a confusion of feelings made them glad they pleased each other.

"I couldn't reach the last buttons," she said. Her eyes dropped as she turned her back to him. He buttoned them for her without touching her skin, but the fluttering touch of the dress on her back raised goosebumps on her arms.

They heard Jonathan whistling his way up the walk then, and Aaron turned quickly to put away the bottle of bay rum underneath the sink. Mary went to the front room closet to find her coat in the small space there. She heard the screen door slam as Jonathan came in, but she stayed where she was, in the darkening room, because the light in the kitchen might reveal her agitated state. She heard the clink of the washtub handles as the two men lifted it to carry it outside.

Jonathan said, "What's the matter with your hand, Aaron?" and Mary glimpsed them taking the tub out the doorway, a wincing expression on Aaron's face.

"Just a bit tender, that's all. Seems I got softer than a patty-cake over the winter."

"Why don't you have Mary rub a little of that ointment on them that she gets from the Raleigh man? That'll fix 'em up in no time."

"Aw, no, they'll be fine. Just gotta toughen 'em up a little, that's all."

But Jonathan was coming back inside as he said, "Mary, get that ointment you keep for—" And there his words died. She had come out of the dimness of the front room into the kitchen light. Her coat was folded over one arm, and she stood very still as Jonathan stared hard at her. Behind him, Aaron stared, too.

Jonathan broke the silence.

"Why, Mary, I didn't know you'd want me to dress up. You should've told me." He always wore his blue cambrics to the hall, but tonight he wished he'd dressed better because she sure looked fine.

He hadn't said she looked good, or in any way noted the effort she'd made for him tonight. Her obvious failure to elicit his admiration made her feel suddenly quite foolish and Aaron saw the reaction parade across her face. He bit his lip to keep from paying the compliment her husband should have voiced.

"That's okay, Jonathan. You look just fine."

"Could you rub some of that ointment on Aaron's hand, Mary? I got the wagon hitched up again, but I'll go get the mare on the buggy while you two get his hands fixed up." He went around Aaron, slamming the screen door behind him.

Mary jerked into action as it banged, and crossed over to lay her coat on the back of a kitchen chair. She found the ointment in a tin under the sink and took the cover off and set it on the table. Aaron still stood just inside the door. She scooped some of the ointment into her cupped fingers and stood waiting. He came over in front of her and extended one hand toward her. He could have taken the ointment and rubbed it on by himself, but instead he gave the hand to her and they both looked down at it self-consciously before she reached out and took it, laying it palm-up on hers. He relaxed his fingers, and she saw tender flesh where blisters had newly broken. She had a sudden, compulsive urge to lower her lips to the spot and, in doing so, heal it. But instead, she touched it with the ointment, then rubbed her flat palm across his, working it in. He kept his hand lax, fingers gently curled upward. He watched small fingers play over his aching flesh as she massaged the hand, curling her own fingers around his thumb, then around the butt of his hand.

When she'd finished his left hand, she reached to the jar to bring up more ointment from it, and the process was repeated with his right. They both kept their eyes on the hand being worked between them, and maybe it took a little longer than it needed to, for the ointment had disappeared before Mary's fingers slid back toward his wrist, then to his fingertips one last time. He realized they would be gone in an instant, and he gently and firmly closed his hand around hers, stopping it in its final pass. It stung, but he welcomed the pain of it. They just stood there with the surging realization of what this handclasp revealed, and there was no way their eyes could meet. He opened his hand, but hers lingered where it was, resting lightly atop his. He could feel the warmth of her flesh burning the tender skin of his own where the sore was.

And suddenly she didn't feel foolish anymore.

This is Mary, Aaron thought, and she's more than my friend. Just then, she moved away from him, turning to retrieve the cover of the tin and screw it back on. When she had put it away again under the sink and washed the salve from her hands, she turned to find Aaron holding her coat for her. She slipped her arms in, then reached to lift the curls off her neck to free them of the coat collar. Her action stirred the scent of lavender and bared the back of her neck once again to the man who stood behind her. The ointment on his hands kept him from caressing her shoulders where he had lowered her coat, and he held it gingerly to keep the ointment from soiling it.

She was, in that instant, a thing that he must never soil.

Abruptly he turned, leaving the kitchen. She leaned over to lower the wick and blow out the kerosene lamp on the table. When she straightened, he had gone out the door, and she followed him after quickly pressing her hands to her cheeks, scolding herself for their heat. When she came into the yard, Aaron had already left in the buggy, and Jonathan was waiting on the buckboard.

Chapter 6

$\mathcal{A}$aron tried to concentrate on Pris as he drove the short distance west. But the trot to her place was too short to give him time to dispel the image of a yellow-clad girl that filled his mind. Had it really been Mary? Mary, who had been there in his house for seven years? Mary, with her child-woman's body, her expression of openness glowing up at him from a face that seemed brand new, hair swept up from that face, fastened in a knot of flowing curls like a schoolgirl's, cheeks flushed pink, lips shining, and tiny hands massaging not only his skin but the blood that flowed within him, sending it coursing to his head and heart like a spring cataract?

Sweet Jesus, had it been Mary?

Aaron reached the Volence driveway in a state of agitation. With an effort he forced himself to a semblance of calm before he reached the house. The door was closed, but the light was bright inside. There'd still be time for Pris to change clothes if she needed to, and they'd get to the hall in good time.

He could hear from inside that someone was playing the organ again in the living room. That must be why nobody'd heard his rig pull into the yard. When he knocked, the organ music stopped and Cora opened the door to him.

Cora had a smile that was as close to smug as any he'd ever seen.

"Evening, Cora. Is Pris here?" he asked.

"She sure ain't. She's gone off to the Bohemian Hall with Willy Michalek. Figgered you woulda seen 'em ride by your place about twenty minutes ago."

But twenty minutes ago he'd been standing in the kitchen with his hand inside of Mary's, and he hadn't noticed anything else. Why hadn't Jonathan seen the rig and said something? He must have been in the lean-to getting the rigging at that time.

"Who's here, Cora?" Agnes Volence asked as she came up behind her daughter.

"Well, Aaron, hello! Don't leave him standin' out there on the doorstep, child. Come on in, Aaron," she invited.

"No. I guess I won't tonight, ma'am, but thanks just the same. I came to call on Pris, but seeing as how she's not here, I'll be on my way again."

He thought he could detect a look of disappointment cross her face as he backed down a step and turned to leave.

"Come on back down again soon, Aaron," she called after him.

What next? he thought as he headed east again. Couldn't a man have a plan turn out in his favor just when he'd strengthened his resolve enough to put it into action? If there was one thing he didn't need tonight, it was to be casting around at that dance hall without a girl to steady him. He'd better pull into his own yard and stay put at home.

When he reached the drive, he stopped the mare under the elms and left her there while he went up to the dark house. It was quiet and bleak inside, and he walked through the kitchen into the front room. Silence and darkness greeted him. He stood in the doorway a moment, then wandered to the pantry door that led off the west kitchen wall. The pantry seemed like her special place; she was in it so often. He hooked his thumbs through his belt and stood with his weight on one foot, the other foot slightly forward, relaxed, as a man might stand who surveys all he has. But Aaron's survey found him lonely and disconsolate. He knew he should stay home, but he wasn't fooling himself one bit that he was going to hang around the gloominess alone. Why hadn't he unhitched the horse and put the buggy away? But he sat down for a minute at the table in the black kitchen. He sighed and propped his elbow on the table. But his hand dropped down, and in the darkness he felt his fingers touch a bit of ointment on the oilcloth. In the darkness around him it seemed that a bright yellow light was reflecting off a dimity dress. He rubbed his fingertips together until the salve was no longer there. Then he went back outside, back to the buggy drawn by that yellow beacon that led him to the Bohemian Hall.

Mary and Jonathan made fast time getting to the hall, in spite of the wagon full of potatoes. She had to laugh at the absurdity of herself all dressed up for the dance but heading there atop a wagonload of spuds. She couldn't laugh, though. There was nothing funny about what had happened back there in the kitchen. She thought how foolish she must have seemed to Aaron, coming downstairs all gussied up for a husband who didn't care enough to compliment her. If it hadn't been for Aaron's own sudden response, she would have died of mortification at Jonathan's tepid remark. But now she was being untruthful with herself.

Hadn't she been so overcome by Aaron that it hadn't mattered about her husband? Oh, please, no! What was she thinking? She had to stop this nonsense right now. In light of Jonathan's plans to leave them alone, she had to get every slightest inkling of these thoughts from her head. Anyway, Aaron was back with Pris again by now, and that was a measure of safety. He'd be spending his free time with her while Jonathan was away.

The hall was filled with noise and music and vibration. The smell of beer from the taps in the back room was pleasant in a yeasty, heavy way. It seemed as if she'd never seen a crowd so large jammed into the hall. Folks from a long table by the west wall were waving to them and beckoning them over. Jonathan led the way through the boisterous crowd, and she followed behind his tall back. When they'd passed several tables, a brown head caught her eye. She thought it was Priscilla. But it couldn't be, for Aaron couldn't have beaten them to the hall. But just then, she saw Willy Michalek come up behind Pris and set a bottle of soda in front of her. Her heart hit her throat, and she felt her face heat up. But she followed Jonathan and sat down at the place cleared for them as the acquaintances at the table greeted them heartily and hands were shaken all around. The ladies were full of chatter about friends and events they all had in common. The men went off to get a supply of drinks for the newcomers, and Mary joined in the talk as best she could in her present state.

It wasn't long before the subject rolled around to Priscilla, and the ladies plied her with questions about the situation between Pris and Aaron. What could she say? The Bohemian women jumped at the chance to glean any gossip they could. This aspect of them had always irritated her.

She was holding her irritation in check but running out of answers when both of the women clapped their mouths shut, like school books at the ring of the afternoon bell. Without needing to turn around, she knew why.

From behind her she heard his voice greeting the two women and asking where the men were. But the men were coming back to the table with glasses and bottles, and it was natural that Aaron was established as a member of their party.

It was the custom at a Bohemian dance for the music to be played in sets of four or five songs, all of the same rhythm. Thus, when the band began with a polka and the two neighbor couples went onto the floor, Mary knew it would be a while before they rejoined the table. It was also a custom that once a couple began a set they would not change partners until the set ended. Sometimes, however, two couples would interchange partners in midfloor as the gaiety picked up and the dancing became less inhibited.

The floor was aswarm with people, but miraculously all moved in one direction, flowing in a smooth circle as the agile dancers cranked their heads this way and that, checking their course as they spun. Once the polka started, no talk was necessary, sometimes not even possible, with the thumping noise all around them.

Mary was grateful for it. She and Aaron sat at the table alone. They could feel more than hear when the bottles and glasses of other spectators came alive in their hands, clacked onto the tabletops in rhythm with the band and the pounding feet. Mary's lemon soda bottle bobbed along with the others, and, listening to it, she began feeling the tension ease away from her body. When the set ended, the steaming dancers returned to their tables and glasses were drained and refilled. More soda bottles appeared. When the new set began, she was asked to dance. Each set gave way to another, and stamping feet pounded the evening on toward midnight.

That night, Aaron chose to drink strawberry soda instead of beer. Beer sounded good, but when he got tight, even slightly, the first thing he wanted was a woman. To be on the safe side, he stuck to soda.

Priscilla was on the dance floor every set, and between sets she seemed surrounded by a crowd of people younger than himself. He danced with some of the women from his table, other girls he knew casually, but he avoided dancing with Mary. When he wasn't dancing, he stood much of the time in the taproom, drinking soda and visiting with whoever was there, for it was always crowded, and everyone knew everyone else. While leaving the taproom he passed Willy Michalek, who was on his way in. On impulse, he tapped Michalek's shoulder and asked, "You mind if I ask your date for a dance?"

Willy shrugged and replied, "Long as it's not the last set."

Aaron approached Pris and asked without preliminary, "Want to dance, Pris?"

She barely looked up at him as she replied, "Not with you, Aaron. Sorry."

There were others around them, and he could tell by her attitude that she was having fun. He could hardly stand there and try to convince her. Nor could he take her forcibly onto the dance floor. All he could do was bow out gracefully, which he did, and then stand with a group of stags.

When the music stopped, he moved with a surge of people to where one of the men had just asked Mary for the next set. Jonathan wasn't in sight. At that moment, Joe Shymek wielded his concertina and announced that it was the last set of the evening. Mary's partner turned apologetically to her and explained, "Oh, Mary, I'm sorry, but my wife will be looking for me, since this is the last set." Not wanting to leave her standing there on the edge of the floor while he hurried to find his wife, the fellow asked, "Where's Jonathan?"

Aaron, whose passage was blocked by dancers filing onto the floor, replied, "I don't know."

And so, unwittingly, the man brought about what Aaron and Mary had been avoiding all night. Pushing them none too gently toward each other, he said, "Well, I'll leave you in equally good hands, Mary." And he scurried off and disappeared, leaving the two standing there, facing each other.

"Do you mind?" he asked.

"No," was all she replied.

A waltz drifted around them as Aaron encircled her waist and began the steps. She found his free hand with hers, not having to look to know it was there waiting. When her fingers touched his open palm, she felt again the blistered flesh she had salved earlier. His steps were not wide and sweeping as some men waltzed. He led her instead in small, precise patterns, the turns so gentle that her skirt scarcely flared. They danced with their bodies apart, but in their nearness each could feel the breath of the other. He smelled of berry and bay rum; she, of lemon and lavender. Times past they had danced thoughtlessly with their bodies much closer than now; this time they made efforts not to look at each other, keeping their eyes on the other couples around them. When the first song ended they stood silently, waiting for the next to begin, the silence between them again a strange thing. With the new song begun, they turned again toward each other, and now he didn't need to reach for her. She was unbelievably close. The space closed between them as they danced and he pulled her lightly to the spot where she fit so well. She dared not close her eyes but left them open and saw, very close, the dark curls on his neck. She thought it a distinct pleasure to be the shorter of the two and have that joy. There was nothing soft about her body as he held her. It was firm, with the suppleness of healthy youth. Even her breasts, where they rested against his chest, were solid. He didn't crush her against him because he didn't need to. The places where their bodies brushed together were alive.

He said just one thing, his breath warm near her ear.

"You're beautiful tonight, Mary girl." And suddenly his using of her pet name took on a new meaning.

"Thank you, Aaron," came her breathless reply.

The song came to an end. He turned her by the elbow toward the edge of the floor where Jonathan stood, and gave her to her husband. For Jonathan there was no escaping the last dance of the evening, no matter how little he liked to dance. But once on the floor it wasn't so bad. She followed him smoothly, and he thought to himself how pretty she looked and that he should've told her so earlier.

"You sure look fine tonight, Mary," he said.

But he was right. He ought to have told her earlier.

Chapter 7

Sunday turned cloudy and cool, and the heat from the kitchen range felt good. Jonathan, Aaron, and Mary sat around the kitchen table with paring knives and bowls, quartering potatoes from the gunnysack on the table-top into bowls on their laps, then dumping the filled bowls into sacks on the floor.

Jonathan was wishing it would rain if it meant to, and clear by morning. They'd need to start planting the spuds tomorrow if they were to get most of it done by the next Sunday. He hated to leave too much of the planting unfinished. Not knowing how many days he'd be gone, he couldn't risk leaving too many unplanted acres.

Aaron was considering his brother's leaving and wondering how he could escape the house next Sunday afternoon and evening. If they took Jonathan to the noon train, he and Mary would have the rest of the long, idle day together. He couldn't go down to Volences' like he used to. Pris had snuffed that idea clear out of his head. There wasn't anyplace else where it'd seem natural for him to show up on a Sunday. Sunday was pretty much a family day. But considering what had passed between himself and Mary the night before, he knew it'd be best if they weren't in the house together with too much time on their hands. Come Monday, they'd have plenty of work to keep them busy, but what would they do during long, idle Sunday?

Aw, hell, he was getting sick and tired of worrying about it. He'd been troubling himself with it all day long, and his head felt ready to burst. There was only so much a man could do before something fouled up his good intentions, anyway. Just like yesterday— "friends" he'd said to Mary, like some asinine schoolboy. Christ! How dumb could a man get? Dumb enough to be sucked in by Jonathan's innocent plans to go off and leave them alone like it didn't mean a damn thing. And how about the other things that happened, which he couldn't control? Priscilla's standoffishness, and that fool who'd pushed Mary into his "equally good hands." All Aaron could think of now was that he didn't want to think anymore. He wanted to sink himself down in a feather tick upstairs and not wake up till Jonathan came home with his damn bull.

In the gray light of Sunday, Mary was calling herself a thousand kinds of fool. Her hair was parted in the center and drawn back to the nape again. Her face was washed clean. But in spite of the return to her everyday looks, she felt like a harlot. Dressing up like a painted doll had been her undoing. Oh, why had she had such an idea in the first place? She should have known that Jonathan wouldn't be warmed by it. Now that it was done, she was ashamed, for she thought Jonathan had misjudged the reason for her finery. He might've thought she'd got all gussied up to turn Aaron's head. Why hadn't she thought of that to begin with? But no matter how hard she wished she hadn't done it, she had, and now she had to live with what followed. The best way to do that was just to go on as if she were the same person as always, but tread lightly around Aaron—her "friend." All she needed was to keep her hair parted down the middle and act as if nothing had happened. In two weeks this would all be forgotten and she'd wonder why she'd ever worried so.

Monday morning, the sun shone clear. The rains of Sunday night had left the earth soft and receptive. Jonathan and Aaron walked down the rows with sacks of seeder spuds on their shoulders. All of Aaron's old resentment for his brother was back again in full force. Even Jonathan's unbreaking rhythm as he planted potatoes riled Aaron. Dropping a piece of potato into the long cylinder on the planter, he'd move a pace up the row and pierce the soil, pushing on the planter with his foot. When he jerked the lever up, the potato was released, and he moved forward again, stepping on the newly interred seed behind him. He never broke the rhythm, but kept it up in four repeating, steady beats.

What does he think about while he works like a machine? Aaron thought. You'd think he had some kind of music playing in his head the way he whistles and keeps beat with those damn potatoes! He's probably thinking of his precious bull . . . among other things.

Aaron's syncopated movements were not lost on Jonathan, who couldn't pretend to fathom the way Aaron ran hot and cold these days. Saturday, on the way home from town, he'd been like always. Today, the way he stomped on the planter, Jonathan could tell he was riled about something.

Potatoes were their biggest cash crop, so the plantings covered many acres. They worked on into the week, refilling their sacks at the ends of the rows, while Mary quartered whenever she found time between her own chores and household duties.

Aaron's hands were healing, for the hardest work now was done by foot. Jonathan worked insatiably. No amount of labor seemed to affect him. His hands were like leather and his shoulders like stone.

As the warm May days lengthened and the first blossoms appeared on the wild plums, there was a blossoming of some intangible thing between Mary and Aaron. They found themselves caught by new awarenesses and a realization of the ties that bound them.

Bending over the laundry tubs, sloshing Aaron's clothes on Monday morning, she felt that she ought to withdraw her hands from the washboard, as if washing the clothes were suddenly as personal as washing the man.

Aaron took note, as he never had before, of all the wifely things she did for him as well as for her husband. He had the urge to thank her. At dinner time, when the washer was still filled with water and the heavy tubs still on the benches, he said, "Leave the water until afternoon, and we'll help you bale and dump it."

When he opened his bureau drawers, he found freshly laundered clothing. When he stretched out between the sheets at night, he knew she'd washed them, too. When he came to the table at mealtime, she had food hot and ready. Looking around his house, he found it clean and fresh, and he couldn't strike the thought of her being there, keeping it that way for him.

At the same time, their unusual triangular tie, Jonathan's and theirs, was brought to them again and again, underlining how they were bound together and to this place in such a peculiar fashion.

He came upon her one day at the well in the yard, leaning over a pail of water, studying three goose eggs floating in it.

"See them bob, Aaron? They're fertile," she said.

"Yes, I know," he answered, then watched her take them carefully back to set under the cluck hens to brood, recalling again how she'd talked about babies that night on the step.

"The potatoes are loaded with eyes this year," he said.

"We should have a good crop, then," she answered as he went out to plant them on his brother's land, her husband's land.

"I'll need extra wood," she said. "I'm baking bread in the morning."

"I'll fill the woodbox for you," he said, and did, using wood from Jonathan's land to stoke his own fire.

"I finished seeding the vegetable garden," she said. She planted the vegetables on Jonathan's land to serve at Aaron's table.

"Good night," he said at the top of the stairs.

"Good night," Mary and Jonathan said together, and they went into the front bedroom of Aaron's house—the bedroom that had once been his parents'— while he walked down the landing and entered his own room, the one he'd shared with Jonathan when they were boys.

As the day of Jonathan's departure drew near, Aaron remembered the stifling closeness of the factory where huge, belching machines stretched and steamed cotton materials, feeling again that forced suffocation. He found that he hadn't valued the farm until he was gone from it, and thinking he might have to leave it again, he realized how terrible that would be. No, Aaron didn't want to leave. Yet the possibility became a real one, drawing him closer to the home ties than ever, warning that again they might be broken for him, and soon.

They had finished eating supper on Saturday night and were lingering over coffee before anyone spoke about the trip.

"You're going tomorrow, then, Jonathan?" Aaron asked.

"Yes," answered his brother. "I'll be going to the

depot after church to wait for the train. That way, we'll save an extra trip to town and you can drive the rig back home with Mary."

"You're sure this is what you want to do?" It was a curious thing for Aaron to ask, but Jonathan had given up trying to figure out Aaron's moods.

"As sure as grass is green."

"Where do you figure on staying?" Mary asked.

"Well, I thought of the boardinghouse where Aaron stayed, but it's probably nowheres near the fairground. Guess I won't know till I get there."

The room stilled again, became uncomfortable, and Aaron said, "Maybe you'll get a chance to eat some of that rare Angus meat you've been reading about, huh?"

"I don't think so," Jonathan said. "I'd probably take mine well-done, just like Mary cooks our pork."

She imagined him in a fine restaurant, eating pink meat from a fine platter with a fine cloth napkin at his throat. Somehow the picture didn't fit Jonathan.

"You'll get hungry on the train. I'll fix you some sandwiches to take along." It seemed a paltry offering, but it was all she could think of at the moment.

"The train stops at Sauk Center for lunch, and I can eat there."

"All you get is cold beans and bread there," Aaron said.

"I'll fix you some of your favorite sandwiches," she insisted.

"If you want to, that'd be fine."

Again it grew quiet. Sunset was complete now, and the dusky kitchen would soon need the lamp. The clock ticked, and a chunk of wood gave way as coals collapsed in the wood stove.

"You'll need my suitcase," Aaron said. "I'll get it down from the granary for you."

Jonathan nodded, saying, "I'd appreciate that, Aaron." Then, as if he'd suddenly had the thought, he added, "Will you be going down to the hall tonight?"

Somehow Aaron really wasn't in the mood for all the commotion down there, but he answered, "Guess so, but I'll get that suitcase first."

When the dishes were done and Jonathan was having his bath in the kitchen, Mary carefully folded Jonathan's shirts, putting spare clean collars with the white one. She was sure he'd wear his Sunday suit the next day, since he'd be attending church before leaving on the train. Not knowing how many days he'd be gone, she was unsure of what to pack. She gave him a pair of overalls, wondering if he'd wear them in the city. He probably would if he'd be around cattle barns. As a compromise she folded one familiar pair of dungarees and a blue cambric shirt.

The clothing was lying in neat piles on the bed when the stairs creaked and she heard a tap on the door. Aaron was standing in the hall with his black suitcase in his hand. When she opened the door he just stood there with it, and she looked at it, then up at his face. There was not room for both of their hands on the one handle without touching. He jumped slightly then and set the suitcase on the floor between them, saying, "I dusted it off on the outside, but maybe you should check the inside before you put the stuff in."

"Okay, Aaron, I will," she said, dipping her shaky knees to pick it up before turning back inside her bedroom, closing the door behind her.

Left in the hall facing the door, Aaron thought,

What the hell's wrong with me, anyway? I've been living with this woman for seven years, and she's my brother's wife. Can't I hand her a suitcase without making a fuss about it?

Chapter 8

$\mathcal{T}$he railroad station was depressing under the Sunday sun. The horses were standing in the brightness, but under the roof of the waiting platform it was chilly. Mary sat on a bench and shivered while she watched the mare flick her tail at some unseen pest. Aaron had saddled the mare and followed Mary and Jonathan to church. The horse now stood tied behind the team and buggy.

The sandwiches she had packed for Jonathan were on Mary's lap. He was inside, buying his ticket. Aaron paced back and forth across the north end of the platform, his shoes making dull echoes on the hollow wood floor. Every now and then he'd stop and glance northward up the tracks for the train, his thumbs caught up in his waistcoat pockets.

There was nobody else waiting to board the train, so the place was dully still. The screen door squeaked into the stillness as Jonathan came out of the building. Mary remained seated against the wall, but Aaron crossed the platform to where Jonathan stood.

"I'll leave the mare at Anson's for you, Jonathan," Aaron said. "That way you can ride her home anytime you get back in." It was essential that Jonathan know he could come home at any hour and find nothing amiss.

"That'll be fine, Aaron. You tell Anson to give her an extra bag of oats in the evenings and I'll pay him good."

"Right," Aaron agreed.

Mary heard the train far off, away up the tracks, and she got up and handed the packet of sandwiches to her husband. "You eat these while they're fresh, Jonathan," she said.

"I will," he answered. "They'll be gone before we reach Sauk Center." They hovered in a tentative, last-minute void as the train sounds grew louder.

"Have a half-cooked beefsteak for us, Jonathan. We'll be expecting to hear all about it when you get home."

Jonathan smiled at that as the train drew nearer. They felt the need to talk, to say the many unsaid things that should have been said during the past week. Instead, the three of them exchanged inanities, ill at ease together, yet dreading the parting.

The engine belched its way past them, and Mary stepped back as near as she could to the wall to protect her dress from the cinders it spit. Aaron shook Jonathan's hand, squeezing hard to assure him, "Don't worry about anything back here." And between the brothers there was a sudden ambiguity to what Aaron had just said.

"No, I won't," Jonathan said. Then he turned to Mary where she stood near the benches, and took a halting step toward her. She moved to him and raised her cheek for the kiss he placed lightly on it. They seldom showed affection in daylight, rarely touched this way when others were near. Aaron picked up the black suitcase, turning away from them as they made their farewells.

"Good-bye, Jonathan, take care," she said.

"You, too."

As the suitcase exchanged hands, the two brothers exchanged an unspoken good-bye, a glance.

Jonathan boarded the hissing train, and the two on the platform saw him through the windows as he walked toward the rear of the car. They stood there until he disappeared but made no move to follow him along the platform. They waited where they were until the cars began to move forward, then saw him pass before them, waving. They raised waves in return as the train took Jonathan away, out of their sight.

"I'll be right back," Aaron said when the last car had clattered away down the track. He went through the squeaky screen door into the depot. In the stillness she could hear him asking the ticket agent what time the trains got in from Minneapolis each day. She couldn't hear the reply distinctly but made out Aaron's thank you before he headed back outside.

"Ready?" he asked, then took her arm and turned her toward the platform steps. The horses were skittish after the train's commotion. Aaron began to hand her up into the rig but said, "I'd better take their heads. I wouldn't want them to bolt."

She climbed up by herself before he got up beside her, gentling the horses as he flicked the reins, "Ho, there. Easy."

They drove to the hostelry on a side street and had to roust Anson from his Sunday dinner in the adjacent house to make arrangements for boarding the mare. After they'd taken the horse inside, the two men returned to the street, where Mary waited in the rig behind the restive team.

Aaron said, "The horses seem a little jumpy since the train pulled through. Mind if I leave them here for an hour or so, Anson?"

"Naw! Don't mind a bit, Aaron. Leave 'em here as long as you want."

"Thanks, Anson." But the hostler was already heading back to his interrupted dinner.

Aaron checked the reins, making sure they were tied securely to the hitching post before coming around to help Mary down.

"I think we'd better let these two settle down a bit," he said, indicating the horses. "It's past noon and I'm hungry." She jumped to the ground at his feet, his hands at her waist. "What do you say to a Sunday dinner cooked by someone else for a change?" He dropped his hands the instant she was safely on the ground.

"By who?" she asked, squinting up at him against the noon sun.

"Well, how about by Annie Halek?" he suggested.

"At the restaurant?" She seemed surprised. "Oh, Aaron—we shouldn't." But her undisguised delight belied her answer.

"Why shouldn't we? We couldn't change that train schedule, could we? Besides, it'll be awfully late by the time we get back home. We'd be mighty hungry by then. And with the horses in such a state, I don't want to drive them till they settle down."

"Well, if you say so, Aaron. I'm hungry, too."

They walked the short distance to Main Street and turned the corner toward the café in the middle of the block. It was dark inside the deep, narrow building after the brightness outside. The light from the front windows was partially obscured by potted plants, which decorated that area. He led the way to a high-backed booth near the front and handed her in, then seated himself across from her. The after-church business was ebbing, so there was no wait before a woman in a long cobbler's apron approached their booth.

"Howdy, Aaron, Mary," she greeted them.

"Hello, Annie. What have you got back there that smells so good?"

"I got the best ham dinner in town," bragged Annie Halek with a throaty laugh. "At least that's what I've been telling myself all morning while I cooked it."

"That sounds fine. Why don't you bring us two of them. Okay, Mary?"

"That sounds good, Annie," Mary agreed.

"You folks seein' Jonathan off on the train today?" Annie inquired. "I heard he's got some idea of buyin' himself a big, fancy bull to bring back."

"Well, I don't know how big it'll be—it's just a calf he's after—but that's right. He's gone clear down to Minneapolis to see a thoroughbred Black Angus."

"Old Man Michalek's kid was in here tellin' us about it the other day."

"News sure travels fast around here," Aaron noted, but Annie must have decided she'd wasted enough time on small talk, for she left abruptly then, saying, "Two ham dinners comin' up!"

When she was gone, Mary said, "After the dance Saturday night, everybody knows all about Jonathan's plans."

But once she said it there was a resurrection of other things Jonathan had planned, other things that had happened at the dance. Their thoughts ran parallel, flashing impressions between them of a yellow dress, a blistered palm, the lingering scent of lavender, the brushing of bodies. They both reached for water glasses across the table, tipped them up in unison, and caught each other in a glance over the glass rims. But that broke the spell, and Aaron knew how ridiculous they must look, acting like adolescents.

"What do you suppose Jonathan would think if he knew we'd seen him off on his way to buy beef, then sat down to a dinner of pork?" he wondered aloud.

"I suppose he'd be jealous, since he's probably choking down his dry sandwich right now." She pictured Jonathan on the train as they'd last seen him, waving.

"Jonathan, jealous? That'll be the day. He's so filled with his own plans that he wouldn't know if he was eating roofing shingles spread with moss."

"Oh, that's just his way, Aaron. He's not as hard as he seems."

"I've lived with him longer than you have, and I know all about his 'ways,' as you call them," Aaron said, "and some of them I don't condone."

Annie approached, bringing bowls of steaming, rich

soup to set before them. When she left, Mary put her spoon absently into the broth, studying it as she said, "Some of them I don't condone, either."

Aaron leaned his forearms on the edge of the table, looking at her. "Mary, we're playing cat-and-mouse with each other, and it isn't necessary. Can't we just pretend we're the same Aaron and Mary we always were and forget Jonathan and all the rest?"

She was still toying with her soup, but flicked a glance up at his face, then quickly away again. "It's not easily forgotten."

And it wasn't.

The rest of the meal was eaten in silence, broken only by remarks on the tastiness of Annie's cooking. They truly had lost the old easiness between them.

Finally Aaron asked, "Mary, if we can't make it through a ham dinner together, how will we make it through two or three nights?"

She hadn't expected his candor, and it stopped her cold. Having her mouth full gave Mary time to think of an answer, but there was none. She didn't know how they'd do it. Swallowing the mouthful, eyes wide, she gulped. "I don't know, Aaron."

They sat there looking at each other and wondering together what the answer was.

"Do you want some dessert, Mary?"

"No, thank you. I think we'd better leave now."

"Give me a minute to pay for this and I'll be right with you," he said, going to find Annie and pay the bill.

Annie Halek was like the town tap: turn her on and she ran off at the mouth until she either ran dry or was turned off. Aaron worried now that she might have read something into his and Mary's attitudes, something to pass on to other customers. If so, there was little he could do about it. He buttered her up a little, anyway, saying, "That dinner *was* the best in town, Annie."

"Well, now, I might get swellheaded at that if mine wasn't the only restaurant in Browerville," the big woman said, laughing. But she had seen nothing around the highbacked booth, and even if she had, Annie Halek would consider it a compliment to her cooking that folks could be so engrossed in eating they hardly spoke a word through an entire meal.

The luxury of a meal in a café was an unaccustomed treat for Mary, and in spite of the uneasiness between herself and Aaron, there was a relaxed air of freedom about the day. As they came out of the dim café into the dazzling sunlight, the day enhanced the feeling. No field work, no cooking, no responsibilities awaited them until evening. They turned to walk the short distance to the end of the boardwalk, but their steps were slow. At the end, when they reached the street corner, he took her arm as she stepped down. He released her elbow then as they walked the block to Anson's place, but once again at the buggy he took her arm to hand her up. His courtesies filled her with a warm, protected feeling. Once again seated in the buggy, Aaron asked. "Would you like the bonnet up before we start?"

"Heavens no, Aaron. I love the sun on my face."

"That's good. So do I."

And heading out of town she reveled in the magic of the golden Minnesota day. When viewed from the height of the buggy seat, it was like gliding along on a low-flying cloud, passing the smells and sights and sounds of the countryside as an angel might ride on her way through heaven. The first wild roses had been too impatient to wait for June. They threw their fragrance from ditches and meadows in tantalizing appeal, competing with wild plum, apple, and lilac. They winked pinkly at the passing rig while great whorls of white blossoms hung half-concealed where copses bordered the road. Katydids played their high-pitched wings in duet with the frogs that thrummed hoarse voices from patches of marshland where red-winged blackbirds bobbed and swayed atop last year's exploding cattails. Crows teased the horses, hesitating at the edge of the road ahead until the last possible moment before rising in awkward fashion, flapping unwieldy wings that somehow drew them aloft. Meadowlarks fluted their elusive clarion call, unaware that it checked human breath until it was repeated. The rig rocked along, accompanied by bugs, blossoms, and birds, and the magic of the day healed something between the two people.

"Imagine living in the city all your life and missing this," Mary said.

"One year in the city was enough for me," Aaron said, "let alone all my life."

"You don't know how lucky you were to grow up here and have all this around you. Sometimes, like on a day like this, I can hardly believe I wasn't born here, too. I feel like I was, like all this was born right into me."

"Don't you ever miss Chicago?"

"It's not the place a person misses, it's the people in it, and there are none of my people left there since Daddy died. Aunt Mabel and Uncle Garner are the only ones now—and they're here. But sometimes I can't help feeling guilty that I came to their house that summer. Like if I'd stayed in Chicago, Daddy might still be alive."

"His death was an accident, and if you'd been there, it wouldn't have prevented it. Accidents happen in the factories like that all the time, but in the city nobody seems to care. That's the worst part about the city—nobody caring." He was pensive, recalling that lonely time on his own. But the day was too bright for sad recollections.

"I'd just as soon not remember it, and I'm sure you wouldn't, either," Aaron said, shrugging off the memories.

But Aaron never talked much about city life, and she often wondered why.

"Didn't you make any friends while you were there?" she asked.

"Friends? Not exactly."

"If not friends, then what?"

"Just . . . acquaintances. Nobody it bothered me to leave when I came back here," Aaron answered, remembering hard women, hard bosses, hard faces in the streets.

"Were any of them women?" She braved the question, suddenly wanting to know.

He glanced at her askance, a partial smile teasing one corner of his mouth now. "What does it matter?" he asked.

She flipped her hands palm-up to signify it didn't matter at all. "Oh, no matter." Then with a sudden shift of her shoulders she adopted the air of a proper city lady, one palm resting on the handle of an imaginary parasol, the other lightly upon the arm of an imaginary escort.

"I'll bet they were. And I'll bet they took your arm as you crossed the street and said, 'Why, Aaron Gray, *wherever* did you learn such fine chivalry?' "

He raised an elbow up beneath her hand, becoming her escort.

"Why, shucks, ma'am," he said in a drawling voice, "way up in Moran Township, but I didn't think you noticed."

"Notice! Why I declare! A blind woman would notice!"

"That's funny, ma'am," he bantered, "all you city girls gave me the idea that the last thing you wanted was chivalry."

"Don't be foolish, Mr. Gray," she answered in her city-girl voice. "We're no different than those country girls back home. We love it."

They laughed then, passing a piece of woods where jays scattered their own raucous laughter back at them, but somehow, as their laughter trailed down, the game lost its lightness. She removed her hand from his arm.

He tended to his driving again but replied, "If you'll pardon my manners, ma'am, I must disagree. There's no comparing the city girls with the ones back home."

But he was dead serious now, and Mary, too, dropped the charade as she told him, "I never meant to compare the two."

"Then you truly must pardon my manners," Aaron apologized.

"There's nothing wrong with your manners," she said. "They're all a girl could ask for."

He considered that for some time before asking

pointedly, "Is that what you thought last Saturday night?"

At the mention of that Saturday night, Mary felt a panic begin to rise within her.

"I wasn't talking about last Saturday night," she corrected. "I was talking about today. I just meant that it's nice to have a man take my arm again and hand me into the buggy or into a booth. Sometimes a husband forgets to do those things."

"All right, so today I'm chivalrous. But what about last Saturday? Was I chivalrous then?"

Her heart beat an erratic tattoo. "I don't know what you mean, Aaron," she denied.

"Yes, you do. I mean was I being chivalrous when I held the hand of my brother's wife in a manner unlike a brother-in-law?"

"It was just the ointment, that's all."

"Like hell it was, Mary." He said it very quietly, the very gentleness of his tone adding impetus to the words. "Was it the ointment at the dance, too? Where was my chivalry then?"

"It wasn't your fault, Aaron. You were practically forced into dancing with me."

"Quit trying to kid yourself, Mary. You know that I wanted you then, and we both know it was wrong. I was about as chivalrous as a fox paying a call on the hen house."

"No, Aaron. It wasn't wrong. We didn't do anything. If you think you were to blame for something, then maybe so was I. I shouldn't have stayed with you through that second dance." It seemed an admission of her wanting him. "It's just that we feel guilty because of the thing Jonathan suggested, that's all." And even as she said it, the rocking motion of the rig brought Aaron's arm next to her own. She knew she must not think about his nearness. Oh, God, why had she let Jonathan go on the train?

"We shouldn't have let Jonathan go on that train," Aaron said.

It was like trying to douse a fire with kerosene, his saying exactly what she'd been thinking.

"I tried not to think about you after that night."

"You ought not talk about it, Aaron," she warned. She willed him to stop now, before it was too late.

"No, I ought not . . ." There he stopped and they rode in silence a while until he seemed to pick up the thread of thought and pull it toward himself. "But if I don't, it would be cheating you."

It did seem like cheating to hold back these feelings, much as he realized the real cheating would be to give them vent. He thought again of how little Jonathan had seemed to see in her that night.

"Would it be all right if I just tell you how beautiful you were in your yellow dress that night?" he asked. But he kept his eyes on the road ahead, feeling her arm bump against his now and then, welcoming it.

"Not if I just said thank you and we ended it right there," she told him.

"I'll end it right there," he said, and tried to mean it.

Once again the motion of the buggy worked its magic and calmed them as it undulated, seeming to sway in rhythm with the trees bordering Turtle Creek. The horses had slowed, sensing their driver's lack of haste. The warm sun, the spring breeze, and the slow pace hypnotized the two riders. But slipping along through a world of bursting blossoms and nectar smells with their arms touching, there began the halting transition from friendship to fervor, for they were lulled out of their common good sense when some magical force, some unseen hand smoothed their brows, cupped their jaws, and turned their faces toward one another. They did not remember doing so on their own. Hadn't they been studying the road, the passing fields, just a minute ago?

But here was Mary, her face upturned toward his. Aaron gazed down at her then, and she back at him. And the goodness of it flooded them both after the days of effort to avoid even the slightest contact. The horses carried them along up the road, and the rocking rig beneath them swayed their bodies in unison as sun-drenched eyes held, brown meeting blue, unsmiling, yet so penetrating.

After they'd had an introduction into one another's eyes, they explored farther. He raised his gaze to her hair and saw the sun radiate off its lustrous richness, and he wondered how it felt when its heavy weight was released into a man's hand. He saw the sun on her forehead, glinting off tiny drops of moisture, and he thought he'd like to touch them with his tongue and know the taste of her. Following the line of her fine, high cheeks he came to her mouth. It hadn't learned to smile at him, but he knew somehow that it would.

She looked at him as if for the first time. With all the glory of the day before her, she saw what she'd never seen before, the sun sending prisms of light from the hairs of his eyebrows, which at last had relaxed from their frown, down the fine, clean line of his nose and the shadow it made on his lip below. His beautiful, wide mouth was relaxed. His breathing was deep. She remembered the strawberry and bay rum smell of him, his breath on her from that other time, and wished for the taste of it now. She studied his skin and saw that the whiskers grew in a pattern that swept toward his jaws. She wished to stroke it in the direction they grew. She thought momentarily of Jonathan's face, wondered if she knew it as intimately as she suddenly did Aaron's, but she could not conjure up his image, couldn't ever remember studying his whiskers, his eyebrows, or his mouth.

Then they became Mary and Aaron again, separate, studying the road, the fields, studying them as foreigners, for it seemed they'd never seen them before.

The horses pulled the rig into the yard and stopped under the elms from long practice. Strangely enough, Aaron did not help Mary alight. They each jumped down from their own side, and Mary went to the house while Aaron led the horses down toward the lean-to to remove their harnesses and set them out to graze.

It was a time without hurry. Aaron's thoughts took their time, as he did, finding small things to do, filling the hours until supper. He found seed corn in the granary and hoisted the sacks onto his shoulder and carried them to the lean-to to wait until morning. Her eyes seemed to be following him as he went, yet she was nowhere to be seen. He went to check the marker, a flat bed of equally spaced two-by-fours used to drag the soil, leaving behind it four clearly marked, evenly spaced checkrows to lay the seeds in. He found it needed tightening after the warping winter, got hammer and nails, and fixed it for morning. And all the while, the color of her honey hair remained in his eyes, nearly blinding him.

Mary had changed her dress for a simple work frock and went to check the goose eggs. They were still brooding under cluck hens, and each day she walked to the well in the yard and pumped a can full of water for them as she did now. She saw Aaron's Sunday suit coat hanging on a fence post down past the granary and wondered what he was busy at. His face came back to her, watching her as she went. Taking the water to the hen house, she turned each goose egg and sprinkled it. She filled the waterers and feeders and looked in each cubicle for chicken eggs, but found only a few, scarce at this time of year. Leaving the hen house, she saw Aaron's coat was gone from the fence post. He'd gone to the house to put dungarees on, and she met him coming out as she went in.

He stepped onto the porch, holding the screen door open for her to pass into the kitchen. On the threshold above him she turned, saying, "Aaron, I'll help you with the milking or anything you want."

He stood a step lower than she, but his brown eyes were nearly on a level with hers. She couldn't see them as clearly as earlier, standing as they were in the shade of the porch. But what details she couldn't make out, she remembered.

He smiled then, not with his mouth but with his eyes. "I don't need any help, but I'd enjoy your company in the barn."

"I'll be there," she promised.

She had enough wood in the box for a new fire, so she laid and lit one in the cold stove, then took the empty pails from the buttery, heading for the barn.

The Fulfillment

They met by the well and walked down together. The cows had accommodated them by hovering around the barn tonight, and when the big east door opened, it took little encouragement to get them inside. The sound of their hooves on the cement floor filled the space as much as the huge bulks did. The barn always seemed so vast when it was empty and so small when the cows came in.

Aaron took a milk stool and pail and evaded a switching tail as he settled in a squat beside the first cow. Mary, too, took a spot beside a cow. When he heard the first ring of the milk in her pail, he said, "There's no need for you to help, Mary."

"Don't be silly, Aaron," she said. "I'm not so helpless I can't give you a hand." But his rhythm was nearly double that of hers, and he'd already moved on to the second cow while she was still struggling with her first. Her unaccustomed hands needed frequent rests. When she'd resumed her stroking, the muscles of her forearms grew hot and tight. She lay her forehead against the warm, wide belly of the cow while she waited for her muscles to relax.

He came around the cow and saw her like that. "Here, let me finish her."

Mary turned her face toward him, her forehead still resting on the cow, and said, "Fine help I am, huh?"

"I told you your company was all I needed. You'd better get out of there before that old gal decides she's all done giving out and heads for the door."

She did as she was told, and while she waited for him to finish the job, found the empty tins and brought them near so Aaron could squirt them full for the eager cats. Standing beside him, she looked down over his bent head as he filled the tins. She came near to putting her hand down onto his heavy russet curls, but he finished and handed her the tins and her hands were saved from folly. She stayed away from him then until he finished, and spent her time trying to coax the unfriendly cats toward her. Freedom had made them skeptics, and they came near enough only to cadge their warm drink before scampering away.

"You go on up to the house. It's getting cool out here, and I'll be up in a minute," he said.

"Okay, but I thought I'd help you carry the milk up," she said.

"I'll bring it when I come. Just go on in and tend to supper."

While she began cooking supper, he came in with the milk pails. Before she could turn from the stove to fetch fresh dish towels to cover the pails, he was there at the breakfront, taking them from the drawer, something he'd never done before. He acted different, with Jonathan gone, almost as if he were playing the master of the house. When he turned to the pump to wet the towels, he found her watching his movements, her back to the stove. She thoroughly enjoyed his doing for her the small task that had always been her duty.

"What are you cooking?" he asked, and she started a bit, as if caught doing something indecent by watching him. But she smiled and turned back to the stove.

"Eggs," she said. "There were five tonight."

He smiled. At this time of year, when the hens were molting, eggs were scarce. The precious few they had were usually saved for other cooking purposes. To fry them and eat them so was as close to lavish as their eating habits came. He figured, and rightly so, it was her way of gifting him, for he loved fried eggs.

When he had covered the pails in the buttery, he went outside, down by the well in the yard, and took off his shirt. Pumping with one hand, he leaned toward the running water and splashed his arms. He had to keep starting and stopping the pumping action several times before he had splashed all of his face, neck, and chest. The water was like ice. It raised goosebumps on his arms. It caused him to suck in his belly with a heaving gulp before he backed off and shook his entire torso like a nickering horse.

He had forgotten a towel, so he came running up the porch steps and burst through the kitchen door like a shivering pup, cold drops of water spraying from his lips as he exclaimed, "Brrr!"

Mary turned from the range, grabbed a towel from the stand at the sink. "You could have washed in here with warm water," she said when she brought it to him, wishing she could rub him warm and dry with it. But the eggs were delicately done and they needed taking up right now, so she threw the towel at him, returning to the stove.

"I thought it might make you uncomfortable," Aaron said, watching for her reaction from the corner of his eye, rubbing himself. She kept her back to him.

He threw his shirt back on haphazardly, leaving it unbuttoned, and sat down at his place. Coming to her chair she saw how the white shirt clung to the skin of the chest where he'd not quite dried it. They began their meal without words. Sometimes they would look at one another, but it seemed as if they had reached the saturation point. Any more gazes would burst an invisible bubble.

She ate one of the two eggs on her plate, then said, "I'm full, Aaron." He half-smiled, covering her hair, eyes, neck, face with one glance, answering, "So am I." But he took the other egg from her plate and finished it before sitting back. She poured his tea, using a small strainer to catch the leaves.

"Why did you make tea tonight?" he asked. He knew why, but he wanted to hear her say it.

"Because you like it best," she answered, knowing he knew why.

Aaron lit the lamp, shut the back door to keep the chill out, and returned to his tea and her.

"You know a lot about me, don't you?" he questioned over his raised cup.

"Like what?"

"Oh, like . . . that I like tea better than coffee . . . that I like fried eggs, things like that."

She shrugged her shoulders, as if suddenly bashful. "We've lived here in the same house for most of seven years. Of course I know a lot about you."

"Yes. But it seems you learned more about me than I did about you. You have a way of knowing a man's needs."

"It's a woman's job to know a man's needs. Besides, all they are is food, clothing, and shelter. It doesn't take much knowing to see how to fill those."

"Is that why you came here—to tend to our food and clothing and shelter? Jonathan's and mine?"

She folded her hands in her lap, hunching her shoulders up and catching the hands between her knees. "I came here because . . . because from the first minute I saw this place I loved it and I wanted to build a life here . . . with Jonathan." Here she glanced all around the comfortable kitchen, bedecked in blue-and-white gingham checks, touched by the hominess she'd created, the plants growing at the windowsill, the crisp curtains at the windows and around the counter that held the sink. "The two of you seemed to rattle around in this house, and I guess it's true that I enjoyed the idea of having it to tend to. And the two of you need a woman to do for you." Here she hesitated again. "But I came here ever so proud to be Jonathan's wife."

Aaron gazed steadily at her. "A marriage should be built on more than pride," he said. "Food, clothing, and shelter aren't enough either. What about love?"

He was leaning back, his chair angled away from the table, an ankle crossed over a knee as he raised the cup to his lips, studying her.

"We have that too," she said, "it's just . . ."

He waited for her to continue, but when she didn't, he said, "You're very different, you and Jonathan. It strikes me that if either of you were to choose a friend, you would not choose each other, yet you chose to marry."

"You don't have to be friends and playmates to fall in love," she stated, her hands still clasped between her knees.

"No, but sometimes it makes it more fun."

"Fun? I didn't need fun. I needed security. When Daddy died . . . well, I couldn't live at Aunt Mabel's forever. And Jonathan needed someone here. Maybe those don't seem reasons enough to marry, but they were at the time, and love came afterward. I didn't think of a husband as a playmate or a friend, and I still don't."

"No, because you've always had me for that," Aaron said.

Their eyes caught and held, and she resisted owning up to the truth of that, lowering her eyes then from his direct gaze. But the lack of anger in his flat statement made it hit home.

"Yes, I guess I have," she admitted quietly.

"But Jonathan has put an end to that, too, hasn't he?" Aaron asked, still in his relaxed pose, one elbow resting on the table edge.

"Oh, I hope not," Mary said, looking him directly in the eye, feeling again how she had missed his friendship these last weeks. His brown eyes darkened, brows drawing together as he met her gaze and held it. Then he sighed.

"Mary girl," he said and, leaning forward, reached toward her hand, which now lay on the tabletop next to her cup and saucer. Touching only her little finger ever so lightly, he confessed, "I find it harder and harder to be only your friend."

She looked at their hands, her heart hammering formidably as his finger slid from hers. He stood up, taking his cup and saucer. "Let's do the dishes," he said, "I'll help."

She got up and gathered dishes in front of her. He did the same, and they went to the stove together to wash them. She filled the dishpan with water from the reservoir and pumped cold water to add to it. She kept the dishpan on the rear of the stove where the water would stay warm while she worked. For the second time tonight, he took a dish towel from the breakfront drawer, and they worked side by side until the kitchen was clean.

Chapter 9

The sun was down now and it was purple outside as they finished the dishes. Aaron went out to get wood for the woodbox so it would be full in the morning. He brought in two big armloads, then said he'd go shut the hen house doors and that he thought he'd left the granary open, too. After he was gone, her mind held the picture of the ridges the wood had made in his chest where he'd carried it against his still-open shirt.

The warm ride from town in the sun and the work in the chicken coop had left her with a grimy feeling, so she took a basin of water upstairs to her room. Without lighting the lamp she washed herself with castile soap. When she had finished, she took a clean nightgown from the dresser and shrugged it on, buttoning the front up to the high, eyelet-trimmed neck and tying the blue ribbon that gathered it beneath her breasts. Then she put on her flannel robe and went down to empty the basin in the backyard. The grass was cold now under her bare feet, so she hurried back inside. She put the basin away under the sink and lowered the lamp on the table, leaving it glowing softly. She made her way upstairs by the faint reflected light it cast around the stairwell.

Aaron was standing downyard, pondering the strange situation they were in when he saw the kitchen lamp dim, then a moment later the lamplight in an upstairs window, from her bedroom, hers and Jonathan's.

Then Aaron went inside to the kitchen and turned the skeleton key in the lock, something unheard of here on the farm, though the key hung loosely in the lock at all times. Then he lowered the wick on the lamp. As it spluttered out, he was left in darkness.

Mary was standing at the mirror brushing her hair, and she counted the familiar creaks of the stairs as Aaron came up. She inhaled deeply. The suggestion of lavender stayed with her as she heard Aaron go on past her closed door. He went down the hall to his own room, and she heard the sound of his dresser drawer opening. She continued brushing and was trying to count to a hundred strokes, but the numbers kept getting mixed up in her head, so she parted her hair freshly down the middle, then went to sit leaning against the pillows, her back against the headboard, as she braided her hair.

There had been no other sound from Aaron's room. When Mary heard a light tap on her door, she jumped as if a rifle had cracked in the stillness. She couldn't seem to force a word up into her throbbing throat, so she just sat holding her unfinished braid as the door opened slowly and Aaron stood there.

"May I come in, Mary?" But still her words would not come forth, and he came to the foot of her bed and stood, watching, while she formed the last braid with shaking hands.

He was wearing light cotton pajamas, and it crossed her mind that she had never washed them for him. Where had he gotten them? She had never seen a man in pajamas before.

"Why don't you take your braids out, Mary?" he asked. "I've never seen you with your hair down before."

And as if his words were the force that controlled her movements, she began undoing the braid she'd nearly finished. He watched her as she freed both of them, then tried to comb through them with her fingers. All the while, her eyes stayed on him. He turned to look over his shoulder and, finding the brush she'd left on the dresser, picked it up and came to stand beside her. She followed him with her eyes, still holding onto the trailing ends of her hair, until he was above her and she was gazing up at him.

He took her by the shoulders and turned her away from him and slowly began brushing her hair. He stroked its full length, to the middle of her back. He touched her nowhere else. All she could feel was the tug of the bristles and the hammering of her heart. Then he put a hand on her forehead and pulled her head backward until her hair hung free against his stomach and the top of her head rested on his chest. Her eyes were closed as he ran the brush over the center part of her hair, and he brushed at it repeatedly until he had obliterated it, and pulled her hair straight back as she'd had it the night of the dance.

In the lamplight he saw the ivory sheen of her arched throat, and it threw his heart into wild disorder. Then his hands slowly went around the front of her neck until, under her hair, she felt his thumbs pushing her head back up. When she had straightened it, she felt the warmth of his body flattened against her back. His first kiss was laid lightly upon the hair he'd just finished brushing.

"I thought I could keep from coming to you, Mary," and his voice was unlike she'd ever heard it, intense and low.

"It's wrong, Aaron."

"It's not wrong yet. All you have to do is say the word and I'll leave. But you have to say it."

It was an effort for her to breathe. "I can't say it, Aaron."

"Are you sure?" he asked, knowing he was being unfair. Standing as he was, behind and above her, he could see her chest breaking with her heavy breathing, knew she wanted him, too, and that he was making her decide for them both.

"There is no such thing as being sure," she answered.

Then she felt his two hands slide from her neck, down over the front of her nightgown, until she was no longer aware of the heat against her back. There was the warmth of Aaron's hands on her breasts instead, pulling all her senses there as he caressed them, moving slowly, slowly, contouring their undercurve, brushing more lightly across the erect nipples before flanking them with his fingers until their hardness became sweet pain. It agonized and thrilled her at the same time. She knew she must stop him, but lacked all will to do so.

He straightened then, put a hand on her back while moving around to sit on the edge of the bed, facing her. He put a hand on each of her shoulders, ran them down the full length of her arms until he reached her hands; then their fingers interlaced, and they sat with palms together, fingers squeezing in near pain, until he forced her arms straight out from her sides. The lamplight glimmered on his russet curls as he tipped his head to one side, but she saw only a brief movement, for her eyes were closing. He kissed her with the soft, light, first touch of discovery before releasing her hands and pulling her nearer. Her arms hung where he'd left them until she felt his tongue lightly tracing a circle over her covered lips.

When at last he felt her arms close around his shoulders, his tongue became more demanding, forcing her mouth open and feeling her response. He chased her wandering tongue with his until he stilled it, explored it, captured it. She was responsive but hesitant, until he nudged her tongue into action and she responded fully.

Separating to look into each other's eyes, she found his face in the lamplight was just as she remembered it. She put both her hands upon it, and his eyes closed while her fingertips traveled over every part of it. They crossed his forehead, starting in the center and separating to cover its breadth of his temples. She laid her fingers gently on his closed eyelids before tracing down his nose and stroking his cheeks toward his jawbone in the direction she remembered his whiskers grew.

"I wanted to do that this afternoon," she revealed.

"Yes, I know." It was no revelation at all, for he'd read it in her face back then. His eyes remained closed.

At last she touched his beautiful, wide mouth.

His eyes opened slowly, and she felt the need to say his name.

"Aaron . . ." Mary said, her head tipped slightly to one side. He understood that after all these years the name was suddenly different to her.

"Hello, Mary." He smiled as if he'd just met her, too.

"I know you far better than I did at suppertime," she said.

"You haven't begun to know me, Mary," Aaron said.

"I want to know all of you," she said.

As if the sweet ecstasy of their gentle introduction could satisfy him no longer, Aaron suddenly changed. He tipped Mary sideways across his lap as he lowered his open, demanding mouth to hers. He pulled her so tightly against his chest that she couldn't tell whose heart she felt pulsing between them, his or her own. When at last he released her, he barely had the breath to groan, "Oh, Mary, Mary . . ." as he cradled her, rocking her.

Never in her life had Jonathan stirred her like this. What Mary was feeling now made the past longings of her life vague promises that had never been fulfilled. The heat in her body was a thing so unreconcilable that it scared her. She'd never felt it before, not with an intensity like this, and she didn't know what to do with it.

But Aaron knew.

He moved away from her and laid her flat across his knees and untied the blue ribbon that circled her nightgown. Using both hands, he started at the high neck of it and began unbuttoning. But when he reached the button under the blue ribbon she put her hands on his to stay them. "Aaron, please turn out the lantern."

His eyebrows drew together, then relaxed. "Let me leave it on, Mary."

"No, Aaron, please." Her heart was hammering with frightful timidity now. In spite of her longing for Aaron, she still felt the stringent restrictions, the proprieties that had always regulated even her most intimate behavior.

"Mary, are you afraid of the light?" he asked.

"Yes," she quavered, and her wide eyes told him it was so.

"But your body is beautiful. Where's the shame in that?"

"Please, Aaron. I can't. I never have, not in the light."

He got up and walked to the lamp and lowered the wick until darkness sank around them. He returned to where she sat on the edge of the bed, and knelt on the floor in front of her. Reaching his hands up to her neck, he again ran them over her shoulders, but this time the nightgown fell from them and in the dark she clasped its fallen folds around her waist, even as the delight of his caress touched her naked skin.

Never had she imagined a man taking as much time as he was now. He touched every inch of her back and stomach, running his hands up her sides and forcing her arms up to his own shoulders so he could run his hands under her arms and over her breasts. At some time while his vagabond hands roamed over her, her neck grew limp, her head lolled backward, and she groaned, "Aaron, what are you doing to me?"

For an answer she felt a warm wetness on her breast, followed by the roughness of his tongue. He loved the sweet smell of her, and as he took his mouth to her other breast, could taste the cleanness of her firm flesh. Her small, hard body was as perfect as he'd known it would be, but he damned the darkness that hid what he could only feel.

It was so dark in the room that all he knew was what he tasted and touched. He felt her tight, small fists clutching the nightgown under his chest. So he stopped kissing her then and put both hands over hers, but he could feel her fists knot tighter at his touch.

"Don't be afraid, Mary," he whispered.

"But I am, Aaron."

"I'll teach you not to be," Aaron promised.

"But Jonathan never . . ." She stopped, realizing what she'd said and wishing she could draw back the name.

"Jonathan never what?" he asked in the dark, and his voice held no rebuke. But she found she couldn't say it. This sort of frankness was totally new to her. In Jonathan's arms there was no talking and, so, no such inhibition.

"Jonathan never what?" he repeated, encouraging her. "Say it, Mary, and don't be ashamed."

She squeezed her eyes shut, as if he could see her in the blackness, and she kept her fists tight on her nightgown as she whispered, "Jonathan never took all my clothes off . . . or talked about . . . this."

"Then Jonathan is a fool," Aaron said.

The Fulfillment

He found both of her wrists in the darkness and, grasping them firmly, stood up, pulling her with him as her gown slid to the floor at her feet.

She stood very still, her eyes growing used to the darkness now. She felt him release her wrists and move a step back from her, then heard a rustle of cotton pajamas falling to the floor. She could see the outline of his shoulders as he took her in his arms again and pulled her to him, tightly and at full length, his body hot and hard between them. And then Aaron began what he'd been doing before, but his hands had a greater territory over which to roam, and they did.

"I'm doing to you what you were made for," Aaron said. Then lovingly, he wielded the magical touch that awoke what had slumbered so long for her.

"Please stop, Aaron. I can't stand up anymore."

He laid her down on the bed on her back. She felt a subtle change begin to tighten her body as his hands continued relentlessly. And when the heat grew until it controlled her every nerve, her hands grabbed at the air, then clasped the metal rods of the headboard as her body jerked in a releasing spasm of warmth, and she heard a voice somewhere calling his name.

She lay then in weak wonder. In the sum total of her experiences there had never been such a feeling, such a myriad of feelings. Yet Aaron had not yet come to her in the way she'd thought he would. His shadowy shape was still leaning over her in the darkness, and she knew by his labored breathing and tense body that he had not yet found release.

He was kissing the soft skin of her temples, then moved across her face as if searching for the perfect place to stop. He tasted the salty trail tears had left on her temples. But he couldn't acknowledge them now, with his own body calling urgently for release.

Pulsing with the want of her, he rolled onto her body, his rigid phallus pressed into the hollow curve below her hipbone. He tore his devouring mouth away from hers, and his voice came loud by her ear, his words jerked from between spasmic breaths, "Mary, are you sure?"

Hands in his hair, her tears now on his own temple where it rested near her ear, she raised her one free knee, and he felt it rub against his hip, then fall aside as she opened herself to him fully. "I want to know all of you," she whispered shakily. "It's what I was made for."

Her response sang through him as he shifted his body to enter the sweet, warm wetness of her, plunging in rhythmic force as she clung to his shoulders, their moans mingling together in the darkness until his final release.

Chapter 10

It wasn't that it was any brighter in the room. Perhaps they themselves had a new brightness. Her head was in a spot where it fit beautifully, and one of his hands rested on a part of her where it utterly belonged. They'd been like that long enough for their breaths to cool, their pulses slow.

"Why did you cry, Mary girl?" Aaron asked.

"I didn't," she denied, not knowing she had.

"There were tears on your face," he said, and laid his lips to the outer corner of her eye to kiss it.

"There were?"

"Yes," he remembered, "I could taste them."

"When?"

"Right after I made you feel beautiful."

She reached an arm around his middle and squeezed him, saying, "Oh, Aaron, you did make me feel beautiful . . . so it must have been a beautiful tear."

"That's never happened to you before, has it, Mary?"

"The tears, you mean?"

"No. I mean what came before them."

"No, Aaron, never before." Her heart was beating rapidly again, realizing that she was openly talking about the act that had always before seemed, if not surreptitious, then at least beyond words. Aaron lay there holding her hand, gently rubbing her arm that lay over his chest, thinking of her body being denied its most precious birthright for her seven married years, and again, silently this time, he called Jonathan a fool.

"What was it that happened to me, Aaron?" she asked, and he pitied her ignorance, yet thrilled to it, knowing he was the first to teach her. He pulled her face close to his neck and moved his jaw across her forehead.

"The same as what happened to me later. Didn't you know, my darling, that for a woman it can be as strong and complete as for a man?"

"How could I know, Aaron?" she asked, pulling her head back to look up toward his face in the dark. "I only knew what one man had taught me. I didn't know there was anything else."

He rolled her onto her back then and leaned across her chest with both of his elbows on the pillow under her, his hands smoothing the hair back from the sides of her face.

"My beautiful Mary girl," he said, "You've come to me as innocent as a bride, and I can't thank Jonathan enough. But I pity him his ignorance and what he's missed in you."

He kissed her face all over then, running its smooth, fine length and stopping at each closed eye to feel the flutter of it under his lips. He came to her mouth, and she reshaped it to fit his. But instead he touched hers in a silent command to be still. But when he lowered his lips near hers, she again was ready for his kiss. When he drew back a second time and laid a finger across her lips once more, her eyelids flickered open in puzzlement. But a curl of hair on his forehead tickled them shut again as she felt the warm, wet tip of his tongue glide over her still upper lip. Her mouth relaxed as the warmth and its following coolness played across her bottom lip, then across one eyebrow and down toward her ear. Then, like hearing the ocean in a seashell, she heard the roar of loud deafness as he licked the inside of her ear.

She squirmed then and rubbed her ear on the pillow under her, and to her surprise, a giggle bubbled out of her.

He backed off a bit and said in mock sternness, "Oh, so the lady laughs at my ardent persuasions."

"I can't help it, Aaron. It tickled. Besides, it made me squirm, wondering who taught you all these wicked tricks."

"Wicked tricks? Up till now my tricks have been making you feel beautiful, and suddenly they're wicked?"

"All right, so they're not exactly wicked . . . but how did you learn them?"

He thought of the women when he'd been to town, the ones who'd demanded no chivalry. But the woman in his arms now was different, more precious.

"Does it matter?"

"No," she whispered. Yet having had what she'd had of him tonight, she wanted to own all his life that had gone before. She knew a vague regret at not having been his first, and he felt a bit of the same for her.

"Don't let it matter," he said.

And Aaron's mouth set out to make it not matter. His lips began again their interrupted meandering until hers began the same "wicked tricks," and their roles subtly exchanged. Without knowing when she began, Mary was kissing him in the way he'd just taught her. His body's response hearkened again to the tune she played on him, and she learned with it that he was not yet finished being her mentor. Within a tightening arm she felt herself swung upward, rolled onto his stomach, his hands guiding her until she was astride him.

"Aaron . . ." she whispered, feeling oddly exhilarated and shamed at once.

"Shhh . . . it's okay. Let me show you."

And for the first time in her life she looked down from above on the act of love, and with sensual delight felt newfound freedom as her body was given free rein. But she was unskilled at his rhythmic caprice, so he murmured to her and guided her and his hands were there on her hips to encourage when she faltered. Her hair swayed across her back sometimes. Other times it fell onto his face and chest. Its silken skeins fell into his open mouth as his head arched back, and she learned from him a new kind of gift, one she could give him. And she gave it as she'd never given before.

Lying once again quietly, only their hands touching, there came the sound of a growling stomach, and Aaron suddenly slapped his belly with an open hand, making a loud clap in the silence. Then he curled his body and rocked up and off the side of the bed in a single action. He felt for their clothes on the floor beside the bed, and when he'd found them, said, "Come here, wench, and let me make a decent woman of you." He reached out in the dark, found an arm, and pulled it until she was kneeling on the edge of the bed in front of him.

"Put your arms up," he commanded, and she did as she was bid. He dropped the partially buttoned nightgown over her head. Then he buttoned up each button, right up to the high, eyelet-trimmed neck, before he said, "You've escaped the eye of the dragon this time, but I warn you, you won't for long." And he put his own pajamas back on, then asked, "Now can I light the lantern?"

"Whenever my lord wishes."

He struck a match, and the room sprang into brightness.

"Your lord wishes some food. He is hungry as a dragon."

"Indeed, I heard the dragon within him roar a minute ago." She couldn't help the giggle that escaped her.

He picked up the lantern, laughing, too, and held out a hand to her. But before leading her out and down the stairs, he took the time to kiss her in the bright glow, holding the lantern aloft.

"C'mon, wench," he said, and she followed him, smiling.

They sliced thick slabs of bread, layered them with butter and gooseberry jam, and drank the fresh milk they'd gotten that night, rich with the cream that had not yet separated to its top. He licked the gooseberry jam from her outstretched fingers, and she thanked him with a hesitant kiss that cleared his upper lip of milk froth. Standing in the pantry slicing their second pieces of bread, she curled her bare toes, and he came up behind her, putting his chin on her shoulder, and told her no wench could run from a dragon with toes like that. When his hands strayed upward, she threatened to do them injury with the bread knife. He admonished her lest she injure instead what lay beneath his fondling fingers, and they ate more bread and jam with laughter in their eyes and finally sat, with sleeves in the bread crumbs, holding hands across the tabletop.

"We have to go to bed now, don't we?" she asked.

"Yes. Even dragons and wenches need sleep."

"Even when they don't want to?"

"Even when they don't want to. Especially when there's corn to plant tomorrow morning."

They got up then and brushed the crumbs from their elbows, leaving more on the tabletop unnoticed, each one a beautiful blot on the kitchen Mary had always left in meticulous order. They went up with arms around each other, the lantern in Aaron's free hand. At the door to the front bedroom they stopped, and he set the lantern on the floor at their feet. The light, rising to their faces from that low angle, highlighted their lips, leaving their eyes in shadow.

Aaron reached out and touched Mary's gilded lips with his fingertips. "I would never sleep with you beside me all night long, and I wouldn't let you sleep, either. If it weren't for that corn, neither of us would care. But I'd better leave you here."

Then the exaggerated shadows of the two became

one on the opposite landing wall before he leaned to pick up the lantern and hand it to her. He went down the hall to the other door, but when he reached it, turned to look back at her. They both stood just so for a long time.

And they opened both doors at once, each turning into a separate room. But they left the doors open, as if the essence of one another might drift through the hall to help ease them into sleep.

When Aaron awoke, it was first light. He came awake as if an alarm had sounded, but none had. He'd slept like something hibernating, after the wearying release his body had needed so badly. The memory of it swept over him now as he got out of bed silently. Before changing clothes, he crept to the open doorway of the room up the hall.

Mary was still asleep, lying on her back, with both hands palms-up on the pillow like a child. Her hair was strewn all over the pillow, and the quilts covered her nearly to her chin. The only parts of her nightgown that showed were the eyelet ruffles at wrists and neck. He went a few steps farther into the room so he could see her features more clearly in the dim, dawn light. Her childlike face looked open, even in sleep, just as it had the night she'd combed her hair back for the dance. He wished she would awaken and raise her arms to him, but she didn't, so he gazed at her, contenting himself with memory.

But the day lay ahead with much to be done, so he went back to his own room, dressed, then crept as quietly as he could down the creaking steps toward the morning chores.

* * *

When Mary awoke, it was slowly, luxuriously, slipping into consciousness to test it, then slipping back out after finding she wasn't ready for it yet. When it finally suited her and she opened her eyes to it, her first thought was that something was wrong. The sun was bright and high and Jonathan had not yet clanged the household awake with the stove lids. Looking quickly down at the clock, she found it had stopped at a quarter to three . . . then she remembered why.

Aaron.

And all the memory of last night followed his name.

How had she ever slept so late? It must be midmorning already! Like a thunderbolt it struck her that she'd forgotten to pump the wash water last night to lose its chill . . . and she'd promised Jonathan to help Aaron plant the corn. How in blazes was she ever going to do all that after getting started so late in the day?

She tore into her clothes, tore the sheets off her bed, and dropped them over the railing in the hall. Before they hit bottom she had already attacked Aaron's bed, ripping its sheets off. Her hair was still flying free, but she didn't stop to put it up now. Instead, she grabbed her brush from the bedside stand where Aaron had left it the night before, and ran downstairs with it. She could do her hair after the boiler was filled and heating. She scooped up the mound of sheets at the bottom of the stairs and turned the corner into the kitchen with her feet tangled in their trailing folds.

There she stopped in surprise. Simmering on the range was the copper boiler, all filled with steaming water. A smile broke across her face, and she hugged the sheets to her, hanging her head back as she whirled in a circle with her feet twisting into the sheets and her hair flying out behind. Just one happy name filled her being.

He had pumped and filled the boiler for her, and now into his favor she read the compliment of his lover's gift. All the years he'd helped her, doing small favors, all the considerations that were so typically Aaron, now found new and untold value in Mary's eyes. She looked at the simmering wash water, and its warmth was nearly hers.

Standing among the sheets, she brushed her hair and, when it was smooth, went into the pantry where there were clean rags on the shelf. Tearing a strip from one, she caught her hair back with it and tied it behind her neck, then began her washday preparations.

During the warm months the washing was done on the concrete porch where the wooden washer was kept. The hot water had to be bailed from the boiler and carried outside. Two tubs for rinsing were set on a wooden bench beside the washer. These were filled with cold water, pumped from the cistern. The first step in washing clothes was always to boil the white clothes in the boiler on top of the stove before turning them into the washer. But today, getting a late start even in spite of Aaron's favor, Mary procrastinated and scarcely felt guilty when she deferred the boiling till next week. Something had to be skipped to save time if she were to help Aaron at all in the fields today.

Standing on the porch in the sun, Mary worked the handle that made the agitator churn the clothes inside the washer. She looked down past the vegetable garden into the east field, but knew Aaron wouldn't be there.

It had already been seeded with small grain. He would be out in the south ten, which was hidden from view by the woods. She looked out toward the south and thought of him there and hurried the day toward him. Through the sorting, soaking, agitating, dipping, wringing, and hanging she worked toward him, breaking only long enough to go into the buttery and dip some fried-down pork out of the crock and put it on the back of the stove to begin warming for their dinner.

The sheets were slapping in the noon wind, the shirts and pants dancing an inverted jig to their own beat. Coming up the field lane beside the woods, Aaron saw the clothes basket turned upside down in the yard and looked for Mary on the porch. But the overturned basket told him the washing was done and she must be inside cooking dinner. He had unhitched the team, leaving the marker at the edge of the field, and had driven the horses up the lane, walking behind them.

The wind carried Aaron's voice as he neared the yard, guiding them into a right turn with a "Gee! Gee" guiding the team. Mary could hear him talking to the horses companionably as he came around their rumps and walked toward the well. She stood a few paces back from the screen door and watched him take the tin cup from the long metal finger on top of the pump. She knew he couldn't see her, but thrilled in anticipation as he leaned his head back to swill the sweet water, all the time looking over the rim of the cup toward the house. He hung up the cup, then pumped the handle again and cupped his hands under the rush of water and splashed his face, running his fingers back through his thick hair. She imagined the texture of it under her own fingers. Aaron turned and began walking toward the house. She skimmed a hand over her hair and turned to look busy at the stove.

"Jesus, girl, you look good standing here," Aaron said, and she understood what he meant.

"It's where I belong."

She put both of her arms around him and felt the wetness of the water on his face. He laid his cheek on hers, and it made smacking noises near their ears, with the moisture between their skins. When he released her, she picked up the skirt of her apron and toweled his face with it, then her own.

"Did you sleep?" he asked, leaning back but leaving his arms around her waist.

"Yes, way too long. Did you?"

"Like a cat who got the cream," he answered, and saw a light blush come to her face. She escaped his embrace and turned her flustered attention to their meal.

"Thank you for filling the boiler, Aaron," she said.

"Well, it's the least I could do for a lady I kept up half the night." He came up behind her as she carried a bowl to the table, and tugged lightly on her tied-back hair.

"I like your hair pulled straight back like that," he said, but she bobbed her head away, saying, "I've never forgotten the wash water before. I don't know what came over me last night."

"I do," he said with a teasing grin. "Me!"

His impertinence had her downright red by this time. Aaron was enjoying every minute of it. She looked as enchanting as a schoolgirl. Last night in the pantry she'd taken his teasing lightly, but today in the daylight she seemed so bashful.

"Mary, if I tease you it's because I'm happy, okay?" he asked.

She stopped in her path from table to stove and looked at him. "Yes, Aaron," she approved, "it's just that it's new to me, that's all."

"Many things are new to you since last night," he said, "but every one of them's fine and good."

"Yes, I think so, too."

"Okay," he said, and they smiled at each other.

They sat down to eat then, but they'd barely begun when Aaron noticed she'd not set the tea-kettle on the hottest part of the stove for scalding their dishes later. "You forgot the kettle," he said, and she started to get up at the same time as he did. He said, "I'll get it," but when he lifted it he felt it was empty and went to the pump to fill it. Coming back to the table, he came up behind Mary and put his lips near her ear, whispering, "Is something coming over you again, Mary? This forgetfulness is not like you." He planted a bit of a kiss on her neck before sitting down again.

She blushed.

In the early afternoon they walked out to the cornfield behind the horses. Aaron had more marking to do, so Mary began the planting with the hand planter while he finished marking the last of the checkrows. He turned the horses free to crop the grass along the edges of the field before joining her with a second planter. Together they crossed and recrossed the checkered field, hesitating at each x to push the seeds into the earth.

They broke to fill their seed canisters and later for a drink of water from the fruit jar Mary had left on the grassy verge in the shade of a rock. He opened the burlap-wrapped jar and handed it to her first. After she drank, she two-handed it straight across at him. But taking the jar from her he turned it until the side she'd drunk from was under his lips, the timeless gesture of a lord for his lady. She turned pink as he handed that jar back to her, but feeling a bit bold when he leaned up close, she kissed him on the corner of his mouth, rather surprising both of them.

They worked through the afternoon, thinking of evening. None of the usual monotony of the job struck them, for monotony is an affliction of the empty mind. Both of their minds were full.

As the afternoon glare wore low, they headed home, with the horses dragging the marker and Mary riding atop it. Chores were waiting when they got back, but this time when Mary had finished her own she didn't go to join Aaron in the barn to lend her ineffectual hand. She went instead to fix supper and take in the clothes from the line, folding and sprinkling them in preparation for tomorrow's ironing.

The last thing left hanging on the lines were the sheets, cut across now with dapples of late-day shadows. Aaron, walking between the outbuildings, saw Mary at the lines with her arms upraised, plucking at the clothespins and gathering the sheets high so they wouldn't touch the ground. At the sight of her there, as lithe and slim as the long shadows about her, he was struck again with the veritable perfection of their place here together.

Taking the sheets fresh from the line, Mary went to remake the beds, doing first her own, then Aaron's. In his room she thought about all the nights he'd slept there, wondered if he'd ever heard her and Jonathan making love, wondered what it would be like when they did it again, as they surely must.

The smell of supper cooking downstairs brought her back to reality, and she finished draping the coverlet over the bed and went down to tend to her cooking. She was busy when Aaron came in. He kept a stream of talk going as they busied themselves, he at the sink and she at the range.

"We got a good start on the corn today because of your help. Thanks, Mary."

"No need for thanks, Aaron. I didn't mind it."

"Still, you must be tired. You're not used to doing double duty in the house and fields."

"The day went so fast it hardly seemed like work. Anyway, I'll be in the fields again at harvest time. This little bit of work will seem like nothing next to shocking grain."

"The day went fast for me, too, Mary. Because you were out there with me."

He had his shirt off, was lathering his chest and arms, and it was all she could do to keep from watching the process, while finally he dried with a towel.

"I missed you in the barn though. The cats asked where you were," he teased. Then his voice changed.

"I told them you were up here putting clean sheets on the bed for tonight." He said it quietly but not teasingly. She picked up Aaron's dirty blue cambric shirt from the back of the chair and was going to take it out to the clothes basket on the back porch, but he said, "Come here to me, Mary." And she felt a flash of heat go to her face.

"I've waited through a million corn seeds and a

hundred hours of chores, and I can't wait any longer." He was standing with the white towel slung around his neck, holding onto its ends.

She let the shirt fall back onto the chair and turned slowly to him. She went to stand in front of him and look up at his face, then back down to his bare chest, where a light mat of red-gold hair lay damp after the washing. Then he flipped the towel off his neck and around the back of hers, pulling her toward him. She put a hand lightly on his chest then and could feel the beating of his heart.

"Don't be afraid to touch me, Mary," he said.

And her hand withdrew a little.

"It's not decent in the daylight," she said.

"It's evening already . . . call it evenlight."

"It doesn't seem right," she repeated.

"Do you want to touch me, Mary? As bad as I want to touch you?" he asked.

Her hand was still poised uncertainly between them. She didn't answer aloud, only nodded in assent.

He took her hand and pulled it back onto his chest and moved it back and forth, across the fine, sparkling hairs, across his hard brown nipples.

"If you want it and I want it, what could be more right?" His hand still guided hers over ribs, navel, neck, jaws, and back down to his chest.

"I don't know," she choked.

"I want you to touch me everywhere, like you touched my face last night," he said, his eyes an intense dark brown.

"Oh, Aaron, you're beautiful," she breathed.

"Am I, Mary?" he asked. "Maybe it's because you're looking with your heart instead of your eyes."

She reached to place her fingertips fleetingly on his lips, saying, "I think I'm looking with both."

He surrounded her then with his bare arms and chest. When his mouth came down on hers, she felt that her hands couldn't pull strongly enough on his back to bring his beauty into her. She rubbed the fingers of both hands straight and hard up the center of his backbone, surprising herself with the motions her hands made of their own volition.

His arms reached so far around her slim body that his hands rested on the soft sides of her breasts under her arms. He spread his fingers and felt the vague swellings there, but when he backed a bit away from her to caress her from the front, she took her mouth away from his and said, "Our supper's burning, Aaron."

"To hell with supper," he said hoarsely, and kept his hand busy as he pulled her closer again and kissed her. "To hell with the light, Mary, don't be afraid of it. I want you."

And for a moment she was tempted to give in, light or no light. "Please don't make me cook another meal, Aaron. If you don't let me go, I'll have to."

He finally realized that there was a taint of burning pork beginning to drift around them. He turned her loose then, cursing the bad timing but knowing she was right about the meal. She caught the food in time to save it, but wished it had been cooked perfectly, as she'd wanted it for him. They had to eat it dry, cutting off the parts that were too brown, but neither of them minded a bit. Aaron had come to the table without putting on a clean shirt, and sat through the entire meal with those impudent nipples daring her to look at them across the overdone food.

After supper they worked together to clean up the mess, and when the kitchen was clean, Aaron picked up his dirty shirt from the back of the chair, picked up the dishpan, and headed out the door to sling it out at the edge of the backyard. Then he leaned the pan against the doorjamb, put his dirty shirt in the basket at the far end of the porch, and walked down toward the barnyard.

He knows what he's leaving me alone for, Mary thought as she watched him go, and he knows I'll do it. And from far off down the barnyard he heard the dishpan clank as she opened the screen door and knocked it over. Retrieving it from its resounding spin, she stopped its ringing and took it inside to fill and carry upstairs for her sponge bath. She wished she could bathe down at the kitchen sink where it was more convenient, but what if he came back before she was finished?

As it turned out, that's just what Aaron did, and on purpose. She heard his footfalls making the old steps creak, and in a rush of near-panic she whipped the wet cloth over her soapy legs, trying to hurry, knowing she'd never beat him if he came in. She stopped her splashing and held her breath to listen. Her heart beat wildly as she saw the doorlatch lift. Aaron stepped inside.

She was standing in the lamplight with one foot in the dishpan and one on the floor. Dear God, she was beautiful. Her skin was glimmering yellow in highlights and dusked to pink in shadow. He caught a flash of one small breast before she turned in a protective half-crouch away from him, putting her arms over her front to shield it.

"Please go out and leave me, Aaron," she implored. He saw her look over her shoulder at the towel lying beside the dishpan on the floor. But she would have had to turn toward him to pick it up, so she left it and kept her guarded position. But when Mary looked up from the towel to Aaron, she saw that he was looking in the dresser mirror at her full reflection. He had missed very little.

"Please, Aaron," she begged again.

"I'll go because you ask me, not because it's indecent to stay," he said, and went out, closing the door. She heard him go to his room, then clump hurriedly back downstairs. As she finished her bath, she heard the iron clank of the reservoir lid lifting and the following sound of the pump handle being worked. She figured he must be finishing the other half of the bath he'd started before supper. A smile teased her lips. There haven't been so many baths taken in this house in any three days since I've lived here, she thought.

With the thought and smile still warming her, she dried herself, dressed, put her dishpan out in the hall, and sat down at the windowsill in the fragrant night to brush her hair.

Aaron was making busy noises down there, and twice she heard him go out onto the porch below her window, but the roof angled there and she couldn't tell what he was doing. The pump sounded again, and after a while he came upstairs to his room, then went back down and outside. She heard the slosh of her bathwater as he dumped it in the yard. She'd forgotten about it sitting out there in the hall! She smiled a little thank-you smile and wondered if he could feel it being conveyed to him through the evening.

*   *   *

When he'd finished, Aaron climbed the stairs for the last time and knocked. She was sitting on the floor at the low sill of the open window. "Come in," she called, and when he did, added, "This is a fine time to knock." But she reached up her hand toward him and said, "Come and smell the night. I think I even smell the first lilacs."

He squatted down beside her with his elbows on his knees, and they stayed awhile, holding hands and smelling spring ease into summer.

"Hey, girl," he said, taking a strand of her hair from her neck into his fingers, "I was unfair . . . but my sense of decency is different than yours. Anyway, you were beautiful."

Soon he said, "Will you come to my room tonight?"

She gave him a short look, then nodded. He got up and blew out the lantern on her dresser, then held his hands out to her and tugged her up. He walked ahead of her down the hall so that she couldn't see into the room as his broad shoulders filled the doorway. But a halo of lantern light radiated from inside, and before she saw them, she smelled lilacs coming from somewhere in front of Aaron. When she was fully into the room, she saw two branches of lilacs in a mason jar of water beside the bed.

"Oh, Aaron. How did you know I love them?" She went to plunge her face among the violet petals.

"I've lived with you for seven years, too," he said, gratified by her pleasure. "I do know some things you like. See here?" he gestured to the dresser. "Choke-cherry wine." There were two small jelly glasses beside the bottle of sparkling drink.

"Another of my favorites!" Mary exclaimed. "Oh Aaron . . ." She gazed across the room at him, honey-hair rich in the lantern light, child's face lustrous with a flush of pleasure upon it. "You have such ways of pleasing. I'm afraid you'll spoil me."

"I'd love to have the chance to try. If I could, I'd buy you wine in the finest hotel in the land, but people might frown and point, so we'll have to drink it here instead, okay?" He cocked his head, waiting for her reply.

"I never drank wine in a bedroom before," she laughed.

"Neither did I," he admitted, and his own rich laughter accompanied her to the dresser, where she filled both glasses. Holding one out to him, Mary said, "Among the things I love, there's chokecherry wine. You're right about that."

She didn't know which was sweeter, the rich red wine or sipping it here with Aaron. They sat on the edge of his bed, and when they had finished, he refilled their glasses. These second ones were shared sitting cross-legged on the bed, facing each other. It was a thing she would never have dreamed of doing two days ago, yet here she was, feeling the glow of the wine and the man.

"Will you let me leave the lantern on when we make love tonight?" he asked.

And again her cheeks took on a little of the claret color of the liquid in her glass. "Please don't ask me that," she said.

"Why?"

"Because it seems indecent."

"Like the act of love itself?" he shrugged.

"I didn't say that, Aaron. I didn't even think it."
She took a small sip from her glass before going on.
"Last night you taught me that it isn't indecent, even
between us to whom it's forbidden. When you made
love to me, it made the act between Jonathan and me
seem the indecent one. How can that be, Aaron, when
Jonathan's my husband?"

"Darling, I don't know about what passed between
you and Jonathan, but I know what didn't pass between you . . . and without that, the act is a sham."

She felt a ripple of delight thrill through her at his
endearment, at his casual use of it when she was so
unaccustomed to words like that. "But I have always
loved Jonathan, and I know he loves me. That should
make it good, but it was never like last night with you.
Why didn't Jonathan know?"

"I can't answer that, Mary. Jonathan never sowed
wild oats. You are probably his first and only. Yet nature should have told him somehow."

Again Mary was struck with the unbelievable fact
of herself and Aaron sitting facing each other cross-
legged on a bed, drinking chokecherry wine and talking about this. She knew it was more than their long
friendship that made it possible, that it stemmed also
from something Aaron had learned in the city, and she
wanted to confirm that, yet she couldn't ask about it.
She looked into her glass of wine, screwing up some
courage.

"It wasn't just nature that told you . . . was it,
Aaron?"

"Mary, if I answer that, you must promise not to
let it matter to you, because it doesn't matter to me."

He watched her nod.

"You know why I went to the city, don't you?" He
didn't wait for a reply, for none was needed. "I felt in
the way here. I thought if I left the house to you and
Jonathan, the two of you might have more success . . .
more privacy. I've always known what it would mean
to both of you to have a family, and I knew that my
being here wasn't helping matters between you. And
so I went. But the city is a hard place, Mary. There
are times a man needs a friendly face, and out of the
hundreds all around him there isn't one, at least none
he's familiar with. It's like a whole different world
there. The factories are nothing but grinding piles of
men and machines. And people are treated as if there's
no difference between the two. You work your shift
with the stink of sweat that's never dried all around
you—no sun to dry it, nothing green. Nobody who
cares a damn if it's you there at the machine the next
day or somebody else. Just a poke in the ribs and a
'get goin', Bucko' from the boss-man when you slow
your pace. It's not Moran Township, Mary."

He paused momentarily, looking into his glass.

"It was the longest year of my life, and the only
thing that made it human was a bit of feeling another
human being was near me now and then. There were
women in the factory who were used to seeing pasty-
faced boys with slack muscles, looking like they'd
crawled out from under a rock. I guess they didn't
mind a bit of me now and again, for at least I had color
and strength from the farm. It was those women who
taught me something about what a woman needs. But
they were just warm bodies to remind me that I was
still alive. They knew their way around men, I'll say
that for them. But not one of them is worth one hair

from your precious head, Mary." And he reached out to put a finger under her chin and raise it so their eyes could meet.

All he'd been saying had created an ache within her, the ache of knowing Aaron's loneliness and the ache of knowing herself to be loose, like those women in the city.

"I'm not better than those women, Aaron, I . . ."

"Don't you ever say that again."

She turned her head to free her lips. "I'm married to one man and bedded with another, and I find I can't even be sorry. I've wronged them both, and I can't find guilt for it."

"You have not wronged me, Mary. What we're sharing is too good, too right to call it wrong."

"And what about Jonathan?" she asked.

"Yes, what about Jonathan? What about my brother who threw you at my feet, traded you off so he could gain a sire?"

"None of that can excuse me or the injustice I've done to Jonathan."

"Injustice? Mary, he deserves every injustice in the book after what he asked of you, and all that hypocritical claptrap he comes up with can't excuse him."

"What about us, though, Aaron? Doesn't the same hold true for us?"

"I'm not making excuses, Mary. I don't feel the need to. I'm not using Jonathan's wishes as a crutch, either. What happened between us happened like a wholesome, growing thing, too good for excuses. I don't need to be excused."

There was a shine of lantern light in her eyes as she looked at him, confessing the rightness she felt about herself and Aaron. Seeing that confession in her face, he said, "Last night you said two people don't have to be friends or playmates to fall in love, remember?"

She nodded silently.

"And I told you that sometimes it makes it more fun."

"Oh, but Aaron, I never knew."

"Mary, until last night I really didn't, either."

The touch of Aaron's hand on her cheek turned her to sweet, shaking jelly as he pulled her forward and kissed her. But their crossed knees got in the way between them, so he took the glass from her and set it on the floor, along with his own, stretching out across the width of the bed to do so. Then he looked up at Mary and reached his hand out to her. And she took it and let him pull her down beside him, beside Aaron, her friend, her teacher, her lover—Aaron, who now seemed all things to her.

He began the magic his hands had played on her last night, but before he could take her gown from her, she sat up and turned the lantern off, knowing he had no intention of doing so himself. They loved again in the dense blackness. It carried the wealth of his murmured endearments, teaching her the way of words before all spoken sounds dissolved.

Chapter

11

$\mathcal{T}$he drone of low thunder brought Aaron awake in the gray, early dawn. It was muffled, but accentuated by a steady rain. He lay very still, hoping it wouldn't wake Mary. She was laying on her side facing him, and the blankets were tucked under her armpit. Some of her hair was way over on his pillow, and if he turned his head he'd be lying on it. He eased onto his side, facing her, moving by inches so she'd not awaken. When he'd completed his quarter turn, he lifted up his arm and held it aloft. Then, moving ever so slowly, he pulled the sheets up and away from Mary's chest. Her arm over the covers held them pinioned to her side, but Aaron pulled gently from his direction, feeling the bedding sliding a cool path across his own body until he had enough slack to lay it all over Mary's arm. Then at last he saw all of Mary, curved and curled up slightly in slumber, as beautiful as he'd imagined her. Her skin was smooth at first, but as he looked at her, he saw goosebumps form on it as the damp, cool air touched her. Watching her breasts, he saw them shrivel, too, with the chill that touched them. He was afraid the coolness would wake her, so he turned the blankets back over her. She roused a bit, turned over on her other side, facing away from him. He curled his own spine to match hers and put an arm around her, pulling her into his warm curve. He went back to sleep that way.

Mary became aware of the cocoon of warmth around her. The only thing that moved as she woke up was her eyes as they opened. She felt Aaron's hand on her breast and his breath on her back, and she closed her eyes once more to better savor everything. She wished his face were in front of her so she could study it in sleep, but she contented herself with his guardian hand instead.

She knew Aaron was awake, too, when his hand began to move, gently fondling, arousing. The first thing he said to her back was, "It's raining, sweetheart."

She hummed, "Mm-hmm," in a lazy monotone.

"We can't plant corn in the rain." His hand kept kneading.

"Mm-hmm." It was hard to remember what corn he was talking about.

"We have lots of time."

"Hm-hmmm."

The nipples on her breasts were getting firm and pointed.

"Mary?"

"Hm-hmmm."

"Put your hand back here."

No answer.

Her hand was resting someplace in front of her, near her face—too far away, Aaron thought. He moved his hand down to her hard, flat belly, and he could feel her suck in the muscles that hardened it even more. Her breathing was fast and shallow. He felt her slowly begin to move her hand. When it got to her hip, under the covers, it stopped. He took his hand from her belly, and captured hers. Sliding his over the back of it, he wove his fingers in between hers and squeezed her palm hard. Then he pulled it slowly down and behind her until it rested on his body. At that instant, neither one of them was breathing, but holding their breaths in anticipation. When he felt her fingers timidly move, then wrap around the warmth of him, he expelled his breath in a near-groan. It was silent for a long time after that, and both of them had their eyes closed.

The next thing Mary felt were Aaron's hands on her shoulders, turning her to face him. She let him pull her around, keeping her hand where he'd put it. When she lay looking him full in the face, he grasped the covers, sheets and all, and very deliberately turned them down to their hips, then kicked them the rest of the way to the foot of the bed.

"Look at us, Mary," he said, but her eyes stayed riveted on his face.

"Look, Mary. We're beautiful. You shouldn't miss anything so beautiful." Her eyelids flickered the very slightest bit but she didn't lower her gaze.

"Just think about how right we are and how good, and how that makes us beautiful. You're beautiful,

Mary. I saw you before you were awake, and I swear to God I've never seen anything as beautiful as you. The only thing that could be better would be both of us together."

When she felt the warmth of his mouth, her eyes closed and her hand began moving down where it still was on his body. The lilac and lavender and rain formed the sweetest ambrosia, and they succumbed to its intoxication.

When Aaron stopped kissing her and drew back, she opened her eyes again, but he was looking down and there was a smile on his lips. She reacted as naturally as a lilac responds to the rain—she looked down, too. And once she looked she was captivated, held.

They explored each other at length, first hesitantly, then more boldly. He knelt on his knees beside her and pushed her onto her back, and his eyes and hands took their fill of her.

"There's nothing in the world as soft as this spot," he said, touching her as he said it. "I think that I can never get enough of it or of you." And he kissed the spot he'd been touching.

What made her think of Jonathan right then? She had a glimpse of Jonathan's shape above her in the dark. She remembered lying beneath him without moving and realized that after two days with Aaron they knew each other's bodies in a way she'd never known her husband's.

"How could I not know all this before? What I knew was such a small part," she said. "All that time . . ."

Aaron rose up on an elbow to look into her face,

his voice softly understanding as he said, "Let me make it up to you, Mary, if only for today."

And he did.

In spite of the rain there were chores to be done and work for both of them to fill the morning. The range was stoked up and it dried and warmed the kitchen, making it the most comfortable spot in the house. After breakfast Aaron said he'd take care of all outside chores so she wouldn't need to go out to the chickens and geese through the rain. He shrugged on a big, loose denim jacket and kissed her with his hands rubbing the base of her spine, then went out. She hummed while she set up the plank for ironing, resting the butt end on the table, the narrow end on the back of a chair. The three irons were heating on the range, and her chore began.

She worked on into the morning. She kept the fire well fed to heat the irons. She put a pan of sauerkraut on the back end of the range, lacing it with caraway and pork. The simmering mixture made a delectable odor. Through it she could smell the hot starch as she pressed the shirts. She protected their freshness by removing them from the kitchen as each one was done, keeping the food smell from them. Later on, she mixed dough and dropped it into the boiling broth, and at dinnertime she and Aaron ate the dumplings and kraut, taking the makeshift ironing board away from the table to make room for their plates.

In the afternoon, with the rain still falling and time on their hands, Aaron brought two big jackets, put one on and helped her into the other, saying, "Come on, I want to show you something." He grabbed her hand

and pulled her along after him through the puddles and showers to the granary. Depositing her inside, he ran out again to fetch the ladder.

He braced it on the rafters over her head, and she asked, "What's up there?" as he climbed up.

"You'll see," he said. He stood above her with his feet astride the beams, testing the weight of the old, crusty trunk he'd found up there two days before, when he fetched the suitcase. "Get me the rope that's hanging by the door and hand it up to me."

She got it and went up the ladder with it slung over her arm, using one hand to lift her skirt as she climbed.

Aaron was above her, looking like a giant as she gazed up at his spraddled legs.

"Be careful!" he warned.

"Be careful, yourself! You're a man, not a monkey."

"Yes, my sassy wench." He smiled down at her, taking the rope.

He tied it around the heavy trunk, grunting as he lifted it to lace the rope through the handles and under it where it rested on the beams. She was still standing on the ladder looking up at him when he finished, asking, "Can you tie a decent knot?"

"Hmph!" was all she replied as she reached toward him for the rope. He tossed it back to her, and she went down the ladder and looped it around an upright, leaving slack in it before tying the end to another upright. Then she came back to the slack near the first post and grabbed the rope, saying, "Okay, Aaron."

He wondered just how okay it was as he watched her apprehensively from above, but with an appreciative smile on his face. Standing below him, hanging onto the rope, she looked like the weight of the trunk would catch her and whip her up and over the beam like a sunfish on the end of a cane pole. But he bent down and began easing the trunk over the beam. Just as it was ready to drop free, he warned, "Here goes!" and lowered it over. Then he quickly dropped to his seat, lowered himself to a hanging position, and let go to drop into the oats below. He was at her side seconds after she'd taken the full weight of the trunk, and he eased the looped rope around the upright with slapping, uncoiling motions until the trunk rested safely in the oats.

"This had better be worth it, Aaron Martin Gray!" she scolded, jabbing at his belly with one small finger.

"Let's find out, Mary Ellen Gray!" And they knelt down in the oats and took the rope off and pushed the trunk around until it lay level on the grain. He opened the lid and folded back some white cotton pieces and exposed a black suit of some dull, heavy fabric.

"What is it, Aaron?" she asked, peering inside inquisitively.

"It's clothes of my mother's and father's," he said, taking the white piece and laying it on the oats as a bed for the black suit and the other pieces to follow. He lifted out the garments and held each one up, all of them plain and wrinkled and dusty. There were sack coats and fitted coats before they came to one dark chesterfield with a matching waistcoat and pants. Below that were women's dresses, all plain until at the bottom, wrapped in its own separate liner, was a garment of crackling ivory satin. When Aaron picked it up and lifted it, Mary cooed a soft, appreciative sound and looked up admiringly as Aaron held the dress raised above them.

"It must've been something in its day," she said.

"It was my mother's wedding dress," Aaron said.

The rucked ivory still had a sheen, even after all the years it had lain interred. The leg-of-mutton sleeves ended in a point at each wrist, where tiny seed pearls trimmed the edges. More seed pearls and satin braid were sewn in intricate whorls across the bodice and down the front, where it narrowed to a tiny waist that flared out in a peplum at the hip. The high choker collar was trimmed in ruching that still stood stiff and firm. Up the center front ran uncountable satin loops that encircled pearl buttons. The skirt was flat in the front, and Mary said, "Turn it around." When he did, she saw the dirndled rear where it must once have puffed out behind the pleated tail of the bustled bodice.

"Oh, Aaron, your mother must have been so proud to wear it."

He lowered it and draped it over the opened lid of the trunk and began unhooking the front buttons.

"She showed it to me once when I was a little boy, but I'd forgotten about it until the other day when I saw the old trunk up here."

Mary picked up the old gray chesterfield coat and asked, "Was this your father's wedding suit, too?"

"I don't know, but maybe, since it's the fanciest one here. Somehow I can't imagine him in it. He was much bigger when he died."

"I wish I had known them," Mary said.

"Oh, you'd have loved them. Pa had an everlasting smile on his face, and he could taste Ma until she'd have liked to throw him out. At least she pretended she'd like to. But in the end they'd always wind up laughing. He could always make her laugh no matter how serious she pretended to be.

"I reckon you got a lot of your pa in you," Mary ventured.

"It'd be nice if I did. I got a little of both of them in my name, anyway. I'm not sure where they got the 'Aaron' from. But Ma's name was Martinek. When her folks came from the Old Country they shortened it to Martin. Pa's family name was Sedivy, but in English that means Gray. Ma was always so taken with the name she gave me, said it was a 'prideful' name."

"What was she like?" Mary asked, seeing his hands on his mother's old wedding dress. Aaron dropped both hands to his thighs as he knelt in the grain, remembering.

"Oh, she was little, like you, and always in a hurry, and she was a hell of a housekeeper—made us help her turn out the entire house every spring, Jonathan and me, and she'd jump around like a banty rooster giving orders and making the dust fly. She could gossip along with the best of 'em, but woe unto the one who spread any gossip about her or hers."

He laughed at the memory. Mary laughed along with him but ended by saying, "I never knew about your name, before, Aaron. I guess . . . well, I guess I'm lucky to have at least part of that prideful name. I think I would have liked them both."

"I know they'd have liked you, Mary. I know they'd be happy at the choice Jonathan made."

At the mention of his name Mary grew sober, but Aaron stood and picked up the ivory gown, saying, "I want to see it on you."

"On me?" She looked wide-eyed back at him with a hand on her chest in surprise. "But Aaron, I don't feel like I should. It doesn't seem right to put on some-one else's wedding gown."

"I don't think my mother would mind. Besides, it was made for a slim little thing like you. Let's give it a treat, after all its years in that musty old trunk."

She looked at it appreciatively and touched the del-icate seedwork on it.

"Do it for me?" he asked.

"All right, Aaron, on one condition. You put on your father's gray chesterfield suit."

"All right, it's a deal," he agreed.

They were still standing in the oat bin. They took off their big jackets and threw them down on the grain. The rain kept falling, and it tittered across the roof, as if enjoying their whimsy along with them. The big door was open, and the misty gray light was enough for them to see by. The cool draft from outside gave them shivers as they took off their outerwear. Aaron had trouble standing on one foot in the shifting grain, so he sat down in it instead, complaining that it bit his skin. He had to pick some oat kernels out of his under-wear before he drew on the gray trousers.

Folded inside them had been a very yellowed shirt with a ruffled front that must have been more than dandy in its day. He put it on under the chesterfield, and when he was all dressed, stood and watched Mary struggling with the numerous pearl buttons on her bod-ice. She had started working them from the waist, so he made his way to her in four mushy steps and began helping her, from the neck downward. The whalebone framing inside the bodice extended up into the high neck and prevented her from lowering her chin with any ease. So she looked up at Aaron and felt her way up the remaining buttons until their hands met. Then she dropped hers and let him finish the buttons.

When he'd done up the last one, he reached for her hand and backed off a step to bend low over it and kiss it, saying, "You look lovely, young wench."

She curtsied deeply and wobbled, losing her balance on the grain. "Likewise, my lord," she laughed.

When she straightened again, he took her other hand and, holding both of her hands loosely between his, said, "I love you, Mary. You know that, don't you?"

Tears suddenly welled up in her eyes, and she didn't try to hide them from him but looked at him squarely and answered, "Yes, Aaron. I know that."

"Do you love me?" he asked, and a tear rolled off her cheek while she tried to stop it from staining the precious old ivory satin.

"Oh, Aaron, I do. I love you so very much."

He gripped her hands more tightly and looked at her, standing slim in the beautiful old wedding dress, and said, "You will always be my beautiful bride. If I could, I'd dress you in this gown for our wedding and give you the rest of my name."

Her tears were falling freely now, and as he took her in his arms, her face was lost in the old yellowed ruffles of his shirtfront. He rocked her as they clung together, and as they swayed, the oats gave way beneath their feet. They stumbled a bit, off balance, but righted themselves again.

The rain was wearing itself out, disintegrating into a soggy mist, when Aaron and Mary packed away the lovely old things in the trunk again. They were sadly quiet. The trunk was too heavy to hoist back up again, so Aaron slid it into a corner of the oat bin, saying, "The mice won't get into it. It's made too well. I'll have Jonathan help me put it back up someday."

They climbed out of the oat bin then and stood in the open aisle in front of the door. Aaron put his arm around Mary, and she dropped her head into the hollow of his shoulder. They stood like that a long time, watching the misty rain outside.

They saw the vague outline of the horse and rider come over the rise of the road from the east and disappear from their view as the barn came between them and him.

"What time did the stationmaster say the train comes in?" she asked.

"Three-fifteen P.M.," he answered, but he needn't have bothered. They knew it was Jonathan. They saw the man and his mount again, nearer now, and Aaron pulled Mary back into the shadow of the granary to hold her one last time. He kissed her so hard she could feel her own teeth cutting into her top lip. Both of her arms were around his neck, and she strained her body into his, feeling nothing but the bulky work jackets between them as he cinched her in arms that were already feeling the loneliness of not holding her, even before it came to be so.

"Just remember that I love you, even though I can't say it or show you how much," Aaron said, his hand at the back of her head, pulling it against him.

"Aaron . . ." she choked, but he pushed her gently away, saying, "Go feed the geese now."

Then he grabbed a gunnysack of grain and tipped it up to half fill a pail standing near the door. He turned up his collar before stepping out and heading for the well in the yard.

Chapter 12

Jonathan had had a miserable ride from town. He'd thought about waiting for the weather to lift, but it looked like it had settled in to stay, so he'd put on his oldest jacket, tied the suitcase onto the back of his mare, and headed for home. Coming up the last stretch of home road, he saw Aaron by the well, raised a hand in greeting, and Aaron waved back. When he brought the horse to a stop near his brother, Aaron said, "You had a wet ride, Jonathan."

"Yup. We're both soaked clear through. I'd better get the horse in the barn right away." And he clicked a sound that sent the mare the rest of the way to the barn door. Once inside, Jonathan took care of the horse thoroughly, disregarding his own discomfort in favor of the animal. He dried her down and brushed her, then caparisoned her with a warm wool blanket as Aaron came in with the milk pails.

"How was your trip?" he asked.

"Successful," replied Jonathan.

"You found the Blank Angus to your liking?"

"I not only liked them . . . I bought one." There was an excited expression on Jonathan's face as he said it. He was drying the saddle kneeling on one knee on the floor. Aaron began the milking.

"Well, that was fast work. Where is he?"

"He'll be shipped on the train at the end of the week. He's a real fine little beauty, Aaron. That he is."

Aaron wondered how long it would be before Jonathan remembered the wife he hadn't seen in three days. He was rubbing the leather off that saddle, and it was well past dry.

"Yessir, a little beauty," Jonathan repeated ruminatively and gave the saddle a slap, then stood up.

"Maybe you better get out of those wet clothes before you catch your death," Aaron said. "I'll do the chores by myself tonight."

"I appreciate it, Aaron. I'm mighty chilly, at that." He left the saddle there rather than take it through the rain to the lean-to. He figured Mary must be up in the house fixing supper, for there was a light burning in the kitchen. It'd sure be nice to get out of these soggy clothes and into some dry ones, he thought.

She turned toward the door as he came in, saying, "Hello, Jonathan. How was your trip?" just like Aaron had asked.

"Fine," Jonathan answered. "I'd like to get out of these wet things before I tell you about it, though."

"Do that and I'll heat the kettle," she said, turning back to the stove.

Upstairs, the dry, warm clothes felt soothing after

the chafing, wet ones he'd suffered on the ride home. It felt good to be home again. The house had the faint, musty smell of sauerkraut, not at all unpleasant. He wondered if they'd had it for dinner. He wondered, too, as he carried his wet stuff back downstairs, how much corn they'd got planted and if it had rained all day today. It'd be good for the new seeds, but at the same time it had probably delayed the last of the planting.

"This rain will sure bring the crops up. Did it rain all day?" he asked, coming back into the kitchen.

"Aha, it's been at it like this since before dawn," Mary said. She was glad Aaron was still outside doing chores. It made it somewhat easier for her to face Jonathan again. He had laid his wet clothing in a heap in the wet sink, and it irked her, for she was busy with the food and supper. Aaron wouldn't do that.

"Would you mind drawing up a chair by the stove and hanging your stuff over it to dry?"

He was the slightest bit taken aback, not because he minded doing it but because she'd never requested such a thing before. She always just took care of things like that. He did as she asked, though, then stayed near the stove to take the chill off himself.

"I bought us that Black Angus," he said, rubbing his hands above the radiating heat, and she was relieved that he hadn't approached her for a kiss of greeting. "He's a real beauty, too. Promises to be a fine, healthy stud."

The remark hung on Mary in a strange and formidable way, and she opened her memory's door for only a fraction of a second to let in the thought that, after all, it was the reason Jonathan had made the trip—to gain a fine, healthy stud. She felt the hot sting of guilt; then she quickly closed that hidden door and answered her husband.

"It's what you went for. I'm happy you got what you wanted, Jonathan." Her voice betrayed none of her real thoughts.

"Wait'll you see him, Mary."

She busied herself cooking while Jonathan raved on about all he'd seen and done at the Cattle Exposition, describing the bull he'd bought, the plans he had for it, talking so animatedly that he was unaware of Mary's lack of response.

Aaron came in with the milk pails while Mary dished up supper, and he went directly to the breakfront and took out clean dish towels to wet and cover the pails, taking them to the buttery to cool. It puzzled Jonathan why Mary hadn't come forward to get the dish towels for the pails as she'd always done, but then supper was on and he forgot about it.

The suppertime talk was all of the trip and the bull; very little about the trip, actually, but much about the beautiful Black Anguses Jonathan had seen firsthand, their characteristics, their assets, and their future. Mary remained quiet, but Aaron encouraged his brother with questions about the calf. They discussed the pasture situation and the extra fodder that would be required for the winter. The barn was big enough to hold the extra animal, but when he began siring calves, their present barn might be outgrown, even though the Angus calves would be marketable at a much earlier age than other breeds.

Talking of the Angus's calm disposition and even temperament, they decided that ringing his nose would not be necessary, as it was with most bulls. Jonathan said that the American Breeders' Association strongly urged that all pure-bred Angus calves that were registered be given a name to make identification easier.

"Since the owner has already registered the birth, his name is recorded as Vindicator," said Jonathan with pride. "I'm sure anxious for you to see him, Aaron. We'll ride in with the double box on Friday to meet that train."

Then a bursting double sneeze issued from him, and an involuntary shiver followed it.

"I think you caught a chill coming home," Mary said.

"Maybe I did. It might be best if I went up to bed with a warm bri-hi-hi-hick-achoo!"

Mary got up to fetch the brick that was used as a door-stop to hold the pantry door open. She put it on the hottest part of the range to hurry it hot, instead of in the oven, as usual. She lifted the lid and used the poker to stir the fire up. She fetched a bottle of camphorated oil for Jonathan's chest, but when she brought it, saying she'd rub it on for him, he took it from her and said he'd do it upstairs if she would give him a rag to tie around his neck. She found one in the pantry, the one from which she'd torn the piece for her hair, just yesterday morning. Jonathan bade them a weary goodnight and left, armed with oil and rag.

"I'll bring the brick up as soon as it's hot," Mary called after him. "The basswood trees are in bloom. I'll brew you some basswood tea, too. That should stave off a cough."

When she turned to begin clearing the table, she found that Aaron had already started it.

*   *   *

Jonathan lit the lamp so he could see what he was doing with the oil and also to give Mary some light to see by when she brought the brick up. When he'd attended to his anointing and tied the rag around his throat, there were steps sounding up the stairs. It was Aaron who came in with the hot brick, however, all wrapped in newspaper and a Turkish towel.

"Thanks, Aaron," Jonathan said, his nose already stuffed up.

"Mary's busy doing dishes, so I thought I'd bring this up."

Jonathan had turned back the coverlet and the bed-clothes, way down to the foot of the bed so he could place the brick parcel there to warm his feet. The sheets were fragrant with fresh-air smell, and he was happy to get back to his own bed once again. Aaron had a blank look on his face as he watched Jonathan put the brick between the sheets. Then Jonathan spoke and Aaron moved to turn off the lamp before he left.

As Jonathan eased his weary body into the downy comfort of the bed, he was remembering the look on Aaron's face. He reached underneath and pulled the header of the sheet out and over the blankets and smoothed it under his arms. As he did so, he realized the sheets were freshly laundered. Had they not been slept on? But hadn't Mary said it had been raining since dawn? If that were so, then she must have washed the sheets yesterday—Monday was always washday, anyway. The fresh-air smell was too pungent for them to have come out of the bureau.

There was no denying it. These sheets had been washed yesterday but not slept on last night. And faster than he could catch it, the idea that had been running around the back of Jonathan's mind since the start of his trip began to take hold. *Mary had not slept in this bed last night.*

Jonathan paused and drew a long, slow breath. The only other bed in the house was Aaron's. The look on Aaron's face, the unused sheets—yes, even a small change of routine in the kitchen. It all came together in an instant, bringing a sudden vast hollowness to the inside of Jonathan Gray. And as he lay in his own fresh bed, that hollowness began to spread, making a place for second thoughts, thoughts it was now too late to consider.

As Mary climbed the stairs later, she was thinking over what Aaron had told her before she left him sitting in the kitchen. On the one hand, perhaps she should have thought about the unwrinkled sheets. On the other, it was as Aaron had said: what they'd done, they'd done, and it was too late now to undo it. Rumpling the sheets intentionally would have been a low, sneaky thing to do, and Mary wasn't capable of it.

She wondered if Jonathan knew now, then realized she'd be foolish to assume he didn't. Whatever the case, Jonathan was back, and she must make the best she could of her life with him. It had always been a good life before, and it would be again. What the outcome between herself and Aaron would be had been a question she'd not delved into.

Lying in the bed beside Jonathan as he slept fitfully, she turned a key in her heart that would lock in forever the beautiful memory of what she and Aaron had shared, and lock out any more of the same. Jonathan was back, and with him had returned her common sense. This was the man with whom she must live, and the sooner she resumed that life, the less hurt would come to all concerned. There could be no question of leaving one man for another.

In the kitchen below, Aaron was trying not to think. Mary was back in bed beside her husband. He, Aaron, was again on the outside. He must take up the question of what to do about himself and Mary, but he would wait a few days. For now he would content himself with the fact that Mary loved him and he loved her.

The rain left Moran that night, and the town awoke under a brilliant late May sun that warmed it for the remainder of the week. Routine returned, and the warm days saw Jonathan and Aaron completing the last of the planting. Mary stayed pretty much to the house and chicken coop. It was nearly time for the chicks to hatch. They would be followed a week later by the goslings, each flock numbering about fifty if all went well. It would bring a tidy profit when she butchered them in the autumn.

Mary neither avoided Aaron nor sought him out, but treated him as she always had in the old days. She was aware of his many and constant considerations for her, and they couldn't help but warm her heart.

In spite of his second thoughts about Mary and Aaron, Jonathan found he could not question either of them about it. Although it hovered around his mind, he was wrapped up with happy expectations for Saturday, the day the bull would arrive. The week seemed to drag until the awaited afternoon came at last. Aaron had agreed to make the trip into town with him, but Mary declined, saying she was tired and would like to wash her hair with the water from the rain barrel while they were gone. But she sent her shopping list along with the men as they set out in the double box wagon.

The subject of Mary never came up between the brothers during their ride, for the subject of fences kept them in conversation all the way as they laid plans to fence off a piece of woods adjacent to the rich, wild hayfield and connect it with gates to a lane leading to the barnyard. The wood for the fence posts would come from the woods themselves, and the proximity to the wild hay would make it easy to turn the bull into that field for foraging, once the initial hay crop had been put up in early July. June would give them time to do the fencing, for their main responsibility then would be only the cultivating of corn and potatoes.

They arrived well before train time in Browerville, saw to the list Mary had sent along, went to the hardware store to inquire about barbed wire, and were at the railway station in plenty of time to catch the drifting sound of the whistle as the wind blew it in from the south. They saw smoke from the pufferbelly before they saw the engine itself. Memories of the last time they'd stood on the waiting platform were in both of their minds, but for both it was easier to blot it out and think about the arrival of the bull.

The door of the cattle car was run open and a ramp put up. The head of a black bull appeared at the top of the ramp. He eyed his reception committee and pulled his head back with a complaining bawl. But Jonathan walked up the ramp then, and the animal stopped his balking and followed docilely down the ramp. Jonathan brought him up near the side of the wagon and tied his rope halter onto the end of it so that he could walk clear around the bull to admire him.

"Isn't he a beauty, Aaron?" he asked, rubbing the sleek black coat on the bull's sides and back.

"He sure is," Aaron agreed.

"You are my little beauty, aren't'cha, Vindicator?" Jonathan asked the bull. "Vindicator seems like a mighty fancy name for a little feller like you, though. How's about I call you Vinnie? Would you like that?" He leaned near the bull's ear to ask it. But the animal became skittish with the closeness of the man and pushed his head downward until the rope was taut.

Aaron and Jonathan both laughed at the feisty creature, trying to look so mean but with the facial expression of a lovable baby.

"Come on, Vinnie," Aaron laughed, "let's take you aboard and get you home. The ladies are waiting."

Mary was sitting on the porch steps as they arrived with the bull. When the wagon was used for small loads, the men put a single tier of planks around it. Then it was called a "single box." Now, decked with a second, higher tier of planks, the "double box" hid the bull entirely from Mary as the wagon pulled into the yard. Her first glimpse of him was from behind as Jonathan lifted the backboards free. He was so thoroughly and completely proud of his creature that she hadn't the heart to do anything less than join in his enthusiasm. She really couldn't see what all the hoopla was about, but Jonathan was certainly agog with it. He called the calf Vinnie already, nicknaming it as he would a child. He patted and rubbed it, admiring its cylindrical shape, and low-set body in spite of the gangly, youthful legs. By the time he and Aaron led Vinnie down to the barn, Mary had heard Jonathan bestow more gentle words on it than he ever had on her. The animal inspired a depth of feeling in Jonathan that she'd never been able to.

During the days when June eased her way over the countryside and Moran felt the full flush of the simmering summer sun, Jonathan and Aaron worked on the fencing project, the subject of Mary still tacit between them. They felled small trees, trimmed them, and sawed them into equal lengths. As the stack of fence posts grew, so did the weeds in the potato patch. Aaron broke the stride of their activity to begin the first cultivating. The change of pace was welcome after the arduous days of woodcutting. Jonathan took his turn at cultivating, too, and when the potatoes were once again weed-free, the corn patch fell under curved blades.

Mary was feeling the strain. It was easy enough for her to say she must reconcile herself to her life with Jonathan, but her mind slipped too often into memories of Aaron. She worked hard, using work as an antidote for depression. She hoed the garden, pinched the tops of the newly sprigged seedlings of vegetables and annual flowers, that pinching of stems tinting her thumb green, that "green thumb" making the garden thrive. But this year she seemed to find less satisfaction in gardening. The strawberries were already ripe, and she put up the first of her summer preserves, putting aside several special jars to give to her cousin Catherine for her wedding. Not even the thought of the up-coming wedding celebration could lift her spirits. Most days, the hard, hot work was wearying, and she felt it wear her down long before the day ended. Sometimes the chore of canning seemed too enormous a task for her to handle. It was a small amount of work compared to what would follow when the bulk of the garden crops matured, but that didn't seem the way of it as the berries continued to ripen and needed daily picking if they weren't to be sacrificed to the birds. She had tried picking the partially ripened berries and holding them in the cellar for a few days, but it made even more work because they reddened at varying times and necessitated an extra sorting and handling each day. They ate as many fresh berries with cream as they could, but still more needed putting up.

She had spent a sickening, hot morning in the berry patch, squatting and stooping until the sun and the posture made her dizzy. When she finally finished picking and went to wash the berries at the barnyard well, the icy water was pure, sweet relief as she dunked her wrists into it. Then she took the berries up to the house and sat at the kitchen table to pick their green caps off during the time remaining before dinner. The house was quiet, and outside sounds were soothing. Here inside the kitchen the strawberries made a pinging sound as they hit the bottom of the dishpan.

It was times like these, lax times when her guard was down, that Mary's thoughts strayed to Aaron. They seemed to move apace with the pinging berries. You know there can be no more between us, Aaron, she thought, so why don't you go off down to the hall Saturday nights anymore? If you went, and I know you should, do you know how it would break my heart? But I have no right to you, nor you to me, so why continue salving so deep a wound when we both know that a swift cauterizing is what it needs? Did you know the lines are as deep as scars between your eyes these days? Your daddy's smile and teasing are gone from you, and I cannot reach to smooth away the worry from your face as I once did.

Jonathan and Aaron had spent a morning of near-misery digging holes for the posts and setting them in under the hot sun. They were more than ready for a good, refreshing meal and a sitdown afterward. Coming in the back door to the kitchen, they saw Mary slumped over the kitchen table with one limp arm sprawled across the oilcloth and her cheek resting on it. Fear flashed through both men simultaneously, and they exclaimed at the same time:

"Oh, God . . ."

"Mary . . ."

Both men were at her side in the second it took to jump from the doorway to her chair. It happened that Aaron gained the side toward which her head was turned, and he saw her slack mouth pushed distortedly against the table-top, opened slightly. A very small, very delicate snore snuffled from her half-flattened nostrils. Her right hand was in a kettle of strawberries on her lap, and her left rested against a dishpan on the table near her head.

"She's sleeping, Jonathan," Aaron said as soon as he recognized the fact. Seeing her there like that, Aaron had a sudden flash of beautiful memories of her asleep in his bed. Too beautiful! He stepped back and let Jonathan awaken her, going to the sink to wash up so he wouldn't have to watch the two of them together.

To his amazement, the first utterance from her as she woke was, "Aaron?" He began working the pump handle to create some diversion in the room, so he didn't hear his brother's reply.

They had an unusually quiet lunch that day, the only real talking done by Mary, who repeatedly apologized for the second-rate meal she slammed together in lieu of hot food. At the end of the meal she promised them a hot supper, but food was not really uppermost in their minds. Both men were hearing again Aaron's name as Mary had murmured it in her half-conscious state. It was the nearest thing to an endearment that Aaron had heard since she'd told him she loved him in the rainy granary. It was the only hint Jonathan had that he might have been right. Mary knew she'd been dreaming of Aaron when Jonathan woke her up, and was glad that dreams could be perceived by nobody but the dreamer. She didn't remember reaching out a caressing hand to Jonathan's face as she spoke Aaron's name.

Chapter

13

$\mathcal{T}$he end of June was nearing. This was the last time of comparative restfulness before the onslaught of long harvesting hours. It was a time that lent itself well to weddings. The entire township was looking forward to Catherine Garner's and Michael Garek's wedding, for everyone was invited. Mary looked forward to it with relief, for it would bring relaxation that she sorely needed.

During the week preceding the great day, she imagined all the activity going on at the Garner house and offered to help Aunt Mabel with the preparations, but the red-faced woman shook her head, wattles rippling beneath her chin, and bellowed, "You done enough for me in years past, girl, and I got a tribe of my own to crack the whip to. You stay home and take care of those two big louts of yours, and don't show your face at my place until you're ready to have yourself a proper fling!" Appealing to her cousin Catherine did no good, either, for Mabel Garner would have her way, so Mary's help was refused.

But the entire Garner family was put to work for days. While Aunt Mabel and the girls cooked and baked, Uncle Garner and the boys prepared makeshift dinner tables and benches, which would seat the crowd in the farmyard. Also constructed was a wooden platform to serve as an open-air dance floor. Those too busy helping in the kitchen on a wedding day often returned on the next evening to take their enjoyment on the dance floor. If it rained, the dancing would be held either in the partially empty hayloft or in the living room of the house. Mabel Garner said she'd be damned if any of her neighbors found a cobweb or smatter of dust behind her furniture, and she pushed her brood of children to work cleaning the already spotless house. But for once they didn't mind because their mother, though an exacting taskmistress, was in the height of good humor.

Across Moran Township, men hurried through their chores before cleaning up and dressing for the long-awaited event. Some of these looked forward to the rarity of being excused from evening chores, having arranged for neighboring youngsters to tend these for them. Failing this, for most of the youngsters would also be attending the festivities, many hoped to convince some young lad to leave the regaling at dusk, long enough to do the chores. As the day progressed and kegs of beer were consumed by the men, they would become generous. Many a lad would end the day with a well-greased palm in return for taking care of someone's evening chores.

*   *   *

Mary wore the yellow dimity dress again, and although she kept her hair in the familiar knotted coil, she wore it pushed higher on her head, sweeping it back from her center part rather than down over her ears. She left Jonathan closing the kitchen windows and door and walked toward the rig. Aaron jumped down to hand her up. She'd pulled on only her left glove. He reached out to take her bare right hand, and as he did so, his back was to the house, shielding her from Jonathan's view. He brushed her hand with his lips, and with a relaxed smile, said, "Mary girl, you look beautiful."

She withdrew her hand as if it had been burned, and quickly pulled her glove on. I've been doing so well all these weeks, she thought. I won't let my resolve slip now. Still, Aaron's manner held a trace of his old brotherliness, so she put on her own old way and responded, "Likewise, sir. The groom himself might feel overshadowed." Then she jumped up into the carriage seat. And everything seemed okay between the two of them again.

Jonathan could hear them bantering as he approached the rig.

"I know what's in the fruit jars I carried out, but what's in the other package under the seat, Mary?"

"It's the bean jar I had you and Jonathan buy last week when you went to town."

"Isn't that just like a woman? Here I've been expecting a mess of pork and beans to show up in that pot on our dinner table, but instead, I find it wrapped for another man's table."

"And isn't it just like a man to buy a wedding gift

and expect to try it out before he gives it away?" she rejoined.

Their laughter seemed genuine, and Jonathan joined in, thinking how good it was that they were all in a good humor again. It seemed as if there'd been too little laughter the last few weeks. He refrained from thinking of the probable cause of the strain that was beginning to show around the edges of their lives. Today the strain seemed to have gone. It promised to be a grand day.

The churchyard was filled with noisy Garners. Waving a greeting to the Grays, Mabel Garner yelled, "Ain't this some day? Somebody said there was a weddin' here today so I come along, but damned if I know whose 'tis. Can't be none of my own, 'cause I sure ain't feelin' old enough to be a mother-in-law yet!"

Uncle Garner was spit-shined and smiling, proud of the robust woman on his arm. "Mother, you don't look old enough," he said, and for once her bellowing was silenced. There was a pleased gleam in her eye as Uncle Garner ushered her toward the church door.

The vows were spoken. Catherine was radiant and Michael was nervous and Mary cried. The church was crowded and stuffy. Women fanned themselves with gloves and prayer books. Toward the end of the service Mary felt the closeness become dizzying. But then the service ended and the back doors opened to let the air flow in. The new bride and groom ran out, followed by their parents and the rest of the congregation, their ears buffeted by Mabel Garner's voice even before they reached the doors.

Everyone repaired to the bride's home, the line of wagons, carriages, and calashes raising dust down the gravel road all the way from the church to the Garner farm four miles away. When all the guests had arrived, the yard was dotted thickly with wagons. The horses were turned into the near, fenced pasture, for they would spend a long day here. Their wedding feast would be the lush June grass. It was a day for children to pick up a prized penny or two by unhitching horses from the pasture when a guest left. At a gathering like this, the kids outnumbered the adults, and the yard swarmed with them. Ladies were kept busy mixing lemonade and nectar at the well to keep the thirsty young horde happy. As the day wore on, some would be sick from too much sweet stuff and some would be tipsy from the beer they'd nipped when glasses were left unattended by grown-ups.

Uncle Garner had tapped the beer kegs under a shady tree and by the end of the day the grass would be flattened there, the mud smelling yeasty where the spigots had dripped. In another spot in the yard, ice cream was being frozen, and the call went up for another able-bodied man to turn the crank. Children ran past the washtub and stole any ice they could lay a hand on, considering it nearly as big a treat as the ice cream would be. Ice was a precious commodity in June. Uncle Garner had chopped it from a frozen pond in March, hauled it from there to his icehouse, packed it with insulating sawdust, and kept it frozen all these weeks.

Mabel Garner's front parlor was converted to a gift room, and the packages were left there. Most gifts were wrapped in brown paper or newspaper, but many were not wrapped at all. Since brides were not showered with gifts beforehand, the collection in the parlor was impressive. A good share of these were homemade: quilts, dish towels, feather ticks, doilies, pillows, and small pieces of furniture. There was also a large assortment of kitchenware, enough to set any new household on its feet. Dishes, crocks, porcelain and iron cookware, churns, paddles, mason jars (most of them filled with home-canned foods), silverware, and a variety of small kitchen tools—Catherine would need all of these.

She cried upon entering the gift room, moved by the magnitude of Bohemian generosity.

But the kitchen was the center of activity as a raft of cooks worked to feed the guests in shifts, starting first with the impatient children. Customarily, the bride's mother was excused from kitchen duty after the week of hectic preparations she'd seen to, but Mabel Garner blustered her way in and out, saying, "That'll be the day, when a bunch of whippersnappers put me out of my own kitchen!" And she helped serve the food she and her girls had been readying all week.

There were platters piled high with *kolacky*, rich, fruit-filled breads; mushroom-shaped *kulich;* roasters filled with meat-stuffed cabbage rolls, called *sarma;* and the ever-present dumplings, studded with caraway seeds and swimming in chicken-cream gravy. Mountains of mashed potatoes were carried to the tables in the yard. Ham in thick raisin sauce raised expressions of approval and made the children's tongues circle their lips in anticipation. Coffee was brewed in two-gallon pots, the freshly ground beans mixed with raw eggs, shell and all, for Mabel Garner claimed the shells made it clear.

When the first shift of adults came to take their places at the table, the coffee had reached perfection. The children's plates and silverware were being washed for the shift of adults who'd be seated at the table next. And the food kept coming.

Above the voices in the farmyard rang the sound of horseshoes. Children had begun making darts of corncobs, sinking long chicken feathers into the soft pith centers and hurling them in contests of distance and accuracy, the corncobs spiraling through the air in perfect balance. In the crowd were master storytellers and comedians. Two buffoons appeared from downyard, one crawling on hands and knees, harnessed in Uncle Garner's horses' gear, pulling a plow manned by his friend. The crowd milled around, and their impromptu comedy gained momentum from the hoots of laughter and knee-slapping of those gathered around.

Again Mabel Garner's voice rang out above all those around her, as she called to the man holding the reins, "Seth Adams, you could plow your fields faster with the nag you're steering there than with those two old pieces of crow bait you call horses!"

And surprisingly, Uncle Garner raised his voice to tease, "Never mind her, Seth. It takes one old piece of crow bait to recognize another!" And Mabel's laughter swooped while her fist shook in her husband's direction.

It was in the middle of this merriment, as Aaron was enjoying the antics along with everyone else, that he felt a tug and, looking down, found Newt Volence pulling on his arm.

"Hi, Aaron," said Newt.

In a spontaneous action, Aaron scooped the little boy up in his arm, and Newt gave the man a big hug, pasting his sticky face against Aaron's as he did.

"How's my boy?" Aaron asked, feeling a keen pleasure at seeing the rapscallion again.

"My belly kinda hurts," the imp confessed.

"Well, I think I know why," Aaron kidded. "If your belly's filled with half as much food as your face is, it's bound to hurt!"

Newt proceeded to rub a grimy hand across a cheek and a corner of his mouth, leaving a smear of dirt plastered where only the food had been before.

"How come you never come to see me no more, Aaron?"

Much as he liked holding the boy, Aaron feared for his suit coat under Newt's grimy paws, so he set the mite down and squatted beside him.

"Been mighty busy with the planting. I had to help my brother get the crops in, you know."

"Aw, shoot, plantin's done a long time ago. How come you ain't come since then?"

"Well, I've been meaning to, but I just haven't gotten around to it lately, I guess." Then Aaron asked, "How're you getting along with that new baby?"

"Aww, he ain't no fun. He can't play with me, and everybody yells at me not to get too close to him, and I can't make no noise in the house or nothin'," the child confided. But he wasn't to be sidetracked.

"Why don't you come to my house no more, Aaron? I like you better'n that old baby, anyway."

"Well, I've just been too busy. You know Jonathan went clear down to Minneapolis on the train and bought a real special little bull calf, and we've been busy building a fence for him."

"Aw, shucks, Aaron, one little bull calf don't take much fencin'."

The child was dauntless, and as Aaron stood up, laughing, he replied, "Shucks is right! I guess Jonathan and I should have thought of that ourselves, Newt."

But just then Priscilla approached, and when she got to Newt she scolded, "Ma was wondering where you were. She said to tell you she saw you snitchin' somebody's beer and you are not to drink any more of it, you hear?"

"I hear," Newt said, scuffling a foot in the dirt, his face downcast.

Pris looked up at Aaron then, squinting into the sun. "Hello, Pris. How have you been?"

"Howdy, Aaron. I'm fine. Busier than ever, helping Ma around the house with the new baby and all."

"I says Aaron should come to see us again," Newt put in here, looking up at the couple standing high above him. "Huh, Pris?" he asked when she made no reply.

"Yeah, sure. We'd all love it, Aaron. We really would." But her voice was noncommittal.

He looked down at her pretty face and felt a lonesomeness for something she and he had missed, something they had missed together, and answered, "I'll do that again someday soon." He was sorry Newt heard it, for the little fellow would take him at his word and undoubtedly wait for the visit that would not come.

Pris gave her little brother a nudge. "Come on. Ma says she wants to talk to you and she can't leave the baby." As she herded the little boy away in front of her, he turned to wave a sticky farewell to Aaron. Aaron then heard Newt ask, his face turned up to his sister as he hurried along with her, "Hey, whatsa matter with you and Aaron?" But he didn't hear her reply.

Mary had been sitting on the grass under a linden tree at the edge of the shaded yard when the pair of comedians raised their hullabaloo. She saw the meeting between Aaron and Pris, and, try though she might, she could not stop a twinge of jealousy from constricting her heart. She didn't have time to dwell on it, though, for Aunt Mabel plopped down beside her on the grass, having finally been turned out of her own kitchen.

"Fetch me a glass of beer, sonny!" she yelled imperiously to a boy nearby. "I worked up a sweat with all that laughin'! How you doin', girl? You havin' a good time?"

"I really am, Aunt Mabel. I don't know when I've felt this relaxed. Of course, it's easy to feel that way at your place. You know, it's just like home to me."

"I still like to hear you say that, girl, and that's as it should be. Ain't none of my own girls means more to me than you."

"Well, then, you should have let me come and help you this week just like your own had to. I can tell an extra hand would have been kept busy."

"Pshaw!" Mabel Garner snorted. "I set them kids to work, and the place never knew what hit it!"

Mary couldn't help laughing. The boy came back with a glass of beer for Mabel Garner and a telltale mustache of foam on his mouth.

"You let up snitchin' that stuff, boy, or you'll be

sicker'n a hog in a barley patch!" she admonished him, then raised the glass to down half its length before smacking her appreciation and wiping her mouth with the back of her hand.

"I suspect you kept yourself busy enough without comin' to help around here this week. I seen them strawberry preserves you brung for Catherine, and they're as pretty as if I put 'em up myself."

"I put them up this week, but just barely! Aunt Mabel, you know what I did? I fell asleep cleaning berries. I don't know what came over me, but I was cleaning berries in the kitchen, sitting at the table, and I got so tired. The men were nearly due for dinner, and I knew it was time to start the meal. But before I knew what hit me, I was sound asleep and Jonathan was waking me up. I've never done a thing like that before in my life. And no dinner ready for Jonathan and Aaron. I felt so foolish!"

Mabel Garner picked a blade of grass and bit on its soft, sweet end, took a swig of beer, and said, "Used to happen to me all the time when I was first pregnant." She was looking off again at the comedians across the yard.

"When you were first pregnant?" Mary's voice was quiet. "Why?"

"Most natural thing in the world for a woman's body to call for rest with all the changes that's goin' on inside it then. Happens mostly at the beginning and the very end."

Of course, Mabel Garner knew how badly her niece missed having children of her own, and she didn't wish to raise any false hopes in her. Yet, with no mother near at hand, Mabel felt it her duty to question Mary.

Anyway, she considered herself the nearest thing to a mother Mary had, after the years the girl had lived with the Garner family.

"You had any other signs, Mary?" she asked.

"No." But she hesitated before adding. "I'm not sure what some of them might be."

"You missed any of your monthlies?"

"Not exactly. I'm a couple weeks longer than usual, but I hadn't thought much of it."

"Well now, mind, I'm not sayin' . . . it could be anything at all, but you been sick? Throwin' up or anything?"

"No."

"You feel unusually thirsty lately?"

"No."

"You get dizzy spells?"

"No."

But after she said it, Mary remembered the day in the berry patch when she'd accused the sun of making her dizzy. She'd spent hotter, longer hours in the garden before which had not affected her like that day.

"Sometimes when I have to stoop over for a time, like berry-picking, I get kind of light-headed, but I figured it was just the heat."

"Did it happen any other times?" Mabel was being very casual now, while Mary's insides were jumping and shaking and doing all kinds of monkeyshines. She sat up and hugged her knees to get a grip on herself, both inside and out.

"Just in church this morning. I felt a little light-headed, is all. But it was awfully close in there."

"You ever feel like fainting in church before?"

"No."

"Well, girl, you sure got the signs of an expectin' mother. How about hungry . . . you been awful hungry lately? You get the feelin' in your throat after you eat like the food's fillin' your whole neck?"

"I—I don't remember. I don't think so."

"Well, you watch for it. It's a sure sign you're pregnant. When you're young, you got a constitution like iron and you can eat anything. But get pregnant and your food likes to roil your insides. Even if you don't get sick, you get that full, burning feeling in your throat."

Mary was sitting there gripping her knees and looking to Mabel Garner, as if the feeling were in her throat right now.

"Now, it's too early to tell, girl. But you take care of yourself and rest a bit between chores until you know. If your monthly hasn't come in a couple of weeks, you can be pretty sure."

"Please don't tell anyone yet, Aunt Mabel."

"Don't be foolish, girl. I wouldn't take that pleasure away from you after all these years you been waitin' to do it yourself."

"Thank you . . . thanks, Aunt Mabel," Mary said, leaning over to kiss the sunburned cheek beside her. "I've got to think for a while now." Then she got up and excused herself.

Mabel Garner wasn't piqued at Mary's sudden departure. She knew she'd planted a seed of mighty long-awaited hope in Mary's heart. A thing like that'd bear some dwellin' on, and she knew Mary needed time alone to do just that.

"The good Lord's been holdin' out on that child long enough," she mused to herself, watching the slim form walk away. "It's a damn sight time He came around!"

There wasn't much space to be alone in the busy farmyard. Mary wandered among the people, returning greetings, stopping to talk when others approached her, but she avoided long conversations for she found her mind swaying with a force of its own. It was impossible to keep from touching her stomach. As if what Aunt Mabel had said was certain, she crossed her arms over her front, pulling her forearms against the place where she thought a new life lived. She knew that if it were true, the life had been placed there by Aaron, for Jonathan hadn't sought her since his return from the city. She hadn't bothered to ask herself why, for Jonathan was not a demanding husband, and found the need only occasionally. She remembered how in days past she'd sometimes had to turn his way first, when she'd been reckoning on Doc Haymes's calendar. She was accustomed to lengths of time sometimes longer than this had been, times he didn't approach her, especially at this time of the year when the field work seemed to fill him.

Jonathan was pitching horseshoes in a foursome and, watching him, she recalled how he'd requested the liaison between herself and Aaron, but it was little consolation now. Would this bring about a rift between the brothers?

He sought her out later and said he was going home to do chores and would return in time for the dancing. She smiled at him, quailing inwardly, wishing she could go home with him, for she again felt dully tired and remembered Aunt Mabel's directive to rest whenever she could. But it would look strange if she were to miss the dance, so she stayed behind. She saw Aaron stop Jonathan as he left the yard, but Jonathan motioned Aaron to stay. It stung her heart. She imagined him saying, "Should I come home and help you with the chores, Jonathan?" and her husband replying, "Naw, I'll do it. You stay." And again she envisioned an end to their brotherliness. Aaron turned as Jonathan left the yard and, seeing her studying him across the way, smiled and raised his chin in a kind of backward nod, a nonchalant greeting. She again put her arms across her stomach.

Darkness fell and lanterns were set around the yard to light the plank floor. Now and then there would be the flash of a dish towel in the lantern light as one of the women was abducted from the kitchen by an impatient partner. Mary took a turn at kitchen duty but no partners came to abduct her, and in her present mood she was grateful. The children danced on the dance floor when they could get by with it, and on the grass when they couldn't. But one by one their number dwindled as tired babies were bedded down on blankets in the straw-filled wagons to sleep while their parents raced the clock into Sunday.

Mary had lost her yen for dancing and spent the night anxious to go home, but Aaron captured her once and insisted on a dance. He was polite, though, and kept his distance. She was glad when the dance was over. He noticed how quiet she was, that she hadn't had any of her usual chatter. He made no comment, for he thought her pleasantly worn out from the day's festivities.

The long day ended well past midnight with Aunt

Mabel calling to all the leave-takers to return next day and help them finish off the remaining food and enjoy some more dancing before the floor was taken up. With the moonlight to guide them, the horses moved off homeward, bearing their weary owners. Some slept, to awaken in their own yards, finding that the horses had made their way unaided by human direction.

In their rig Mary rode home sandwiched again between Jonathan and Aaron, her stomach sometimes gently buffeted by her husband's elbow while its side rested softly against Aaron.

Chapter 14

$\mathcal{T}$he waving pastures of wild hay had begun trading their verdure for the yellowing hue of dry ripeness. Jonathan knew it wouldn't be long now until it could be cut. Standing in the hay near the edge of the pasture, he listened for the sound of it. When it was green, it whispered a sibilant s, but when it touched his ear with a *shh,* it would be ready to cut. It was saying something in between right now. He broke a piece between his fingers and found it not quite ripe enough. He tasted it. If the weather stayed dry, he'd be able to drive the team over the rich peat soil to cut the hay within a week. If it rained, the peat would hold the moisture like a sponge. The horses would sink and flounder.

He said a little prayer of supplication for good weather. Glancing at the new fence in the adjacent wooded pasture, he added another of thanks. The fenced land was a source of great pride to Jonathan. It was a reminder of Vinnie and the goal Jonathan aimed for, begun with the purchase of the black bull. In the weeks he'd been here, Vinnie had grown considerably, feeding on the plentiful, rich grass. After the cutting of the wild hay, that pasture, too, would be his to forage.

Jonathan was happy in Vinnie's company, happier than he was at nearly any other time.

Jonathan called to Vinnie and trilled a high whistle as he approached the fenced pasture where the bull was grazing. Bending to separate the strands of barbed wire, the man stepped through, then, still whistling, approached the shining black beast. When the bull blinked and Jonathan drew near, his whistling stilled and his soothing voice lay mellow on the animal's ear.

"Won't be long now, and you'll have the wild hay all to yourself. Won't be long now, and I'll know the truth about Mary . . . and Aaron. You see, I brought it about between them, so I got no cause to complain, do I, boy?" The man's calloused hand caressed the animal's black ear. "I heard tell that your kind sometimes don't lunge at the ladies like they ought. That's how it is with me right now, too. Guess you might say I got to wait till I know for sure. Don't reckon I could spend the rest of my life wondering who sired the child—if there is one. This way, I'll be sure. Some men might rather live with the doubt instead of wanting to admit their own shortcomings. But I'm not made that way. I'd have to know the truth, eh, Vinnie?

"Well, if it turns out there's a babe and it's not mine, we still got you and your strong seed. You just keep on like you are, a-growing strong, and between us we'll work things out."

The Fulfillment

With a last affectionate scratch behind an ear, the man left the pasture. Coming toward the yard, he glanced toward the sumacs behind the outhouse. They were now in full leaf, and he had no way of knowing whether she'd dried her cloths here, concealed from sight, or not. But it had been nearly two months now, and if she carried a child, she'd have to tell him soon. He wondered how long he ought to wait before he could be sure she didn't carry one. Awhile longer, he thought.

And meanwhile, Jonathan's life remained full because of Vinnie and his fields and the ripening grain. The absence of sexual fulfillment caused him no discomfort, physically or otherwise.

Mary's discomforts grew daily. The feeling that food was stuck in her throat was one of Aunt Mabel's predictions that had come true. A sudden implacable burning was there each time she ate, and to make matters worse, she ate all the time, with the hunger of a starved person. She was constantly tired. She never got a full night's sleep because she had to go to the outhouse so often during the night. Waking up in the mornings, she would drag her body from the bed, feeling she'd left her consciousness still in it. When any jot crossed her up, tears would spring to her eyes. It made her feel foolish, yet she couldn't control the tears.

One day in July she had spent at a most unpalatable but essential task, killing potato bugs. The orange-and-black insects were an inescapable plague of the farmers. As sure as potatoes were their biggest cash crop, the potato bugs were their greatest enemy. If not dealt with, the bugs would eat the fresh green leaves of the plants and sustain a healthy life, laying eggs on the undersides of the leaves so that the yellow baby bugs would continue the cycle.

Carrying a pail and stick, Mary had spent the day walking up and down the rows knocking against the potato vines with the stick and catching the falling insects in her pail. The insects were then covered with boiling water before the disgusting mess was buried in the woods behind the house.

The day had left her tired and miserable. Even a sponge bath in the late afternoon had not washed away the crawly feeling from a day spent among the bugs.

She had gone to do her evening chores, feeding and watering the goslings and chicks who were all over the barnyard these days. She filled the shallow pan with water and left it in the coop while she went to the granary for feed. But when she returned to the coop she found that the larger birds had clumsily fought for a place at the watering pan and in doing so had managed to spill the whole thing. She stood there in her long cotton skirt, hitched up into the waistband to keep the hem clean, and she felt the bird droppings that she trampled under her bare feet. She gaped at the empty pan and watched it grow watery as tears filled her eyes. Didn't those stupid chickens know how it caught her stomach muscles when she worked the pump handle these days? And those miserable geese were no better. "Look what you've done," she wailed at the dumb birds. "You spill everything I feed you, and you crap all over the yard, so I have to shovel behind you! Stupid, squawking, weak-witted . . ."

She was crying and sniffling while she poured mental imprecations on the animals, all out of proportion to the injustice they'd done her. She grabbed the pan and crossed the dung-splattered yard to the pump. Her tears came faster than the water from the pump. She was choking on her inhalations, and her limp efforts at the pump handle were made sorrier by her hanging head and slumped shoulders.

Then someone was there, taking her hand off the pump handle and turning her before she felt what she needed most—warm, comforting arms around her and a hand pulling her head into a shoulder. She buried her face and bawled, arms hanging limply at her sides under those which encircled her.

"What's the matter, Mary?" It was Aaron's voice.

She jerked up and reached for her apron pocket, but there was no handkerchief there, so she raised the apron and wiped her nose and face with it.

"You shouldn't b-be h-holding me li-like this out here," she choked in huffs. He turned her loose but kept his hand lightly on her shoulders as she struggled to clean up her face.

"You shouldn't be crying, either, so we're both doing what we shouldn't."

"I couldn't he-help it. The dumb chickens spilled their water again."

He took the pan from where she'd put it, far from where the water had been falling, and, centering it beneath the pump's mouth, began pumping.

"Spilled water shouldn't make you cry like this. What's wrong, Mary?"

She watched his feet.

"Everything's wrong," she said, hoping he'd stay his distance instead of touching her again. It had felt too good the first time.

"I know—and it's my fault," he admitted. "I can see you feel caught in the middle between Jonathan and me. I'm sorry, Mary. I mean to talk to Jonathan about it and somehow see our way clear of this situation. I've put it off because it may mean leaving this place, and this isn't a time of year the farm could stand that without suffering a loss."

"No, Aaron. You mustn't talk to Jonathan about this at all." She looked up at him then with her swollen eyes, and it was like a soothing balm to see his face, filled with concern for her. "Just let it go, Aaron. There's no other way." But the look on his face told her Aaron didn't want to let it go.

She was sure by now of her pregnancy and also that the baby was Aaron's, but she feared that by revealing it she might force him to leave, just as before. That thought was unbearable, yet she knew that the fact of her pregnancy bound her even tighter to Jonathan, for now there was even more disgrace to be suffered from leaving her husband. If she were to do that, everyone would guess that the child was Aaron's.

All these thoughts were upon her as she looked at Aaron. She thought of a life with his baby, but without him, and the misery of it was reflected in her eyes, which welled once again with tears.

"Don't, Mary . . . don't," he pleaded, seeing her tears. He felt like a puppet who'd made a careless move and entangled itself in its own strings. "You're tearing me apart. If you don't stop, I swear I'll grab you again and kiss you right here before God and my brother both."

She knew if she didn't control her tears he'd make good his threat—his promise—so she got the upper hand over her tears again, but still looked bruised. She realized the injustice of her withholding from Aaron her precious secret. Whatever it cost her, she must tell him and tell him first before Jonathan. It was the only consolation she had to offer him.

She looked quickly toward the barn, but it was quiet, the cats sitting outside the door. Oh, please, God! Don't let Jonathan come out yet, she thought before looking up at his brother, hoping that her face revealed the depth of feeling she had for him.

"What I have to tell you is the most important thing in the world to us, Aaron, but the most painful."

He took a turn glancing down at the barn before turning a puzzled, questioning look at her.

She drew in a ragged breath and tried to erase the strain from her face so that his memory of her telling him would not be grim.

"Aaron, I'm going to have a baby."

She caught the full impact of his surprise as his mouth dropped open at the same instant Jonathan emerged from the barn with two milk pails. Aaron looked thunderstruck but struggled to regain a casual countenance as Jonathan approached. But it didn't work. Aaron had been gone from the barn long enough that Jonathan had guessed something was amiss. Mary picked up her chicken water and hurried away toward the coop, thinking she was fleeing like a coward, but unable to stop herself. Aaron was left to fill the void hanging between himself and his brother.

"I meant to come back down, but Mary needed a little help with the chickens and geese. Sorry, Jonathan."

"Yup. It's all done now, anyway," answered Jonathan, heading for the house, leaving Aaron there alone to damn the poor timing, which had cut Mary away from him again, and at the most inopportune moment.

For several days, no chance came up for Aaron to question Mary. It wasn't a conversation to be picked up with the risk of interruption, or with the risk of being observed.

The work that Jonathan did, Aaron did beside him, so they were together most of the days. The wild hay was cut and left to dry. Tying the hay into bundles in the hot, dry field, Aaron went over and over again the simple statement Mary had made.

Aaron, I'm going to have a baby. Not "Jonathan's baby" . . . not "your baby." Just "a baby." Would she know whose it was? Was it his own or Jonathan's? If she didn't know whose it was, it would be torture for them all.

Mary had the advantage of knowing who the father was, but it was little consolation, for she was feeling Aaron's confusion as keenly as he, and was impatient to answer his unasked question. Her impatience was compounded by her wish to be able to tell Aaron that Jonathan hadn't sought her out in bed since his return. She truly didn't understand why he hadn't, but knew it wouldn't be long before he did again.

She felt compelled to tell Aaron the entire truth before she broached the subject with Jonathan. If this should be impossible, Mary would feel a kind of disloyalty toward Aaron. This was what confused her, for in her heart she knew Aaron could never claim the baby outright. Yet Jonathan would, even knowing it wasn't his. Why, then, the disloyalty toward Aaron? Shouldn't she feel it toward her husband, instead?

Jonathan was the only contented one of the group. Harvesting any crop always filled him with a sense of fulfillment, and this year the taking of the wild hay meant a new pasture for Vinnie to forage in.

Vinnie.

Yes, Vinnie was the bright spot in Jonathan's life. Not a day went by without his stopping by the wild hay to admire the bull and play the imaginary game of watching a hayfield filled with Vinnie's pure-black offspring fattening for market. When the bull caught the flicker of any motion, his head came up and his red eyes followed the movements as he stood dead still. The alert pose was accented by the breadth of his powerful body, which was growing fast in the rich, nurturing Minnesota summer. Vinnie's stance would be held until Jonathan neared the fence. Then his natural curiosity would take over, and he'd approach the fence with an unblinking eye, studying the familiar man. The man and the bull would stand eye to eye, at ease with each other while they carried on a conversation.

"Hey, big boy, you're lookin' fine. Come on over." And Jonathan held a clump of fresh, long grass invitingly toward Vinnie.

But the bull took his time, studying the man, listening to his soft, low voice.

"Come on, now, it's the least you can do to step over to the fence after I come clear down here to see you."

The bull relented, made a low grunt, flared his nostrils, and stepped nonchalantly toward the proffered grass.

Jonathan scratched Vinnie's face, enjoying the grinding sound as the bull scratched the grass.

"You like that good stuff, huh? Good. You just eat to your heart's content because we gotta grow you up and get you breedin'. Any breedin' to be done around here's gotta be done by you, you know. There won't be any done by me. But it don't matter, Vinnie . . ." And after a long, quiet pause, the bull's head jerked a little as if he wondered why the man had grown quiet. Jonathan seemed to hear the bull's question.

"I don't mind. She hasn't told me yet, but I'm pretty sure of it now."

The bull stretched his head forward, then shook it, rolling it left and right.

"Hey, I said it's all right, didn't I? Of course I'm hoping it's a boy. If it is, then between you and me, I guess we'll have pret' near everything we could ask for, huh?"

A heavy hoof on the ground answered him.

"All you gotta do is grow up a little more, and by next spring we'll start building a herd for my son, okay?"

Sometimes a snort came from the bull while Jonathan stood deep in pensive thought before shaking himself alert once more.

"Yes . . . all a man could ask for . . ."

And so the two became friends, and Jonathan poured out his feelings and expectations, both of which seemed to grow in proximity to the bull's pasture. To the bull Jonathan could speak with ease, and he always felt understood, his tongue becoming glib while the bull listened.

Jonathan was content, feeling the fullness of life.

He saw this fullness in the maturing bull. He witnessed it in the ripening fields. He sensed it in Mary. But he blocked out Aaron's part in it and trusted that everything would somehow work out for the best.

One evening while the men were both in the barn finishing chores, a strange rig drew into the yard. Mary stepped out onto the porch to greet the driver. As he stepped from his wagon, she thought his face was slightly familiar.

"Hello," she called from the porch.

"Hello, Mrs. Gray," the man greeted her as he started through the gate and came toward the house. When he reached the steps he extended his hand and said, "I'm Aloysius Duzak from over in Turtle Creek Township."

"Well, of course." Mary remembered him now. "How are you? What brings you up this way?"

"I tell you, Mrs. Gray," Duzak said, "I hear your husband bought a prize-winning bull, and I drove over to see if I could get a look at it."

"I don't know why not. Jonathan's so proud of that bull, he'd be happy to show it to anyone." Mary came down from the porch, and they began walking toward the barn as she continued, "He's still out here doing the milking. Come on down and talk to him."

"I sure appreciate this. I've been hearing so much about the animal, I wanted to get a look at it for myself. It's a Black Angus, isn't it?"

"Yes, it is. And he's Jonathan's pride and joy. He went all the way to Minneapolis to buy him and had him shipped up here on the train."

"That's what I heard," Duzak responded.

When they got to the barn Mary introduced Duzak, but Jonathan and Aaron both seemed to know him already as they got up to shake hands with him.

They exchanged greetings before Jonathan asked, "What brings you up this way?"

"A little curiosity about that new bull of yours. Wondered if I might take a look at him." Duzak rocked back on his heels as he asked the question, and Jonathan clapped him on the shoulder, saying, "Sure thing. I'm just finishing up here."

But Aaron interrupted, saying, "Go ahead, Jonathan. I'll finish up. We're nearly done, anyway." And he resumed his hunkered position beside the cow he'd been milking when Duzak came in. The cows were never tied and the barn had no stanchions, so as Jonathan turned to leave the barn, his cow sensed the man's leaving and began backing up to head for the open door to the barnyard.

Jonathan flapped his hands at the cow and slapped her on the rump saying, "Hold it, boss, you're not done yet." Then he called to Mary, who was already out the door. "Can you come here and hold this one until Aaron gets a chance to finish her?"

Mary came back into the barn and held the cow the only way she could—by taking her place on the milk stool and making milking actions that yielded little milk but kept the animal pacified until Aaron could take over.

The voices of Duzak and Jonathan trailed away as they left the barn.

The two cows chewed their cuds, and the comfortable sound soothed Mary. Everything else was quiet. Mary had a tranquil sense of going back to the beginning, sitting there in the barn with the pair of cows and Aaron, just like that first evening after Jonathan had left. Her milking was ineffectual, as it had been then. The closeness of the barn created the same earthy intimacy as it had last spring. The same feeling of expectation was in the air.

Aaron had little milking left on his cow, but it seemed to take an eternity while precious minutes alone with Mary were slipping away. He figured they might have half an hour together while Jonathan walked to and from the wild-hay meadow. His hands worked like pistons, and his heart seemed to be doing the same. He had to get these damn cows out of the way before he could talk to Mary. This was too important to risk being distracted, even by the cows, so Aaron hurried, hurried.

There was always something special about looking at Mary when they were alone together, as if Jonathan's absence gave Aaron the right to her. Seeing her squatting there on the milk stool, his heart responded to the scene being repeated in so much the same way as their first evening together. She looked up at him silently, then they exchanged places.

No matter how firmly Mary had resolved to get through this without breaking down and touching him, it was like it always was. She stood beside him and crossed her arms over her stomach to keep her hands off him. He began the milking, then raised his eyes to her, and they looked at each other while the steady rhythm of the milk fell into the pail, Aaron not needing to watch it to know where it would fall.

"Aaron, I'm not very strong-willed," she confessed.

"That's because you love me, Mary," he said.

But she drew her fists up and pressed them against her temples, saying, "Don't say that, Aaron." And she stepped back a step, as if by moving away from him she could combat her feelings. "I have to get over it, that's all."

"Tell me about the baby, Mary. I've got to know."

He stood up and lifted the pail safely away while the cow moved toward the door, separating him and Mary for a moment. When it was quiet and they stood facing each other again, she said simply, "The baby is yours, Aaron."

He heard it many times, though she said it only once. It seemed to resound off the barn walls, and the more he heard it, the weaker he became, until he thought he'd drop the pail of milk. So he set it down on the floor.

Then, like a fighter who has suddenly had the wind knocked from him, Aaron's breath swooped out. "Jesus Christ."

He covered the space between them in a leap, lifting her off her feet. He held her suspended, crushed against his chest, and swayed back and forth with her until she felt an ache in her groin from hanging that way so long.

"Put me down, Aaron. It hurts," she said against his neck.

He reacted swiftly, guiltily, setting her on her feet and turning her loose in one swift movement.

"Oh, Mary, I'm sorry. Are you all right?" He looked like the ache had struck him instead of her, and he dropped one big hand to her belly, covering it and her own two hands that were pressing it.

"Yes. It's all right," she assured him. "I just have

to move a little slower to keep that from happening lately."

She stepped back then and started talking before he could reach for her again.

"Aaron, I wanted you to know about it first . . . before Jonathan. He doesn't know yet, but now I'll be telling him. After that, I'm not ever going to talk about it with you again."

"But, Mary, it's my . . ."

She cut him off. "Let me finish this, Aaron, or I never will. There's only one way it can be. Jonathan hasn't touched me since he came back, so he'll know the baby isn't his. I won't have to tell him so. But I'm going to promise him it won't ever happen again between you and me, and I'm going to try with all my might to keep that promise."

"You can't mean this, Mary," Aaron said. But she stopped him again by rushing on.

"I have to mean it, Aaron. There's no way you and I could live, trying to get over the disgrace, if we admitted the baby is yours."

"There are other places we can live besides Todd County," he said.

"There's no place," she said with finality.

"The hell there isn't," Aaron argued, half in supplication and half in anger.

"We knew it when we started," she said.

"When we started, I didn't know this would happen. It changes everything."

"It doesn't change the fact that I'm Jonathan's wife."

"But it's my child."

"At his request," she stated, hating herself for having to say it.

"Are you saying you believe all that hypocritical claptrap he threw at us that I owed him this? Or are you saying you made love with me because he asked you to?" His facial muscles were drawn up hard, and it hurt her that he'd become angry.

"No, Aaron. Oh, don't be angry. I didn't say you owed the child to Jonathan. I . . . I'm pregnant because I love you and not because Jonathan asked what he did. But I have to get over it and make a new life with Jonathan."

"And my baby?" he asked simply.

But she dared not look up or answer.

"I'm asking about my baby," he repeated. "Can you look at me and say you want to give my baby to another man?"

Tears came to her eyes, and she pleaded, "Don't, Aaron."

But he pulled her chin up with his hand and she was forced to meet the hurt in his eyes. "Don't, Aaron?" he asked quietly. "Don't fight for my life? It's my life you're carrying, and you say you're going to give it away to another man."

"It's not just another man. It's your brother. How could we be allowed to live in peace, knowing—"

His words covered hers again, though. "Brother be damned! At least we'd be living. Apart, we're dead."

"What would we tell the child when he grows up?"

"The truth," he answered. "That he's ours because we loved each other."

"While I was married to your brother?"

They stood with their eyes locked, the weight of her question pressing on their consciences.

"We can go away to another state. It's a big country. We can live anywhere in it."

"How?" she asked.

"I have some money," he said, "and the house."

"Do you believe Jonathan will pay you for your house so you can run away with me?"

They stood in hurtful silence together, slowly realizing that she was right.

"You tried the city once, Aaron, but you told me how you hated it. It's farming that's your way of life. How could you go away from the farm? This is where your life is."

He came near her again and placed his hand gently on her stomach. "This is where my life is. How can I live here without it and you?"

In the end she was the stronger of them. She pushed him gently away, saying, "Even if I learn to love Jonathan again, it won't mean I loved you less. I'm telling him tonight about the baby, and everything will change after I do."

She slipped out the barn door then, and was gone. He stood there with everything aching in him.

It was dark when Jonathan went up to bed. Mary was already there, but no lamp was lit. He felt his familiar way up the stairs and undressed. When he got into bed beside her, something told him that she was still awake. After he had sighed his usual bedtime sigh and settled onto his back, she coughed softly in the dark. It was quiet for a while before her voice came to him.

"Jonathan?"

LaVyrle Spencer

"Ahuh," he grunted.

She lay with the blood pounding in her ears, her throat tight, and her palms damp. He could hear her breath, short and shallow, and he knew before she said it what she had to tell him. When she didn't go on, he turned his head toward her in the dark. "What?"

"I'm going to have a baby."

With the words came a sharp pain of disappointment that caught at her hammering heart, giving her voice a catch. After all the years of waiting to tell her husband this, telling him now was empty, bitter.

"I reckon I knew it already," he said, and her relief was great.

She wondered what all he'd guessed about herself and Aaron, but still didn't really want to know.

"It's what I wanted," Jonathan said.

"Yes."

"I'll be . . ." Here he swallowed. "It'll be ours. I mean, people won't question that I'm the father," he said, telling her that he knew the child was Aaron's.

She was silent, guilty.

"It's okay," Jonathan assured her, but, less than assured himself, felt the truth swiftly burn through him as if a new rope had sizzled through the slack grip of his innards. "It's okay," he repeated.

But Mary lay beside him thinking nothing would ever be okay again. She'd been squandered by her husband, had compromised herself, and had denied Aaron the right to claim his baby. How could conceiving a child in the midst of such deception be okay?

Mary slept fitfully at last, but when she did, Aaron was there in front of her. He held his arms out and smiled at her, an invitation to his embrace. She ran a few steps toward him, but Jonathan came riding across her dream on the back of a large black bull. The bull came between her and Aaron, and she knew it would charge her if she took another step.

"Be careful, Mary," Jonathan warned. "Be careful with my baby."

"It's my baby," came Aaron's hollow voice from beyond the bull. The bull and its rider blocked Aaron from her sight, but she could hear him calling that hollow cry over and over again, and soon the cry was mixed with her own and with the laughter of Jonathan as he sat on the bull's back. The confusion of sound grew to a great din, and the bull became riled and wild and he charged off in a strange direction toward a waiting green field of hay, taking Jonathan with him. It was a long way to run to Aaron and she ran and ran and it hurt her distended stomach but she knew that when she reached him the hurt would be gone . . . I'm coming, Aaron . . . She held her belly to keep the pain away . . . Aaron's arms were so near . . . but just as she reached him she found herself confronted by an army of potato bugs and she slapped crazily as they neared her ankles.

Her dream actions lapped over into semiconscious brushings that roused Jonathan. He awoke Mary, but he was too sleepy to wonder what had caused her to thrash around, and she was left alone once again.

Chapter 15

$\mathcal{A}$ugust bore down without consideration for a pregnant woman. It came on hot and dry, pleasing the farmer instead. While Mary labored for long, sweat-drenched hours over the boilers that held her canning, the men toiled in the dry dust of the wheat and barley fields. Coming in only for noon dinner and at the end of the long afternoon, Jonathan and Aaron rarely saw Mary bending and stooping over the endless vegetable rows in the garden, but at the end of the day they both saw the redness of her skin from the sun and the neatly placed rows of filled fruit jars that stood on the tabletop, waiting to be carried into the root cellar under the pantry. Sometimes there would be dishpans of cucumbers on the porch or pails with the second crop of string beans. Then they would sit together in the last evening hour, snapping beans or scrubbing the cukes on the back porch for pickling the next day. The three of them never talked much anymore, but it was easy to chalk it up to the fact that they were all exhausted.

Aaron often found small jobs to keep him away from the house in the evening if there were no vegetables on the porch. None of them mentioned the night of Al Duzuk's visit, when Aaron had taken a bottle of wine out to the granary and finished it off all alone, drinking himself into a sick stupor that took two days to wear off.

By late August, Mary's usual trim, flat belly had begun thickening perceptibly, and she sometimes unbuttoned the top button of her skirt and petticoat to make breathing and bending more comfortable. It wouldn't be long now before she would be asked the reason for her newly blossomed shape. Few women would make any bones about coming right out and asking if she was pregnant. She wondered whether she'd mind it when the first one asked. Some penchant for privacy made her want to hug the knowledge to herself for just a little longer.

The one person who knew was Aunt Mabel. After church one Sunday, Mary had told her, "You were right, you know. I'm going to have a baby." Then she quickly warned, "Shhh, I haven't told anyone else."

"Laws! How happy you must be, child. I can't believe it myself. Now you remember what I said about takin' it easy, and no overworking, you hear? I'll come help you at threshing time, 'cause it'll take a heap o' cooking for those galoots who'll help thresh. You seen Haymes yet?"

"No, not yet."

"Well, I had mine without no doctor badgerin' and probin', but Haymes is a good man. You go visit him and mind what he says—we don't want you droppin' this one early on."

"Yes, dear." Mary placated her with a small laugh.

"And don't go overdoin' when those threshers are due. I'll get there and do the heavy work, mind!"

"I'll mind," Mary agreed, thinking Aunt Mabel was being overprotective, but loving it.

Uncle Garner owned a steam engine and threshing machine that crisscrossed the county at harvest time. The threshing crew traveled with the rig, slept with it, ate as much food as it ate wood. With Uncle Garner gone so much of the time now, Aunt Mabel looked forward to spending a day or two in Mary's company and at the same time helping her with the heavy cooking necessary for the threshing crew.

The grains were ripe and waiting: oats, barley, and wheat. Every farmer worked from dawn until dark, driving the horses that pulled the binder. As Mary walked behind the binder during the hot August afternoons, she alternately loved and loathed the chore of shocking; loved it because it put her near Aaron, loathed it for its backbreaking weariness. Aaron and Jonathan alternated jobs, sometimes driving the team, sometimes shocking, with Mary's help in the afternoons. Much as they were concerned for Mary, the men knew her help was needed if the grains were to be ready when the threshers arrived.

Driving the team, Aaron spent much time looking behind him, keeping a constant eye on the twine box as the twine was payed out to tie the bundles. True, the twine box bore watching, but it wasn't necessary to watch it as much as he did. Aaron craned around to catch a look at Mary, to wish she needn't brush grasshoppers and spiders off her legs.

Jonathan worked and whistled a lot, now and then catching some chaff in his throat as he inhaled. Aaron's neck grew stiff from its craned position, and he was relieved when it came his turn to shock.

Six bundles were stood up and a seventh was spread on the top, the flared tail of the top bundle holding the uprights in place. The fields of shocks made a continuous pattern that grew each day, the number of shocks increasing until the pattern was complete, the shocking was done, and the stacking could begin.

When the shocking was done, the bundles had to be pitched up onto the hayrack by hand, the rack inching up and down the field behind the horses, the three workers filling and refilling it after each ride to the barnyard where the stack was made. At long, weary last, the golden stacks stood hunched in the barnyard, kernels turned centerward, where they lay in a final sweat while nature loosened the grain for threshing.

The sweat might be final for the grain, but not so for Jonathan, Mary, and Aaron. They had all hoped for a respite from the hard work, but word came that the threshing rig was nearing, and Mary sent a letter off to Aunt Mabel on the day they finished stacking, telling her they expected the threshing crew any day now. There was no telling when the rig would appear, creeping up on the horizon like a giant prehistoric monster. It moved along from farm to farm at its best harvest pace. Aunt Mabel preceded it by only one day.

She bustled into the yard, and a tired but healthy Mary took one glimpse out the screen door at the rotund figure alighting from the carriage and flew outside to be hugged against her aunt's generous chest.

"Aunt Mabel!" But no words could tell how happy Mary was to have her there. The great, loving bear hug was as welcome as the threshing crew would be.

"Well, it looks like I beat your Uncle Garner here," were her first words.

"I'm happy you did," said Mary as she backed off with happy tears reflecting the late harvest sun from her eyes.

The men were working downyard, stacking wood to feed the steam engine when it arrived, but a shout from that direction brought a halloo to Aunt Mabel and she waved back at the men. They stopped their work to glance at one another, one of them thinking, Help is here for Mary at last, the other thinking, The threshing crew can't be far behind now.

The specially fattened hens were in scalding water, raising the stench of wet feathers to mingle with the aroma of baking bread. The two women came into the mixture of these smells as they entered the kitchen.

"Looks like you been busy, girl," said Mabel Garner. Her presence filled the room in a homely way. She was plucking feathers before Mary had crossed the room to carry her grip into the front room. Mabel's special status gave her a right to questions Mary would have resented from others, and it didn't take Aunt Mabel long to start.

"You're lookin' mighty good, but you better take care of that sunburn, girl."

"I'll put some salve on it tonight," said Mary as she came to join her aunt at the feather-plucking.

"Tonight, my eye!" Mabel scolded. "You do it now

and leave this mess to me. You been out there shocking, have you?"

"Well, the men needed a hand if it was to be done
in time." Remembering her aunt's admonition to take
care of herself, Mary turned away as if to make light
of her heavy field work.

"What do them men think you're made of, anyway?
You got no business out there in your condition."

"It didn't hurt me at all." But Mary was pleased by
her aunt's concern. She enjoyed being coddled, which
she rarely was.

"Well, it took you so long to get that way, we don't
want no grain crop undoing what it took you and Jonathan seven years to do."

Mary had pulled a tin of ointment out from under
the wet sink, and Mabel Garner saw her niece holding
it in her hand and looking at it in an odd way. Mabel
thought, Something's troubling the child. But when she
said as much, Mary brightened. "No, nothing's wrong.
How could it be when you're here at last?"

The older woman's affection for this slight, sunburned lass with the new roundness at her middle
made her answer a bit gruffly, "I'll give that Jonathan
more'n a little piece of my mind for settin' you to field
work like that!" Then, with a specially hard tug at a
clump of feathers, she grunted, "Humph! Damn them
men, anyhow!"

But when Uncle Garner appeared, it was a different
story. His threshing rig appeared over the east hill the
next day at midmorning. Mabel Garner waited in the
yard along with the three Grays, and it was hard to tell
who was the most eager for the rig to pull to a stop.

Jonathan pointed down to the new woodpile, and Uncle Garner waved to his wife with a smile as he drove his team down that way and finally pulled up with a "Whoa!"

Mabel Garner unabashedly hugged him as he stood beside the wagon. He planted a neat kiss on her cheek, slapped her on the rump, and said, "Got work to do, woman!"

"Damn if you don't, Mr. Garner!" his wife laughed. Both of them had happy, wholesome smiles on their faces, which spoke of feelings rich with their age and their years together. Aaron didn't miss it, and neither did Mary.

The threshing crew numbered nine, and when the slick, long belt was eased onto the pulley, the men in the farmyard became a part of the machine. The stoker loaded wood into the woodbox that fired the boiler. Aaron fed bundles into the thresher. One of the men who'd arrived with the rig was tending its operation, another was leveling the spewing grain around in the double box as it filled. Another double box waited to be filled while the first was driven to the granary, where one man shoveled it in and Jonathan waited to push it into the farthest corner of the bin.

The straw pile, cast off to one side, grew in proportion to the dwindling of the grain stacks. The men sweated outdoors while the women sweated indoors. The heat of Mary's sunburn was multiplied by the radiating heat from the stoked range, yet the cooking went on.

Noon dinner was only the first big meal. It seemed the hungry workers could put away mountains of spuds, gallons of gravy, quarts of pickles, dozens of rolls, and roasters full of chickens. But appetites were totally whetted again by midafternoon, when an enormous lunch of sandwiches, pies, cakes, and hot coffee was wolfed down while the big engine kept puffing away under a full head of steam. By evening the chaff covered the yard with its dusty coat and the men scratched ineffectually at the pesky stuff where it mixed with sweat and encrusted their skins. No part of the body was immune to it.

"Them men ain't gonna have no armpits or crotches left, they go on scratchin' like they was at dinnertime," Mabel Garner commented wryly, making Mary laugh.

"Look at Tony. What's he doing?" The two women were standing in the kitchen doorway, the men down by the well washing up for supper.

"I'd say he's feelin' his oats!" Mabel Garner laughed as Tony Vrensek danced a crazy jig, scratching and rubbing himself in disgustingly funny places. Suddenly Vrensek catapulted for the cattle tank and dove in, startling a cow, which backed off with a complaining moo. The man came up spluttering, wearing a cap of green moss from the cow tank. The men hooted their enjoyment.

"What is it makes them men go crazy when threshin's over?" Aunt Mabel questioned no one in particular, enjoying the scene down at the cowtank and Mary's laughter.

"Well, girl, we'd best get the platters loaded. They'll be ravenous. Especially Tony, after takin' that swim!"

It was completely dark by the time they finished supper, which meant that the crew would wait until morning to move on to the next farm. They'd finished this one, and the haymow was filled with snores and snorts as the weary men bedded down in the sweet wild hay, thinking nothing of its itch after what they'd already been through.

The crew was fed breakfast before dawn and moved on, leaving full grain bins. Even so threshing left a curious empty feeling in its wake, the void of a thing completed, the hesitation before stepping into winter with hands idle. Even Mabel Garner felt it and hadn't any of her usual rackety chatter as she sat with Mary over a final cup of coffee.

"Guess I never got a chance to get after that Jonathan, did I? You see that you take it easy, Mary."

It grew quiet, and from outside somewhere came the sound of the grindstone as one of the men sharpened an ax. It brought to mind the coming of winter, the wood to be put up, the separations that lay ahead.

"Jonathan and Aaron will be going to hire out in Dakota again this year," Mary said quietly, and Mabel heard the lonesomeness in her voice, as if she were already alone.

"Are you worried about being alone in your condition?"

"No, not really worried. I just dread the loneliness, like every year."

"Yup. It ain't easy bein' without your man."

If only you knew, Mary thought. But she said, "This is the last year I'll have to be completely alone, though."

"Aw, that's the spirit, honey," her aunt replied. "I've been expectin' you to do more talkin' about the baby but since I been here you hardly said a word about it. Somethin' botherin' you, child?"

The truth of what was bothering her welled up in Mary and brought with it a desire to tell Aunt Mabel the whole thing. But such honesty would only cause the other woman unnecessary concern. Mabel would worry herself sick if she knew. So instead, Mary reached over to pat the workworn hand that lay on the tabletop. "I'm just tired, I guess. We've been too busy to talk since you've been here, and now that the work is done, it's time for you to leave. I just hate to see you go."

"If you ain't talked about the baby, I guess it's because you're scared like we all are when it's our first one," Mabel offered.

"I'm not scared, really," Mary said.

"Then what? You sure ain't happy." Mabel Garner had that way of getting at the eye of a thing.

"I'm just not used to the idea yet. It takes a little time, I guess."

"Well, you'll have plenty of time when them men leave. Meanwhile, you cheer up and try to think of the blessing you been handed here and what a joy it'll be when these here dull days're done. It's only natural, you bein' a little blue now, but wait and see—it won't last." Mabel Garner knew that for a fact. She'd been through it enough times herself to know the feeling, and she worried about Mary being left alone while the men went out to Dakota.

"Are the men going to the same place as last year?"

Mary hated the thought of their going, but there was nothing she could do about it. "Yes, the same place. Jonathan's already written to Enderland, and he's just waiting for word to come. He and Aaron will leave when the grain's ready out there."

This time it was Mabel's turn to pat a hand and say with gruff affection, "Chin up, child, the time'll pass before you know it."

The morning that Martha Culley finally put her oversized Bohemian nose in Mary's business, she did it when Aaron was within earshot. They were all out in the churchyard again on a Sunday in late September. The women were clustered near enough to the knot of visiting men so that Aaron heard every word.

"You've put on a little weight, haven't you, Mary?"

Aaron's ears had already pricked at the voices behind him.

"A little, I guess."

"Couldn't be you're pregnant at last, could it?"

At last! Aaron thought. Why, that insufferable crow bait had her nerve to say a thing like that. He had no way of knowing Mary was wishing she could spit point blank in the middle of Martha Culley's eye. Aaron heard Mary answer coolly, "Why, I believe it could be, Martha." Then, like a gaggle of excited geese, the women flapped and squawked and wrapped their wings around Mary, then broke ranks to gather their ganders in and tell them the juicy news. Aaron thought the congratulations would go on forever after the first shrill voice announced, "Mary and Jonathan are going to have a baby." He stood there among the well-meaning men and women with a rock in his stomach, and ground his teeth behind his pasted smile. Someone said, "It took you a while, Jonathan, but better late than never." And Jonathan nodded and rocked back on his heels like a strutting rooster. Mary's smile was tight, and she kept her hands crossed loosely in front of her as if shielding her unborn child from the carping flock. "I suppose you want a boy, eh, Jonathan?" another voice asked, and Aaron heard his brother reply, "Sure thing." Then there was laughter and back-slapping before someone whacked Aaron on the shoulder, saying, "So you're gonna be an uncle, Aaron! What d'you know about that!" He kept his smile broad and thought, I know a damn sight more about it than you'll ever guess. But he answered, "They waited a long time for this," which was true enough yet feeble enough that he could force himself to say it. When his eyes flicked across Mary's they both smiled a little bigger, but the others couldn't tell these were forced smiles. To add his old touch of brotherly affection, Aaron dropped his arm lightly around her shoulders for all to see, squeezed her arm, and said, "She'll be a hell of a mother." Then dropped his arm while he smiled at Jonathan convincingly and said, "Congratulations, Jonathan." Jonathan nodded, and the babble went on around them.

Jonathan felt good. He was lying beside Mary under the warm eiderdown comforter. The chill of early autumn that touched the air couldn't touch him. He was full of plans. It had never occurred to Jonathan that the baby might be a girl. Whatever misgivings he may have had about the expected baby were all gone, replaced by hope.

Mary was still awake, he knew.

"Mary?" he said softly, but even so, she jumped.

He wondered why she'd flinched like that and asked, "You okay?"

"Yes, Jonathan. What were you going to say?"

"With the money I earn in Dakota harvesting, I figure I can buy an Angus cow and start breeding a herd in the spring."

It was the last thing in the world she expected him to say. All day long, since the scene in the churchyard, she'd been aware of the feeling generating in him, and she guessed it to be pride. She was baffled. Not once had he blamed her, acted jealous or hurt. How was she to generate any kind of feeling for him if he accepted her faithlessness so easily? She needed to feel loved enough by him to bring out the feelings any normal husband should feel. She had made an effort to please him in the past weeks, trying to recapture a sincere affection for him. But he seemed cold, and that coolness was reflected in her. She was prepared for him to say nearly anything but what he'd said.

"Buy a cow?" She sounded puzzled to Jonathan. And then she said a curious thing. "Could we talk about something important, Jonathan, just for once?"

He sensed an even deeper irritation in her than her voice held, and wondered what had brought it on.

"This is important, Mary. For the baby."

"Ah, the baby!" she said with a quiver now quite discernible in her voice, "Now there's an important item."

"What is it you want me to say?" he asked.

"Whatever you want. Just say something."

"All right." He paused, searching for the words. "I'm happy about the baby."

"How can you be happy, Jonathan?" she asked.

"Well, I reckon I'm happy 'cause the Lord saw fit . . ."

"The Lord! What about you, Jonathan?" She sat up and pounded her fists into the eiderdown.

Jonathan was unprepared for her sudden burst of anger and didn't know how to deal with it, coming as it did so suddenly. Not knowing what she expected of him, he repeated her question, confused, "What *about* me?"

"Don't you want an explanation, an apology?"

"I figure it's best we don't talk about it," he mumbled.

"But Jonathan, what I did was *wrong*. I wronged you. Why don't you blame me for that?"

"I said once I'd take the blame myself, and it's between me and the Lord to straighten it out."

"Leave the Lord out of this, Jonathan! This is about human beings and their feelings—yours and mine."

"All right, Mary, but you're making yourself too upset."

"I am upset. I'm upset because my husband doesn't care enough about me to be jealous."

"Jealousy is a sin, Mary."

"So is adultery."

A verse from the Bible entered his mind then, but he wasn't going to bring the Lord into this again. She was too worked up, and she had him confused, so he remained silent.

But she was insistent, demanding a response. "I said, so is adultery, Jonathan."

He didn't understand the reason for her anger. "I heard you, Mary. But I don't know what you want out of me."

"I want some jealousy, some reaction, some sign that you care. I want to talk about it."

"The time for talking is past. Now it's time to make plans."

She sat, still and silent and angry, not knowing how to elicit from him feelings he apparently didn't harbor.

"You know, Jonathan, that's always been our trouble. We never talked about anything. I mean anything important. Like how you felt about needing a baby so bad. I knew it, but why couldn't you say what you felt? And I wanted so many times to talk about what Doc Haymes says, but you'd get silent as a fence post if I'd bring it up. That's not right. In order for two people to know each other, they've got to talk about the things you can't see, not just those you can—like bulls and crops and fences and new barns! Don't you see?"

"No, I don't. You want me to talk about bein' jealous when I ain't, and about wantin' a child when we're gonna have one. You don't make any sense. Besides, I'm not much for talkin', anyway. You got Aaron for that."

She couldn't believe he'd say a thing like that now. Rather than try to work out an understanding, he'd go on as if nothing had changed.

"You're my husband, the one I ought to talk with."

"Well, we been talkin' here, haven't we?"

"Yes, in circles."

"I don't think you're acting like yourself tonight. Maybe it's being pregnant does it to you."

She couldn't help it, she burst out laughing. Only it wasn't amused laughter, it was harsh, dry, hurt. But Jonathan didn't even seem to understand her laughter. He reached up and pulled at her shoulder, saying,

"Come on, lay down here and let's forget it," and she let him pull her back to her pillow and take her in his arms. Her anger was gone, and she was wondering what to do with the big, aching emptiness that was left in its stead. Jonathan's hand on her breast did nothing to fill it. She lay still under the big, moving hand, waiting for some sweet, flooding emotion to begin at his caress, but none came. His petting gave her a feeling of vague revulsion, and she swallowed hard and made a soft sound behind her closed lips, which he mistook for passion.

Mary lay waiting. Waiting to discover whether she thought Jonathan did too much or not enough. His sudden mounting seemed no longer enough, yet it was more than she could bear. While his body worked against hers, she did what she'd vowed to herself she would never do, she imagined he was Aaron. She remembered the swirling, velvet releases of her climaxes with Aaron, but when her husband withdrew from her body, she was left with only that memory and a throbbing emptiness. She was afraid to ask herself if she desired that fullest draught of passion with Jonathan. Her answer might be that it was a pleasure she wanted only from Aaron, and from no other man.

Chapter 16

$\mathcal{A}$aron could see his breath this morning, and the chill October air made the ax handle cold. Autumn was his favorite time of year, and he hated the thought of leaving these radiant, rolling hills for the flat, colorless prairies of North Dakota. Minnesota was a myriad of changing colors, at its best now in the full flush of fall. It even smelled better this time of year. It smelled of tucking in, of getting ready, like the squirrels were. They were all getting ready. Mary was getting their clothes ready, he and Jonathan were getting the wood ready . . . and I'm getting ready to leave Mary, Aaron thought.

She was coming out of the house with the clothes basket slung on her hip. Her hip didn't jut out anymore. She was bigger already. He wondered if the child moved inside her yet and what it felt like when that happened. How he wished he could ask her. Sometimes, thinking of her, his unasked questions made his throat ache. The forced restraint made him seek out the hardest physical work. But wood-chopping was a cold substitute for shared intimacies.

Mary was wearing an oversized red plaid jacket, and he watched her hang clothes while he chopped. He thought of how it would feel to slip his arms inside the jacket and hug her, feel the baby between them. She hung the last wet shirt and blew on her hands to warm them. He kept up the wood-chopping, wishing he could go to her, open his shirt, and warm her fingers against his chest. She dropped the basket beside the path and headed for the outhouse. As she walked along, the plaid jacket blended with the scarlet sumac and she became a part of the fall foliage. Sometimes at night he'd hear her get up and go out there, and he wished he could get up and just walk with her, wait for her, and walk her back in, ask her if the baby made her uncomfortable. He didn't think she'd been sick, but he knew there were lots of discomforts involved with pregnancy. He wished he could share them with her, if only by talking about them.

When she came back down the path, he shouted in her direction, "Don't lift that wash water, Mary!"

"No, I won't, Aaron." He could see her breath as she called across the October morning.

The depressive moods of her first pregnant months had gone away weeks ago, but Mary was having difficulty keeping the lump from her throat this morning. The letter with the Enderland, North Dakota, postmark had arrived yesterday afternoon. The men had delayed leaving until today to give Mary a chance to get their things ready and also to allow them time to get a load of winter wood into the yard and chopped. They had cut the timber in the woods and spent the day since the potato harvest sectioning it with the crosscut saw. If it was to dry, it needed chopping, but it looked like winter would catch them before they finished the job. Whether or not the wood supply ran out would depend on how long they stayed in North Dakota. If Mary got low, she could ask a neighbor to chop a supply for her. Thank heaven for neighbors, he thought. He'd miss Mary, but he needn't worry about her.

The morning warmed quickly, and the day promised to be a beauty. Jonathan headed the horses in with the last load of wood and stopped at the near pasture, where Vinnie would stay until the winter snows pushed him into the barn. The bull approached the fence and stopped full-face to Jonathan.

"Howdy, big boy." The clean, cylindrical lines of the bull were already nearing maturity. His smooth black coat gleamed in the sun. His red eyes gleamed from his dished face. Looking at the beautiful creature who represented so much of Jonathan's hope for the future, the man found good reason in leaving his farm to work on another man's land.

"I'll be bringing home money to buy you a missus. Now what do you think of that?"

The red eye blinked.

"No. You wouldn't yet, but come next spring when your sap is up you'll thank me."

The eye didn't blink this time.

"Sure hate to leave you, Vinnie. You'll do fine, though. Plenty of pasture time left before winter."

Again it was between the man and the bull as if they talked the same language. Vinnie made a snuffling, low noise. "I'll miss you, too. But just think about growin' up, and by the time I get back you'll be a little heavier." Then he added, "So will Mary."

His thoughts of the future held the image of his son and Vinnie's sons growing together on the land. It made his leaving easier. Turning his back on the bull, he hoped for no unseasonably early snow this year. No one would be here to put Vinnie in the barn while they were gone. Checking the azure sky of October, he felt the weather would favor him. Vinnie'll do fine, he thought, making his way up the lane toward the yard with the last load of wood.

The house had a curious stillness to it, as still as the autumn air that scarcely stirred the woodsmoke away from the chimney. It was the kind of brilliant noon that would usually be invigorating, Indian summer having its last fling. But this flawlessly perfect day had the opposite effect as the three of them waited for the sound of wagon wheels on the road. The faint remains of the dinner's aromas tinted the air with hominess, but nobody had eaten much. Nobody'd said much, either, just the necessary last-minute instructions, the necessary lonely things. Some ashes gave way as a log collapsed in the cookstove. Aaron came clumping down the stairs with his gear under one arm, and Jonathan said, "They're here." A buckboard full of men pulled into the driveway, and the men hoisted up bundles, jackets, bedrolls, keeping their eyes from Mary. Any last-minute thing they thought to say seemed pointless. Neither of them liked leaving Mary alone in the house. Mary led the way to the door and stepped out onto the porch with a too-bright smile.

Aaron came past her first and kissed her cheek, leaning past the gear that encumbered him, saying, "The time'll go fast. You'll see." Jonathan came next, weighted down, too. He lightly kissed her quivering mouth, and they both said, "Take care," together before he made for the wagon. Aaron was already climbing aboard. The other men were in high spirits, feeling the fraternity of this all-male adventure. Their voices accompanied the sound of rocks being spit from under the wagon wheels as they left the yard.

Then it was quiet. Mary stood on the porch with tears silvering her cheeks. She blinked hard, trying to clear her vision, but the faces of the disappearing men were blurred. Finally she raised her apron, wiping her eyes dry momentarily, and saw Jonathan and Aaron squinting into the sun as the wagon jostled them with its motion. She realized they couldn't see her on the shadowed porch, so she came down the step into the sunny yard and waved as the wagon disappeared over the crest of the first hill. A long time later, it reappeared, climbing the second hill, finally disappearing for good.

Mary stood, tears washing over her cheeks. Her wet lips widened silently at the uncaring sky as she dropped to her knees in the middle of the silent yard, cradling her swollen body. And for the first time the child became someone, no just something. Inside her was a growing body, alive, someone to be with her through her aloneness. Kneeling in the yard with her arms around her middle, she rocked and cried until she had quieted, then spread her hands wide upon herself. "Are you awake in there? I need your company. I know I haven't given you much of my good thoughts, have I? Maybe this time we spend alone—just the two of us—will help us get to know each other better. Sorry I cried. I guess I'm the last one who should feel sorry for myself."

The grainlands of North Dakota sprawled flat, the farms so large they took weeks to reap. The small farms of Todd County, after giving up their golden grains, gave up their men to these sisterlands to the west. It was a common practice for these harvest-hardened hands to hire out as threshers on the larger Dakota farms. Seven men were in the group that day. None of them relished leaving their homes behind, but a good year might find them returning with nearly two hundred dollars after a month's work. Since bunk and board were provided by employers, the only expense incurred was the price of the train trip, probably only as far as Fargo. From there the men caught rides to the outpost farms.

Jonathan had been returning to the same farm for several years. Aaron had, too, with the exception of the year he'd been to town. So they'd been expecting the letter from Enderland. Wallace Getchner's farm was as good as any, better than some. They remembered years when they'd hired out at places where the grub was bad, flies and filth in kitchens as slovenly run as the farms were. Sleeping accommodations weren't important—any mow with a decent spread of hay would do—but ample, good food was a must, for the days were long and the work hard. Getchner paid fair wages, and his wife knew how to lay a good spread of food. There's a thing about a misplaced man and good cooking that can take him closer to home than anything else. It brought the men back to Getchner's year after year.

They'd ridden by train and buckboard, reaching the Enderland farm in the early evening. Getchner had hired six hands for this year's harvesting. Three were already there when the buckboard arrived with the remaining three. Getting settled took little time, not much more than tossing their bedrolls into the haymow. Their small packs of extra clothing and personal articles were kept there, too. Washing up was done at the well in the yard in tepid water warmed by the teakettle Mrs. Getchner sent out. Meals were taken in a crowded fashion around the family's kitchen table.

They began shocking the grain the following morning. Here the farms were so vast they weren't measured in acres but in sections, these sections stretching away endlessly across the flat prairie as far as the eye could see. Unlike the Minnesota harvests, which were threshed in the yards near barns and granaries, these crops were threshed where they grew, in the fields. The threshing rig ate its way across the sections, chewing up shocks as it went, filling wagon after wagon with grain. Tiring day followed tiring day. The only thing to buck up the spirit was the promise of profits and an occasional letter from home.

Jonathan had written to Mary, a short note stating that they had arrived safely, telling of the good weather conditions, the number of workers Getchner had hired this year, ending with, "Aaron sends his best," and signed, "your loving husband, Jonathan." He wrote the same two letters each year, one right after he arrived, one just before leaving for home. If Jonathan was inarticulate in speech, he was equally so when putting his thoughts on paper. Only his closings indicated they were personal letters. Mary had always treasured these closings, for they were the only written words of love she had ever received from Jonathan.

Mail was speedy, for trains ran with great regularity, two or more per day passing through Browerville from either direction. So Mary got Jonathan's letter the day after he'd sent it. She'd been sitting on the porch step in the noon sun, cracking hazelnuts with a tack hammer. The nuts, in their spiny husks, had been spread to dry on the roof of the granary, safely out of reach of the ever-searching squirrels.

It was another golden day like the one on which Jonathan and Aaron had left. The sun was warm on Mary's arms and face as she rapped the shells. She dropped another hazelnut into the fruit jar as an inquisitive squirrel rustled through the leaves, stopping a safe distance away.

"Hey, you," she beckoned, but he scurried a bit away at the sound of her voice. "Bet you'd like some, huh?" She tossed one near the squirrel, and its tail flinched, gray and shiny in the bright sun, before the animal grabbed it and hid it away inside its cheek. "If it weren't for you, we wouldn't have had to dry those nuts up there on the roof. Now you pretend you're too shy to come and eat them." Then she talked to the baby, as she'd begun to do often. "You know, little one, Jonathan would have a fit, and so would Aaron, if they knew I'd been up that ladder after those nuts. You won't tell, will you?" Then she popped a hazelnut into her mouth. "How do you like hazelnuts, huh?" she asked her unborn child. The squirrel was back, looking for more nuts, his head cocked cutely to one side. "Well, who do you think I'm talking to?" she asked it. "All your babies are grown up now, but you're not the only one who can have babies. I'm gonna be a mama, too, so there." And she gave the squirrel one more hazelnut. "And don't look at me as if I'm crazy. I got to talk to someone."

Oh, she was lonesome, no doubt about it. But since the men were gone she'd found an unusual response to the child that helped fill her days, while at the same time setting her mind straight about Jonathan and Aaron. The longer they were away, the easier it was to detach herself from the emotions that pulled her in opposite directions when they were both around her. She was able to analyze what she'd done and what was the right thing for her to do in the future, and there was less and less doubt that she had wronged Jonathan. Even if he'd asked for it, she'd been wrong to turn to Aaron, and she realized that she'd never asked for Jonathan's forgiveness.

She wasn't trying to delude herself into believing she didn't love Aaron. She did, but she was also convinced that she could find the old love she and her husband had shared. She wondered if Aaron could ever forgive her for the choice she had to make or if he'd come to think she'd used him to get the baby. But if that were so, it was the price she'd have to pay. This had cost them all so much. Not only was Mary determined to set things straight between herself and Jonathan, she was determined to make him see that he must do the same between himself and Aaron. She told Jonathan so, that day, by letter.

Dear Jonathan,
 I received your welcome letter today and am happy all is well there. Here, too. Amos and Tony

are handling the stock just fine. They refuse to let me make them a lunch before they leave, though it's midmorning by the time they finish. I'm already missing the cooking, but of course they have chores of their own and can't humor me just because I'd like company at the table. In the evenings they come after supper, and it's dusk by the time they leave.

Soon you'll be gone a whole week. I've had time to get clear of mind since you left. It's not good that we haven't made some kind of peace among ourselves, you know? You've got to accept what I have to say now, knowing it's long since time it was said. Our being part could heal some wounds—I know you think you don't have any, but you do. And Jonathan, I'm sorry I gave them to you. I'm deeply sorry. What happened between me and Aaron will not be again. He and I have made a sort of peace, but you and I have to, too. And I believe you and he have to do the same. You know that if left to fester, this thing will become enmity between you, and I can't let that happen. Jonathan, you were brothers long before I came between you. You have to be again. Maybe this time in Dakota was meant for you and Aaron to sort of sift the chaff from the grain in your lives while you sift in the fields. I'm like a bit of bothersome wind when I'm around. I blow the two together. But now with me here and you two there, why not let the distance serve a purpose? Let it sift away your differences and get you back to being brothers again.

I've told Aaron that I'll stay true to you from

now on. He knows, too, that the baby will be yours—that there is no other way. We all have to find peace for the unborn one. For you and Aaron that can't happen till you two talk. Then he can start in building his own life and so can we.

But now, for all of us, please do as I ask, Jonathan. But mostly for your sake and Aaron's. Let me not add this to my guilt—that I tore you forever apart.

Please return my best to Aaron.

With deepest affection,
Mary

Jonathan slipped the letter into his cambric pocket when Mrs. Getchner handed it to him, to wait until he was away from the kitchen flurry before he read it.

It was dark when they finished eating and headed for the barn. Jonathan claimed the lantern, sitting apart from the others, who jawed awhile before turning in. The floor of the loft was swept clean in a wide circle around the lantern to prevent fires. Jonathan knelt on the floor, holding the letter toward the lamplight, haunches low, hands high, as he strained to read the words in the flickering glow. A smiled creased his eyes as he pictured Mary inviting Amos and Tony in for coffee. Nobody could make a cup of coffee like Mary, he thought.

But then his expression sobered as he progressed through the letter. When he finished reading, he lay it lightly on his lowered knee, holding it there loosely between two fingers. His other knee was raised, and he braced it with an elbow as he sat motionless, pondering. A picture of her as she must have looked while writing came to him. Then he looked toward the cluster of men, reclining in haphazard poses on the hay. Aaron was smiling, listening to Joe telling some story about how his kid had harnessed a chicken. A burst of laughter filled the loft, and as Aaron leaned his head back to join in, he glanced over to find Jonathan studying him. Jonathan's face was serious, unsmiling. Aaron's immediately became the same. He rose and came to Jonathan, asking, "Everything all right at home?" He knew the letter was from Mary.

"Yup," Jonathan answered, snapping out of whatever had sobered him. "Mary sends her regards."

The men settled down, climbed into their rolls, grunting and yawning and shifting around to get comfortable. Someone turned out the lantern, and Jonathan considered again what Mary had said. She was right, but he needed time to sort his mind. Tomorrow was Sunday. They'd work the day as if it were any other, for crops came before worship this time of year in Dakota. But they'd probably cut the day short. He and Aaron'd have time to talk then.

As Jonathan expected, they came in from the fields a couple of hours before sunset the following day. The men were invited to stay in the kitchen to pass the evening, and Mrs. Getchner got out the tin popper and popped corn at the range, where the men settled to enjoy both the corn and the warmth.

Jonathan was thinking of asking Aaron to walk out toward the barn with him when Aaron stretched and said he guessed he'd turn in early. It saved Jonathan from making unnecessary excuses for their leaving.

They went to the loft together, going through the familiar ritual of lantern and bedrolls.

It was darkly quiet, the dusty, sweet smell of the hay pleasant and familiar. There were few night sounds to be heard, but Jonathan could hear his brother's breathing, could hear his own heart beating at a stepped-up pace. He wanted to say things right, knew that if he failed, it could drive the wedge deeper between himself and Aaron. He began, with the words still unsure in his mind, "Aaron, you awake?"

"Yeah," Aaron grunted.

"It appears we got some things to settle between us," Jonathan began.

"I figured this was coming."

"Yeah?" The way Jonathan said it, Aaron knew how hard this was for him.

"What took you so long getting around to it?" Aaron asked.

"Thought it might settle itself." In his halting way he added, "Didn't, though."

Aaron wondered what Jonathan wanted of him, wondered what had finally prompted him to speak. He asked, "Did Mary say something in her letter?"

"She, ah . . ." Jonathan cleared his throat, giving himself time to make his thoughts clearer. "Ah . . . she thinks it's best we talk about it between us, sort of, settle the air a bit." He paused, then added, "Reckon she's right."

Still, Jonathan didn't mention the baby. Did he want Aaron to admit he was the father or what? Aaron knew how hard this must be for his brother, and at last Aaron prompted, "About the baby?"

"Yes." But still Jonathan didn't say more. He

wanted to but couldn't. They lay side by side in the dark, listening to each other breathe, make small movements, thoughts of Mary glimmering through their minds. Thoughts of their brotherhood came, too, of the rift they'd suffered, how the rift had become a chasm. The silence grew lengthy, and Aaron waited in vain for Jonathan to say more. Drawing a deep breath, feeling a mixture of trepidation and release all at once, he said, "Mary said the baby is mine."

"Yeah, I knew that," Jonathan said, his heart hammering fit to burst.

"We didn't intend it, Jonathan. It just happened, that's all."

Another silence weighted them down while both men sought for an understanding.

"I'm sorry, Jonathan," Aaron said, reaching his own understanding.

"I am, too," came Jonathan's voice. "I thought I wouldn't be, but I am."

The trepidation easing, Aaron asked, "What made you ask it of us?"

"At the time it seemed the clear way. I guess I talked myself into it being the clear way."

"Have you got any idea the pain it caused Mary . . . and me? We didn't see it in the same light as you did, Jonathan."

"I reckon I know that now. Even after I asked it I never thought you'd do it, you were so mad. But it's a funny thing how it worked out like I asked, anyway, about the baby and all. I can't say I ain't happy about the baby. Guess I gotta thank you for that."

"If it was the other way around," Aaron said, "I

don't think I'd be thanking you. If she were my wife, I'd kill the man who laid a hand on her."

Jonathan, in the darkness beside his brother, realized then the depth of feelings he'd been author to. He'd been so sure there was nothing between Aaron and Mary before the start of this. Chances are there hadn't been. But what a fool he'd been to think a thing like that could happen and leave people the same afterward.

"You love her, then?" he asked, dreading the answer.

Should he lie and add to the damage already done? Or would the truth do more damage? Aaron plunged the rest of the way. "I love her, Jonathan. I can't deny it. I reckon she's what I was looking to find—only I never knew it till this happened. She was always too close for me to see."

A pang of sudden regret and fear hit Jonathan, his fear of losing Mary becoming a real possibility. "What about you and Priscilla?" he asked hopefully.

"We tried, Jonathan, but it just wouldn't work for us." After a pause he admitted. "We never really loved each other. We were just convenient, I guess."

"Seemed for a while there, you two got on just fine," Jonathan offered, but he knew it was wishful thinking.

"It's not hard to get on fine with half of Moran Township marching you up the aisle before you know what's happening. With everybody pushing and shoving at us, I guess I thought she was probably the right one for me. Aw, hell, I don't know, Jonathan. Sometimes I thought maybe I loved her. But I guess we don't always pick who we love. If we could, Pris and I would be married by now."

"You don't intend to patch it up with her, then?"

"No. Priscilla just doesn't measure up anymore. Mary's your wife. You should know she's not a woman you . . ." But Aaron found that any way he tried to say what he meant would reveal too much. "Aw, hell, Jonathan. I just need some time to get over this, that's all. I could no more rebound back to Pris right now than you could tell the good citizens of Moran that the baby is mine."

Oh, that hurt, but Jonathan guessed he deserved it. He knew it meant an even deeper involvement than he'd first suspected. At least on Aaron's part. And in spite of himself, he wanted to know the truth about Mary's feelings, too. "And what about Mary?" he couldn't help asking. "Does she love you, too?"

Aaron found he couldn't strip every shred of pride away from Jonathan by saying yes. "Like I said, she's your wife. That's for you to ask her, for her to say. What did she say in her letter?"

"That there'll be nothing more between you and we'll say the baby's mine. She says you'll find things will work out best this way."

Of course that's what she said, Aaron thought. Hadn't she already told him the same thing that night in the barn? She was right, of course, but that didn't make it any easier. Still, it was up to him to confirm it to Jonathan. "That's how it'll be, then, Jonathan, and I swear that's the truth."

They could hear voices near the barn and knew the others would be mounting the ladder soon. But there was one more thing Aaron had to make sure of. Would Jonathan understand that even though he gave up any claim on the baby he was still concerned for the child's welfare and happiness?

"About the baby . . ." Aaron started, then hesitated.

And for once in his life Jonathan grasped Aaron's feelings intuitively. "I'll love it, never fear. And it'll never know the truth from me."

"Jesus, it'll be hard," Aaron admitted in a husky voice. Thinking of the life he'd helped create, of giving it up before it was even whole, he added, "It'll be hell, Jonathan."

The men arrived then, cutting short the sifting of the chaff. Both Aaron and Jonathan lay awake for hours, thinking.

Work made the day go faster, and Mary kept busy in an effort to hurry them. She'd put off making winter sauerkraut until this time when the men were gone. She'd stored the largest, firmest heads of cabbage in the root cellar and now sliced them, added salt and caraway seeds, and beat the mixture with a stomper, smashing it into its own juices and leaving it to ferment.

Navy beans from the garden had been drying since picking time. She spent a day winnowing these in the windy yard, pouring the beans noisily from dishpan to roaster many times until the dried pods were gone, blown free by the October winds. She stored away the cleanly blown kernels.

She dug up gladioli and dahlia bulbs from the garden, tearing their dried tops off, washing and storing them until next spring. The frosts had finished all but the last few resisting chrysanthemums, and she picked them and took them into the house for a bit of cheer. She burned the pile of dead stalks and leaves from the garden on a late, cool afternoon, feeling the days cooling toward winter, the westering sun lowering earlier each day.

She cleaned the coops, the last time before the snow flew, and went down to the barn to visit with Tony and Amos when they came to do the chores. But they'd never take time to come up to the house for a cup of coffee. They had work of their own to do and couldn't take time for pleasantries. So the house remained too silent, the tabletop too free of crumbs, the early-morning fires too lavish for just one.

She talked to the baby, referring to herself often now as "Mama," but never calling anybody "Daddy," feeling that she couldn't yet give that name to either Jonathan or Aaron.

The evenings were the worst, the time right before supper when families should be a-gathering home, but when she had the urge to feel sorry for herself she quickly talked herself out of it, saying again, "I'm a fine one to be feeling sorry for myself!"

She waited until she thought they'd be coming home very soon before she washed blankets and bedspreads, giving them their last prewinter airing. Hauling the heavy things up the stairs late one day, she made up her and Jonathan's bed first, then took the other fresh things into Aaron's room, where the slanted rays of sun sliced low through the west window. Tugging at the sheets and laying the fresh quilts and coverlet on his bed, she thought again of the night she'd spent there with him, of all it had yielded and all it had cost. She caught herself doing more than just dropping the pillows into place, then shook herself and freed her mind of Aaron once again.

Chapter 17

𝕀t seemed like the answer to all their problems when Getchner approached Aaron in early November, saying, "The threshing'll be done the end of this week, but I could use an extra hand around here till Christmas or so, if you'd care to stay on."

The other hands were all married. Aaron, being single, would be more likely to agree.

"The missus'd like to visit our girl in Fargo and do some shoppin' for the holidays. Need somebody to see to the small stock if we go. Machinery needs a good goin' over after harvestin', too." Getchner hurried on, " 'Course, you'd sleep in the house. Gettin' too cold to expect you to stay in the barn." Getchner couldn't know that right now Aaron would have slept in the fields for such an offer as he'd just made. "Pay'd be as good as if you was threshin'," Getchner added.

Aaron smiled, offered his hand, and said. "You've got a man till Christmas, sir."

"Getchner offered to keep me on for a few more weeks—as kind of an odd-jobs man, you might say." It was the night before their return. There was a holiday feeling among the men, a camaraderie created by their eagerness for tomorrow. "I told him I'd stay on," Aaron finished, watching as Jonathan folded and rolled his extra clothes, preparing them for morning.

Aaron's statement slowed Jonathan's hands. He knew this was a blessing in disguise, yet an emptiness crept through him as he replied, "The pay's good here. Getchner's a right fair man."

"That he is." Aaron kept his tone light. "I'll have full pockets, come Christmastime."

Jonathan continued fiddling with the clothes un-necessarily, keeping his hands busy to cover his con-fused feelings. He and Aaron had changed since their talk. What they shared might not be exactly peace, but it was an understanding of feelings that was new. The mellowing had sweetened their relationship, strength-ened their brotherhood. Jonathan felt that new close-ness now. He'd miss Aaron at home, and he knew it. Under this newfound amity, Jonathan was still at a loss to say what he felt, the turmoil within him still beyond expression. The closest he could come to voicing it was, "Have I put you out of your own home, then, Aaron?"

"No, Jonathan," Aaron assured him offhandedly. "No, why—hell! It's only a few weeks."

"You'll be home for Christmas, then?"

"That depends on when Getchner's through with

me here, huh?" A fleeting picture of the Yuletide living room at home limned Aaron's memory, but he pushed it away.

"Mary'd be lookin' for you," Jonathan said, meaning that he would, too. But he simply couldn't say so yet.

Aaron chuckled and answered noncommittally, "We'll see, we'll see. Meantime, I'll need a few more winter things. Could you ask her to pack them up and send them out to me?"

"Anything, Aaron," his brother offered.

They spent the time before the lantern dimmed making verbal notes on what should be sent to Enderland, guessing it wouldn't take but a couple of days for a carton to get out there.

As if the morning knew the men's jobs were finished, it signaled their release with the first, fine-flown flecks of snow. Getchner, at the seat of the buckboard, hitched his collar tighter to his red neck, anxious to roll. The men were arranging their packs on the crowded wagon, jostling one another in good spirits. Jonathan tossed his roll up, saying, "Stash that for me, Joe, will ya?" Then he, too, hitched his collar up, turning to Aaron. His breath was white in the crisp air as he admonished gruffly, "Now, you take care of yourself, boy, you hear? And we'll be lookin' for you, come Christmas."

Aaron stood jamming his gloves on tighter, taking longer than necessary, jabbing the left hand against the right long after the gloves were snug. At last he reached one toward Jonathan, who clasped it tightly as

Aaron said, "You've got a sight more to take care of than I do. You see to it, brother."

"Don't worry, I will." And as he said it, they pitched together, roughly slapping each other's shoulders, their gloved hands making dull thuds before Jonathan broke away to jump onto the buckboard. It jerked to life with a lurch as Getchner slapped the team into action. Aaron stood with shoulders hunched, hands in pockets in spite of the gloves. The wind blew from the northwest at the wagon's tail, hustling it as it went, ignorant of the loneliness in the man who watched it go.

The men had been gone twenty-six days, but it seemed like a year. Then, at last, Jonathan's letter arrived, saying they'd be in on the late-afternoon train. Amos and Tony had come to do chores for the last time this morning. Clem Volence took the rig to town and left it at Anson's. All that was left to do now was wait.

The day had flown by. Mary had cleaned the already clean house, baked bread, and butchered a fat hen for noodle soup. It was a joy for her to be doing again for the men. It seemed as if the house itself took on an expectant air. The warmth of the range, the aromas of the foods, the scrubbed and polished rooms extended a welcome.

As the day flew, the last hour crawled. Mary's footsteps returned again and again to the east window, where she watched for the rig. The weather had turned suddenly cold during the night, and she worried about their warmth, as if Jonathan and Aaron were children.

She smoothed her apron for the hundredth time;

then, glancing outside, she caught first sight of the horse topping the hill. As if surprised at finding herself in an apron, she flew to the pantry, tearing at the ties to remove it as she went. Returning to the window, she saw the rig pull over the nearer hill, but the bonnet was up and she couldn't distinguish any figures inside. Where was her shawl? In the living-room closet . . . She charged there to retrieve it and quickly threw it around her shoulders, gaining the porch steps just as the buggy drew up under the elms.

Jonathan was stepping down, his back to her and the wind, and she flew down the yard, down the wind, calling his name. His big, welcome arms circled her small shoulders, and his face was cold against her warm cheek. His mouth, though, was warm on hers as he tasted her welcome.

Releasing her, he scolded, "You'll catch your death, girl. Get back inside." And he turned to grab his roll from the buggy.

But glancing into the empty conveyance, she said, "Where's Aaron?"

Jonathan swung back to face her, the roll between them as he answered, "Getchner asked him to stay on awhile." He watched her face, but no glimmer of change marked it. The wind threw a stray strand of hair across her cheek, reminding him that she had only a light shawl on. "Get back up to the house," he ordered easily. "I'll be up as soon as I stable the mare."

When he entered the kitchen she was kneeling beside his opened bedroll, picking stray wisps of hay from it. His spare clothes were in a pile beside her. She looked up and smiled at him, and he saw what he had not seen outside, how much she had grown. Her belly had rounded, and her thighs, as she knelt, formed a cradle for its bulge.

"You brought home half the harvest," she smiled, sweeping the transient pieces of hay into her hand.

He turned to hang his jacket on the hook behind the door, chuckling as he crossed the kitchen to where she knelt.

"Maybe," he said, reaching a hand toward her, "but it doesn't need raking right now." He made a tug at her hand. She rose and he noticed a new awkwardness that her added weight caused now.

She lifted the stove lid and brushed the hay into the fire, a jumble of thoughts and feelings threading her mind. In the five minutes he'd been home, Jonathan had shown a solicitousness to her that was unlike him. The hardness seemed gone from him. Was it because he'd missed her, or because Aaron hadn't come back, or what?

He sat down in the rocker by the stove, sighing, "Ahh, home."

She put the bedroll at the foot of the stairs and, coming back into the kitchen, caught Jonathan's eyes on her stomach. As if acknowledging his glance, her hands went to it. She was suddenly self-conscious and could no more hide it than she could hide her newly acquired girth beneath her splayed fingers.

Jonathan cleared his throat.

"Mary," he began, and she knew he was having his usual difficulty voicing his thoughts.

"Yes, Jonathan?" she urged.

He rocked forward, resting elbows on knees, rubbing his palms together as if he might find the words between them.

"Everything's all right between Aaron and me." He paused, then went on haltingly, "We talked . . . we talked like you said, and it's good we did."

"Then why isn't he here?" she asked as gently as she could, but her question still cut into him. Some quiver of muscle at his temple told her he mistook her question, and she hurried on, "Oh, Jonathan, don't look away from me. Didn't I promise in my letter that there was no more between me and Aaron? Will you look at me like this every time I mention his name? He's your brother, Jonathan. This is his house we're living in. I must know."

"Getchner asked him to stay on till Christmas or so. He didn't know exactly how long. We settled our differences, though, and Aaron'll be back before long."

"To stay?" she asked.

"I don't know," Jonathan admitted. "It's a two-man farm, Mary."

But she knew that. Instead of replying, she walked toward the pantry and got the coffee grinder. "I'll get supper," she said quietly, "and then you can tell me all about Dakota."

She was on her way back to the stove when Jonathan rose slowly from the rocker, a look of near-agony on his face. "Dakota was lonely," was all he said, but it stopped her in midstep and she whirled to reach her arms toward him.

"Oh, Jonathan," she crooned as her arms went around his neck. He felt the coffee grinder dig into his shoulder blade, but he didn't care. He crushed her against him, murmuring her name against her hair. The coffee grinder fell to the floor with a splintering crash, but they remained as they were, holding each other, sharing a new bond.

"I love you, Jonathan," Mary whispered, and she found it was true. It was easier to love this warm Jonathan, easy to think he loved her, too.

Her words brought a quickening to his loins and a quick wish to his mind. I wish I could take her up to bed right now, he thought as he ran his hands over her back, bringing her body tightly against his. But he forced a calm to himself, burying the thought that seemed suddenly prurient again when he opened his eyes to the kitchen light. Releasing her, he almost felt that she'd have responded, regardless of the time of day. He chastised himself, reluctantly turning Mary free, wondering what folly had captured him to even think such a thing, especially with Mary in her condition.

Mary turned to her supper preparations to hide her chagrin. Her body felt suddenly chilled, abashed at being turned away so abruptly. She had offered herself to Jonathan, and he'd denied her. Would this be the way of it forever? Her needs had been so simple before Aaron. She longed to return to that state, to quell these urgings that now overtook her without warning. But what had lain asleep in Mary had lain too long, rested too well. It seemed it would stay aroused for a long time to come.

Aaron's decision to stay on in Dakota necessitated some changes in the early-winter planning. The serious snows had held off, but November's temperatures dropped down below freezing, cold enough to keep meat, bringing butchering time. Jonathan and Clem

Volence made plans to exchange help with the chore because it required two men. They butchered at Jonathan's place one cold day in late November, out on the south side of the granary where the steam rose from a huge cast-iron pot. In spite of the chilling cold, the fire under the pot warmed Jonathan's hands as he added ashes to the simmering water. A pulley and rope hung in the sturdy oak tree that had been pressed into such use many times before. Together he and Clem slew the hog, bled it, and hoisted it into the oak with the aid of the pulley. A large wooden barrel leaned on a cross-prop beneath the carcass, forming a kind of chute that held the boiling ash water. It regurgitated belching bubbles as the two men lowered the pig's forequarters into it. The drenching and scalding continued as they slid the carcass up and down, removing bristles as it scraped against the barrel staves. The process was repeated on the rear end, with more scalding water and more scraping. On a table of sawhorses and planks the carcass was laid to be knife-scraped until the hide was clean and hairless.

"This time of year I wish I had a boy to help out," Clem confided.

"Yup. A boy Priscilla's age would be mighty helpful," Jonathan agreed.

" 'Course, I wouldn't trade Priscilla. She's been a big help to her ma since the baby came and all. We thought for a while there we might lose her to Aaron, but he sure ain't been around much lately." Clem squinted a look at Jonathan as he replied, but Jonathan remained his stolid self, scraping away at the carcass.

"Reckon Aaron doesn't know what he wants right now."

"That young Michalek has been hangin' around a lot. Agnes don't think near as much of him as she does Aaron. That don't faze Priscilla none, though—she just tells her ma to quit worryin'. Just the same, we miss seein' Aaron around."

"Mary misses seein' Priscilla, too. Used to get together a lot on Sundays." Jonathan stopped his scraping then and looked at Clem from under lowered brows. "Guess it's not for you nor me to say what they do, though." Then he reached for a board and drew it through the hog's ankle tendons and said, "Let's hoist 'er up now. She's ready to be split and drawn," and the subject of Aaron and Priscilla was put aside.

Mary came downyard, swaddled in mittens, scarf, and coat, a dishpan of salt water propped on her hip. "I came to get the heart and liver for soaking," she called. They needed immediate attention if they were to be edible.

"We got 'em out," Jonathan said, pointing to the tub at his feet.

Mary had suffered little nausea during her first six months of pregnancy, but at the sight of the unsavory tangle of innards in the tub, her stomach gave a sickening lurch. She took what she'd come for and hurried back to the house. But the chosen sections of gut also needed cleaning and scraping for sausage, and she finished her day with the gorge threatening to erupt from her throat. Even the fresh liver she fried for supper lost its usual appeal, but Jonathan ate heartily.

"You're not eating much," he noted, looking at her plate.

Involuntarily her hands went to her stomach and

she said, "When the butchering is done, I'll feel more like eating again."

He was surprised. She never got sick at all. This was something new, and he realized the peculiarities of pregnancy were something they hadn't shared at all. He wondered if there were other things that bothered her.

"I can finish scraping those sausage casings after supper," he offered. And in spite of her queasy stomach, Mary smiled. It was so unlike Jonathan, and she understood his full intentions. His concern was all she needed right now.

"They're all done, Jonathan, but thank you, anyway." And he returned to cutting the meat on his plate, a bit flustered by a new, expansive warmth inside him.

The following day, he brought the quartered carcass into the kitchen table and sawed it into meal-sized pieces. These he placed on planks covered with dish towels, and left on the back porch to freeze overnight. Hopefully no wild animals would brave coming that near, even for a free dinner.

The hams, bacon, and side pork Mary put into brine crocks to soak and turn red as the saltpeter did its work. Slabs of lard, too, were cut and frozen in preparation for rendering. The grinding and frying down of the fat permeated the house for days with a heavy odor. Jonathan had packed the frozen meats into a barrel on the north side of the house long before Mary's job was finished. The sausage-making took on a more pleasant aspect for her, although Jonathan mercifully boiled the hog's head in the caldron in the yard. But when she cooked the meat from it with pearl barley and spices, it filled the house with a pungent garlic aroma, reminding Jonathan of the coming holiday. "It smells just like when Ma used to cook it at Christmas," he said.

"I'm saving it for then. We won't have our first taste till Christmas, just like when you were boys."

"How'd you know we always saved it till Christmas? I never told you, did I?"

"No, Aaron did one time."

"Oh . . . sure," he said, glancing at the kettle that bubbled away on the stove, then back at Mary again.

"Do you suppose he'll make it home for Christmas?" she asked.

"I hope so," Jonathan answered, and he truly did.

"Me, too." And for once her husband didn't feel threatened by her words.

But the hams were smoked in the smokehouse, tied into sacks Mary had sewn for them and plunged deep within the loose oats in the granary, for storage, and still no word had come.

At Getchner's farm, a changed, quiet atmosphere filled the days. Aaron was kept busy, but the work was lighter, the days shorter. After the frenzied harvest activities Aaron felt the abrupt loneliness.

The Getchners took their trip to Fargo, and Aaron was left alone in the strange house. It might have warmed or charmed him, for it was a comfortable place, but it wasn't his home and it left him wanting and lonely, remembering his own place.

It was a week before Thanksgiving, and Aaron pictured the kitchen at home, the table covered with geese being readied for market. His nostrils seemed to catch the smell of wet feathers and melting paraffin.

How he hated picking pinfeathers! But he'd do it gladly to be home right now.

The slow-moving days brought Thanksgiving. He spent it alone, his thoughts miles away. The late-found understanding between Jonathan and himself had left him missing his brother and Mary equally. He found he was again thinking of them as a pair, and the longer he was away, the less he singled out one or the other in his thoughts.

The Getchners returned, and December blustered across the bleak Dakota landscape, the raw winds sweeping its flatness. Christmas was nearing, and Aaron waited for the word from Getchner, word that he was no longer needed. It couldn't come fast enough. He'd had enough of the flatlands, the emptiness.

Some years, Jonathan and Mary had traveled as far as Osakis to find the best market for Mary's dressed geese. This year, though, Jonathan sold them all in Browerville. Mary had kept back two for themselves, one for Christmas dinner and another to be hoarded until midwinter, when it would be a welcome treat after a steady diet of pork and wild game.

They'd had no word from Aaron, and with Christmas only a week away, both Mary and Jonathan were anxious. Mabel Garner had written, inviting the Grays to join her great, raucous, crowded family on Christmas Day. But Mary's condition forced them to decline. Also, they didn't know if Aaron might make it home. So they waited uncertainly, not wanting to be gone if he arrived without warning.

*   *   *

In the wintery dusk the streets of Fargo were shimmering with lights. Motorcars and horses shared the roadways, parked or tethered, chugging or trotting. The backs of the horses gleamed wetly under melting snow. The hoods of the autos were dusted with it.

There were two hours to fill before the night train departed. Aaron had tried rare beefsteak at the Comstock Hotel, finding it surprisingly flavorful and juicy, as Jonathan had read it'd be. Wait till I tell Jonathan about it, he thought. Every thought now was of home. Passing ladies in their hobbled skirts, he tried to imagine Mary hobbling around the kitchen in one, and laughed at the thought. How could she jump the porch steps in a getup like that? Childish voices drifted along the street, and Newt Volence's face came to him, one tooth missing. Through a bakery window he saw decorated delicacies, and he could almost smell the kitchen at home. Mary would be making holiday breads, he thought. The sound of a carol wafted through the evening as the door swung open. He paused and entered the department store where music was spinning off a gramophone. Standing before it, listening, he was approached by a mustached man who moved like a chipmunk.

"May I help you, sir?" the chipmunk chirped.

"How much for this gramophone?" Aaron inquired.

"This, sir," the mustache twisted, "is the newest Edison grraph-o-phone." The little man enunciated each syllable, rolling the r's like an outraged pedagogue.

"How much for this Edison grraph-o-phone?" Aaron repeated, rolling his r's, too, superbly, but with a smile twitching his cheek.

"The device sells for a mere nine dollars." But as

the chipmunk said it, the music wound down and he had to crank the handle to speed up the singing voices until they, too, sounded like chipmunks before settling once again to a human cadence.

The little man ruffled at Aaron's open amusement, but relaxed when Aaron said, "I'll take one anyway, and some records to go with it." The salesman scurried away to find a carton for the purchase, looking even more like a chipmunk in his brown, striped suit.

Aaron also bought a pair of soft kid gloves for Jonathan and a length of white organdy for Mary. For himself he bought a heavy, warm sheepskin jacket, spending a sizable lump of his earnings but enjoying it.

When Aaron at last boarded the train he was weighted down with packages like many of the other homeward-bound holiday travelers. It was hard to contain his excitement amid the babble of voices around him. But darkness passed the train window and he thought of the two who waited for him at home. He pictured the rolling snow-covered hills, the contrast of black tree trunks against them. The yard, the house, the barn—all the familiar, loved scenes lulled him to sleep along with the clacking of the rails beneath him.

Tomorrow would be Christmas Eve, and still no word from Aaron. Every day, when the mail carrier came without a letter, it was hard to keep the disappointment from showing. Mary was preparing dried fruits for her Christmas *hoska* when she heard the chug of the mail car coming over the hill. She finished chopping the last few cherries, then went to fetch a jacket. She was reaching for the door when it opened and there stood Aaron. His face was red and snowburned, but he wore a huge smile as he threw his bedroll inside and followed it to scoop Mary up in an engulfing hug, booming, "Merry Christmas!"

She was so stunned she could only give herself over to the bear hug, stammering, "Aaron, where did you come from?"

"I came from Dakota!" he laughed, swinging her around in his exuberant hug while she struggled to push out of it and look at him.

"But how did you get here?"

He finally released her and answered while he leaned to pull a large carton in from the porch, "I rode the milk train and caught a ride in the mail car—and here I am!" As he finished, he knocked the door shut with the heavy box.

"Milk train? Mail car?" She couldn't believe it yet. "Why didn't you write and have Jonathan pick you up?"

"And spoil a good surprise?" His booming, exuberant mood was infectious. She still had a surprised gape on her face, and he reached out a finger and pushed her chin up, saying, "Good thing it's not summer or the flies would get in there."

Her mouth closed then, but it took on a scolding pout while she shook her finger at him as if he were a naughty schoolboy. But she couldn't fool him, and she couldn't hold a straight face. They eyed each other, snickering; then the merriment grew and blossomed into rich, free laughter. Aaron hooted unabashedly at just being home again.

When they stilled a bit, they looked each other over, noting the changes the last two months had made.

With a little raise of the eyebrows and a perfectly calm expression, Aaron surveyed her rounded shape. "Well . . . look at you."

She spread her hands on her belly as if measuring its growth, shrugged her shoulders, and smiled. "Big, huh?"

He nodded. "But pretty as ever."

"Oh, I don't know about pretty," she corrected. "Clumsy and slow, but not too pretty anymore."

He laughed at her description as he shrugged out of his jacket. She noticed it was new as she reached for it automatically to put it away.

He waved her hand away. "You don't need to fuss and do over me, Mary." And he hung the jacket on a hook behind the door. "It's a Christmas present for myself," he said.

Aaron looked around the room then, saw where she'd been working at the table when he came in. There was a dish towel covering a mound atop the warming oven, and he asked, "Making the *hoska*?" Everything was the same as always, and a rush of contentment filled him.

"Aha," she answered.

"Where's Jonathan?" he asked.

"Down in the barn someplace. Probably with Vinnie. Why don't you walk down and find him?"

"Soon as I get my fill of this kitchen." She watched him as he walked around, touching things, warming his hands at the stove. He acted as if he couldn't get enough of it.

"We didn't think you'd come." She busied herself with the bread while he took care of the things he'd dumped on the floor.

"Getchner kept me busy. I wasn't sure myself when I'd leave."

"What's in the box?" she asked as he took it to the front room.

But instead of answering he complained from beyond her sight, "What? No Christmas tree?"

"It's not time yet, Aaron. Tomorrow's Christmas Eve. Jonathan says he's got a perfect beauty picked out, though."

"When the tree is up, you'll find out what's in the box," he informed her. He had returned to the kitchen, bringing his teasing grin with him.

"Is it a present, Aaron?" she asked, turning to him with floury hands, unable to conceal her curiosity and anticipation.

"Tell you what," he said with the air of one about to make a generous offer. "If you let me poke my finger in that dough, I'll consider telling you." The elastic white puff was mushrooming over the edge of the crock, ready for its last kneading.

"What?" she said, amazed.

"Well, once when I was a kid, Ma let me do that, and it was so much fun. But after that when I asked her she said it made the bread tough, and she never let me do it again."

"Has anybody ever told you that you never grew up, Aaron Gray?" she teased, then stepped aside. "If it'll delight your immature whimsy . . . by all means, have at it." And she made a sweeping gesture, giving him leave to indulge.

He rubbed his palms together. "Oh, boy!" Then he took aim and sunk one finger in the airy puff and watched it deflate and collapse while they giggled at their own absurdity.

"Now get away and let me shape it before it's ruined," Mary scolded, still giggling, then began slicing, flouring, studding the dough with jeweled cherries and golden nuts while Aaron left to find Jonathan.

The *hoska* was baked and cooling before Jonathan and Aaron returned to the house together. Mary heard their voices as they came, and cleared the steam off the east window with her forearm, watching them as they approached. Their bare heads were lowered as they came; then Jonathan's rose as he laughed at something Aaron had said. Aaron threw a loose arm around Jonathan's shoulder for a moment as they reached the back porch steps. Everything must be okay, just like Jonathan said, Mary thought. And she opened the door for them both, loving the sound of their laughter-filled voices.

The gay, careless mood in which Aaron returned affected them all. His first evening home, the house seemed transformed by the voices, the holiday preparations, Aaron's spirit of fun. Mary strung popcorn and the men ate from her bowl while she playfully scolded them until another batch had to be popped. They talked of rabbit-hunting in the morning, the invitation from Aunt Mabel Garner, what Aaron had done for Getchner in Dakota, what they'd earned from the harvest, an Angus cow in the spring, and of course about Aaron's first taste of rare beef.

In the morning Jonathan found a fat cottontail when he checked his snares in the woods, so the hunting wasn't necessary after all. Rabbit was their traditional Christmas Eve meat, and it had taken Mary many failing attempts before she'd learned how to cook it the way they remembered their ma and their grandma cooking it. It was simmered in a stock laced with onion, bay leaf, and prunes, then thickened with spicy chunks of gingerbread. The aromas were heavy in the house when, in late afternoon, the men brought in the pungent pine.

The box Aaron had brought remained mysteriously sealed, the source of much amusement, for Mary refused to give up about it.

"You promised to tell what's in it if I let you have your way with my bread dough," she niggled.

"I did no such thing as promise," he teased. "Jonathan, didn't I tell you it's my dirty laundry? Tell the woman it's my dirty laundry."

Jonathan chuckled. "You'd better watch what you say there, brother. She does up the laundry around here, you know."

Then when they returned from milking, a hurried affair that evening, Aaron found one corner of the box turned back, although nothing of its contents showed.

"O-ho!" he bellowed. "Some sneaking cur has been chewing on my private possessions!"

"Sneaking cur!" came a shriek from the kitchen. "You said yourself it was just dirty laundry, so I merely put it in a tub of lye water to soak." And she heard laughter from the front room.

Mary hadn't peeked into the carton, but she'd pushed it across the floor a bit to see how heavy it was, and she'd found it was excitingly weighty. For all the give-and-take, the box had her giddy with excitement. She fairly squirmed through supper, willing everybody to hurry up. She barely tasted the food, eating a small portion while the men took exasperating second helpings, then agonizing thirds. Normally, she would have been gratified, but tonight it only held them up.

Even Jonathan could see her impatience and played along with Aaron, tipping the tureen sideways and peeking inside, saying, "This stew wants finishing, brother, and you know how Mary's always after us to clean up the bowls."

She jumped up then and snatched the spoon from Aaron's hand, saying, "Just you try it, Aaron Gray, and you'll draw back a stub!"

She flew through the dishes while the men stood the tree erect in a pail of water in the front room. At last, free of her kitchen duties, she joined them.

They trimmed it with tiny candles, each in its own miniature holder, the popcorn Mary had strung, tiny wooden figurines from Jonathan and Aaron's childhood, molasses gingerbread men new this year. At the top went the painted cardboard angel with white horsehair halo, the same as every year. The candles remained unlit until Christmas Day, but the glow of the kerosene lantern lent a rosiness to the room. Small packages had mysteriously appeared, but with the time at last here for their opening, Mary held back, saying, "I don't want to open them yet."

"Leave it to a woman to change her mind, huh, Jonathan?" Aaron winked.

"I hate to have it over so fast," Mary added hastily. "It's been such a wonderful day." She expressed what they'd all been feeling, drawing them close but making the men momentarily uncomfortable with emotion. But the moment passed, and they sat to open the collection of packages. The small ones from Mary yielded necessary items, bought with her money from selling the geese, mostly socks and plaid flannel shirts. Jonathan's luxurious kid gloves brought a gentle rebuff to Aaron—"These are pretty fancy for Moran Township"—but he was pleased, and his eyes showed it. At the length of white organdy, Mary cooed, "Ooo, it's so fine and soft," then draped it around her shoulders like a shawl. From Jonathan, Aaron received a new bottle of bay rum, Mary a woolen scarf.

Aunt Mabel had sent a package that proved to be a selection of homemade kimonos, saques, and bibs for the baby. While Mary was pulling them out, examining each one, even putting them to her nose to smell the newness of the fabric, Jonathan quietly left the room. There was a moment of apprehension as Mary and Aaron looked at each other across the tiny clothes that lay on her lap. Jonathan's absence was brief, however, and as Aaron began to rise to go after him, they heard the porch door close. Then Jonathan came back in, bringing with him a wooden cradle. He stepped inside the doorway, and there seemed to be a faint flush on his cheeks as he stood there, holding the cradle self-consciously.

"I . . . ahh . . . here . . ." he began haltingly. "Well . . . I dug this out of storage and painted it up a bit," he finally managed. He looked at Mary while he said it, and her face registered her delight as she came to her feet, exclaiming, "Jonathan, your own old cradle! And look how you've done it up!"

He set it down, and she was beside it, touching it

to make it rock, walking all around it to view it from all sides, happily expectant as she circled it. "It's just perfect. I'll have to make a mattress for it. When did you paint it? How could you get it done without me knowing? It's small enough to fit anywhere, and we could move it around the house to any room we want. I have enough yard goods to make sheets for it, too. Oh, Jonathan," she finished, wide-eyed with delight.

Aaron hadn't seen her in this jubilant maternal mood before. He sat on the sofa, elbows on knees, studying her in an element he couldn't share. He smiled as he watched and listened to her, but a hollow yearning settled in the pit of his stomach. He'd known it would happen at times like this, but this was the first time, and he hadn't expected the force of it. She was radiant in her excitement, glowing with her plans, pleased and proud of Jonathan. As he heard her exclamations he looked at the cradle, and Aaron thought of how he'd slept in it as a baby, too. That ought to be some consolation, but it was none at all.

Jonathan beamed at Mary while she jigged around the cradle. He'd felt the awkward moment pass with her exhilaration. He'd been unsure if it was wise to give it to her in front of Aaron, but seeing Aaron's relaxed pose and smile, he was glad now that he'd done it. It seemed like another barrier safely crossed.

"All right, enough now, Mary." He stopped her and pointed to Aaron's carton. "Maybe Aaron will let you look inside that thing now."

Aaron rose from the sofa, hiding his morose reflections behind a smile, and pulled the carton into the middle of the floor. "Who wants to do the honors?"

Mary was kneeling beside him in a minute, all grinning and eager. Aaron gave her the go-ahead with a wave of his open hand, indicating the carton. He winked at Jonathan as they watched her pull it open, voice high with excitement as she asked, "Oh, Aaron, what did you get?"

When she got to the last layer of enveloping cardboard and pulled it back, she sucked in a breath and covered her mouth with her hands in surprise as she exclaimed, "A gramophone! Aaron brought a gramophone!"

"Not quite," Aaron corrected. "I was told it was an *Edison grraphophone!*" And he rolled the words off his tongue, imitating the salesman. "I bought it from a chipmunk! And he made it very clear that only an idiot would call it anything else."

He described the fussy, brown-striped gent and his haughty treatment. They all laughed and repeated the word "grraapho-phone" over and over while they examined the records, the knobs, and the crank on the machine. They played all the records. There were two Strauss waltzes, the Christmas carol Aaron had first heard playing, and a Sousa march. They took turns cranking the machine as it needed it, laughing when it slowed to a distorted growl. The music wound down, then back up. Mary wanted to dance.

"Aw, you dance with Aaron," Jonathan dissented. "You know I'm not much for it."

So she and Aaron spun a few slow circles around the room, leaning and swooping exaggeratedly as if they were in a Vienna ballroom while Jonathan shook his head, enjoying their antics. Aaron bowed at the end of the dance, and Mary curtsied, holding her dress away from her bulging sides.

"Thank you, Mrs. Gray," Aaron said.

"Likewise, Mr. Gray," she laughed. "Ahhh," she sighed as she sunk down tiredly into a chair, "what a gift you brought, Aaron. But it wore me right out."

"I guess we all need rest. Tomorrow we can celebrate some more," Jonathan said.

"Why don't you two go up and I'll bank the coals and fill the woodbox?" Aaron said, then watched Jonathan lead Mary toward the stairway.

When they got there, Mary turned toward Aaron again. "Merry Christmas, Aaron," she said.

"You, too," he answered.

On their way up the steps, she said to Jonathan, "It was the best Christmas ever, I think."

"Are you glad to have Aaron home?" Jonathan asked.

"Oh, yes," she answered, and she reached behind her to take Jonathan's hand.

Downstairs, the door closed as Aaron went out to the woodpile.

Chapter 18

$\mathcal{T}$here were many small preparations to fill Mary's last weeks before the baby was due. She hemmed flannel for diapers, made small blankets and buntings, prepared the necessary rigging for the cradle, and completed the baby's layette with the clothing she thought it would need.

In the evenings during these longest nights of the year, they all sat around the kitchen table with bags of washed goosefeathers beside their chairs. Featherstripping was a tedious job, but it brought in good money when they sent the feathers off to a buyer in Chicago. Perfect goosedown brought a tidy price with little work, but the larger, coarser feathers had to be stripped, drawn between thumb and forefinger to take off the fine, soft fuzz, leaving the bare quill to be discarded. As the nights wore on, Mary would rise from her chair more and more often, bracing a hand against her back, arching it to remove the cramps of discomfort before returning to the feather-stripping. She seemed to grow extra inches daily, and the men never left her alone for long now. When it was necessary to go to town, Aaron went alone, leaving Jonathan home with Mary.

The only hint of discord among them came when Aaron returned from town one day in late January. He'd had time to ponder during his ride. Lately there'd been times when they all sat around the table and his eyes would wander to Mary's girth, seeing for himself the commotion of the baby within her. Her belly at times heaved in ballooning fashion under her dress as the child shifted and rolled. She would hitch herself up on the chair then, tightening her stomach muscles to still the action within. He'd catch himself wondering if it must not hurt her, but she never complained.

He had never heard her ask for anything regarding the baby or the birth and wondered what plans she and Jonathan had made. He was sure Aunt Mabel couldn't leave her large brood to come to Mary for the length of time she'd be confined. Most wives had mothers or sisters to help out, but Mary had neither. He'd hesitated to ask questions, not wanting to ruffle the smooth relationship among them. But the questions nevertheless lay heavy on his mind, and when he returned home that day, he cornered Jonathan in the granary to ask him.

"Who's going to help Mary with the delivery?" Aaron kept his eyes on the grain Jonathan was shoveling into a pail.

"We'll get the midwife," Jonathan answered, and Aaron felt his ire rise.

"No, Jonathan," he said with quiet insistence, "no midwife. She'll have Doc Haymes."

Jonathan stopped shoveling, and their eyes met. "Haymes is an old fool," he said.

"Mary doesn't think so," Aaron argued. "You know she'd feel easier with Doc Haymes. With two of us here, I can go to town easily when the time comes and get him."

Jonathan's eyes seemed to level, but not relent, as Aaron, too, stood fast.

Aaron spoke. "I haven't staked any claims. I haven't asked anything—but now I'm not asking, I'm telling you, Jonathan. That's how it'll be. She'll have Haymes, and nobody else."

The shovel bit into the grain again, and Aaron knew he'd won his way. He softened then as he offered, "If it's the money, I've got it to pay him."

Jonathan felt the barb and couldn't let it pass. "You know it's not the money, Aaron," he defended himself.

Aaron knew it was true. He knew Jonathan resisted because he'd never liked Doc Haymes much. "Yes, I know that," he admitted. "But I'd pay if you'd let me. I'd like to," he finished.

"That's for me to do," Jonathan said in finality, and Aaron had to accept that.

They'd each taken a little and given a little. While the conversation had caused the first rift between them since Aaron's return, they knew they would overlook it, for Mary would need them both in days to come.

There was nothing extraordinary about the day it started. The feared snowstorm of Aaron's dreams was nowhere in the offing. The sky was true blue, the roads rough but dry. As he drove to town, he wished they had a telephone, but nobody out their way had a phone yet because the line hadn't come out that far. The closest phone was nearly in town, so he might as well go clear in to Doc's office to fetch him. Suppose Doc was out in the country on a call? I'll just go track him down, Aaron thought, while his mind raced. But Doc Haymes was in his office and acted almost casual in light of Aaron's anxiety.

"First one takes some time a-comin'," he reminded Aaron, collecting his bag, stuffing some strange-looking things into it while Aaron chafed at his slowness. Finally he donned his coat, clapping Aaron on the shoulder to push him ahead out the door. "It's usually the father gets the jitters. Now calm down, Uncle Aaron," he chuckled good-naturedly as they headed for the rig.

It seemed forever that the tensing pains had been flowing and ebbing through her. Mary had walked the floor until an especially severe spasm caught her, made her grab her belly, and give in to the bed at last. Jonathan hovered near her, then left the room again to check the road for signs of the rig.

Aaron arrived with the doc and dropped him off, saying, "You might need help. I'm going to fetch Agnes Volence." A woman's presence might be comforting to Mary, whether the doc needed her or not. He hadn't consulted Jonathan, hadn't really thought about what he was doing—just acted on instinct.

There was no dallying when Agnes came to the door and heard what he'd come for. She didn't stop to question or give orders to the family she left behind. She just said, "You see to everything here, Pris," and

Aaron was following her stubby shape toward the buggy.

When Mary saw the reassuring, familiar face at the foot of the bed, she sighed, "Agnes," before another pain took her breath away.

The two visitors took over, Doc Haymes issuing orders, Agnes carrying them out. They prepared the bed, spreading layers of newspapers to be covered by soft, absorbent layers of something that felt warm and good beneath Mary. Doc Haymes hitched straps to the foot of the bed, and the sight of them gripped Mary with a sudden, repulsive fear. Agnes stroked her hair back from her forehead, calming her wild-eyed fear with a quiet voice, "No worry, girl, you'll be happy to have them when the time comes. Rest now while you can." And Mary closed her eyes to do as Agnes said, happy the woman was there.

The pains subsided a short time later, and Mary seemed to be resting fitfully. Agnes left her to see how the two downstairs were doing. Jonathan looked gray, so she made coffee, encouraging him to drink. It seemed there'd be a wait yet and no sense in his hanging around, looking like a whipped pup. "You got something to keep you busy outside awhile, Jonathan?" she asked. "Might do you good to get away from the house a bit."

"I ain't leaving now," Jonathan retorted sharply.

But Agnes explained, "She's resting for a spell. Why don't you get a breath of air, and Aaron can come and get you if something happens?"

Aaron was agreeing and Jonathan didn't care to battle both of them, so he grabbed his jacket and swung out the door, going down to talk some sense with Vinnie. Vinnie always listened.

He stayed in the barn, talking to the bull, a long time. If he'd been a drinking man, he'd have had a snort right now, and he told Vinnie so. He hadn't thought about this waiting around before. This was hell! He could tell him anything, old Vinnie. Never before had he appreciated the black ear quite as fully as he did now.

Aaron sat in the kitchen, his chair propped back, studying the snowy yard. He let himself think of the baby trying to come into the world right now, of Jonathan as shaken as any father might be, of Mary and the pain she'd soon bear. But he permitted no thoughts of himself. He remained locked outside himself, a muscle twitching in his tense jaw while he waited.

Jonathan was cleaning Vinnie's stall when he heard Aaron enter the barn with the milk pails. At his questioning glance, Aaron answered, "Everything's the same. She's quiet." They started the evening chores together.

Mary came awake with a gasp. She'd been drifting and dreaming in a pictureless place when her eyes flew open at the pain and she saw Doc Haymes's face near the bed. She didn't know how long she'd lain quietly, but as if her body had enjoyed sufficient peace, it now dictated battle. The contractions built and swelled, leaving less rest between each one. She felt a gush of wetness and realized her legs were bound, her body exposed.

"What is it?" she gasped.

Agnes was there, holding her hands. "It's just your

water." How did Agnes get here? Doc Haymes was supposed to come. Then she felt other hands on her and realized he was there, too, before a jagged pain made her clutch at the hands she held. She felt her hands being placed on the cool iron of the bedstead above her head, and she grasped it and pulled.

She was aware of calling out Jonathan's and Aaron's names as the undulating contractions came and went, but her senses soon became blurred as the pushing pains started. Someone was telling her it was all right to scream, and she heard the rasping growl of her own voice as her legs strained, her arms pulled, and a rush of warmth washed the baby from her. She felt its feet kicking against her thighs before she slipped past the ether into unconsciousness.

Jonathan was in the kitchen, pale as the porcelain coffeepot on the table before him. Aaron sat beside him, a cup in his hand. He had raised it to his lips when a muffled sound of pain drifted through the house from the bedroom upstairs. Aaron shot from his chair to stand before the window, his back to the room, his thumbs hooked in his pockets. He heard the cry increase in volume and strength, and his own breath matched it, slowly exhaling, silently pushing the air from his lungs, while the wail above drew out interminably.

During the minutes he stood there, the baby had no part in his thoughts. Only Mary. She labored with a pain too deep for him to comprehend, and all he could do was futilely wish to share it, ease it some way. She possessed him in that time as surely as if they'd spoken vows. The false front he had shown in these past weeks had worked so well he'd convinced himself he was nearly free of her. But now, hearing her give birth to their child, she gave birth again to his love for her.

He'd been so tense that even his eyes had dried out from his unblinking stare. When suddenly Mary's voice was stilled, his shoulders lurched forward and his head dropped. He gulped for air suddenly realizing he'd matched her breath for breath. The sound of a baby's gusty cry brought such exhaustion to him he sank into a chair again. His knees had buckled.

Jonathan was standing at the foot of the stairs when Agnes stuck her head over the upstairs banister. "It's a girl, Jonathan."

"A girl," he breathed. He stood in hesitation, one hand on the railing, one foot on the stairs.

"Should I come up, Agnes?" he whispered.

"No, later. Mary's asleep right now."

"Is she . . . are they . . . all right, I mean?"

"Fit as a fiddle, both of 'em." Jonathan knew it must be so by the pleased grin on Agnes's face.

"That's fine," he said, more to himself than to her, "just fine."

Jonathan came back into the kitchen, and the two men saw each other's haggard faces. "It's a girl," he said. Aaron's face remained unchanged. He thought that he didn't give a damn what it was as long as Mary was okay.

"How is she?"

"Both fine."

In this intimate minute while they both drew deep gulps of air with eyes locked, the two brothers found an even deeper understanding. Aaron remembered

Pris saying there's no time when two people feel closer than after a birthing—and he knew now, fully knew, how true that was.

Then Aaron quickly covered his feelings, afraid to have Jonathan see any more. "You'd rather it was a boy."

"It doesn't matter," Jonathan said, going to the sink to pump a glass of water, uncomfortable now with what had passed between them for that instant.

"I'll take Agnes home whenever she's ready to go," Aaron offered.

"That'll be fine," Jonathan agreed, slipping back into familiar ways again.

It was nearing midnight when Doc Haymes left and Aaron returned Agnes Volence to her home. By admitting to himself that he still loved Mary, he'd exposed himself to more torment. Now there was the baby, too, to add to it. A girl, he thought. Agnes had said she had lots of curly hair. She's got my curls, he thought, then shut out the thought.

"You look like you did as much fretting as Jonathan did," Agnes said.

"I guess no man feels at ease with birth."

Agnes laughed tiredly.

"No, that's for sure. But you still got the worst one coming—when it's that first one of your own. Tonight's fretting will seem like child's play then."

It cut into him, but he replied, "That time's a way off yet, I guess." And of course they were both thinking of Pris.

"You know, Aaron, I always favored you for Priscilla. I was sorry when you stopped comin' around.

Now mind you, I'm not pryin'. I don't know what happened between you two, but she lost a good man when she lost you, and I just wanted you to know, that's all. I wish . . ." She stopped then and heaved in a breath of the cold night air. "Mothers sometimes talk too much," she finished, and Aaron felt a closeness to Agnes Volence then, wishing things were different.

When they got to her house, he took her hand, and mittened though they both were, there was contact of a close sort. "I just can't thank you enough for coming down, Agnes," he said. "It means a lot to me . . . to us."

"Don't mention it," the woman said, sorry all over again that circumstances had drawn this man away from her daughter.

"You're sure Mary's okay?" he asked one last time.

"You don't have to worry about Mary. She might be tiny, but she's tough. She bent two spokes of that bedstead out of joint. Don't worry."

"Okay. Thanks," he repeated.

"Good night, Aaron."

"Good night."

He rode home in a tangle of thoughts that played tricks on his mind, appearing and disappearing so fast he couldn't grasp any one of them. Mary's hands pulling on an iron bedstead hard enough to bend it . . . a head full of brown curls . . . a different head of honey-colored hair swaying over bare skin . . . Jonathan's face when he said it was a girl . . . then, hands bending iron rails again . . .

The house was dark when he got there. He made straight for the cellar and brought up two quarts of chokecherry wine. He took them to the barn to do the honors, as he ironically put it to himself. When he'd finished the first quart and reached to uncap the second with stiffly moving fingers, he bellowed into the quietness, "Don't tell me when I've had enough!" as if someone had scolded him. But there were only the animals and himself, and his voice softened as he blubbered, "Man's gotta right ta get drunk whenniz wife az a baby." He'd forgotten she was someone else's wife. The wine had done its work.

Jonathan found him there in the morning. Aaron's sheepskin jacket was pulled up around his ears, his knees drawn up for warmth. In the hay beside him the second bottle of wine stood, nearly full, straight up. Not a drop had spilled.

Jonathan took the bottle and dumped it in the gutter. He went back to shake Aaron awake and smelled his fetid breath as his brother snored, unaware. He felt a sort of pity for him, but realized that this kind of self-indulgence would gain them all nothing. The deed was done. They had to proceed.

He leaned down and shook Aaron's shoulder, resolution in his voice as he ordered, "Wake up, brother, I need you. C'mon, let's do chores!"

Aaron opened his bleary eyes and did a most surprising thing. He got straight up, as if he'd been caught napping during a sermon. But when he was upright he wavered a minute, then slammed back down.

"Gotta get started with the chores," Jonathan said, and turned away, leaving Aaron to locate his equilibrium.

Aaron pulled it off with wretched aplomb. He got up, straightened his jacket, joined Jonathan with not so much as a whine. But he felt as if he'd been horse-kicked.

They couldn't work in the close barn without words between them. After all, Aaron had left the house with little news of Mary or the baby.

"How's everything up there?" he asked, with a nod in the general direction of the house.

"They're doin' okay," Jonathan replied.

"Must be some things that need doing in the house . . ." But before he could finish the thought, Jonathan was nodding, "Yup. Agnes says the women from around here will be comin' up each day to lend a hand."

"Good," Aaron answered. But he felt a ripple of regret that events were already flowing on, out of his hands. The women were coming to help out, and there wouldn't be much need for him to. He'd gladly have helped at any unaccustomed job. It would've made him feel closer to Mary and the baby.

"I'll tend to the chickens and geese," he obliged. That, at least, was Mary's job. But even that wasn't much now in the winter with the dwindled flocks.

The first day was oblivion for Mary. She never re-membered a sleepiness as heavy as she felt that day. She slept for long hours at a time and was awakened when the baby was brought to suckle. But Mary fell asleep with the warm, wet tugging at her breast, in a deep, delirious contentment. She ate something once when the sun had circled past the south side of the house, drank huge glasses of milk when she was told to do so. It wasn't until the second day that she awoke, refreshed, at first light, to the tiny sounds from the cradle beside the bed.

The house was silent. Jonathan must have slept on the couch or in Aaron's room, she thought.

She reached an arm out and, without leaving the bed, pulled the cradle up close. The baby was lying on her stomach, and all Mary could see of her was a silken cap of brown curls on the back of her head. Tiny, disgruntled complaints came from the wriggling bundle, and Mary recalled how that same wriggling had felt inside her own body. A surge of feeling coursed through her at the moment as she reached to pick up her daughter. She thought, How can I contain all this joy when it grows into love? A giddy sensation of completeness aroused everything maternal in her as she cooed to the babe, examined her perfection.

"Hello, precious girl. Look at you, all wet and complaining. Mama has to learn everything, so be still while I get this off you." Inside, she found the skinny, bowed legs, the perfectly formed toes. "Princess, you're beautiful. Yes, I'm hurrying," she said, reaching for a diaper from the foot of the cradle, "I'll get faster when I learn." She continued the flow of soothing talk until she'd changed the baby and settled her at her breast. Then she ran her forefinger over the delicate earlobes, the eyebrows that looked no more than a fine mist. The baby's perfection seemed a miracle.

Oh, Aaron, she thought, how can I ever repay you for giving her to me? And how will you bear it not to share her? Her newfound feelings still imbued her with this sense of fulfillment, making her sharply aware of what Aaron would suffer. With the living reality of their baby in her arms, she admitted the magnitude of the sacrifice he was making. But she was helpless to change it.

Jonathan came to the door at midmorning, as spit-shined as a boy in a school play. She couldn't help chuckling. "Jonathan, I've been waiting for you," she said, reaching a hand out toward the door.

He came in and took it, but she thought if he'd had a hat in his hand he'd be turning it nervously by its brim. "How you feeling?" he whispered, dropping her hand.

"Fine. Sit down," she said, moving her legs over.

"Oh, no," he said as if she'd accused him of something.

"Did you see her yet?"

He shook his head, and she couldn't tell if he meant yes or no, he was so nervous.

"Don't be scared, Jonathan. She's only a baby."

"Yeah, I guess so," he said, peering into the cradle.

"Sorry it couldn't have been a boy for you."

"Oh, no, it don't matter. She's . . . she'll do just fine."

"I reckon she'll have to."

He stood above the cradle, nodding repeatedly as his arms dangled uselessly at his sides. Then one hand reached out tentatively, jerked back again in doubt.

"It's okay to touch her," Mary said. "She'll be waking up pretty soon, anyway."

"He touched some of the brown curls with his large knuckles. "She's sure small," he said. When he turned, he caught Mary wiping quickly at a tear, trying to get it gone before he looked at her. All he could do was clear his throat, but it sounded like thunder in the quiet room.

"Could I get you something?" he asked.

"I reckon I've got all I need," she said.

He cleared his throat again. "Mrs. Orek is cooking up some dinner down there," he said, not able to think of anything else. "Why don't you sleep awhile till it's ready?" But when he'd left she couldn't sleep at all. She couldn't forget Jonathan's big brown knuckles on the baby's hair.

That first week brought a steady parade of neighbor women each day. The house seemed invaded, overrun. No matter that they came one at a time. You never knew who you'd run into next, Aaron thought, and stayed away most of the time. Priscilla came one day, and he made a special effort to remain outdoors so their paths wouldn't cross any more than necessary. They were civil to each other at mealtimes, but each felt distant from the other.

Aaron had pulled himself together after that first night, but it took a full day for his body to return to normal after the abuse he'd done it. He put off seeing the baby for the first time, not wanting to disturb Mary during her first uncomfortable days. He chose the time carefully, waiting until he was armed by the presence of others in the room.

Mrs. Hawkins was there that day, with her perpetually flapping jaw. He knew she would run plenty of interference for him during his visit. Jonathan was in the bedroom, too, when Aaron stepped to the door.

Mrs. Hawkins was changing the baby's diapers, and for once Aaron was grateful for the woman's chatter.

"Well, lookit here! And if it isn't the proud uncle. Now don't you be rude and put up a fuss when your uncle comes to see you. Yeees"—she drew the word out in the pouting way some adults talk to babies—"yes, yes, we're nearly through here, little one."

Mary was sitting up, wearing a silk bed jacket. Her hair was tied back but unbraided. He remembered the night she'd taken her braids out because he'd asked her to. She turned a radiant smile to him as he stood in the doorway and Mrs. Hawkins jabbered to the babe. But Mary's face gave away no secrets, and neither did his. Except maybe that he couldn't keep his eyes from the metal rods of the bedstead, and sure enough, it was easy to see the two that were bent a bit out of line.

"Aaron, you've come at last," she chimed. "Jonathan and I couldn't guess why you waited so long."

Aaron stepped inside the room, throwing a wink at Jonathan as he declared, "The wee ones are a bit overpowering to us bachelors."

Mrs. Hawkins guffawed as she brought the wrapped bundle and thrust it toward him. "This little thing ain't but a mite. You hold her, Aaron, you'll find out."

But Aaron staved her off with open palms. "You can hold her, Mrs. Hawkins. I'll just look over your shoulder." That brought their laughter on him as he peeked inside the concealing blankets. He could see dark eyes that didn't seem to focus on much, a tiny mouth that sucked at nothing. He kept his hands folded behind his back and rocked forward on his feet as if cowed. Actually, he knew it'd be folly to touch her, especially that curly brown hair.

"What'll you call her?" he asked.

"Sarah," Mary answered. "It means princess. That was the first thing I called her, so it seemed right for her name."

"It's a pretty name." He nearly said it aloud to hear it—Sarah Gray. But he bit off the words, saying instead, "She's mighty pretty, Mary," then added tardily, "Jonathan."

Jonathan cleared his throat. "Mrs. Hawkins cooked a fine-smelling meal. Reckon I'll go have a bite."

Mrs. Hawkins made for the door, and Jonathan followed her. Aaron turned, too, but Mary stopped him, saying, "Aaron, can you stay for a minute?"

He thought, I could stay forever, but a minute is harder.

"Sure," he said.

When the others had left, she said, "Jonathan told me you went after Agnes, and I just wanted to thank you. You can't know how happy I was to have her here that night."

"We all felt better having her here," he returned, and his eyes went to the spokes behind Mary's head. "Is everything okay? I mean . . . you?"

She just nodded, that same brilliant smile on her face.

He wanted to say, "Call if you need me, let me know anything you want and I'll get it for you, do it for you, buy it for you." But instead he just said, "Good. Be seeing you, okay?" And he hurried from the room.

Most women stayed in bed for two weeks after giving birth. Mary refused to be pampered, coddled, or cajoled longer than seven days. When Doc Haymes came around, she asked his okay to get up and start doing for herself again. He realized the willful girl would do as she pleased, anyway, and judged it wisest to give her rein and at the same time some sensible advice to go with it.

"All right," he agreed, "but no lifting, no straining, and plenty of short rests for a couple of weeks."

"Oh, I promise, Doc Haymes," she conceded. "The neighbors have been grand with their help, but I can do most of it now, I'm sure. And Jonathan and Aaron are here to help, too."

"Well, see that they do, young lady," he warned.

She chuckled at his grudging, grumbling warning, hearing, too, the concern behind his words. On an impulse, she stayed him with a hand on his arm, saying, "You were right, Doc."

His grizzled eyebrows raised questioningly to her. "About what?" he asked.

"About the time of the month. I tried it till it worked."

She was happy she'd told him when his wizened face broke into a smile. He patted the small hand on his arm, gave it a squeeze as he spoke. "Good for you, girl, good for you."

He'd seen many babies into the world, but few had been wanted as much as this one. It was heartwarming to see the couple blessed after seven fruitless years. It was downright gratifying, he thought as he walked through the kitchen on his way out. Jonathan was waiting for him there. "I'd like to settle up with you," he said.

"No need to be in a rush, Jonathan," the older man answered.

"It's not my way to let debts go for long," and he

seemed intent upon having it done. He held a number of bills in his hand.

Doc Haymes named his fee, and Jonathan placed the proper number of bills in his palm, abrading the corner of each between his callused fingers as he counted.

The doctor folded them in half, then looked at the man as he thanked him. But before turning to leave, he said, "You have a fine daughter, Jonathan . . . and a hell of a fine wife."

"Yessir, I do," Jonathan agreed.

Chapter 19

$\mathcal{A}$aron made his decision the day he first saw Sarah. Folly, he'd thought it was to touch her. And folly it was to stay here any longer. He should have left last summer when common sense told him to the first time. But something had kept him here until he was sure everything would be okay. Now that the baby was born and she and Mary were both doing all right, he knew he had to leave. Jonathan had stepped into the father's role so smoothly there was no doubt that Aaron wouldn't be needed around here anymore. Mary treated Aaron exactly as she always had. But the difference now was that sometimes when she turned to say, "Aaron, hand me that wash cloth," Sarah was there on her arm. He stayed away from the house as much as he could, but he began to hate the granary steps where he sat and shelled corn or mended harness or did nothing in the evenings. He began going down to the hall again. But he made plans to leave as soon as he could.

Farmers all over the state would need field help soon, and he could find work anywhere. He'd been to Douglas County before and liked the look of the land out that way. He remembered once when he'd taken a load of geese to Osakis, passing farms much larger than those around here. The land west of Alexandria bore farms of even greater acreage, and besides, the country there was as pretty as here, not flat and desolate like Dakota.

He subscribed to the *Douglas County Courier* and waited for the first paper to arrive by mail so he could read the want ads.

Meanwhile, spring moved closer. Jonathan was again full of plans for Vinnie. He never tired of searching the farm journals for information on Black Angus cows and seemed obsessed with the idea of buying one soon. The bull had matured over the winter and broadened in its wide, powerful shoulders. Aaron had to admit he was a beautiful specimen as Vinnie's coat glimmered in jet sheens. Jonathan had a right to be proud. The way the bull handled for Jonathan was a thing of beauty. He could walk near the animal and say some mysterious thing near the smartly angled ears, and as if the animal truly understood the man, he followed, doing as he was bid. His polled head would turn in response to Jonathan's nearness and his throatlatch would tighten as he became alert to the man.

They started preparing the fields for seeding but an early April blizzard unexpectedly forced them all inside for two strained days. When the mail came again, Aaron had two replies to his inquires from Douglas County. The pay wouldn't be as good as in Dakota, but it would do. He wrote back inquiring when he could start work. Then he and Jonathan found their days frenzied with spring activities, and Aaron waited for his reply.

Aaron could hear the grindstone downyard where Jonathan was sharpening implements. He walked toward the sound, and Jonathan finished honing the piece as Aaron approached. Jonathan looked askance at his brother as he poised a harrow spike over the wheel. Before he lowered it, Aaron spoke. "I've decided to leave, Jonathan."

"Seems you're always leavin'. But you always come back. So why not just stay?"

Aaron hunkered down, elbows on knees, and picked up a stone, tossing it repeatedly as he answered. "It's different now. I've got to go now."

Jonathan started the wheel up again, his foot rising and falling in smooth rhythm. The blade touched the wheel, sending sparks and swarf spraying around it. He had to shout to be heard above the whining noise. "There's still room for you here."

"Three's a family—four's a crowd," Aaron replied.

"What?" Jonathan yelled.

Aaron raised his voice. "Never mind. I'll be gone in early May."

"What?" Jonathan yelled again.

Aaron put his foot on the paddle, stopping the wheel. "Stop that damn thing, will you?" he demanded gruffly. "I got a job in Douglas County. I'll be leaving in early May."

Jonathan had felt more comfortable with the noise of the grindstone grating around them. "It's a two-man farm," he reasoned.

"Not anymore," Aaron said. "You'll just have to let some lie fallow. Vinnie's calves will bring in plenty extra cash to make up for it."

"What about the house?" Jonathan asked.

"We'll settle that when we must. I'll get my room and board there, so for now let's let it ride."

"I want to buy a cow this year," Jonathan said, meaning he couldn't pay for a house, too.

"We'll let it ride, I said." And with that Aaron left. The wheel shrilled behind him once again.

Mary knew what was coming before she was told. She'd seen the *Courier* arriving for Aaron, then those two letters right after the blizzard. It could only mean that Aaron was after a job.

Jonathan told her it was true one night at bedtime while they whispered in the dark, not wanting to awaken Sarah, who slept beside them. He seemed to accept it quite readily, even to using the house again without settling anything on Aaron for its use. It rankled her that Aaron shouldn't even realize a bit of rent for it. But she didn't say so, for there was one thing Jonathan had a fixation about and that was building his Angus herd. He could start that only if the house came free.

But she made up her mind that she would not see Aaron pushed away from his home without any compensation at all. She knew they couldn't continue this way but felt a guilt at her part in forcing him out. She began thinking about asking Jonathan to build another house, maybe down in the woods west of this one. She expected him to balk at the idea, but why should Aaron get cut out? Knowing how he felt about this place, she thought of him leaving it again and formed questions she would put to Jonathan. But she and he were getting along so well, and if she argued in Aaron's favor, what would Jonathan think? She thought of the money she still had from selling the geese. More had come from the down they sent to Chicago. She decided she'd offer it as a start. Maybe Jonathan wouldn't doubt her sincerity.

Aunt Mabel and Uncle Garner came at last. They arrived in a buckboard one hot Sunday in late April, bringing their entire troop of kids and half of their larder along for a picnic. Mary was ecstatic. Her confinement and the time since Sarah was born had left her little time to feel lonely, but she often missed Aunt Mabel.

The big, mothering woman took over the house and the new baby with a largess of familiarity that left Mary in a compliant, amused frame of mind.

"Why, this child is damn near as pretty as my Bessie was when she was born!" Mabel raised the baby aloft while Mary wondered why Sarah didn't cry, suspended as she was.

"Land! Girl, you got this tyke so wrapped up you're lucky she ain't mummified!" Mabel Garner loosened the blankets and freed the baby's feet, removing booties, chuckling and talking to Sarah. "This here's one hell of a hot day for April. 'Lizabeth, fetch that blanket!" she ordered one of her children. She used it to make a pad on the floor in the living room to lay the baby there.

"Won't she be too cold?" Mary fussed.

"Cold! Must be eighty-five degrees! She ain't no different'n you, child! Give 'er some air! Besides, a-trussed up like she was, how's she gonna find room to grow?"

It was impossible to feel criticized. The big woman had an air of authority and homespun good sense that couldn't be denied. As if to prove the point, Sarah slept peacefully. Mabel drove her own brood out into the yard, giving orders for laying out the picnic dinner. And they weren't the only ones she raised a tongue to. Jonathan, Aaron, and Uncle Garner heeded her gusty orders, too. Nobody gave Mabel Garner short shrift. Mary alone took her leisure for this one day, thoroughly enjoying the unaccustomed vacation.

The heat intensified as the day wore on, surprising everyone into lethargy with its unexpected force. It pushed a lusty wind ahead of it, graying the sky. After their meal and a rest on the lawn, Uncle Garner said a walk would feel good and told Jonathan he'd like to walk out to the south pasture and see Vinnie. Jonathan was more than happy to oblige, and the three men left the yard together.

When they returned to the house it was late afternoon, and the Garners made ready for their long ride home. When the hugging and handshaking was done, the buckboard pulled away under a lurking sun. The heat had sapped everyone. Sarah slept unusually long, and even Jonathan lay down on the sofa in the front room to rest a bit.

Aaron's suit jacket had blown off the fence post, but he was nowhere to be seen. Mary sat in the kitchen, watching the colors changing outside. She saw the dish towels standing straight out from the line, and suddenly one let loose, flew like a kite, and was plastered against the woodpile downyard. Sitting inside, out of the wind, she'd been unaware of its growing force. Aaron appeared then, fighting his way against it, and she rose and opened the screen door, but it was ripped out of her hand and flung against the porch wall.

"Get Jonathan!" he called against the wind, "We have to get the stock inside!"

The baby awoke and began crying as the sudden cold draft gusted through the house. Jonathan awoke at Sarah's sudden squalling, flew off the sofa, and scooped her up off the floor, depositing her in Mary's hands on his way out the door. She put Sarah in her cradle and ran to the porch door again as the men headed for the yard. Aaron had turned his head to protect his face from the wind that now was blowing bits of flotsam before it. With his head screwed around, he saw Mary making as if to follow and knew she must be heading to the chicken coop.

He motioned her back inside, but his words were garbled by the wind. She heard him say "chicken coop," so he must have shut it up already. Sarah was squalling inside, and she went back in to pick her up, holding the baby against her, as much to settle her own thumping heart as to still the child.

"We've got to herd the cows inside," Aaron shouted.

"Vinnie!" Jonathan hollered, jabbing a finger repeatedly, pointing at the south pasture.

Aaron grabbed his arm and tried to stop him. "It's too far!" he screamed, but Jonathan wrenched his arm away. Aaron grabbed Jonathan around the neck and yelled into his ear, "You can't make it—too far!" But again Jonathan pulled away. The jaundiced sky had turned the color of an old bruise, an unearthly yellow tinged with green. Aaron felt Jonathan wrench away from him, saw him break into a run toward the field lane. He cupped his hands to his mouth and shouted, "Come back, Jonathan," but the wind had swiftly shifted to the southwest and blew his words back down his throat. He knew the cattle would stand facing the storm as always, letting it knock them senseless. He had to get them into the barn.

"Damn Jonathan!" he cursed. But he couldn't follow his brother. He had to get the stock inside.

Jonathan felt the first rain riveting into his face as he ran down the lane. The trees were arching toward earth as if rigged for snaring animals. He cut sharply across a stubbled cornfield, away from the line of trees on his right, and the rain began to slash at him. When he reached the south pasture, he had to struggle with the gate. It was no more than barbed wire strung between two posts and secured by a loop of wire off an adjacent post, but the wire loop slipped from his wet fingers and he had to grasp the post to keep from blowing over. He opened it at last, but the wind was a wall of violence now that knocked him from his feet. He could make out the black, hulking shape of Vinnie and began crawling toward it, his clinging, wet clothing dragging him back.

"Vinnie!" he screamed into the banshee wind. "Vinnie!"

But the relentless force swallowed his sound. A

slashing bolt of lightning cleared his view, and he saw the animal above him. He struggled upright on his knees, waiting for the slightest ease in the gale so he could reach for the animal's halter. His only thought was of forcing the animal down to the ground, forcing Vinnie to lie where he'd be somewhat protected from the fury around them. If only he'd put the ring in Vinnie's nose, he could give it a yank and make the animal lie down instantly. But there was no ring, only the halter, and he straightened his arm, straining his body upward, seeking it, groping blindly while the rain blinded him and the wind pushed him flat.

The bull danced in dumb terror as the twister threw itself in crazy commotion, carrying leaves, wood, branches in its gaping maw. The scream of the wind became an earsplitting rumbling as the tornado hit them with full force. The animal swayed in a terrorized dance, its hooves striking left, then right, its powerful chest rippling, its eyes bulging in fear. Vinnie had no horns to meet the force that tried to grasp him from below, while the sucking wind pulled at him from above. So the bull struck at it with his hooves instead, stamping at its softness, knowing only terror. The wind howled and the animal stamped—left and right, left and right—until both the wind and the bull quieted at once.

In the barn Aaron shivered inside his wet, clinging clothes. There was a small, cobwebbed window facing the house, but only the main door facing in the direction Jonathan had gone. If he opened it, it would be torn from its hinges. He rubbed the dust from a pane and peered toward the house, but he couldn't even define its outline in the pounding torrents. He could hear objects striking the barn as they were driven by the wind, and his mind flashed from Mary to Jonathan to the Garners in their open buckboard.

The cattle were restive, the storm making them shift and low noisily. He'd brought the pails down earlier. It might soothe them if he started milking. It would soothe him, too. There was little he could do for the others, and the milking had to be done sometime. Jonathan would be in no shape to help when he came back. What a fool thing to do! Chase after that bull in a storm like this. There was no denying Jonathan had a way with that animal, though. Aaron thought, I wouldn't be surprised to see him ride Vinnie in bareback. The idea made him smile as he tried to shake off the worry that was nagging him, worsening the longer Jonathan was gone.

He left the pails in the barn, for it was still raining when he finished. The howling wind had waned to a less fearsome strength, and the rain had eased off.

When he opened the kitchen door, he could see the trapdoor open on the pantry floor. He called Mary's name, and she came running from the other room with Sarah in her arms, her face pale.

"Are you all right?" he yelled. But he could see that she was. His main concern now was for Jonathan.

"Yes," she assured him. "I had the cellar door open in case we needed to go down . . ." Then she stopped abruptly. Her voice became intensely quiet. "Where's Jonathan?"

"I hoped he'd come back," Aaron said.

"Back from where? Wasn't he in the barn with you?" She clutched the baby closer.

"Don't worry, I'll find him." Aaron's voice was trailing him as he ran back out into the rain.

She held the door open and pulled the blanket over Sarah's head as she shouted after Aaron, "Where did he go?" But Aaron was already halfway across the yard. She could see that he was heading in the direction of Vinnie's pasture.

Aaron had hoped that somehow Jonathan had gotten back to the house. Now as he ran he knew it had been a foolish hope. He could see ahead of him strange shapes on the edge of the woods. A fear clutched his gut as he identified the broken boles of trees.

Jesus, it must have been a tornado, he thought, realizing only now just how bad the storm had been. The house had gotten only the side winds, but the path of the funnel was easy to mark.

He began to call Jonathan's name, and the longer he called, the slower he ran. He jogged around great gnarled roots that had been ripped up by the storm. He reached the end of the lane and swerved east, toward the pasture.

He could see Vinnie standing with his rump to the rain. He had slowed to a walk, his fear crystallizing as he approached the gate that lay loose where it had fallen.

The bull moved when he heard the man coming, and Aaron saw a shape on the muddy earth in front of Vinnie. He knew it was Jonathan before he could discern any more than that. He ran toward the two and gave the bull a vicious kick in his wide belly.

"Git away from him!" he screamed as the bull pranced sideways, surprised.

Aaron dropped to his knees beside the inert figure that lay crumpled facedown in the mud. He knew before he turned the lifeless body into his arms that Jonathan was dead.

"Jonathan," he cried as he saw the rain falling on his brother's battered face and chest. "Jonathan, why didn't you listen to me? Jonathan . . ." He pulled him up and shielded Jonathan's face and railed at the sky, "Stop that! Don't rain on his face!" But the rain splashed on the torn, bloody face and ran over Aaron's shirt sleeve, staining it a weak red. "Oh, Jesus. Oh, Jesus, no. You can't be dead. *Jonathan. Wake up!*"

The bull took a step nearer, and Aaron pulled the still form closer in his protective embrace while he railed again, "Keep away from him, you bastard!" But his words ended in sobs as he rocked his brother. The bull stood by, watching.

He carried Jonathan beyond the fence and locked the gate again. It was too far to carry him back to the house, so he stripped his own white shirt off and covered Jonathan's face with it.

He ran across the cornfield at an angle this time, taking the shortest way to where the lane joined the yard. Before he reached the edge of the corn, he saw Mary standing in the lane waiting for him.

Runnels of rain were trailing down the strands of hair that washed over Aaron's forehead. They camouflaged his tears as he ran. But there was no hiding his bare chest. She saw it, saw how hard Aaron ran to meet her, and her hands flew to her mouth, stifling a cry.

Aaron panted to a halt just short of her and saw

her open, silent mouth beneath her hands, her wild, frightened eyes above them. He choked, "Oh, God, Mary."

As if his words tore her loose from the spot, she lurched, trying to pass him, screaming, "Jonathan! Jonathan!" But he caught her shoulders and stopped her. She tore at his hands, scratching his chest, screaming again, "Let me go!" She fought with a mindless strength and tore herself loose, her arms flying free as she spun from him. She was racing down the lane when Aaron caught her from behind and stopped her flailing arms, pinning them to her sides in an encircling grip.

"No, Mary. You can't go out there. Jonathan's dead." His words at last took the fight from her. "Vinnie . . ." But he didn't need to finish it. Her head dropped back against Aaron's chest, a keening wail beginning as she lost control. The rain licked her face. Her body was consumed by sudden, violent spasms that quaked through her limbs with such force that Aaron could feel his own body being jerked by hers. She began slipping down, and he lowered her to her knees in the wet grass. He knelt behind her, and she suddenly fell forward onto her hands, knelt there on all fours, sobbing Jonathan's name over and over again. He surrounded her waist with his arms and leaned his face on her back, trying to still her shaking but unable to. For he was shaking, too, as they both cried for the man they loved.

It was hard to tell what time of day it was, though the rain had stopped. Aaron saddled the mare. He knew he had to go for help, but what about Mary?

"I can't leave you alone here," he said again.

"I'll be all right," she answered, "just hurry!" But she was still far from under control.

He slapped the reins, and the horse shot forward. Hooves thundered beneath him, but to Aaron it seemed he moved on a treadmill. When he had barely started down the road, doubts assailed him. Should he have left Jonathan like that in the field? Oh, God, why hadn't he brought him up to the house? But he couldn't do that and leave Mary there to see him. Mary, Mary . . . I shouldn't have left you alone. But you said you shouldn't take the baby in the rain. No matter, you shouldn't be alone. What should I do?

As he rode, one thought recurred: he couldn't leave Mary there alone while he made the long trip to town. At a curve in the road he slowed the mare to turn around and go back for her. He could take her and Sarah to a neighboring farm. Why hadn't he thought of that before?

But before the mare had completed the turn, a miracle took place. The buckboard full of Garners appeared around the curve. They pulled up, hands waving and voices calling Aaron's name. The children were babbling about the tornado. Mabel Garner silenced them with a quick word as she and her husband saw Aaron's face.

"What is it, boy?" Uncle Garner demanded.

"It's Jonathan," Aaron's voice quaked. "He's been gored by the bull."

"How bad?" The terse question cut through Aaron's shock.

"He's dead."

The instant he said it, the Garners took over. Aaron

felt the easing of a weight as Mabel quieted the children and left Garner to question Aaron.

"Where's Mary?" he asked.

"Back at the house. I was going back to get her, take her to a neighbor's." Aaron was sobbing pathetically now.

"And Jonathan?"

"In the south pasture," Aaron began, but his voice broke, faltered. "I didn't know what . . ."

"It's all right, boy. You turn around and follow us back."

Uncle Garner stopped at the first house he came to and sent the neighbor to town for help. When they reached home, he saw to Aaron's horse and everything else.

The Garners' presence during that endless night was the loving thread that held them in one piece. Uncle Garner drove the buckboard out to the pasture and brought Jonathan in, then saw to the arrangements when the undertaker arrived.

Aunt Mabel took over the house, dispatching her children to collect eggs, see to the milk that still sat in the barn, make beds in the loft, help lay food out. She forced order where, without her, chaos would have threatened. She made them drink coffee when they would have no food, made them put on dry clothes when they'd have sat damp, made them rest when they would have resisted. Somehow they all made it through the night.

Chapter 20

$\mathcal{M}$oran Township folk always turned out for weddings, births, and deaths with a great show of strength, their understanding making them a people unequaled in generosity.

The tragic death of Jonathan Gray brought out these good people with full hands and full hearts. In the days before and after the funeral, they filled the house, bringing comfort, companionship, and food. They saw to it that Mary had company and Aaron had help. They helped him put in his crops. Some came to call at chore time, even helping for the first few days. Someone else pastured Vinnie, knowing his presence on the Gray farm was unthinkable. Someone came with crosscut saws and took care of the fallen trees, repairing fences where needed. Someone else offered to repair the roof of the chicken coop, but Aaron finally refused, saying they'd all done enough already. They all had work of their own to do, and many of them had suffered damage from the tornado, too, and had let their own repairs go. But the neighbors had done what they set out to do. They made those first days possible.

Aunt Mabel stayed several days after Jonathan's funeral, but she had her own family at home, and soon had to return to them. "Y'know you can come live with us, girl, and we'd be happy to have you," she told Mary.

But Mary knew that two more additions would be a hardship to the family now. The Garner children were bigger now, bigger eaters and bigger helpers. Mary wouldn't be needed, as she once had been. "I need time to decide what to do," she answered.

" 'Course you do, dear," Aunt Mabel said, accepting the girl's refusal with understanding.

When everyone was gone at last and things were quiet, Aaron came into the yard and found Mary kneeling listlessly near some green things sprouting in the garden. She held a trowel forgotten in her hand.

"It's too damp on the ground. How long have you been kneeling there?"

She sighed and began absentmindedly chucking the trowel in the dirt. It made a rhythmic scratching sound as she did it. He knelt down on one knee and stopped her arm. "We have to talk about . . . some things," he said.

He pitched the tool in the dirt and said, "Come on."

She shivered and got up to follow him into the house. He went to the stove and did something to the fire, then said, "Sit down. We've got to talk about the farm, Mary, and what we should do." His eyes looked sunken and completely out of place in his already tanned, healthy-looking face. When she saw how haggard he looked, she felt worse but didn't know what to do for him.

"Well, I don't know," she began lamely.

"I can't stay here anymore," he said, his sunken eyes avoiding her swollen ones. "It wouldn't do. I've had several offers to stay with neighbors. I can take my pick, so I guess I'll take Dvorak up on it. They're about the closest ones I'd want to stay with."

She hadn't thought she had much left in her for tears, but she was wrong. There were enough left to wet her eyes again, and they stung her swollen lids, already raw. "Oh, Aaron, isn't it bad enough without you going, too?"

"I've got to go. You know that."

She nodded dumbly but said, "Sure, you've got to go again. I've got to push you out of your own house again. Why should you be the one who has to go?"

He leaned an elbow on the table, shutting his eyes and squeezing the bridge of his nose with thumb and forefinger. "Mary, let's make sense. You aren't making this too easy for me, okay?"

She squared her shoulders and wiped her eyes with her sleeve. "Aunt Mabel told me I could go to her place. Why don't I go there?" she suggested as he released his squeezing fingers and faced her again.

"Now listen, that doesn't make any sense at all. They pack a baker's dozen into that house and this one should stand empty while you go to their place? It makes more sense for me to go."

"But I . . ."

"Hey . . . I want you and Sarah here. You need the

house worse than me. I mean, I won't see you crowded in where you're not needed."

"If I say I'll stay here, then what?"

"Well, I'll write and say I'm not coming to that job I planned to take." She was relieved that at least he wouldn't be pushed that far. "I can come and work the place here days and sleep at Dvorak's nights."

"You'd do that, Aaron? You'd keep the place going when it's not . . ." But she couldn't say it wasn't his.

". . . not mine?" he finished for her. "The crops are more than half in. Who's going to take care of them if I don't?"

She just shrugged dismally.

"I didn't mean that like it sounded," he consoled, seeing the shrug. "I don't know anything but this farm, and anyway, I really didn't want to go to Douglas County to work. You knew that, didn't you?"

She looked at her lap and nodded, then, smoothing her skirt repeatedly over her knees said, "I appreciate it, Aaron. I mean, I don't know what's going to happen here." But then she became upset and waved a flat palm at the kitchen around them. "Oh, it's all so mixed up. The land and the house—just everything."

"It usually is when somebody dies," he said, looking at her squarely. "But we'll take it a day at a time, and for now I'll go to Dvorak's and see if I can't get the rest of the crops in and a new roof on the chicken coop. Okay?"

But she was silent.

"Mary?" he asked.

"Who gets the profits?" she challenged.

"The land is yours, Mary," he said.

"The house is yours," she said stubbornly, "and so

is the chicken coop, for that matter, the one with my hens in it. I'm not taking everything free, and I mean it."

"Okay," he agreed, "okay. We can work that out later. There won't be any profits till fall, and by that time some decisions will be made. But for now I go, and that's final."

"Okay. So you go for the time being, but if you handle the crops, you handle the money. What do I know about the price of seeds and . . . well, everything? Jonathan took care of all that. The land is worthless to me since I don't know how to run it."

"It's not worthless. You can sell it."

He was serious, and it nearly made her laugh. "Sell it?" she asked, stupefied. "Do you think I'd sell the farm right out from under you?"

"Well, it's yours," he said, "or it will be as soon as it's probated. Maybe then I could buy it . . ." But that sounded too ridiculous even to his own ears, and he finished, ". . . or something."

"Aaron, can't we just keep on like we were for a while till I know what to do? I mean, do what you want, run the farm however you want, and keep what you need of the money or whatever. It'd be kind of like payment for me and Sarah living in the house."

A muscle twitched in his jaw. "I don't need payment for you and Sarah living in my house," he said.

"Well, how're you supposed to live . . . on what?" She had him there.

"People are so damn nosy around here. We just have to do our best to keep them from talking till we settle the . . . estate." The word was so forbidding.

LaVyrle Spencer

"Aaron, I can't think about this any more tonight. I'm just too . . . can't we decide tomorrow?"

She looked whipped now, and of all the times he'd had to turn away from her, tonight would be the hardest.

"Mary, you don't seem to understand. I can't stay here tonight. With Aunt Mabel gone, I'll have to go to Dvorak's tonight. That's what I came up to tell you."

"Tonight?" She swallowed. It was so quiet in the kitchen. He nodded silently.

"Will . . . will you wait till after supper?" she asked. He sighed and leaned back on his chair, running a hand through his hair.

"I've got to get some clothes together to take with me. You can get supper while I do that, okay?"

She agreed by nodding again, and the force of old habit made her want to please, so she asked, "What would you like? There's all kinds of stuff people brought. There's ham and hot dishes and . . ." But she stopped, the question sounding so silly now.

"Anything," he said gently. "I'm not too hungry, Mary." And she knew he'd probably rather not be faced with food at all, that he was doing it because she'd be lonely when he went.

She fixed some food while he went upstairs, and his footsteps sounded menacing above her, only because she knew they soon wouldn't be there anymore. The sound of his heels back and forth on his bedroom floor marked off the minutes that were flying too fast, and soon he came back down, gathered a few items from underneath the sink, his comb from the comb holder on the wall.

She struggled with tears all through supper and finally said in a shaky voice, "Aaron, you come home for your meals. There's no sense in putting the Dvoraks out any more than necessary."

"I . . ." He wanted to say he'd eat only noon dinner with her, but she looked so forlorn, was having such a hard time keeping the tears in check.

"Please, Aaron," she begged, "what will I do here alone?"

"Okay," he agreed, and she seemed to deflate, releasing the breath she'd held while waiting for his answer.

He was all finished eating, and she asked over-anxiously, "Why don't you have a piece of marble cake? Agnes brought it."

He just shook his head no, but she got up anyway to get it from the pantry. He stopped her with a hand on her arm. "Tomorrow will be easier. It's just this first night alone, but don't worry." He got up and went over to the door and said, "I'll put this key up above the outside sill, and you lock up from the inside with this one. But you don't have to be scared of anything here, Mary."

It wasn't fear she dreaded, just loneliness—so much more final than when they'd gone off to Dakota and left her alone.

He gathered up his things from the seat of the extra kitchen chair, and she said, "Wait, I'll put them in something for you," and went to get brown paper to wrap them in. But then she couldn't think of any more excuses to keep him there.

"I gotta go now, Mary girl, okay?" he asked at the door, and his lips were quivering. "Hey, it's okay," he added, as much for himself as for her. "Now lock the door, and I'll see you in the morning."

She breathed only half-breaths, fearing that if she relaxed any more than that, her whole chest would collapse and she'd burst into tears again.

He squeezed her forearm, then turned at a run and was gone down to the lean-to to saddle the mare. When he galloped out she was in the doorway, and he raised a hand but never slowed. She watched the road long after she knew she wouldn't see him on it again. Then she went into Aaron's house, where everything reminded her of Jonathan. She went over to the comb holder and stared at his comb, then walked to the living room where his coffin had been, but the furniture was all back in its usual order. Just when she thought she'd surely break, Sarah started crying upstairs and she ran up gratefully to her.

But later, lighting the lantern, she couldn't make herself go up to the bedroom, hers and Jonathan's. She sat holding Sarah long after the baby should have been put in her cradle. Finally, when her head lolled where she sat, she gave up and went upstairs, but at the door of the first bedroom she found she couldn't go in. Taking Sarah, she hurried on down the hall to Aaron's room and climbed into his bed, putting Sarah beside her for the night.

Just for tonight, she thought, just till I get used to the quiet. Aaron's pillow smelled of bay rum, but she lay stiff and lonely on it, thinking of the empty room down the hall.

There were too many things to confront: the cold, quiet stove in the mornings that Jonathan had always had hot and snapping when she came down. The silence, when the house used to ring with stove lids. His clean, folded clothes in the dresser drawers beside hers and, worse, his few dirty ones she found the first time she did the laundry. His old jacket on the hook behind the door. The coffee grinder he'd fixed after she dropped it. She never used it now. His chair stared at her across the table.

After a first awful week, she realized she'd have to overcome his absence, and she began moving back into their bedroom. She dug out an old comforter to change the look of their bed, and rearranged the furniture, moving the bed away from the wall. Each night she got to sleep a bit easier.

She began laying a fire in the stove when the coals had died in the evening, so all she had to do was touch a match to it when she came down in the morning.

When she found herself listening for his whistle, she'd crank up the graphophone and put the Sousa march on again and again, sometimes even waking Sarah with the racket.

She washed his clothes and put the cambric shirts up in Aaron's dresser. It took longer before she could pack away all the other things from their dresser.

She took a leaf out of the table and left only two chairs at it, putting the other two beside the breakfront.

People noted Aaron, working around the place but, finding no signs of his belongings around the house, nodded heads in approval, commanding him for the way he kept the farm going when everyone knew it wasn't even his. And giving up his house that way to Mary and her baby—why, what would the girl have done if it hadn't been for him?

He rode the saddle horse over the rim of the east

hill at the same time each morning, never surprising her early or inconveniencing her late. She would have breakfast ready for him, the baby already fed and asleep before he arrived. She'd see him gallop into the yard, passing under the elms and taking the horse to the lean-to where he left the saddle before turning her out to graze. It gave Mary time to get the food on the table. He always knocked on the door before he came in, and she knew how foreign that must seem to him.

They talked about the crops, the work he planned to do that day, the neighbors, the weather, the work she'd do during the day. Nothing personal.

At noon he came again, this time stopping at the well to wash his hands, giving her time to know he was on his way up.

One noon when he came in for dinner, Mary seemed nervous about something, and it wasn't long before she said, "A letter came this morning from a lawyer in Long Prairie."

"Can I read it?" he asked. He laid down his fork and read the letter, taking a drink of tea while he continued reading over the rim of the cup. "It looks like you'll have to go to Long Prairie, huh?" he said, putting the letter back into the envelope.

"Do I have to go?" she asked.

"It's nothing to be afraid of, Mary. Hunt was the one who made out my pa's will before there were any lawyers in Browerville. He says it's just a formality that you sign the papers. You don't even have to go to probate court, but he needs your signature on record. That's the law. Then the land is yours for good." He began eating again, apparently unconcerned.

"But how can I go—what about Sarah?"

"Maybe one of the neighbors can take her for the day."

"For the day! How long does it take to get there and back?"

"Well . . . why does it matter? You can stand to get away for a bit. It will do you good."

She glanced self-consciously out the window and said, "I'm nursing her, Aaron."

"Oh . . . oh, sure." He was suddenly totally absorbed in cutting the meat on his plate. "Well, that's a pretty long way to take Sarah in the buggy. Maybe you could take the train."

"Aren't . . . won't you come along?" she braved, uncomfortable asking him to do any more.

"If you want me to, of course I will. You pick the day. Hunt says you can come anytime."

"When would be best for you?"

"It doesn't matter."

"Should we go tomorrow and get it over with?"

"Okay. But you'll have to get Sarah ready early in the morning. I'm not sure just what time the train comes in, so we'd better get there early, just in case."

"We'll be ready," she said.

The next morning was damp and chilly, and Mary bundled Sarah into layers of blankets to keep her warm on the way into Browerville. Even so, Sarah was crabby all the way, and tiny though she was, Mary's arms ached from holding her.

Once on the train for Long Prairie, Sarah settled down, and Mary was grateful to rest her elbows on the padded armrests of the coach seats.

They found Alfred Hunt's office easily, only two

blocks from the train depot. When they opened the outer door, they found an empty desk in front of them with its roll top pushed up and ledgers, documents, and scraps of paper ever so precisely arranged.

When Aaron called hello, a portly, balding man with a jolly face came around the doorway. "Good morning! Good morning!" he said merrily.

"Mr. Hunt?" Aaron asked.

"One and the same," replied Hunt, extending his hand and creasing into a smile.

Aaron smiled, too. "I'm Aaron Gray. This is my sister-in-law, Mrs. Jonathan Gray."

The man's face sobered. "Ah, Mary Gray it is, then. Please accept my sympathies—both of you." Then, glancing at the baby in Mary's arms, he added, "My deepest sympathies. I'm sure it has been difficult for you to come. I'm sorry you had to make the trip. I wasn't aware that you had a baby, Mary." His using her first name made him seem a friend. He did it to put her at ease. "So sorry my clerk was out and you were left standing. Come inside and we'll get the business done in no time."

He ushered them into an inner office that was the antithesis of the one they'd just passed through. There were plants and books and ashtrays with pipes sitting on windowsills and atop anything that would hold them. The desk was a clutter of business-looking things, but the overall feeling of the room was one of comfort and familiarity. Mr. Hunt pulled up two old, cracked leather chairs near the heaped desk. "Sit . . . sit," he invited. "This is just a formality, you understand. The property does of course belong to the widow in a case like this. However, I'm happy to see you make it official with your signature. It'll insure it for the future of the young one there." He indicated Sarah by glancing over the smudged spectacles he'd fastened behind his ears. He unfolded some papers and dug through the disorder on his desk until he found a pen. "The land will be officially yours now, Mary, in the event you'd want to sell it." Mary nodded, intensely uncomfortable at the mention of selling the farm, which seemed so much more Aaron's than hers. Alfred Hunt handed her the pen and pointed to the spot where she should sign.

"I'd like to read it first before Mrs. Gray signs it," Aaron said, and she stopped, realizing she should have done so herself.

"Well, of course, you ought to." And while Aaron looked over the relatively simple form, Hunt went on. "I only met your husband once, Mary, shortly after the death of his parents, but he impressed me as a man with a level head on his shoulders and one who'd keep a place up to snuff. If he kept up the property like I suspect he did, it would be worth a good deal now. If you should ever want to sell it, I'd be most happy to represent you."

The train was late getting in, but Mary began to relax again when they were on their way. Then, suddenly, she felt it. She sat very still, willing it to stop, but knowing it wouldn't, knowing she had to act fast.

"Aaron?"

He turned his face toward her, wondering why she had whispered. "What?" he whispered back.

Her eyes were enormous, as if she were afraid.

"Aaron, I have to feed Sarah."

Is that all? He thought. "She's not complaining. Why don't you wait until she does?"

"I can't wait." She was still whispering. Suddenly enlightened, his eyes dropped to her breasts where a telltale spot had already seeped through the gray cotton and dampened a tiny round circle at the crest of her left breast.

"Jesus," he said, gaping, learning fast. "Hold on." Then he was up and gone, swinging down the aisle between the seats, disappearing out the door at the head of the car. She sat like a ramrod for what seemed an eternity, holding still to keep from flowing.

Then a Negro porter appeared, bending across Aaron's empty seat solicitously. "Your husband has asked if there's a private place where you can be with the baby. If you'll follow me, I'll show you the way." She followed him gratefully, catching sight of Aaron reentering the car from the opposite direction. She was shown into a plush private compartment with two seats facing each other and red-tasseled shades on the windows. Thanking the porter profusely, she sank down and began loosening her blouse as the door closed behind him.

She heard the call for Browerville before Sarah was done, and hurriedly composed her clothing before going back to their seats. They were pulling into the depot as she came up behind Aaron, and in the hubbub of gathering Sarah's trappings, wrapping her for outside, and leaving the train, they were spared embarrassment. But the friendly porter was at the door tending his portable step when Mary put her foot down onto it, and he reached up to take her arm, smiling broadly. "I trust you found the compartment satisfactory, ma'am?"

"Yes it was—most satisfactory. Thank you," she answered.

Aaron was right behind her, and he reached a hand into his pocket, asking, "What do I owe you?"

But the congenial porter smiled again. "There's no charge for the service, sir. Just happy to have you all aboard, sir."

"Ah . . . thank you . . . thank you kindly," Aaron replied, tucking some coins into the black palm as inconspicuously as possible. The porter nodded appreciatively. "Thank *you*, sir, thank you."

Turning to take Mary's arm, Aaron asked, "Do you need anything in town before we start back?"

"No, just get me home fast," she said, then blurted, "Thank you, Aaron."

Chapter 21

$\mathcal{T}$he days returned to unvarying sameness. For Aaron they were long, hard days, days in which he missed Jonathan beside him. The neighbors' help had made the first plantings easy, but they'd planted more than they should have of some crops, and now Aaron worked long and hard at the cultivating. The milking wasn't bad in the morning, but at the end of the day when he was worn down, his arms ached before he finished.

When Aaron came up at suppertime one evening and slumped into his chair with a heavy sigh, Mary put the food on the table, then sat down, studying his weary look. "I've been thinking, Aaron," she said as she spooned food, being careful not to look at him. "I'd like you to teach me to milk." She tried to make it sound offhand.

A wry, amused look flickered over his face. "You're not the best at milking," he said.

"Well, I could learn," she offered.

"I can handle it alone."

She grew piqued. "Well, if you'd give me a chance, I'd like to learn! I'm the only woman for miles around here who can't milk a cow!" She reddened slightly and sat looking down at her plate.

"Okay . . . okay," he gave in, slightly surprised.

She instantly softened. "I could try tomorrow night. I've got washing first thing in the morning, but I'd have time in the evening."

It was settled, and he left that night thinking the milking would take twice as long tomorrow. He'd have to do it all, anyway, after waiting for her to try her hand at it.

But she was a determined woman. She kept trying in just the way he explained, watching him first, then trying again until it was less difficult. Within a few days she could do it passably well, although she tired far faster than Aaron.

Sarah was a problem, though. Mary left her in the house alone a couple of times, but she hated doing that. So she asked Aaron if he could make a light box of some kind for her. "I hate leaving her inside when I do the gardening," was Mary's excuse. She was afraid that Aaron might think it too great an inconvenience for her to help with the milking.

Aaron made a light, small box with lattice sides to let the air through and a handle like a grape basket. When Mary brought Sarah to the barn in it the first time, the baby was asleep, and Aaron peeked at her, in pale green blanket and yellow bonnet, declaring she looked like a cob of corn all ready for market. Mary put the basket on two upturned milk pails, saying, "Aaron! What a thing to say about your own daughter!"

She could have bitten off her own tongue. It had slipped out. She hadn't meant to say it. She turned away, stammering. But Aaron covered the uncomfortable moment. "I see she likes the basket all right." He turned to his work, but a pleasant tingle of warmth shivered through him.

The mayflies paid their short-lived visit, and the deerflies came in June. One evening during milking, Mary and Aaron and Sarah were in the barn as usual when a sudden, frantic cry came from the baby, who had been asleep in her basket. Aaron had been on his feet between cows, and before Mary could break free of the pail, her skirts, and the stool that hindered her, Aaron had whisked Sarah out of her basket in alarm.

"What is it?" Mary cried while the wails continued in full force. But as she reached Aaron, she saw the growing welt on Sarah's face.

"A deerfly," he said. "She'll be all right."

Yet the little mouth squared and quivered and squalled, and Aaron kissed the welted cheek, murmuring to the baby. "Here, Corncob," he said. "You'd better go to your mother." He handed the baby to Mary.

"I'd better put some soda paste on it," she said calmly, then added, "Sorry, Aaron."

Then she left him in the quiet barn, looking at the empty basket. Why had she said she was sorry? Sorry for the disturbance? Sorry to leave him with the milking? He decided *he* was most sorry she'd had to take Sarah from him. Holding her was not unpleasant. As a matter of fact, he'd liked it very much.

When he returned to the house, he took the basket, too. "How is she?" he asked.

"It was just a bite, like you said. If Sarah's going to live on the farm, she'll have to get used to bites."

Wondering how long Sarah would be living on the farm, Aaron left again, saying, "I have to get the rest of the milk."

The next day, Aaron worked until noon and then went to town. For Mary it was an endless day. She gave him a list of supplies and watched him head away, wishing she could go. It had been so long since she'd been to town, but the ride was too hard with Sarah. She was still nursing the baby, and couldn't leave her with a neighbor.

The afternoon dragged on. She weeded the garden to fill the hours. It seemed an eternity ago when she had first grown dizzy, stooping over the garden rows. She took Sarah back into the house when the garden was done, and cleaned herself up to start supper. Aaron should have been back by now, she worried, and found herself returning time after time to the porch rail, to look eastward.

When she saw the rig coming, a feeling of relief swept her, and she raised a hand in welcome. Aaron saw her on the porch waiting and hurried the horses. Her waving, waiting figure seemed to beckon him home in a way he'd never felt welcomed before.

"I thought you'd never get here," she called. "Hurry in! Supper's ready."

He unharnessed the team and carried the box of supplies to the house.

"What took you so long? What's in here?" She was

pulling at the brown paper before he could set the box down.

"Back off, woman," he scolded with a smile, "and give me room to set this down."

But she grabbed the parcel and tore the string, saying, "I didn't order anything like this. What is it?"

She found a length of cheesecloth inside. "It's not for you. It's for Sarah—to keep the deerflies away."

It was so unexpected—his buying the netting for the baby. She floundered for something to say, but all she could think of was, "Why didn't I think of that?"

No answer was needed, but Aaron knew she was pleased.

She peppered him with questions about town, wanting to hear all the news, asking whom he'd seen. Aaron relayed what he could, and of course there were good wishes for her from everyone he'd seen. He could tell she was aching to go to town herself again.

That night, it was hard to leave. She seemed dejected as he left her on the porch. He stopped under the elms and called back to cheer her, "Next time I go to town, you're coming along. It's no man's job to buy things for a baby." Then he heeled the horse, wondering if she'd find some excuse not to go with him because of what had happened on the train.

After that, he had no need to knock on his own door, for she was usually standing on the porch when he arrived. Sometimes at noon he'd see her under the clotheslines, stretching her arms up to hang clothes. There were always diapers and little clothes now. He loved seeing them there. She still did his laundry, refusing to have it any other way. She said it was the least she could do.

One evening when Aaron was leaving for the Dvoraks', she called, "Wait a minute, Aaron, you forgot your laundry," and came from the front room carrying the brown parcel. "Try not to smash it now," she said, as she usually did. Then she handed it to him, one hand on the bottom of the parcel, one hand on the top. As Aaron reached for it, her hand brushed his palm. Their touch was like an electric current, and Mary reacted as though she'd gotten burned. She jerked her hand backward and grabbed it with the other. Realizing what she'd done, she shot a look at Aaron, her cheeks flaming.

"It's not necessary for you to do my clothes up, Mary," he said. "Mrs. Dvorak offered to do them for me."

"Don't be silly, Aaron," she argued, "I love doing them."

But once again her response seemed to tell a secret. Aaron sought to cool the flame that suddenly leaped through him. He stepped fully out onto the porch, closing the screen door between them, and said, "I appreciate your doing them for me. Thank you, Mary."

When he was gone, she put her palms to her cheeks and called herself every kind of fool. She resolved to control herself from now on.

Haying time arrived, and Aaron began staying in the fields at noon to save time. The first day he did this, she came walking with his dinner in one hand and the basket-in-cheesecloth in the other.

When he saw her coming, he pulled up at the end of a row to wait. She set the basket down and handed him the covered plate, collapsing onto the grass.

"It's too far for you to come way out here. Tomorrow, just pack me a sandwich and a jar of water in the morning."

"A sandwich and a jar of water! A man can't work on scraps like that." But she was puffing from the exertion.

"Sarah's getting too heavy to carry around in that thing." He pointed at the basket with his fork, then looked inside and said, "You're gonna break your mother's back, Corncob!"

"Aaron! That's the most disgusting nickname I've ever heard!

But Aaron leaned toward Sarah and said, "Hey, Corncob, you tell your mother that she did the naming and a papa should at least be able to pick a nickname." He'd been thinking of it ever since that time in the barn when Mary had slipped first and called Sarah his daughter. He knew Mary's face must be scarlet, for she turned her back on him fully, Sarah's little face over her shoulder, wide-eyed as only a baby's can be. The baby was all milk and honey and brown curls, and he'd have given anything to reach out and touch those curls, just once, on purpose. But he ate his dinner and studied her instead, immensely pleased, thinking he could make out a resemblance to himself.

When he finished eating, he said, "Okay, Corncob, tell your mother she can have the plate now—and tell her it's rude to keep her back to a person all that long. At least she's taught *you* some manners."

But Mary picked up the basket and took off down the lane without turning around again, saying, "Tell your father he can carry his own dirty plate back!" But Mary was smiling from ear to ear.

The next day Mary delivered Aaron's lunch in the wheelbarrow that also held the baby's basket.

When she arrived where he waited, Mary stated, "Sarah wishes you to know that she has no intention of breaking her mother's back."

He retorted, with a twinkle, "The point is well taken." Then reaching for his dinner plate he whispered loudly to Sarah, "Tell your mother she's a hussy," and a smile tugged first his cheek, then Mary's.

During the long, hot days when the horses worked like drudges, Aaron traced the fields behind them, dreaming of owning a tractor.

He was pondering this when a tug strap broke. Silently cursing, Aaron examined the damage. There was nothing to do but drive the team back up to the lean-to and exchange harnesses.

Back at the yard, while the horses drank, Aaron thought of how Mary usually kept cold tea around for a quick, cool drink. The baby must be sleeping, he thought, nearing the quiet house. He opened and closed the screen quietly, the spring on it twanging softly as he went into the kitchen. He found a fruit jar of cold tea in the buttery and carried it with him, raising it and taking long, deep swigs as he strolled absently around the kitchen. It was very quiet and cool inside the house. He strolled, still drinking, to the doorway of the living room, and there he stopped dead, his mouth filled with tea that he couldn't swallow. The heater stove was gone from the living room for the warm season, and the kitchen rocker had taken its place again. Mary sat in the rocker nursing the baby, who lay on a pillow in the crook of her arm, Sarah's skin as milky white as the breast that fed her. They both seemed asleep, Mary's head leaned back and to one side against the hard back of the rocker. But as if she sensed someone looking at her, she came awake with a start, and as she jerked, Sarah did, too, then began sucking again, one hand pushing against the breast.

Mary saw Aaron's crimson face, then saw his Adam's apple move as he swallowed the tea. "I thought you nursed the baby upstairs . . . or I would have knocked," he stammered.

"It's cooler down here," Mary explained, her heart hammering. But she made no move to pull the baby away. Sarah was still sleeping as she suckled. "I only do it here when you're sure to be out in the fields."

He stared at the baby for a moment longer while his throat worked again. Then he spun from the room and hurried out of the house with the screen door slamming behind him.

Sarah awoke with a start when the door banged. The baby's eyes flew open, her chin quivered for a hesitant second, then she wailed, choky, milky-mouthed, with gusto.

"Shh, Princess," Mary soothed. "Did your daddy scare you? Me, too, darlin'. Me, too." While she cooed soft words to quiet the baby, she thought, Did Aaron really scare me, or do I fear myself? Do I fear the weakness that I felt just now, and did he see it written all over my face? Being here together all the time, it must seem to Aaron that I expect him to look after us and support us, Sarah and me. Does he think I'm coyly playing my hand, trying to force him into a role he doesn't want?

Aaron talked out loud to the horses to cool his heels: "What a flea-brained dimwit I am, charging into the house!" He mulled over what Mary's feelings must be. She'll think I asked her to stay on in the house so I could weasel my way back into her confidence, maybe even her holdings, and eventually her bed. She needn't stay here to exist! She has property, capital—that gives her independence. Suppose she saw the lecherous look that must have been plastered all over my face. Suppose she spooks and runs—runs with Sarah, too. Mary came to me willingly once, but it's different now. If I push too fast, too soon, she'll think I'm an opportunist. It can't be like that. We walk a fragile line, Mary and Sarah and I. I'll do well to bide my time so as not to snap it.

When Aaron came that evening, he again knocked on the door, even though he could see, through the screen, that she was only putting supper on in her usual way. She had purposely stayed inside, not waited on the porch as she'd done lately. She set the food on, and he watched her out of the corner of his eye. When she reached to set the dishes onto the center of the table, her dress molded itself to her swelling breasts, more generous in maternity than before. He had a mental flash of their naked whiteness as he'd seen them that afternoon, and the want of her crept over his skin, touching him in tremulous, forbidden places. But he warned himself: Down, Aaron!

"There are some things I should get in town for Sarah," she said. "She's growing so fast, she's nearly out of her little saques. I ought to have supplies to make more for her."

"Like I said, that's a woman's errand. When do you want to go?"

"When can we?" She tried for a careless tone but couldn't bring it off.

"Saturday?"

"Saturday . . . Yes, Saturday." But a quick doubt puckered her brows. "What about Sarah?"

"Well, what about her?" He sobered his face, raised his fingers, using them to count on. "Now, let's see . . . she's one, two, three, four, five—going on six months old. High time she learned how to travel without complaining, don't you think?"

"Do you really think it would be okay to take her?"

"You ah"—Aaron cleared his throat, made a vague gesture toward her shoulder somewhere—"don't have much choice, do you?"

Mary colored, but he missed it, for he was studying his plate just then.

"How will we take her? The basket is okay for a short while, but she's nearly too long for it. It's an awful long way for me to hold her on my lap. And what if it rains?"

"Hold up a minute, all right?" he calmed her. "Now, if it rains, we'll wait and go another day. You'll have to let me think on how she'll ride."

"Okay." Then excitement got the best of her again. "But Aaron, it can't rain on Saturday. It just can't!"

On Friday evening Aaron rigged a plank as a divider, creating a small crib on the single box right behind the rider's seat. He filled it with soft bedding straw, followed in his every move by Mary, who was giddy with anticipation for the coming day's trip to town. Watching her come arunning with a quilt to cover the straw he realized how long it had been since she'd been anywhere, that he should have seen to it she'd gotten away before this. He promised he'd see to it more often from now on.

She felt as if she should take credit for wishing up the perfect day. It dawned flawless. The myriad colors of the sunrise blushed the hills with rosy gold. Wrens warbled Mary awake, as if scolding her for tardiness. The pungent smell of wild baby's-breath lay heavy in the dewy dawn. Aaron came early, and yet it seemed an endless time before his morning work was finished. The dew was drying when he came up to the house to wash and change clothes. He knocked, and she beckoned him inside instantly.

"I thought I'd wash up first and put on some other clothes?" He was asking her permission.

"There's warm water in the reservoir. I'll be ready when you are." She went upstairs with Sarah on her hip.

She washed only his work clothes, dungarees and cambrics. His better clothes, rarely needed, were still in his own room upstairs. There was a certain sensuousness about the two of them changing clothes, getting ready in the same house alone. She couldn't put it from her mind as she heard the sound of his washing. Hearing the sounds, she found her mind filled with the memory of Aaron, bare-chested, shivering from the icy well water, then standing with a towel slung around his neck while she touched his bare chest. She chided herself for remembering and hurried to finish dressing.

She wore a lavender sprigged muslin that cinched

her trim waist, and her breasts, too. Although the neckline was demure, her bodice seemed unchaste because of its tightness. She smoothed her hands over it critically, then compromised on a light shawl over her shoulders to camouflage the tightness.

Aaron finished dressing before she did and went past her door again on his way out. "I'll bring the wagon up," he said as he passed.

When she and the baby came out, he was tacking a dish towel over the small area that would act as Sarah's crib. He had already spread the quilt beneath a sunshade.

She was pleased by his ingenuity. A thrill of pride rippled through her as she complimented him, "You think of everything, don't you, Aaron?"

"I try," he grinned. "There's a length of canvas under the seat in case it rains."

"I left Sarah's things in the house. Can you hold her while I get them?" And before he could answer, Sarah was on his arm. She blinked up at him from under a scalloped bonnet, silently studying his face before she reached out one inquisitive hand and caught the corner of his lower lip. It was a kind of introduction, one that caught on his heart and made him purse his lips to kiss the tiny hand. This was his daughter, whom he'd never kissed before.

When Mary had shut the house and returned, he laid Sarah in her spot and handed Mary up. It was a perfectly polite excuse to touch her hand, but their touch was brief. She clustered her sprigged skirts, stepped up, and they were away.

The ride couldn't last long enough for Mary. Eager as she was to get to town, the ride was probably the better part of going. There was a growing feeling of rightness about the three of them being together. Their increasing awareness of each other was at once multiplied and mellowed by the common, everyday thing they were doing, going to town like an ordinary family.

Unconsciously, Mary found herself counting the months since Jonathan's death. When she realized what she was doing, she brought her thoughts up sharply.

Both Mary and Aaron acted with the utmost propriety in town that day, knowing that curious eyes were on the new widow appearing in public for the first time. There was no hand to help her down from the wagon seat this time. Mary herself lifted Sarah from the wagon bed. She and Aaron separated on the boardwalk before the dry-goods store, he going to the barbershop for a haircut and the latest gossip, Mary going to select goods for the baby, staples for the pantry. While looking through the bolts of cloth, her eye fell on one of a creamy ribbed faille. Its soft sheen tempted her fingertips, and as she touched it, she gave in to temptation and asked Sam to have a length of it added to her order. Next she went to the bakery and indulged in a jelly-filled Bismarck, giving Sarah a taste from her fingertips. The baby was the center of attention wherever she went. The taste of the jelly made Sarah demand more, and Millie Harmon at the bakery invited Mary to avail herself of the living quarters at the rear of the building so Sarah could be nursed.

The nursing finished, Mary walked to Doc Haymes's office to ask his advice on what to feed the baby. Sarah was growing fast and needed more than a liquid diet.

LaVyrle Spencer

Doc Haymes greeted Mary in his gruffly affectionate manner and chucked Sarah under her double chin. Noting the baby's obvious robust health, he advised Mary, "You should wean her now." At Mary's look of surprise he went on, "Babies get too fat when they nurse too long. Make it easy on yourself and better for Sarah, here." He instructed her on getting the baby used to soft foods, on binding her breasts and taking in less liquids when the time arrived, and finally sent her to the drugstore for Lydia Pinkham's Patent Medicine, to be taken for the discomfort.

Aaron was waiting at the dry-goods store when she got back. Sarah was grumpy after her long, unaccustomed outing.

"Do you want a bite to eat before we head back?" Aaron asked.

Mary remembered the ham dinner they'd shared together once, but wistfully declined this time. "Sarah couldn't take it, I don't think, and anyway, I had a sweet at the bakery."

The baby was spluttering noisily now, complaining aloud.

"It sounds like she's tuning up," Aaron joked.

"You're right. We'd better roll."

The ride back went faster than ever, for they talked all the way. After getting away from the townspeople, once again a natural ease fell between them.

"I splurged on a length of faille," she confessed.

"Oho!"

"But I still save by making it up myself."

"You don't need to make excuses, Mary. You can buy anything you want, and it's okay with me."

"Yes, but I really have no need for it."

"You deserve it," he declared, angling a half-smile sideways at her before adding, "Besides, needing it takes all the fun away sometimes."

She smiled at his impracticality. "You're right, Aaron. I'm not going to worry about it or make excuses . . . just like you said."

"So what else did you do?" he asked.

"I visited Millie Harmon at the bakery and ate a big, fat Bismarck, and gave a taste to Sarah."

"And what did she think of that?"

"Oh, she loved it! She fussed when I wouldn't give her any more."

He screwed his head around to glance at the sleeping baby behind them, smiling at the picture of Sarah eating Bismarcks. "See that you don't give in to her and spoil her. Nothing worse than a spoiled kid."

It was the first confidence about child rearing they had ever shared. She marked it in her mind for future reference.

"We went to visit Doc Haymes, too," she said, changing the subject.

A fleeting look of concern puckered his brows as he glanced at Mary. "Is something wrong?"

"Wrong? Oh, no. I just had to ask him about feeding her . . . ah . . . other foods, that's all."

"Already?" He seemed surprised.

"Well, you know Doc Haymes. He never prescribes the usual thing. Sometimes I think he amuses himself by shocking his patients. He's usually right, though." Then, quickly shifting, she pulled a knee up on the seat and faced his profile, asking, "So what did you do?" Surveying his hair with a twinkling eye, she noted, "I see you got your ears lowered."

"That I did," he laughed. "Also got 'em filled. According to the boys at the barbershop, we can be expecting another wedding around here."

"Whose?" She leaned toward him expectantly. But he hesitated and Mary thought he was teasing her again, so she grabbed his earlobe, pulling it. "If you don't want this lowered some more, you better tell me and tell me quick!"

He let her pull, feigning helplessness and pleading, "Okay, okay, let loose and I'll tell!" But she held on until he revealed the names of the lucky couple: "Priscilla and Willy Michalek."

She released his ear then and quickly faced front again. He could sense questions forming in her mind. They were quiet for some time before she ventured, "How do you feel about that?"

"I'm happy for them," he answered without hesitation.

"Nothing more?"

"What else should there be, Mary? There's nothing between Pris and me."

"But there was once."

"Yes, I won't deny it. You know what there was between us because I told you."

"Well, it's not a thing you take lightly, Aaron. I just wondered if you had any regrets about leaving her."

"None whatsoever, Mary," he assured her. "Do you believe me?"

She looked at him then, studying him momentarily before shrugging. "I want to." Looking away again, she asked, "When is it supposed to be?"

"Right after harvest, I guess, if you can believe all you hear in the barbershop."

"That's a nice time for a wedding," she commented. "It should give you a chance to wear that new dress you're talking about making."

She cheered a little at the thought, and they talked of other gossip the rest of the way home.

Sarah was still sound asleep when they got there. Mary turned to pick her up, but Aaron asked, "Could I carry her in to bed, Mary?"

There'd be no harm in that, she thought. "Of course, Aaron."

It was turning dark when he left that night, acting as though he hated going. She walked down to the elms with him, twiddling some grass between her fingers, sorry he had to leave.

"Aaron," she said, looking at the blades she toyed with, "you're awfully good to Sarah and me. Not just today, the trip to town and all. I mean . . . every day. I just wanted to thank you."

He steeled himself to keep from pulling her into his arms. "Hey," he told her quietly, "I told you once there's no need to thank me. You just somehow make me want to work for you. You do that to a man, Mary girl."

At his words a cherished, protected feeling stole over her. She crossed her arms and rubbed them under her sprigged muslin sleeves and for a moment imagined he held her. The words brought warmth, but she wished, too, for the warmth of his real arms around her.

But seeing her full, swelling breasts where she hugged them, he left quickly before he gave in to himself.

Chapter 22

Late summer eased its bountiful self upon the land, bringing harvest. For Mary and Aaron this was a healing season. The busy summer had worked to diminish the horror of Jonathan's death. They still felt his absence, but time and activity began diminishing grief.

Jonathan had requested Mary and Aaron's first liaison, and had gone away to permit it. He was gone again, but this time his absence held them apart. The proprieties that they observed so strictly served to heighten their awareness of each other. Their relationship was all new.

Sarah's presence was an added dimension for them both. Mary became aware of Aaron's wish to play a father's part the night he asked to take Sarah to her bed. She realized the depth of feeling he had for his daughter and felt he had purposely hidden it. Propriety again!

But after that night a subtle change was effected. It began one noon when Aaron came to the house for dinner to find Mary in the midst of making currant jelly. Dinner wasn't ready. The table was lined with scalded jelly glasses waiting to be filled. A dish towel filled with boiled currants still hung suspended, like a punching bag, where she'd drained the juice. A large kettle of simmering juice sent fruit-scented steam billowing over the range. The baby was on the floor in the middle of the confusion.

Mary threw him a harried look, apologizing, "I'm sorry, Aaron. This took longer than I thought, and I couldn't let it overboil or it would be ruined. Your dinner's not ready."

He didn't seem to mind. He stood inside the door watching the steamy confusion, smiling at the mess. Actually, he was enjoying the scene before him. Mary's hair had slipped its coil, so bits of it clung to her temples and neck in inviting tendrils. The heat from the stove had heightened her color, giving her a rosy hue. The fruity aroma filled the room like ambrosia.

Sarah wasn't pleased by it at all. She'd had enough of being ignored on the floor, and squalled in protest.

"Aaron, will you pick her up so she'll stop crying? My hands are full."

"So I see," he chuckled and lifted the complaining Sarah saying, "C'mon, Corncob. Your mother wants me to spoil you a little bit." He rested her on his suntanned arm, where the contrast of her whiteness captivated Mary. She watched him while she stirred the jelly. He took Sarah's hand in his free one, smiling into her eyes. Sarah looked into his face in a steady, unblinking way, as if she were deciding something for herself. Then she made a spitty sound that came out, "A-bah," and smiled up at the man who was her father in an enchanting, two-toothed grin. He gently pumped the delicate hand he held and said, "Hi, Sarah." Then he realized Mary was watching him, and he turned to catch her gaze. She smiled at Aaron, and her heart seemed full enough to burst as he smiled back at her with the same wide smile Sarah had just used on him. "She's beautiful, Mary. Isn't she?" he asked.

"Yes, Aaron. She is," Mary answered, and the music in her heart could be heard in her voice. Wanting to give him more of what he'd missed, she suggested, "Why don't you take her outside where it's cooler? I'll be done here in a minute, and we can have lunch out there."

When the jelly glasses were filled, Mary sliced ripe tomatoes, brought vinegared cucumbers from the buttery, added cheese, cold meat, and bread, and carried it out to the shaded yard on a wide breadboard.

Aaron was lying on his side in the cool grass while Sarah braced against his chest to stand up. She was babbling and drooling and bobbing up and down on wobbly legs. He caught her when she lost her balance, stood her upright again with a "Whoa there, Princess!"

"You talk as if she were a horse," Mary teased him.

"Well, I don't know much about talking to babies."

"You'll have to learn," she said. His face was lit up with pleasure, and when Mary came, it made the circle complete.

"Here comes your mother to take you," he said to Sarah.

"She's happy where she is, if you don't mind."

"I don't mind." It was the first time she'd charged

Sarah to him, and there was a feeling about it of sharing her at last. They didn't talk much but watched
Sarah and laughed at her cub clumsiness, growing used
to the togetherness it evoked.

After that, he held her every chance he got. She
was always awake at noon, growing out of one schedule and into another, in which she napped following
dinnertime. Aaron would pick her up from the floor,
out of Mary's way, as soon as he came into the kitchen.
Mary purposely delayed the meals, giving him time to
play with Sarah while she set dinner.

One day Aaron suggested, "There's a high chair
up in the granary rafters. Shouldn't I bring it down
for her?"

"Oh, yes, it'd be a blessing. She's always underfoot
now that she's outgrown her basket."

He took down the old piece of furniture and
scrubbed it to get the years of dust from it, then set it
in the sun to dry. The following evening after the day's
work was done, he painted it on the back porch while
Mary and Sarah sat on the steps and kept him company. Mary waited until Aaron was at the house before
she put Sarah into it for the first time. They made a
little ceremony out of it, and Aaron was alight with
pleasure. He brought the baby a piece of toast to initi-
ate her into her new spot. After that, the high chair
became a permanent fixture at the table.

The day came when Mary knew she had delayed
the weaning long enough. Doc Haymes's orders were
long overdue, and Sarah could hold her own at the
dinner table now.

She stopped nursing Sarah one morning and bound

her breasts as tightly as she could. When Aaron arrived that morning, he noted her new, flat shape but said nothing. At noon Mary seemed quiet and moved more slowly than usual. By evening she was listless and said she was tired and wanted to go to bed early, so he left right after supper, worrying vaguely, unsure of what he could do for her.

The night was endless for Mary, a fitful string of hours during which she dozed and woke repeatedly to the throbbing that increased as the hours wore on. She changed her bindings, and the new one added some comfort, but soon the aching beat through her breasts again. She felt fevered and hot and dreamed of great drafts of water. She awoke knowing she could drink nothing. She tried Lydia Pinkham's medicine, but it did no good. The hours of the night crept on to dawn as her discomfort became gnawing pain. She dozed again, but even Sarah's light stirrings awakened her. She lay listening to the sounds from the crib, thinking it was worth all this just to have Sarah, but distressed tears sneaked from behind her eyelids.

When she heard Aaron come, she rolled to the side of the bed, but found herself completely milk-soaked again. She sat on the edge of the bed, clutching the heavy, wet bindings through her drenched gown, biting her lip to hold back the tears.

Aaron saw the closed back door and ran the rest of the way to the house, leaping the porch steps in one bound. When he tried the back door and found it still locked, panic gripped him. He reached above the door-sill for the key they always kept there. He dropped the key in his haste and cursed at his inept fumblings before he finally worked the key and swung the door wide.

The kitchen wore a morning chill that permeated his heart. Why wasn't a fire lit? Where was Mary? He paused only a moment to scan the quiet, empty room, and then he was bounding up the stairs, fear pushing his legs in giant strides as he hollered her name in the stillness.

Her bedroom door was open, so there was nothing to hinder his entrance, yet he stormed the doorway as if he'd smashed through a barricade to reach her.

She was sitting on the side of the bed, clutching her wet, sticky chest, and he read the misery in her eyes immediately.

"Oh, Aaron, it hurts so much," she whimpered. He was at once relieved at her safety and distressed by her pain.

"What can I do?" he questioned, coming to her side immediately.

She shook her head, still holding herself, and his heart hurt at the sight of her.

"Tell me, darling." He knelt down on one knee in front of her. "Tell me what to do," he entreated. "Here, you're all wet. We have to get you a dry gown and some dry bindings. Where are they?"

"I use dish towels," she confided, "but I can't get them tight enough by myself." It was so good to have Aaron here that she gave in gladly, letting him insist that she wash while he gathered fresh towels for her.

Sarah had awakened when Aaron made his noisy entrance, but she sat contentedly, watching this strange new scene in the bedroom.

Aaron helped Mary, doing as she instructed, cinching the towels until they bit into the soft flesh of her armpits. It pained him to bind her so tightly, but she insisted, saying it felt better already.

When she had her fresh gown on again, he pulled her hair from inside its neck, and as it fell free outside, he put an arm around her shoulders, guiding her toward the bed. "You had a wicked night, my love. Now maybe you'll sleep better."

She began to object, "But Aaron, I have to . . ."

He placed a finger on her lips, stilling them and ordering her, "You have to rest and let me out of here so I can take care of Sarah."

She spluttered, but he'd have it no other way. He nudged her again toward the inviting bed, and she acquiesced, sitting down. From there she looked up at him and asked, "What would I do without you?"

He reached to push her hair behind one ear, saying, "Pray, love, that you never find out." Then, cupping the back of her head in his hand, he leaned to kiss her mouth lightly, feeling her lips quiver beneath his.

He went to the crib then and picked up Sarah, saying, "Come on, Corncob, you need drying out, too."

The day Aaron spent in the house put him a day behind in the fields. Threshing was starting earlier than last year, for the grain had filled out sooner. He not only had to make up the lost time but spent some days helping Dvorak get his crops in. The arrangement benefited both men, for Dvorak would help Aaron at threshing time.

Those following days kept Aaron too busy to idle in the house. Until Uncle Garner came with the rig, he saw Mary and Sarah only at mealtimes, and those were hurried.

Mary improved so fast it amazed her. It seemed her body was easily dissuaded and her comfort grew greater each day until, by threshing time, she wore her old shape, slightly filled out.

She'd spent many hours remembering the endearments Aaron had spoken, recalling the way he had charged into her room, the concern on his face, and his kiss. But he hadn't touched her again.

The end of threshing was approaching fast, and when she thought of Dakota, Mary got a sick feeling in the pit of her stomach. Aaron hadn't mentioned it at all, but she knew they couldn't avoid talking about it much longer. She waited for him to bring it up, but when he didn't, she knew she'd have to.

It was a heavy, gilded morning with the sun slanting low through the east window and the kitchen door, backlighting the dust motes that ever hung now in the harvest air. Aaron had taken a kitchen knife and sliced a sliver from a piece of firewood in the woodbox to use as a toothpick. He was heading straight outside, but something made him stop and look back at her. She was standing with some things she'd gathered from the breakfast table; only she wasn't moving, just following him with her eyes.

"Is everything all right?" he questioned, stopping in front of the window.

"You haven't mentioned Dakota," she said.

"No, I haven't."

The sun was at his back, on her face, and she couldn't make out his expression when he spoke. His voice didn't tell her much.

"Are you going this year?"

"I haven't decided."

"You've been thinking about it then?"

"Yes. I never wrote Getchner about Jonathan. I suppose he's expecting both of us."

"Oh." The things in her hands got heavy and she set them down again on the table.

"Do you want me to stay?" he asked, giving her the chance to keep him here with a single word.

"I . . . I just wanted to know, because I'll have to find someone to help around the place if you go."

His teeth were clamped tightly on the wood sliver and she could see the silhouette of his right jaw against the gold glow behind it, could see the muscles tensed, but he stood as if the rest of him were as pliable as warm butter, softened in that sunlight.

"You didn't answer my question," he said quietly.

"Do we have to have the money?" she asked, and he made no comment about the way she now seemed to lump the money as both of theirs. Instead, he turned his head slowly, from side to side. As he did, indicating no, it made shadow, sun, shadow, sun, play across her face.

"Do you want me to go?" he repeated, and this time it was she who turned her head, silently, left and right, left and right. And as she did, the sun repeatedly glanced into her cornflower eyes, again . . . and again . . . and again.

She saw him reach up and thought he took the toothpick from between his teeth. She thought he was moving toward her, but it was just the sun in her eyes creating the illusion.

"Then I'll stay. I wanted to be here to take you to the wedding anyway," he said. "Will you go with me?"

She was momentarily confused by something she'd expected, some other thing she hadn't, and she questioned, "The wedding?"

"Priscilla and Willy's" he reminded her. "Will you go with me?"

She wanted to say simply, yes, she'd go anywhere with him, but instead, she answered, "I don't know what I'd do with Sarah."

"Bring her along," he said, and then more sternly, again, "Will you go with me?"

"Yes."

And he moved away from the sun, leaving black spots before her eyes from its brightness, a heat in her heart from its fire, from him. But he never touched her, only said before leaving the house, "I like it when you tie your hair back and let it hang that way."

Mary made up the ivory faille into a slim skirt that sheathed her hips, then flared to drift and swirl above her ankles. She ordered a new pair of high-button shoes. From the white organdy that Aaron had given her last Christmas she made a blouse of full sleeves, pointed collar, and tucked bodice, trimmed with black shell buttons. A black cummerbund completed the outfit, and she eyed herself with approval as she waited for Aaron on the morning of the wedding, late in October.

Mary hurried to gather the baby's things. "Oh, Princess, aren't we gonna dance?" she asked Sarah. "Your daddy loves to waltz—you'll have to learn how, too. Here, let's get your blanket . . . he should be here any minute." Mary pulled it from the crib, added it to the stack on the bed. It was impossible to be patient, to keep her feet still, to keep from squeezing Sarah too hard.

Finally she heard Aaron pull into the yard and collected the stuff she'd readied, scooped the baby up in her other arm, and went down to meet him.

He had somehow acquired a new suit without telling her. It was sienna-brown serge with pale pinstriping. The smartly cut jacket lay open to reveal a waistcoat that hugged his lean torso. A golden chain spanned the open area, disappearing inside a hidden pocket. His round ivory shirt collar was the perfect contrast to his summer-tanned skin and burnished hair. He looked to Mary like some harvest god, his coloring so like the colors of the season. She swallowed hard as she took in his flawless elegance.

Aaron drank in the vision before him. In ivory and white, she could have been the bride of the morning. Her hair was lit by the morning sun, its simple, pristine lines more alluring than any elegant tresses would have been. He recognized the white organdy he had given her, felt a tingle of appreciation at how it looked on her narrow shoulders and rounded breasts. Through the opaque lightness of the blouse a hint of skin was discernible, and he could almost smell it, remembering lavender mixed with her own scent.

Suddenly Sarah demanded attention. Aaron swept an elegant bow to break the electric silence that lay between them.

"You shall be the most beautiful woman at the wedding, and I shall be the luckiest man," he bantered in a theatrical voice.

She came out of her reverie, lifting her skirts in a curtsy. "Then let us away!"

The morning was brisk but warming, an autumn stillness enhancing it, for most birds had left, save the crows and the hidden pheasants that now and then carped their barking cry. They savored the ride to church, knowing it could be one of the last pleasant jaunts before winter.

They took their accustomed pew and for a moment felt Jonathan's absence from his familiar spot. But Sarah was there now, and, like all babies in church, took some managing. While they waited for the ceremony to begin, Sarah was busy looking at the unfamiliar surroundings and the faces of those in the pew behind. When she made loud, babbling sounds that resounded in the quiet, Mary and Aaron glanced at each other and smiled, the newness of this experience as exhilarating for them as it was for Sarah.

The organ music captivated Sarah, however, and she became a well-mannered lady as the service began.

When Mary saw Pris coming down the aisle, a knot came to her throat. Pris was radiant in white satin, smiling as she came forward on her father's arm. Mary's thoughts slid backward to a night long ago when she and Aaron had sat on the dark summer steps. She heard his voice again, saying it takes two to do a lot of things—to make love and to get married—and she wondered again about their intimacy, Aaron's and Pris's. Now here she was, more beautiful than Mary had ever seen her. Aaron's eyes followed Pris, too, and Mary wondered, Is he sorry after all? But as if he divined her thoughts, Aaron's russet head turned away from the aisle and his glance flickered over Mary, reassuring her somehow.

As the ceremony proceeded, Aaron thought of the mysterious tether that held him from marriage with Pris. What had held him was that he didn't love Pris. He knew it for a fact because now he knew what it felt like to love someone fully. He was struck by the irony of his search for that love of his finding it in the place from where he started: at home. Hearing the vows, he knew he'd waited long enough, played the passive brother and acquiescent uncle long enough. Today was the perfect time to begin his suit. The public be damned. He'd wait no longer.

When the service ended and the congregation rose, Mary hitched Sarah onto her arm, but before she could struggle to her feet, she felt Sarah being lifted from her and looked up in surprise as Aaron held Sarah with one arm and reached his other to her elbow, helping her to her feet. She still worried about the delicate balance of propriety. But that balance was inexorably tipped when Aaron kept Sarah on his arm as they entered the aisle, further confused when he took Mary's elbow solicitously on their way out of church. She didn't pull away although her confused mind insisted on querying, What will people think? But Aaron's lucid mind knew they would think exactly what he wanted them to—that the period of mourning was over!

In the buggy she affected a light tone, though her heart was unnecessarily jumpy. "You mustn't be so . . . so polite and helpful, Aaron. People will talk."

He just tossed his head up and laughed, undismayed. "Didn't I tell you, you do that to a man, Mary girl?" he teased.

She didn't know what to make of it, after all the careful months of avoiding the slightest scandal. He suddenly seems to be laughing at the wind, she thought. If she didn't know better, she'd swear he'd been tippling.

He kept it up all through the day. Her heart did crazy things, and she knew she should still it, but couldn't.

Aunt Mabel commented on how good Mary looked. Seeing the girl's eyes seek out Aaron in the crowd, she realized why. At dinnertime he brought her a plate of food and took Sarah so Mary could enjoy her meal. In the afternoon he paid a young girl a half dollar to take Sarah off Mary's hands for a while so she could further enjoy her day. When the line formed for the men to kiss the bride, he was in it. But when he had kissed and paid the bride her dollar, he scanned the crowd for Mary and found her watching him. He winked at her, and she dropped her head to attend to something Aunt Mabel was saying.

They both danced with many people. Sarah was asleep by then, and Mary was free to join in the revelry. Aaron asked her to dance and kept up the gaiety, teasing her about the others she'd danced with. The quarter moon was high before the festivities ended. A heavy chill crisped the air. As the rigs left, the voices that called goodnights carried across the autumn air, ebbing away as the night ushered them home.

In Mary and Aaron's rig, it was quiet. Sarah slept on Mary's lap. She was grateful to have the baby there asleep. It seemed a plausible reason for their sudden silence with each other. There was little time for thought. The ride home was too short.

Aaron took Sarah from Mary before she could protest, and carried her upstairs to her bed. When he'd laid her in the crib he stood a moment, thinking of Mary downstairs, a pounding in his veins. He took off his jacket and hooked it with two fingers, slinging it over his shoulder. Drawing a ragged breath, he went downstairs.

Mary had lit the kitchen lamp, but she was in the pantry. He saw the hem of her skirt as he stood just inside the kitchen doorway. She moved then, knowing he stood there, and gazed at him from across the room. He still held the jacket slung over his shoulder, making no move to leave.

She became self-conscious under his steady eyes and dropped her gaze to the floor.

"I would like one more waltz with you," he said in a disturbingly quiet tone.

"I . . ." But she couldn't finish, seemed not to know what to say.

He crossed the room slowly and reached for her hand, led her across the kitchen and into the shadowed living room. He threw his jacket across the rocker, then released her hand and went to wind the graphophone. The hushed strains of the Strauss waltz glimmered in the room. She saw Aaron against the light from the doorway, saw his hand reach for her again.

She felt the silken back of his waistcoat as she placed a hand on his shoulder, then the rough texture of serge as he pulled her into his arms. They moved a few steps to the music, but it went on as they stilled.

She felt his hands at her hair, pulling the pins from it, but she stayed where she was, her temple against his chin. She heard the pins drop onto the floor behind her. Then his hands turned her face and he lowered his mouth to hers. Her arms came around him of their own volition, and her mouth slackened under his.

The kiss was as familiar to Mary as if she'd shared his kisses every day. But the surge of emotion pounding through her seemed as new as if she'd never been kissed before. Its warmth became heat. His tongue became a coal inside her, setting her afire with its insistence. He twisted his mouth over hers and clamped her body against the hard length of his own. His arm lowered from the small of her back to her hips, and he pressed his own hips against hers, lifting her to her toes.

He tore his mouth away then, and his shaking voice was at her ear. "I meant to go slow, darling, but I've waited so long, loved you so long."

She grasped him against her, protesting in spite of her demanding body, "Aaron, we can't do this again."

"Don't say it, Mary." And he stopped her words with his mouth.

When he freed her lips again, she said unsteadily, "I've felt so guilty about what we did to Jonathan."

"I have, too," he said. "But Jonathan is dead, and we can't keep him between us forever. We're alive, Mary. You and I are alive, and it's wrong to deny it any longer." There was pain in his voice, and hunger, and longing. And as always, he made her do what he wanted because it was what she wanted, too.

There was no denying the shivering weakness that possessed her starved body as his hand slid to her breast and she leaned into his palm, groaning as he caressed her. She could no more stop what was happening than she could stop the turning of the earth.

She felt him release her and begin to open the buttons of her blouse, up the back. With her lips still on his, she undid the buttons of her cuffs, behind his neck.

They parted long enough for him to pull the blouse from her shoulders. It was tucked into the waist of her skirt, but he let it drop over her hips, remain tucked in. He pulled the straps of the chemise over her shoulders and pushed the garment to her waist, his hands gliding down her warm sides.

Then he circled her waist with one arm, forcing her to kneel on the floor with him. She felt his mouth hot and wet on her breasts, and pulled his head harder against them, feeling his soft hair against her skin as he moved from one to the other. Her fingers were in his hair, and he felt them clutch and pull it as he licked a line down the center of her chest to her lowered chemise.

When he reached for the hem of her skirt, he touched her high-button shoes. Gripping her bare arms again, he pulled her to her feet, begging, "Take your shoes off, Mary, please." He turned her toward the kitchen, and she clutched her chemise as she went away toward the lantern light.

He heard her searching for the button hook. After a length of silence she returned barefooted and stood silhouetted in the doorway, her hair forming an aureole around her. He had taken off his vest and shirt and stood barefooted. He raised his arms to her, and she padded noiselessly across to him, making a soft, pained sound as they touched.

"I love you so much, Mary," he whispered. "I've loved you so long."

"I've known it, and I'm so sorry I had to fight it,"

she said softly, "but I promise I won't fight it anymore. Aaron, oh Aaron, I love you."

It was a kiss of rejoicing when their lips met again, magnified by the long wait they had both endured.

This time she tugged at him, pulling him down onto the hooked rug, taking his hands and placing them on her breasts as she knelt before him. But his hands lingered there only a short moment, then lowered to the buttons at her waist.

A pandemonium of pounding blood clamored through Mary's head and pulsed through his body. When her skirt fell and he pulled her hard against him, she could feel him, hardened with desire.

"Touch me, Mary, love me, too," he begged in a strained, throaty whisper, and her hands made their way to the band at his waist. She felt the buttons where they strained against his lean, hard body, and they opened beneath her fingers. The muscles of his buttocks contracted as she ran her hands over their firmness, pulling his trousers away as she smoothed his skin. Then she recognized the familiar heat against her belly as he clasped her to his manhood, her hand there between them. Still holding her so, he fell, pulling her down with him onto the rug. She could feel cold hairpins touch her warm side as he rolled her over, searching with his hand along the soft, warm skin of her inner thigh.

She uttered his name in faint, muffled tones against his neck as he explored and awakened her, finding that she had come to him in a heightened state, as ready for this as he was. He murmured to her, nuzzling her bare shoulders, his joy and passion mounting with hers.

She whimpered as he worked his loving magic on her, a magic remembered from so long ago. When her body trembled and arched, he rolled over her and entered her in silken strokes, grunting as the force built, answering her in sounds only she could understand. At last, fulfillment overtook them and he collapsed onto her, arms outstretched over hers.

In those first intimate afterminutes, with his body still warm in hers, she lay thinking that this was the highest accolade a man and woman could give each other and that words were insignificant in its wake. She felt rich with his gift, as if nothing greater could be afforded her.

But she was wrong. For the next thing Aaron said erupted inside her, lavishing her with an unbelievable plenitude.

He rolled her with him onto their sides, rubbed his knuckles lightly along her jaw, and said softly, "Mary, girl, will you do me the honor of becoming my wife?"

He felt the muscles of her cheek shift as she swallowed. His heart hammered painfully when she remained silent, but Aaron heard her swallow a second time. As if his proposal lacked full import, he added, "And will you bring our daughter along and let me be her father?"

Her arms suddenly clung to him and his face was lost in her hair as she choked, "Aaron, oh Aaron, I thought you might not ask." She felt like singing and crying at the same time.

He clutched her against his chest, rocking in a timeless motion of relief as his voice cracked. "And I thought you might say no."

"You should know by now I can never say no to you."

There was a pause. Then Aaron said, "I thought you might have changed your mind about me . . . with Jonathan gone."

"I was afraid of what people would say, Aaron. I tried not to love you because it seemed we could never be allowed to without scandal."

"I could see that happen to you, and it put me through hell, girl. Seeing you every day in my house with my daughter and not being able to claim you both. Oh, God, Mary, it was hell leaving you two at night."

"I did so well until I saw you hold Sarah that first day by the wagon. Remember?"

He chuckled ruefully. "I remember every day of these last six months. I remember choking to keep from asking to hold Sarah. I remember the pain in my gut from wanting to hold you." He was running his hand again and again over her hair, as if stroking away the memory. "And when I'd come in the morning and see you waving from the porch, it was you I was coming to, not the work or the house or the farm. Just you—and Sarah." He felt it was a miracle, their being together at last.

She turned her face to kiss the palm of his hand and confided, "Right after she was born, I thought you were sorry about her. I tried to tell myself it didn't matter, but you wouldn't even look at her. But even then I could never think of her as Jonathan's baby, like we agreed. I looked at her and saw you."

"The only way I could get through all the pain was to stay away and not touch."

Mary knew what he said was true, that of all of

them he had borne the most pain, and she wished she could change what he'd been put through. "Darling, I'm sorry for—"

"There'll be no more regrets from now on, right?"

She shook her head, not trusting her voice at that moment.

He chose his words carefully, knowing they must be said to free them of Jonathan's ghost. "Mary . . . I'm not saying Jonathan willed us together that first time. We had minds of our own. We made choices. But we can't go on feeling guilty about Jonathan. If he could, I think he'd give us his blessing."

In Aaron's voice she caught a fleeting intonation reminiscent of his brother's. And it seemed almost as though Jonathan had spoken. "I think so, too," she said.

Sometime later, they became aware of the October chill around them. Aaron made a fire in the heater stove, and they opened its front grate so the flames licked lights across their faces where they huddled before it.

Their muted voices came and went, and the quiet periods lengthened as fewer words were required. Then Aaron and Mary let their bodies do the speaking, and they celebrated each other once again.

"Let's go to bed, love," Aaron murmured.

"You can't stay, Aaron." Mary's sleepy voice came from some buried spot in his shoulder.

"Oh, Jesus, don't turn me away again," he begged.

"I have to if you want our neighbors to respect our

marriage. There'll be enough raised eyebrows as it is."
She couldn't resist a chuckle. "If only they knew."

"Who's to say I didn't bunk in the loft over at Volences' with the overnighters after the wedding?"

She shook her head slowly, pivoting it on a spot
just under his chin where her hair was warm on his
chest. Then she turned in his arms.

"No, my love, you'll not have your way with me
again until the deed is done. I want to have a wedding
night to cherish."

He held her from behind, an arm around her middle, another over her shoulder.

"You told me a little while ago that you could never
say no to me."

She moved his hand beneath her own, feeling its
warmth and protection on her breast. "I've not said no,
my love . . . only prolonged saying yes."

In the end, she had her way.

But he was back in the morning, and he caught
her sleeping, long after the sun had risen. Sarah slept
soundly, too, after the tiring day before.

Aaron watched them for a long time before his
gaze awakened Mary. She opened her eyes to him, and
a thrill of remembrance whipped through her, arousing
her body with sudden intensity.

He came to sit beside her on the bed and leaned
above her, an elbow on each side. "I came for my
breakfast," he whispered, smiling and nuzzling. She
could smell the fresh air in his hair as he bent to kiss
her throat. He pulled at the covers, pushing them
down, away from her. He lay his face in the softness

of her breasts, and Mary felt his warm breath through her nightgown.

Not wanting to wake Sarah, she whispered, pushing at his shoulders, "Aaron, I told you last night, no more till we're married. Now behave yourself." But there was such a natural goodness about his coming to her like this, finding him here in the sun. "We seem to work so well together without even trying. What if I get pregnant as easily as the first time? What will the good people of Moran say then?" And it worked. He backed away from her a bit.

But there was something she'd never told Aaron that she thought he ought to know now. "Aaron, I said we work together without even trying, but that's not exactly true." She hesitated uncertainly, then went on, "Doc Haymes told me a woman has a right time that comes every so often, and she can plan it by the days of the calendar."

He gazed steadily at her but didn't reply.

"When Jonathan went on his trip, I knew my time was right, Aaron." Still, he hadn't said anything. "I mean, I thought I could conceive then, and I did."

"And you came to me, anyway?" he asked, and she feared he might be angry.

She said, "Yes. Are you angry?"

"Angry?" But there was jubilation in his word. "Don't you see it makes Sarah all the more precious to me? She was what you wanted, and I could give her to you, and I never knew till now anything about what you and Doc Haymes talked about."

"I thought if you knew, you might think I just used you, but I didn't, Aaron. Honest."

"I know," he said, kissing her neck again.

"We really do work well together, don't we, Aaron?" she asked.

He raised his head and looked into her girl's face, loving every plane and curve of it, not wanting to stop. "Yes, we work well together," he agreed, charmed by her simple way of saying it, "so well that I'll be wanting you morning, noon, and night for the rest of our days. And what will you think of that?"

"I think I will love it," said Mary.

He felt smothered in happiness and closed his eyes, loving the graze of her touch on his face. His eyes remained closed as he kissed a finger that slid past his lips. "My God, girl," he whispered hoarsely, "how I love you."

She leaned to his bronzed face and laid her mouth lightly on his, knowing at last the fullness of their mutual harvest as she whispered with tears in her eyes, "We love you, too."

The days that followed were a heady beginning, harbingers of joys to come. For Aaron there was the pleasure of Sarah as well as Mary. He indulged in all the foolish, fatherly things he'd thought of, giving free rein to the love he felt for her.

For Mary there was an awakening of pride such as she'd never known before. He was so natural with Sarah and with her, although she held him at bay, his hands, arms, and mouth constantly wanting her.

He bought a tractor with the money he got from selling Vinnie. Aloysius Duzak bought the bull, and the sale was recorded under the animal's registered name, Vindicator. Duzak admitted he'd probably call the animal by his old nickname, then became self-conscious after he'd said it, remembering that the bull had killed Jonathan.

There was money left over after buying the tractor, and Mary used it for new curtains and wallpaper for Aaron's bedroom, informing him with an innocent look that Sarah would sleep better if she had the old front bedroom to herself.

Aaron couldn't resist teasing, "It'll be quieter there for her, too," loving the blush that came to Mary's cheeks.

As Mabel Garner so often said, weddings come in threes. This one was the third, and the most unexpected.

They were married in November. It was a small ceremony, but all the Garners were there to admire Mary in ivory satin, trimmed in seed pearls.

Mabel Garner told everyone later, "Damned if she wasn't the prettiest bride I ever seen!" Rumor had it that Mary had worn a lovely ivory gown of quaint design, but nobody knew where it had come from. Surely if it were an heirloom, she'd have worn it at her first wedding.

It gave the women of Moran Township food for a whole winter's gossip. They recalled Mabel Garner's telling them how she and Garner had found Aaron wandering the roads in shock after his brother's death. They recalled how he'd given up his home to Mary and Jonathan more than once, how he'd worked the land after Jonathan died, asking nothing in return. Long before spring, their husbands had tired of hearing the merits of "that boy" and how he'd married the girl, providing for her—with that young baby and all. They never failed to say, "What would Mary have done without Aaron?"

On their wedding night, after putting Sarah to bed, they tiptoed down the hall by lantern light. At the doorway Aaron picked up his bride and kissed her before carrying her into his old room, which wore a new look. When he saw the room, colorful and clean, he thought how Mary loved this house, how she felt so right in it and in his arms, and how neither of them would ever have to leave it again.

Setting her on her feet, he asked, "My darling, what would I do without you?"

"You'll never have to ask again," she replied, pulling him toward the bed.

And their lantern burned brightly, long into the night.